NEMESIS

NOVELS BY THE RS PERRY

Off The Edge
Over The Line
Out of Time
Ecuador
Nemesis
Remilious

NEMESIS

JIM JOHNSON'S GREATEST CHALLENGE

RS PERRY

ISBN (Hardback) 978-1-989938-09-6

ISBN (Trade Paperback) 978-1-989938-11-9

ISBN (Paperback) 978-1-989938-10-2

ISBN (Large Print) 978-1-989938-33-1

ISBN (e Book) 978-1-989938-12-6

ISBN (audio) 978-1-989938-13-3

Published by Penelope Ltd.

The author wishes to thank E. Beach for use of her poem Kestrel.

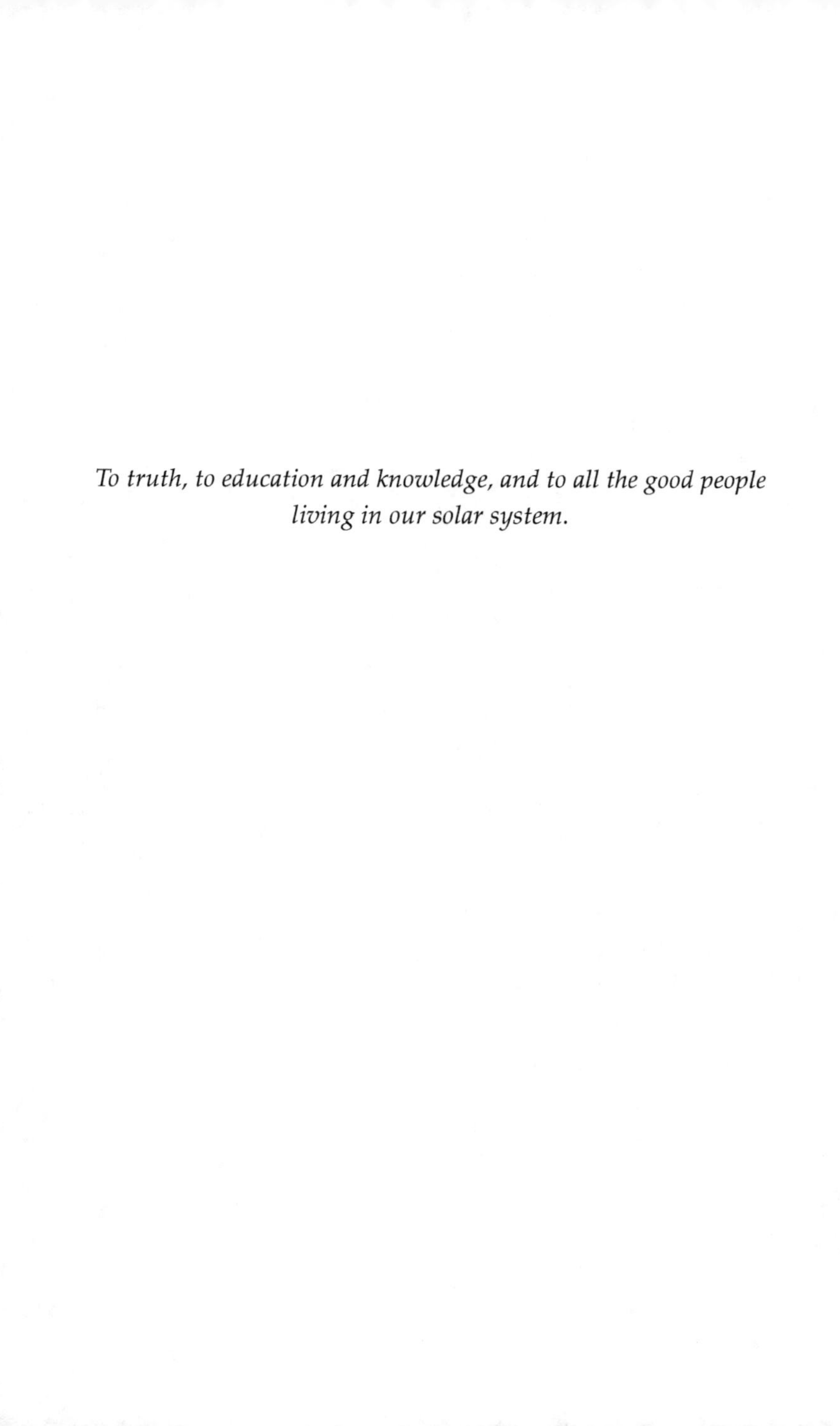

To truth, to education and knowledge, and to all the good people living in our solar system.

NEMESIS

RS Perry

. . . Heather made a fist and held it in the air. Something she had learned from Jim. She turned and put her finger to her lips. Then she pointed down the canyon and slightly to her right.

Pedro and Roy inched their horses forward until they could see the deer with her small fawn. Suddenly the neck of the doe stiffened and grew longer, and her head froze as she looked at the intruders. The horses stood uncharacteristically still. No one moved.

The mule deer must have reasoned they were not a threat as she, followed closely by her fawn, walked further down the canyon. She stopped and looked back. Then she pawed at the snow to expose the grasses beneath. She moved a few more feet, then nervously nibbled a bush, with her youngster imitating her.

'I've never seen a baby that small this time of year,' Roy whispered.

'Yeah, it's lucky to be alive. It doesn't look to be more than two months old,' said Heather.

'Must've been born in that bit of Indian summer we had in late October.'

As they watched the mother and her little charge, the mule deer's body froze. She sensed the cold eyes above. Suddenly, her rear legs kicked the snow as she tried to push herself into a run. It was too late. The huge tan cougar landed on her back and dug its claws in. The weight buckled her knees as the powerful mouth closed on her neck. The fawn sprinted a few feet away and then back toward its mother.

'Oh my God,' said Heather.

'Help it, Mama. Don't let it die,' cried Pedro.

Heather could only shake her head.

Roy said, 'It's not our place to interfere, even if we could.'

Pedro kicked his heels in to move to the rescue, but his horse wanted only to go away from the life—and—death scene, not toward it. Roy's horse, QT, was a nervous horse by nature. She stamped her feet and tried to turn. Fortunately, Pedro's horse, Blacky, unwilling to go forward, and Roy's horse, moving sideways into Pedro's, allowed Roy to grab Blacky's reins.

Heather watched, stunned, as she tried to keep Dawn from bolting. Within seconds, the deer yielded to the cougar's superior strength. It was as if the prey's mind removed itself, became anesthetized, succumbing to its eventual death without further struggle. This was something they had all observed before. They called it the fright factor. The fawn, however, was still unsure what to do and was jumping back and forth. Its instincts told it to stay with its mother; it didn't yet know enough to run further from the predator. Fortunately for the fawn, the big tawny brown cat had lifted the mother's neck clenched tight in its teeth, shoulder muscles rippling, and pulled the lifeless body a few feet closer to the canyon's wall. She had no interest in the fawn. She had a much larger meal to give her the energy she needed.

'What can we do, Mama?' asked Pedro with tears streaming down his cheeks.

'There is nothing.'

'Can't we take the fawn home?'

'No way to catch it.'

'It'll still be able to eat without its mama, won't it?

'No, sweetie. It needs its mother to survive.'

'Please, Mama. Do something. Look, it is walking toward us.'

Heather looked at Roy.

'I can try. Maybe it will come close enough,' he said.

'Try what?' asked Pedro.

'Roy is going to try to rope it. Don't get your hopes up, but because it is so narrow in here, the fawn might get close enough. Roy might be able to do it.'

'Please, Roy, please.'

'Stay quiet, so it won't be frightened.'

The small, late-born fawn stumbled on toward the riders.

'It's in shock,' said Heather.

The lasso that Roy always carried on his saddle went round and round as he spun it, waiting for just the right coincidence of events to occur between him, the rope's motion, and the target. Roping was an art, not a science. Intuition and long practice would tell him when to let the lasso fly.

Pedro watched transfixed as the lasso flew through the air. The fawn seemed to notice it coming closer and lifted its head. It was too dazed to move away. The rope, with luck, went over its head. One part landed on the baby's rump; the other slid down the fawn's front legs. The rope was stiff and intended for cows, not tiny fawns.

Roy quickly pulled it toward him. QT was skittish but had been well trained in a feed lot. She backed up as Roy squeezed her sides with both heels. The fawn jumped forward, and the back part of the lasso slipped completely over its rump. Heather bit her lip. The baby was going to walk out of it. A perfect throw, she thought. A sad ending. It will starve or freeze to death.

Roy knew before the rope slipped over the little fawn's rear what would happen. His only chance would be to pull it tight before it slipped to the ground. Partly because of the slow motions of the shocked fawn, and partly because of Roy's skill, the rope tightened around the fawn's legs. The youngster fell on to its side, with the rope holding all four legs.

Pedro jumped down from his horse. Without him, Miss Blacky immediately turned and ran back out of the canyon toward the safety of home.

'No, Pedro! The cougar. Stop. Please stop,' shouted Heather.

The cougar lifted its head and tensed. Its snarl sent shivers down Heather's spine as Pedro ran in its direction. Roy didn't want to drag the little deer, but he did so, just a few feet, getting it further from the cougar and closer to Pedro, who raced to the fawn and dropped down beside it.

Without looking, Heather tossed her reins toward Roy, jumped to the ground, and raced after Pedro. Roy secured the rope and managed to grab Heather's reins. The cougar snarled, tensed, but went back to tearing at the warm flesh. Her hunger overcame any fear she had for these two clawless creatures.

As small as it was, the fawn was too large for Pedro to carry. Heather put Pedro's hand on the fawn's shoulder as she nervously watched the cougar.

'It's a little boy. Hold him down while I loosen the rope,' she said as she surrounded its legs with her arms and lifted the small fawn.

The captive fawn lay still, suddenly thrashed with its legs, and went still again.

'Walk easy, no quick movements, back toward Roy,' she said.

As they approached, Roy lowered the 30-30 Winchester from his shoulder and put it back into the scabbard.

Heather looked up at Roy as if to say, I don't believe this.

'We were lucky,' said Roy. 'If it wasn't for the doe, we might have been dinner.'

'That's not what I told Pedro when we walked down.'

'Ain't no way to know now anyhow.'

Pedro kept rubbing the fawn's neck and head.

'Will it be okay, Mama?'

Heather lifted it to Roy. The tiny fawn kicked weakly as Roy pushed it inside his heavy coat.

They had entered the canyon with three horses and left whit two, with Pedro mounted behind Heather. He never took his eyes off Roy and the small bundle held under his coat.

That's the second time Pedro has watched a mother die. His, and now the fawns. Heather covered Pedro's hand with hers, wondering about the awful effects witnessing what he had would have on him, or anyone.

Her thoughts were broken when Roy's horse twitched and kicked the snow, and he said, 'Settled down now. You'll get home soon enough.'

'I can't believe you got your rope around that small of a target, Roy,' Heather said with admiration.

'It was lucky. All that can be said about it.'

'You teach me to rope?' asked Pedro.

'Sure, we can practice when it warms up. The fawn's settled down some.'

'Mama, where are we going to keep him?'

'We'll talk about it tomorrow, sweetie.'

'Now.' Then more softly, 'Now, please.'

'Roy, you okay with him for tonight?' She turned her head back toward Pedro, 'Roy will take good care of him, and we'll pick him up in the morning.'

'Mama, please.'

''It's too far to carry him, and it's too cold. We're going to try to spot that hoot owl again.'

Heather gave Roy a look that said, 'Don't you dare say you'll drive us tonight.' Then she said, 'You have enough to do with the fawn and taking care of three horses. You have to catch Miss Blacky.'

'She ain't no problem. She'll be standing by the barn, waiting to get her saddle off.'

Heather wanted to walk up in the twilight, then a shiver went through her body as she thought about the cougar. *No, I won't let it change me. The night has always been my friend.* Heather desperately wanted to know how Pedro was accepting what he had witnessed. She was afraid to say anything. This is what children learned on a ranch or farm —death, breeding, and babies were a part of their everyday lives.

Pedro pushed it from his mind. It was complete denial. As the cougar brutally killed the doe, his mind flashed to scenes of the evil lady killing his family. It was too much for him to deal with. Too many parallels. He had survived; the little boy deer survived. He didn't yet comprehend the difference; the cougar simply followed its natural course and needed to eat; Najma killed his family for pleasure. One day, he would understand.

'You should get a going up the road before it gets completely dark,' Roy told them.

'Good idea.'

Pedro's spirits were lifted by the thought of having the fawn to take care of. He didn't want to walk, though. He didn't like the night like his mother did. It scared him.

'Thanks, Roy. We'll be fine. It's never dark with all this white stuff reflecting the stars. The moon will be up soon, too.'

Yes, thought Roy. *All true. Maybe if I can get everyone settled in, secure this little guy in the shower stall, and then trail along behind them. The night can be dangerous as we just saw.*

Heather put her arm around Pedro and nudged him. They both waved at Roy, walked down the drive to Balky Hill Road, turned right, gaining a few feet in elevation as the road rose above Beaver Creek and met its namesake— Beaver Creek Road.

Heather felt comforted by the oversized 'sat' phone in her rucksack. She had no way of knowing that she had missed one call from Jim just as they had entered Pipestone Canyon, and another just after his plane took off from Colombia. She knew he would not break his promise to be home soon.

After they had locked the main gate and walked past the large, scraggly, old homesteader's apple tree, she stopped before the wooden plank bridge and looked up the old road. There was only a hint that it had ever been a road. Bushes and branches intruded through the white snow swath. Only a few feet away was the Secret Meadow. She smiled, remembering the special times there, and the less than joyous last visit when she had prepared the special picnic welcome for Jim.

Her expectations for that day months ago had been dashed. With their newfound understanding, she realized that she had been wrong to expect Jim, dead tired after a mission, to feel the same way she did about their reunion. *He needed rest and understanding. I should have realized,* she thought. *Later, I could have had what I needed.*

A nearly full moon rose over her right shoulder. With the snow, the moon, and the Milky Way, it would be a spectacular walk.

A flashing memory of the cougar caused her to pull Pedro in close.

The trees rustled in a slight breeze. The cool night air settled as the sun-warmed air molecules slipped into the atmosphere. Suddenly, she felt a chill as a moonlit shadow passed and she heard the crunch of snow behind her.

Soliloquy - The next morning

Jim felt a warm glow. He was facing backward in the Globe Master III, racing northward from Colombia toward Fort Lewis, Washington. His feet were up, his head was back, and he wore a headset connected to the extensive comms on the Biological Warfare Center's long-distance response plane. Without success, he had called Heather. *Out of range,* he wondered. Or, had Heather forgotten to charge the batteries. Thinking about her foibles made him happy.

Heather was as smart as she was capable. She also had several personality quirks, which he unequivocally liked: stringing three questions together; routinely forgetting to charge her phone; picking up anything that crawled; and possessing an undying love of pangolins, cats, bats, dogs, llamas, and her favorite, Sharifa, a pregnant dromedary camel.

Jim would arrive at Fort Lewis in less than six hours. He called Master Sergeant First Class Williston who assured him his Piper Seneca was fueled, the oil and tires checked. Jim intended to exit the Globe Master; do a quick inspection of his tan, red, and white twin-engine plane, and make the sixty-five-minute flight up and over the Cascades to his home airport in Winthrop, Washington.

He tried Heather one more time. No answer. Not able to reach her, he called flight control, received a weather report, and filed an instrument flight plan from Fort Lewis to Winthrop. The weather was good and using visual flight rules would be more than sufficient for when he cancelled the IFR plan before descending into the valley.

He took his headset off and set it on the side table next to his recliner. For the first time since their flight to Ecuador, he relaxed, stretching out in the lounge chair with his feet up. The physical comfort of the lounger was in stark contrast to the uncomfortable catch-when-you-can sleep that he had become used to in his work. Jim was weary from their extended mission. His weariness abated at thoughts of the upcoming holidays with Heather and Pedro. Thoughts of warm fires, good food, and sound sleep danced inside his head. It would be good to be home.

The last several weeks in Ecuador, Colombia, and Brazil had been hectic. The expanding mission had kept Jim and his team busy; tracking the source of a smallpox outbreak, uncovering an insidious military plot to kill thousands of FARC rebels, and rescuing young Shuar girls from a group of brutal miners in the Amazon. An image of Tshui's smile and round face grew large in his mind's eye. She had immediately become his favorite as he had become hers.

A limited mission to rescue the Ecuadoran president's daughter in the Amazon had turned into one mission after another. The daughter, Angélica, had gone missing. Three days later, a ransom note had been delivered to her father in Quito. Jim's mission to rescue her had been arranged with extensive backup. It turned out, however, that she hadn't needed to be rescued. She had been easily recruited to the cause as well as to the leader's bed. Angélica Noboa Perez's kidnapping had lasted all of three minutes before her attraction for Jago, the rebel leader, had taken hold of her body and mind.

The seemingly straightforward mission had then degenerated into a series of complications. Once started, Jim's thoughts cascaded through a series of memories: gold mines, swamps and alligators, VX gas, the Colombian army, and the FARC rebel band that had become unlikely allies: Jago, Lobo, Cherry, and Chico. The team had also suffered the loss of two of the young FARC rebels as well as of their long-term friend Gaston, whose luck had run out in a jungle firefight with Ecuadoran soldiers.

Jim was more than ready to go home to Heather and to his adopted son Pedro. He used to think that home meant Heather and the ranch. But lately, they had been accumulating people—Lola, a stout Mexican woman, rescued along with Pedro from the cartel. And there was Old Man Shuskin, a vagrant who once haunted the mountain wilderness during the summer.

Jim sighed happily. He would be able to keep his promise to Heather and Pedro to be home for Christmas. He had come close to not keeping that promise. The festivities were only three days away. There were times during the last couple of weeks when he had wondered whether he would be able to keep his word. But making it is making it.

Jim closed his eyes and settled into the recliner. The plane's engines hummed steadily in the background. There was no turbulence. Drifting off to sleep, he thought of Tshui and Pedro, and Maria Dakine's interest in the Shuar head-shrinking process.

CHAPTER 1

SIX MONTHS EARLIER – SEPTEMBER 2000

Najma opened her eyes to the sound of decelerating helicopter blades. She blinked, trying to clear her vision. Only inches away, the face of her nemesis, Colonel Johnson. She reached over, wanting to check his pulse. She raised her arm, but the pain in her gut and shoulder made her dizzy. She started to perspire, closed her eyes, and tried to force the pain away. Had she killed the colonel?

She willed herself to check again. She had to be certain. She lifted her arm again, despite the pain, but the sound of someone walking outside the hangar stopped her. She forced her mind to clear. Her knife lay at her feet in pooled blood. Her clothes and hair were drenched with blood. On the smooth concrete floor, her blood co-mingled with the colonel's blood. Moaning, she reached to retrieve the blade. She knew one thing for certain; whoever was outside was her enemy. In agony, she forced herself to stand and survey the hangar. There was nowhere to hide.

My only chance is to ambush someone entering. Najma hobbled to Jim's Enstrom. Lazaro's body was still stretched out on the floor. He meant nothing to her. She turned her head back toward Colonel Johnson and managed a small smile. A large pool of blood was expanding near him. *Dead. I killed him. If I could only remember how. What happened?* Then an odd thought: *Is this what I wanted? To kill him? Yes. But do I want him dead?*

The thoughts swirled through her brain, nearly causing her to fall. She wanted to go back to him. To lie beside him. To feel the hard floor beside him. Footsteps brought her back to reality.

She leaned against the white chopper, listening. Whoever was outside was moving purposely at the back of the hangar. Below her hand, she found a small panel ajar. The downward tilt of the helicopter kept the panel closed. She opened it and peered into the darkness. Eighteen inches square, it extended to the other side of the Enstrom. Too small for most humans.

As she squeezed herself inside the helicopter's luggage compartment, Najma closed her eyes against the pain. The space was so small she could barely pull herself forward. Fingertips tenuously holding onto rivets, she pulled herself into the darkness. The effort left her exhausted and faint. If anyone discovered her there, she would be unable to defend herself. Her feet inside, the lightweight cover drifted shut. The square metal enclosure pressed against her. She was stuffed so tightly inside that a small sliver of light passing through the door hinge didn't penetrate past her hips. She closed her eyes in torment. Then she reopened them to the black void. Footsteps. Someone was entering the hangar.

A male voice said, 'Shit! Jeff, in here. Now.' She heard

running. 'He's still breathing.' *He's not dead.* In the darkness, Najma smiled.

General Crystal pressed his eyes closed. 'Status?'

'Bad, sir.'

The general knew he couldn't do anything for Jim. He gripped the helicopter's door gun and scanned the area, searching for a target. The only movement was Jeff running toward the hangar.

'Stay alert,' said Neilly. 'There's blood from someone else next to Jim.'

Mac scanned the inside of the hangar. He looked inside the Enstrom's cockpit. 'Blood trail from Jim comes in under the helicopter's tail. We're clear in here.'

They weren't clear. But stuffed in the narrow cubicle, Najma was no danger to them. She was bleeding internally. The two .25-calibre bullets' entry holes had coagulated, stopping the flow outside. Her wounded shoulder bled slightly, staining her clothes.

The trail of blood originated from Jim's entering the hangar, not from someone's exiting it. Forensics would later determine that Mac had been correct in his assumption.

'Three hangars north, two locals are hunkered down in a hangar,' said Gaston. 'No sign of anyone else.' He stood at the back of the hangar and searched the brush and hillsides, looking for Najma or any remaining cartel members.

The black Suburban skidded to a stop near 'Techie' Tom Bryant. Glenda, Marilyn, Gaston, and Joe jumped out. Joe covered Gaston as they ran to Tom.

'There's a body behind the colonel's hangar. It's Major McGuire.'

Glenda bolted toward the rear of Jim's hangar. Marilyn

ran behind her, turning and scanning, attempting to protect Glenda from an ambush.

The Medivac helicopter thundered overhead and set down not far from Techie Tom and the jet.

Glenda Rose skidded to a stop and dropped on her knees next to Brush. Marilyn scanned the area while JP moved down the hangar line, searching for cartel members.

'Brush doesn't look good,' said Glenda.

Will closed his eyes for a moment. His two special agents were injured and possibly dying at the hands of Najma. His BWC could never replace them. That was his rational side. He was a tough battle-worn commander, however, who was used to subduing his emotions. There were several people he had been fond of throughout his career, including Bertrand and Martin at the CIA. As they worked together, they became friends. He had never had a woman in his life. He had entertained the thought of Sheilla once, but his inexperience kept him from pursuing her. The same inexperience with women prevented him from realizing that, although Sheilla liked and respected him as her boss and friend, she would never love him as a companion.

Long ago in Vietnam, he had met Jim and Brush, his two closest buddies. Young, they had survived that war together. Will was their senior, both in age and rank. Nevertheless, the three had bonded as only those who have survived battles together can bond. Through the years, that bond had deepened. While the general outranked the colonel, who outranked Major McGuire, there was never a doubt in their minds that they were all equal. As hardened as he was, the general knew he would never be able to replace them in his life. The thought scared him.

The airport secure, he decided it was no longer necessary to stay on the door gun. Will jumped out and jogged toward Jim's hangar.

After a shot of morphine, Jeff left Techie Tom. Techie was wounded, but he would be okay. Jeff needed to check on the others. He ran toward the wrecked Enstrom helicopter, cutting to a jog as he neared it. He called Glenda about Brush's status.

'He looks bad. But the dumb Canuck is talking to me.'

Jeff ducked under the Enstrom's tail and rushed over to Jim.

'A lot of blood.'

'Money still says it's from two people,' said Neilly.

Jeff tore open a medical kit, cut off Jim's sleeve, and managed to insert an IV.

'Mac, I need you to hold the bag. He needs fluids before he goes into hemorrhagic shock.'

'Mac, look for Najma,' said Will. 'I'll hold the bag.'

Jeff lifted Jim's shirt and inspected the wound in his side. 'There's an exit hole in the back. He's lost a lot of blood and I have no way of knowing what his internal damage is. The scalp wound is ugly-looking. A big gash.' He pulled the wound together with his fingers, securing it with a butterfly bandage.

Two medics slid a stretcher under the Enstrom's tail and rushed over.

'Let's load him onto the chopper, get him oxygen, and see what his blood pressure is. Pulse is thirty-two. He needs a hospital. Now,' said Jeff.

'You want him to go to the west side?' asked one medic as they maneuvered Jim onto the stretcher.

'Omak is closest. He's just barely alive. Get him there and see if Fort Lewis can get one of its trauma docs to the hospital. Load Tom. I'll take a look at McGuire while you're getting them loaded. We need to hustle.'

He turned toward General Crystal. 'You want to take over for me, sir?'

'I haven't practiced for a long time,' said the general.

'Do your best, sir. Mac, Joe, get a stretcher for McGuire. I want to be in the air in two minutes,' said Jeff.

He ducked under the helicopter's mangled tail and rushed around the hangar to Glenda and Brush. He inspected Brush. 'Mac, hustle up, and get him on the vac with the other two.'

Despite his injuries, Brush was conscious. 'Who's the two?' he asked Glenda, hoping it was not Jim or the general.

'The colonel and Techie. Jim needs help ASAP.'

'Don't worry about me. Just get Jim where he needs to go.'

'Shut up, you dumb Canuck. Let the medics call the shots.'

Brush smiled slightly, mumbling, 'I love you too, honey,' before losing consciousness.

Marilyn stood guard until Brush was loaded onto the stretcher. As soon as they started toward the chopper, she moved back to the tarmac.

'He'll make it,' said Jeff more convincingly than he felt. The major's pulse was steady near sixty. He would probably survive. It was the colonel that worried him.

It took all Najma's willpower to remain still. The pain amplified as she lay pressed inside the metal chamber. If she passed out, her foot might push the compartment door open, exposing her. If she moved, the lightweight metal might make a noise, giving her away. They would have her, and it would be back to a Guantanamo jail cell. This time with no chance of escape. Guillermo would have someone terminate her. She had to stay the course. Silent and unmoving.

The voices disappeared. The Medivac chopper lifted off simultaneously with the Blackhawk. To allay the searing pain, Najma tried to shift her body. Instead, she passed out. Her foot relaxed, pushing the compartment door open to an empty hangar.

She regained consciousness to agony and blackness. There were no sounds. She gritted her teeth, pushing herself out of the compartment. She fell to the floor and passed out again.

∼

General Crystal monitored Jim's vital signs in the Medivac helicopter. *Heart rate thirty-nine. A bit better. Blood pressure forty-nine over thirty. Not good*, he thought. There was nothing else he could do. The medics fussed over Jim doing what they could.

He sighed and decided he had to call Heather. Waiting wouldn't help. She needed to know.

'Heather, we're flying to the hospital in Omak.'

Heather held her breath. At least he had not said Jim was dead.

'How bad is he?'

'It's serious, Heather.'

'I'll send the Medivac to bring you over as soon as we land.'

'Shoot. Why is this happening? We're waiting for the vet for Rosie O Twisp. Too many shootings.'

'It's worse. Brush is also seriously wounded.'

'Don't tell me. Najma got away. Can I talk to Jim?'

'He's unconscious. Try not to worry. We'll get him to the ER. We have one of the army's best docs on his way to Omak from the army's special trauma unit at Madigan hospital.'

'Oh, God. No.'

Techie Tom managed to get himself to the Medivac but could not get in. The two medics, followed by Glenda, Mac, and Jeff, were doing a fast walk to the chopper with the unconscious Brush. Mac ran ahead and helped Techie in. Loaded, the Medivac rose to a hover before dipping east.

The general said into his headset, 'Redline this bird.' He didn't need to add 'or else.' The pilots knew his connection to the injured passengers. They pulled in maximum power and did exactly as the general ordered.

The two medics shifted between Techie, Jim, and Brush. Glenda sat next to Brush, holding his hand. The general continued to monitor Jim and made sure that the Mid-Valley Hospital, where he had recovered a year ago, had its ER teams standing by. The staff had fond memories of their famous patient and prepared for the incoming patients. However, their ER was not staffed for three emergencies. The head nurse located an additional experienced doctor and nurse and ordered them to the emergency room.

'Three minutes out. They've cleared the parking lot near the emergency entrance for us to land,' said the pilot.

'Sheilla, our army doc's status?

'Forty minutes away, sir.'

'I want search teams on the ground pronto. Forensics, FBI, whatever or whoever else you need. I want to find that killer. She's close. She doesn't get away this time.'

'On it, general. I sent the Blackhawk to remove the prisoners. Mac is at the airport and guarding the jet. Carter is flying to the airport with his team. The FBI and forensics are on their way. I've asked for sat coverage. The local cops are setting up roadblocks. We'll find her.'

General Will Crystal sat brooding with a stethoscope affixed to Jim's chest. A medic attached EKG leads. Will sat brooding. They had lost Sergeant Mason. Jim and Brush were wounded, and Jim might not make it. Even Pedro's dog, Rosie, shot. *Jim lost his little chopper. I lost my bird. How much damage can one woman do? And she's still on the loose. Jesus, what a day.*

Violent shivers forced Najma into consciousness. She lay on the concrete floor below the Enstrom. The floor was cool in the late summer. The induced hypothermia saved her life. Her mind started to register what had happened and what had not: she had not been captured.

She turned her head to where she and Colonel Johnson had lain. He was gone. *Why am I still here?* Her mind churned. She tried to focus, listening for voices. There was only silence. *Why?*

The Medivac pilot brought his helicopter in fast. *No delay.* The orders from the general rang in his ears. No hovering or turning. The emergency staff stepped back, worrying that the pilot would fly into them. But the pilot executed a perfectly coordinated running landing that stopped short of sliding into them as the skids scraped along the asphalt.

'General, I've patched the incoming doc into your comm. He wants to speak to the emergency doctors.'

General Crystal pulled his earpiece out and offered it to the lead doctor. The doctor ignored him. A booming voice stopped everyone short.

The doctor smiled, recalling his past patient now barking orders at his staff. Glenda stepped in, hooking her mic and earpiece up for Dr. Green as he held his gloved hands in the air.

'General, you need your comm. I can spare mine for the doctor,' said Glenda, who abruptly turned to Brush.

Dr. Green said, 'Fluids heated and warmed oxygen. Stat.'

A voice entered his earpiece. 'Stop.'

'Who is this?'

'I'm an army doctor. I'll direct you. Reverse the warming. I want you to induce hypothermia.'

'That will kill him.'

A louder voice commanded, 'Do as he says, Doctor.'

'It's your man on the table,' said Dr. Green. 'Okay, reverse that. No warming.'

The voice in Dr. Green's ear continued while they worked on the patient.

The general watched as Dr. Green reduced the IV flow.

'General, this is Lt. Colonel King. I presume you are monitoring. What is the status of the other patients?'

The general moved to the bed where Brush was being worked on. He relayed what he saw from the EKG monitor.

'He appears stable.'

'The third patient?'

The general didn't bother to give Techie's vitals, pulling a dividing curtain aside. Techie Tom was conversing with the staff attending him. 'The third patient is fine and talkative.'

'My ETA is less than five minutes.'

'Explain why you wanted to keep Colonel Johnson hypothermic?'

'Battlefield experience. Hemorrhagic shock during the golden hour is normally treated by fluids and warming core temperature. I've lost dozens of patients with that protocol. I researched it. We changed our battlefield treatment. I've written this up.'

'Explain.'

'Induced hypothermia protects tissue and organs in bleeding polytrauma patients and increases intact neurological survival. Reversing has to proceed slowly. It's a double-edged sword. Too much or too little can kill. The treatment has to be nuanced and combined with reduced fluids. In short, first repair vascular injuries, maintain hypothermia, then slowly restore temp, and replace fluids. In that order.'

The door burst open and a tall black man walked in wearing camo fatigues. 'Where do I scrub?'

CHAPTER 2

Najma realized the airfield was temporarily abandoned. She knew it would not stay that way long. The time was now. Accept her pain. Escape while she could.

The odds were not in her favor. Many would be looking for her. They would have air, satellite, infrared, and perhaps dogs. There was no hiding here. She had to get away and not leave a trail. Even with all her skills and wits, she would need a large dose of luck.

She moved under the Enstrom's tail, hugging the wall. She peered outside. The cartel men remained where they had died. The jet was parked fifty meters in front. There was a movement in the cockpit. She pulled her head back. For a moment, she wondered how far she could get hijacking the plane. The idea evaporated as a man carrying an MP-7 moved into the doorway. From his manner, it was clear he was part of the Special Forces unit. In her condition, she was no match for someone with such training.

Her vision started to blur. She felt faint and suppressed

a wave of nausea. The man disappeared from the plane's door. She willed herself to move around the corner and toward the back alongside the hanger. Surfacing through the pain and her swirling brain, a thought slipped out. *The colonel was not dead. She would not die. There would be a return engagement. This time on her terms.*

As she stumbled toward the rear of the hangar, visions of holding him captive kept her from fainting. Thoughts of teasing him, feeling him inside her, and watching his pain grow, gave her the strength to move. Move where?

At the back of the hangar she looked in all directions. The ditch where she had shot the colonel's partner. The other side of the ditch. The road. She knew from experience that the road led to Winthrop to the north and Highway 20 to the south. She looked up the hill. It was dry. Only weeds. No trees.

No cars on the road. Three hang gliders circled in warm updrafts on a distant hill. Flying away like a bird would prevent dogs from tracking her. She could soar for miles. But the gliders were too far away, and there would be too many people for her to handle.

Far down the road, a glint. Sunlight reflected on chrome. She evaluated for a second. Law enforcement. army, or civilian? She had no choice. Luck would win or lose this gamble. She moved through the ditch to the road and lay down in the middle of the pavement. For a moment, doubt consumed her. She reached to her ankle and found the .22 pistol. She felt for her double-edged knife. She found it in her back pocket in its black leather sheath.

She relaxed. It felt better to be lying down. The moment of truth awaited. A blue pickup truck slowed, then pulled up next to her. A large man jumped out and came to her side.

'Are you all right?'

'Better than I was,' she replied as she pointed the small .22 at the man's face.

'Be a gentleman. Help me up. No funny ideas or they will be your last.'

Murray reached down and took her outstretched hand. He assessed whether he could move out of the way fast enough. The woman grimaced.

'Get me in your truck.'

'I've watched a lot of movies. Best time to put up a fight is right away in the beginning. The further I go with you, the worse off I'll be. I'd rather take my chances here where we stand.'

'Look, mister. I'm not going to hurt you or shoot you unless you make me. There are some bad people on the loose here and one of them shot me. I don't know you and don't trust you. Until I do, you do as I say.'

Murray re-thought and decided to take his chances with her.

'Where are you shot?'

'Do a U-turn. I want to go to Wolf Canyon Ranch. You know where that is?'

The man laughed. 'It's like a second home. I do vet work there all the time.'

'I was taking the short cut to the ranch. Over Balky Hill Road. You want to go the long way around, it's fine by me.'

'Okay, smart guy. Quickest way.'

If she wanted to go to the ranch, she can't be all that bad, he thought.

'You know Jim?'

'I work with the colonel,' she lied. 'Quit ass-poking.'

'Where are you from?' Murray laughed at her reversing the slang phrase poke-assing.

He stepped on the gas pedal while winding up the long hill. His old pickup didn't like the steep hill any better than the mules did in pioneer days.

'Drive. I don't want to talk.' It took all her willpower to remain conscious.

They descended the hill toward the lower ranch house and Beaver Creek.

'Sheriff from Omak is down there. Big goings-on at the ranch to bring him all the way over. Jim's dog is shot. Can you tell me what happened up there?'

'I will. First, I need to tell you that I work undercover for the general and the colonel,' she smoothly lied again. 'There was an attack on the ranch led by a Mexican cartel.'

'What do they have to do with anything in these parts?'

'You really don't know? Obviously not. I have to make this quick, so you'll understand what I am going to ask you to do.'

Murray started to get nervous again. 'Ask me what?

'That sheriff down there is on the cartel's payroll. He won't say anything about me when we drive by, but those military guys might. I can't be seen. I need to protect my cover. I'm going to get down. You drive by and wave. Keep going. Don't stop. Don't go slow. If they try to stop you, yell emergency at the ranch and keep going.'

'This isn't making any sense.'

'I can't afford to fuck around here. Does this gun pointed at you make sense?'

'Like I said before, I'll take my chances. I'm stopping. You shoot me if you have to.'

Najma would have liked to do just as he'd said. Instead, she said, 'You're one of the good guys. Not everyone down there is. I have to find out who, so they don't kill Heather, Pedro, or anyone else on our side. You want to be responsible for that? And for telling Jim why you let Heather and Pedro get killed? Because that's what these guys were sent here to do. Unless we stop them, they'll find a way to do it.'

Murray drove fast. His old truck rattled down the dirt road, shaking every nerve in Najma's body.

'You need a new truck, bud fuck.'

He waved at the sheriff, pointed frantically toward the ranch, and mouthed 'emergency.' The sheriff tried to wave him to a stop. Murray didn't stop. The sheriff would have chased him down, but he was here to block traffic, not to stop the local vet from driving to the ranch.

Over the bridge and at Beaver Creek Road junction, Najma said, 'Thanks. You did the right thing.'

'Turn left.'

'What? You said we were going to the ranch.'

'We will, Mr. Vet. What's your name?'

'Murray,' he said, listlessly. His mind was on Rosie. A dog he had grown fond of through the years.

Murray's cell phone rang. Najma needed him. She wanted him to trust her.

'Answer it. Please don't mention me.' She lowered the gun.

'Thanks for calling, Heather. He'll be okay. He's a tough guy. Wish him well for me, will you.'

'Who's going to be okay?'

'She said Jim was in the emergency room in Omak. A chopper is going to take her and Rosie to the hospital. I don't need to go up.'

Najma tried not to smile as she said, 'Shit. I told you. Just what I've been trying to get into your head. Now they got Jim. Bad people. I'm glad for Pedro that his dog will get attended to. How bad is Jim?'

'Not good, I think.'

'I want to contact him, but I can't break my cover. God, I hope he is okay. You ever operate on a person?'

'Jesus. You can't ask me to do that. I'll take you to the hospital with your boss in Omak. They'll fix you up.'

'Look, you. For the last time. I'm undercover and need to stay that way.'

Beaver Creek ran alongside the road on the left. A steep drive appeared on the right.

'Where does that go?'

'A mobile home that Jim bought.'

'Empty?'

'Maybe the Twisp chief of police lives there. Jim rents it to him. We can go check if you want.'

Najma shook her head as he passed the road.

Another driveway went up the hill. 'What's up that one?' asked Najma.

'Abandoned house. Used to belong to the Baptist preacher. Belongs to the county now.'

'Drive up.'

'Yes, ma'am. You're sure a bossy one for such a little thing.'

Najma looked at the vet's hands. He was a big man with big hands.

'You sure you can perform delicate surgery with those hands?'

'I do okay on animals.'

Najma opened the door. Mice droppings littered every surface.

'Looks like hantavirus heaven,' said Murray.

'Open up your vet kit. Give me a surgical mask. I might die from you operating on me. I accept that. I don't plan to die from a mouse virus.'

'I told you. I'm not operating on you.'

'One step at a time. Open your bag. Wipe the table down with alcohol.'

Najma walked close to Murray. 'I know you don't want to. I have a job to do, but not with these bullets in me. I need your help. Do the best you can. I trust you.'

With dark eyes and hair, she looked up at his six-foot three-inch height, using her most beseeching look. He was eleven inches taller than she, and twice her weight.

'You were never going to shoot me, were you?'

'I sort of doubt I was. Please, though, help me. Help Jim. Help the general.'

Murray looked big and rough around the edges, but he was a kind and gentle man. Najma had pegged him correctly. If he thought he could help Jim, he would and right now this confusing lady needed help to do just that.

Murray's face showed he had acquiesced. 'First, I need to get some things from my rig.'

CHAPTER 3

'Glenda, I want to talk to you,' said the general. 'Let's step outside.'

'How's Jim?' asked Glenda.

'I don't know. It depends on if he has organ damage. They're prepping him.'

'The surgical staff is prepping Brush too. The trauma doc you brought over looked at him. He says, Jim first and then Brush. He said Brush would be better off if he waited for him to do the surgery. He'll last. The local ER team is tending to Techie Tom.'

'Sheilla has marshaled the FBI and local law enforcement. The lead FBI is Jurgen Shultz. You know him?'

'Yeah. I do. He's about as good as it gets. Different and better than most.'

'I'd rather have you out there, but it's not fair to ask you to leave Brush. I'm going to stay here until after Jim's surgery and then fly back to Methow Valley State. The control center will be located there. We'll keep in contact.'

Glenda was thankful the general was letting her stay.

She understood that he would want to know how Jim and Brush were doing. And he would want her back to track Najma as soon as possible.

'Thank you, sir.'

The general was caught off guard as Glenda gave him a tight hug. General Will Crystal, the tough combat commander, hugged her back.

'They'll be okay,' he said. 'We'll all be okay.'

Glenda brushed aside a tear and patted him on the shoulder before she walked back to Brush's room.

'General Crystal. Special Agent Jurgen Shultz, I'm onsite. We're setting up an operations headquarters in Winthrop. I didn't want to take time to airlift in modules to the airport.'

'My departure is in eighteen minutes.'

'The address for your pilot is 51 North Highway 20. It's just north of the town about a mile. I'll have a landing zone marked in a small park next to the building.'

'The pilot has the destination. From my GPS, I make my ETA 1756.'

'Sorry, General. I should have realized you'd be the pilot.'

'Bring me up-to-date.'

'We have all local law enforcement sitting at roadblocks on major routes. Until we get more agents, we can't cover all the roads. There are dozens of forest service roads. We've typed the blood at the hangar. It matches Najma Hussein's. We also have fingerprints and DNA matched from the hangar.'

'What about satellite coverage? Anything in real-time?'

'No, sir. We have a fair estimate of when she left the hangar. She was there hiding while your agent Colonel Johnson was removed.'

'Explain, Agent Shultz.'

Jurgen ignored the lack of Special Agent prefacing his name. 'She managed to squeeze into a small luggage compartment in the helicopter. From the blood, forensics was able to estimate when she left. I've questioned the Special Forces that were in the hangar and cleared it. The compartment door looks like an inspection panel. It's only eighteen inches on a side. They were not familiar with the Enstrom's configuration.'

'Damn it to hell.'

'She's injured. There were two .25 auto shell casings that forensics says were probably point-blank next to where the colonel lay.'

'That's a backup pistol that Jim uses.'

'Pretty low-impact weapon?' questioned Jurgen.

'It's a backup pistol. Anything else?'

'I'll keep you updated. I know the importance of this. I'm in contact with a Martin Pearson at CIA and Sheilla McCarrick. They're both monitoring all area communications, police bulletins, missing persons, and stolen cars. Ms. McCarrick, who I hear you recruited from the FBI, is getting a drone moved to the airport. A Special Forces SAD team is en route. SWAT teams from the FBI are even closer with an ETA of twenty minutes.'

'You have one of the best SF teams already on-site.'

'The one that overlooked the perp in the hangar?'

'Set it aside, Agent Shultz. That team's as good as it gets.'

'Here's the breakdown,' said Sheilla. 'Colonel Johnson and Major McGuire are both in critical condition in Omak's Mid-Valley Hospital. The general is en route to Winthrop where the FBI is setting up a command post. Fred has summarized relevant locations in the briefing sheets.'

'On the computer display monitor in the hot room, I've installed several variations with both terrain and road maps. They are tied directly to each workstation. Each workstation is synced to the large display. Your choice which one to view.'

'Thanks, Fred. Our primary mission,' Sheilla continued, 'is to monitor all communication in the surrounding area. Law enforcement included. Additionally, I want to monitor Siastra Cartel communications, specifically in Mexico and eastern Washington State. But I don't want to limit us. Let's get back into their headquarters. If they're helping her, we might get some info. Misa, as we speak, is installing a keyword search to aid you. Focus on local law enforcement that are on the cartel's payroll. Known specifics and names are in your briefing sheets. I want one person to monitor security cams at stores, rest stops, the Canadian border, and truck weigh stations. We're working on a facial recognition program. Fred will make the assignments. Get rid of any assumptions. Think outside the box. Let's find her.'

Sheilla waved Katarina over. 'I'd like you to propose ways Najma might escape. You've profiled her in detail. You know as well as anyone how she thinks.'

'It won't be possible. She will be opportunistic. Respond to the situation and turn it to her advantage.'

'I understand. What I am hoping is that, as we begin to

track her, you can determine her next move. I know it's guesswork.'

'It's likely she will evaluate her choices and not make the choice we would expect. She will call the shots. It's a battle of wits. She's alive because she's good at this.'

'So are you. Get into her mind. Stay a step ahead. Direct us. Even with all the data we'll have, I'm willing to bet that your input will be how we catch her.'

'We will have to be lucky to catch her in the first place. She'll be like a trapped animal, only smarter. When she ascertains the chips are down, she will take as many with her as she can.'

'What do you mean?'

'It will be her game. It's not in her makeup to be cornered. She will become the aggressor. As dangerous as a wildcat with the intelligence and survival skills of an Einstein.'

'You think Neilly is no match for her?'

'He will be if he gets it into his head that she does not play by his rules. We need the colonel's input, and you've seen, even with him, what has happened. Jeez, Sheilla, I hope he survives,' said Katarina.

'Ditto.'

The general had uncharacteristically remained silent. He heard the discussion on the edge of his thoughts. Sheilla's voice brought him back into full focus. General, can you write something that won't offend him, but let him know what he's up against?'

'I will. One thing. Don't assume she won't go after Colonel Johnson in the hospital.'

Sheilla went back to her office and took several spins in her chair before calling General Crystal.

'Is Jim going to make it?'

'Something tells me he will. He always does.'

'The major?'

'Doctor says he'll be okay.'

'Katarina is going to try to predict what Najma will do. She says it's hopeless until we get some information about her current path. Also, she'll not rule out that Najma could go after Colonel Johnson in the hospital.'

'Glenda is staying at the hospital. Alert her. I'm ten minutes ETA Winthrop. Martin is coordinating with RCMP and CSIS. I'll make sure that Shultz has what he needs. I have to be in D.C. late morning. Stay live comms with Martin and Shultz. I'll take the plane back from here.'

'Got it.'

'We just flew over a roadblock on Highway 20 and Beaver Creek Road. Another on Balky Hill Road and Beaver Creek Road. Tell Agent Shultz to get names and license numbers for cars as they pass through.'

'Hey, Mac,' said Neilly. 'I was in the hangar too. I never looked at the cargo compartment. But who would? I didn't even know that the Enstrom had one.'

'Turns out it can hold ninety pounds for flight,' said Mac.

'Put it behind you. Not your fault. The general just called. We're first up if they get a fix on her. You can redeem yourself then. Get some sleep. I need you ready and focused.'

'You can't handle this without anesthesia.'

'Look, big boy. Local only. I'll take the pain. You just find those two bullets in my gut. After, disinfect my shoulder and stitch it.'

Dr. Murray Lundqvist wondered if his Viking relatives had ever been as tough as this lady. *Probably not,* he thought. *She won't be as tough as she thinks she is when I start digging around in her belly.*

'I don't have any anesthesia anyway.' *What I do have,* he thought, *is Rompun. That will put her out if I can get it into her.* Murray filled a syringe with Xylocaine.

'What is that?'

'It's a local. I have to numb the area, or you'll jump. I might rupture an intestine or worse.'

'What's it called?'

'You have to trust me, little one. I don't even know your name?'

'What is it? Then you can have my name.'

'It's Xylocaine, or lidocaine. It will numb the local tissue. Pull your blouse up and your pants down some.'

'It's Sally Lopez.'

'You don't look Mexican.'

'That's because I'm not. My mother was. You're wasting time.'

'It will take a few minutes for the lidocaine to take effect. Relax.'

Najma lay back on the table. Murray worked the needle into her abdomen and injected the Xylocaine. He filled another syringe with Rompun. Luckily, Najma didn't look. He would have preferred to have given the Rompun IV, but with her watching, an intermuscular injection would have to do. *I wish I had some ketamine to add with it. That would shut her up good.*

'I'm feeling a little dizzy. What did you give me?' Najma started to lift herself and pointed the pistol at him.

'Put it down. I gave you a lot of local. It's making you faint.'

Murray took the top off a seven percent iodine and poured some on her wounds. She winced.

'I told you.'

Najma let go of the pistol and went limp as the Rompun took effect. Even without the drug, she'd been ready to pass out.

Murray took a deep breath before he pinched and probed near the bullet wounds. His beefy fingers were surprisingly delicate but the openings were too small for his finger. He enlarged them with a scalpel. After some poking, he located both bullets and with forceps managed to get them out. One had lodged in her kidney. The small-caliber bullet had been slowed as it passed through her clothing and muscle. He thought she would be all right if she didn't get an infection.

He sprinkled on a large amount of antibiotic powder and an injection of his best broad-spectrum antibiotic. After suturing the incision and entry holes, he sat down on the floor, leaning against a wall. He looked at her lying there then pulled out his cell phone thinking about what she had said, about not being able to trust anyone. *Could the enemy be listening?*

'I think I did good for my first human surgery,' he said to the dozens of listening mice. *If she lives. If it helps Jim.* The phone slid from his hand as the strain took hold of him, and he fell asleep.

Slices of rose-orange penetrated the dust-covered windows. A shaft struck her eyelid. It wasn't the light that woke her. It was the sound of ear-rumbling snores. *I'm too groggy. He gave me something else.*

She laid her head back on the table. She raised herself and looked at her stomach. Much of it was covered with orange-purple iodine glowing in the evening light. The stitches looked neat. She closed her eyes and shook her head. The snoring was irritating. Her head throbbed.

It took several minutes before she was able to sit and then stand. She kicked him in the leg.

'Who did you call?'

'Huh?'

'Give me your phone.'

Standing on unsteady legs, she took the phone in her right hand and kept the .22 aimed at him. She backed to the table and pushed recent calls. There were none.

'You are being a good Norwegian.'

'My family was Swedish.'

'What do you have in your bag of tricks to keep me awake?'

'That would be dangerous.'

'I have little time. What do you have?'

'Ritalin.'

'Get up and get it. If you hadn't done such a good job, I would have shot you just to shut you up.'

'Snoring, huh?'

'If that is what you call that cacophony. I like the sound of the word. I hate noise.'

At the sound of a helicopter speeding along Beaver Creek Road, they both stopped talking.

'Get me the drug. We need to leave.'

'Where to?'

'Conconully.'

'That's all dirt roads if we keep going this way. The bumps will kill you. We could go back to Highway 20. It's smoother that way.'

'No. Let's move.'

'What's there?'

'Move it, Doctor Murray. Wait. Stop. Give me a pain pill.'

Murray reached in his bag and pulled out a plastic container.

'Give it to me. What is it?'

'Oxycodone and Motrin are all I have. My clients don't normally require it. They're for me. I've been banged around a bit, mostly with large animals.'

Najma studied him for a few seconds.

Murray said, 'The pills will help.'

She reached up and touched his cheek. 'Thank you for fixing me. Let's go. I need to hurry.'

They drove north on the gravel road along the creek. Murray tried to avoid the washboards and holes. Najma held herself as rigid as she could. The pills mitigated the discomfort. This man was okay. She even sort of liked him. His body had been punished. He knew what pain felt like. Something they had in common.

The road turned away from the creek and started uphill.

'You sure you know the way?'

'I go hunting up here. Not many people do.'

'Why not hunt up Wolf Canyon? Deer, bear, and cougar from what I saw.'

'Jim doesn't like hunters.'

Najma stifled a laugh. *Her arch enemy. The killer didn't like to hurt animals. Didn't make sense.* It was impossible for a psychopath to understand someone like Jim. They were on opposite ends of the spectrum. It was just as difficult for Jim to understand someone completely lacking in feelings for living things.

They climbed up the hills. The sky deepened to blue-gray. Orange smudges filtered through the trees to their west. They were heading east away from the sunset when they came to a cleared area that had been logged several years ago. Small Douglas fir grew four to five feet high. Mixed in were dead trees already cut but too small to take to a mill.

'I don't know why they do this,' said Murray.

'Do what?'

'Deforestation. It's as if a square tornado dropped from the sky and decimated everything growing. 'Heather hates these forest clearings too. We often talk about logging and overgrazing while we work on animals together. A long time ago they cut all the good hemlocks. The trees here now are Doug firs. Heather called them a weed but was fond of their name *Pseudotsuga* menziesii. Used to say it all the time and the only reason I remember it. The loggers think trees are to be cut, whether they need to be or not. Maybe just like your cartel members. Kill just for the sake of it.'

Najma understood. She smiled. 'How far to Conconully?'

'Over the ridge ahead the road widens out and drops straight down to it.'

'Pull over the other side of the clearing.'

'I could use a break too.'

They got out of Murray's truck. Scattered dents and small rust spots merged with oxidized paint. Murray paused, looking back toward the surrendering orange sky. A sliver moon hung just above the mountains to the west. It stood vertical, kissing the horizon's edge with the point of its sickle.

'You have a woman, Murray the Viking?'

'Huh? Ah, I do. She is bedridden from a horse-riding accident. Paralyzed.'

Najma walked over to him. 'You've seen my stomach and my intestines. Those may not be my best parts.' She looked up at him as she undid her blouse. She was braless.

Murray didn't, couldn't say anything. He hadn't been with a woman for years. His mouth hung open. Najma reached over and softly, slowly massaged his penis until it grew hard. Murray felt dizzy.

'Lay back on the ground.' The dim warm light curved over and around her breasts. She massaged a nipple and it became erect. Murray was mesmerized by the vision, the dream that stood over him. Najma rubbed herself and looked down at him. She liked this man. She did something unusual for her. She lowered her pants and pulled one leg off. Orange reflections danced on iodine. She continued stroking.

Sensuality, heightened by pain, pleased her. Her dark eyes and hair blended into the shadows. Her eyes closed as she held herself tight for several seconds. She dropped onto both knees over him. She reached in her back pocket and removed her double-bladed knife from its leather scabbard.

'I have told you a lie, Doctor. My name is not as I said. It is Najma Hussein.'

Still dazed, Murray looked into the darkening night air. The evening held no more color. Only dim shadows.

'I see you do not know that name.'

She reached behind her as she had done so many times before and began massaging his penis. He was as hard as a tree stub. She peered into his eyes and positioned the knife above his larynx.

'I am the one that shot your friend Jim. I'm the one everyone is looking for. I am no Mexican. I'm Iraqi.'

Murray was confused. What Najma said barely registered. A female was playing with him. Something he had not felt for a long time. His body tingled. His breath was short. The woman had said she was the killer. An Arab on the run.

She watched his eyes. They were no longer blue. A white spark from the moon bounced off his pupil. He felt the knifepoint at his throat. As was her custom, she reached below for his throbbing member and grasped his testicles. She squeezed slowly at first. Then, harder. Murray's eyes registered the sickening ache that took his strength away. She was the killer. He was going to die.

'But I helped you,' he protested before the knife cut through his vocal cords, making its way to his cervical spine.

Najma didn't smile. Her mouth opened slightly, and she closed her eyes as the life drained from him. She pressed herself on his lifeless body. Slowly, back and forth. The sensations soft and wonderful. Her mind on an oxycodone pleasure binge. His limp body under her, she opened her eyes again and stared into the darkness.

CHAPTER 4

While Lieutenant Colonel Bart King operated on Brush, Glenda wandered aimlessly down the hall. On her right was an open door with a sign that read "Prayer Room." It was empty and quieter than the hall. Glenda Rose, closed the door, and stood for a moment, as tempted as she had ever been to pray.

'If you are real, God, please do the right thing with Brush.'

An old upright piano sat to one side. Glenda had taken lessons as a young girl, but she could no longer play. She could, however, read the bass and the treble clefs on simple pieces, and she could still pick out fragments of songs she had learned as a child.

She pulled the bench out and hesitantly fingered the first piece that came to mind, a song that always made her feel good. Tentatively, she drifted from one note to the other. The tune had been written two years before she was born and had been made famous three years later by Frank Sinatra.

She hummed and sang along as she played. *When I was seventeen. It was a very good year for small-town girls and soft summer nights.* She could barely remember the words. *When I was thirty-five. It was a very good year for blue-blooded girls ....*

Suddenly, the day caught up with her, and she broke down crying. 'Please let him be okay,' she implored the empty room. She sat unmoving, her mind a blank.

The door opened. Lieutenant Colonel King filled the door frame.

Glenda took a deep breath and held it.

'He's okay.'

'Thank you. Thank you.'

'They're both going to be okay.'

'Can I talk to the major?'

'I believe he would like that. That is, assuming you are Glenda Rose? I'm Bart King, Lieutenant Colonel King, by the way.'

'How did you know my name?'

'Patients sometimes talk when they are under sedation. I think it would be wise not to mention everything he said. Glenda Rose was mentioned several dozen times.'

'Spreading our personal lives around, was he?'

'Don't worry. I would say you both are lucky.'

'The men are not safe here, sir. When can they be moved to the base hospital?'

'The major and the colonel both need several days or weeks recovery time. How urgent is it?'

'Unknown. The sooner the better.'

'If we treat them with TLC, they can move tomorrow. If it's important, and I take it it is, I'll stay till tomorrow and go back with them.'

'Thank you again. The truth is, they will be checking

themselves out if we keep them for more than a couple of days.'

'We get them back to my hospital next to Fort Lewis, and I'll keep them in there until they are fit to leave. I'm used to persuading the survive-anything-macho types. They think they can bear any pain and survive any challenge until they find out it just ain't true.'

Near a parking lot with dozens of government vehicles, a sign announced *The Barn*. A Blackhawk was sitting in a grassy area, separated from the large wood building. Men were lounging around the helicopter.

The general positioned his approach, thinking he didn't like the looks of the Blackhawk. *And it's what I'm flying now.* As the general approached, the soldiers stood.

He settled onto the grass next to a picnic table. One of the men started toward him as the blades slowed.

'Sir, we turned the prisoners over to the FBI. We heard you were flying here. Sheilla told us to stay until you arrived.'

The general returned Captain Carter's salute and walked rapidly toward the oversized building with Carter in tow.

'She was right. We need all the bodies we can get. What's with your team? I almost said manpower but rejected that thought. You don't have a woman among you? What gives?' asked the general.

'No prejudices, sir. Just the way it is.'

'Consider rectifying that, Captain, if you find someone appropriate.'

'Our immediate supervisor is a woman. Then there is Ms. McCarrick and Agent Stuart. I will, when the right person pops up.'

They burst through the door into the center of the room. It was a large, empty space, a refurbished barn as its name implied, used by the community for everything, conferences, meetings, and even as a cowboy dance palace. Now men and women were setting up computers, monitors, printers, and faxes. A large composite map had been tacked to one wall. Two men turned from the map. One of them, a short man with cropped gray hair, walked toward them.

'General Crystal, Special Agent Shultz. Pleased to meet you, sir.'

'Bring me up-to-date.'

'I was just checking the roadblock locations. We don't have sat coverage yet. Two light surveillance planes are en route from Fairchild Air Force Base. The Special Forces A team is at Methow State, searching in detail.'

The general caught the nuanced reference to Neilly's crew having overlooked Najma in the Enstrom. His look was enough to convey to Shultz that it would be the last time he cast any barbs their way. Shultz took the hint to heart, not wanting to antagonize the director of the CIA.

'Agent Shultz, meet Captain Carter. He is part of a special response team we work with. His team is standing by outside.' Shultz might be an old-line respected FBI agent, but knowledge of the BWC and of Carter's headquarters was outside his security clearance.

'We can use them. For now, I want them to stand by. We have one lead so far. A dog team was given Najma Hussein's scent. They followed it outside the hangar to the access road, where it stopped. She was picked up there.

That leaves three possible directions. We have roadblocks at all three. All vehicles have been thoroughly searched. Nothing so far. She might have stopped short of the road-blocks. She could still be close by. Unless she swims the river, I don't see any other way for her to escape.'

'Don't count anything out. Run every driver and vehicle through your computers. There could be a link.'

'Your assistant just called me about that.'

The general didn't correct him.

'Along with the SF team, the dogs are working their way down the road. It's several miles, so it will take a while to survey both sides to the roadblocks. There is one gravel road that goes over the hill toward Wolf Canyon. There are no roads off it, but lots of spur roads. All eventually dead-end. It will take some time to look over. In our favor, there is not a lot of cover. I plan to have air surveillance check that area and both sides of the river. As I get more agents, we'll interview everyone along the routes and on both sides of the river.'

'We're monitoring all communications and videos at stores,' said General Crystal. 'She should still be in the vicinity. Let's not overlook her.'

Shultz nearly said "again" before he caught himself. The general was well respected. His short brief on him showed General Will Crystal to be a battle-tested soldier. He was not a politically appointed head of the CIA. If he thought as highly of Neilly's team as he seemed to, so be it. He would adjust his opinion.

'I'll wait outside with my men,' said Carter.

'You won't be long,' said Shultz. 'The general said you were rapid response. I'll have you wait where you are, then

I'll assign you to the search. When I do, keep your team together in case we locate her. I'll want you to be able to act fast. Live up to your name.'

CHAPTER 5

Sheilla's long auburn hair lifted slightly as she spun in her chair. *I like being a Whirling Dervish. Maybe I missed my calling.* She stopped, walked out her door and down the hall to the computer center.

Fred shook his head as she walked in. 'Nada. Nothing.'

'She's on her own,' said Sheilla. 'That's something new.'

She opened the door to Misa and Vidya's *Cave*. 'You want to chat. Get a coffee maybe?' she asked as Misa turned from her computer screen.

'Let's go into our *sitting room*,' said Misa.

'I sometimes forget you are British,' she chuckled at Misa's word.

'What's up?'

'Nothing really. I think we're wasting our time. She isn't going to communicate with anyone. The cartel pukes are all caught. Najma won't trust anyone else.'

'We might pick up on some news if she kills someone.'

'Maybe … You miss the sun, Misa?'

'You don't get out much yourself.'

'Never bothered me. But I've been thinking about it lately.'

'Vidya and I don't mind being hermits. Or, this far underground. It feels cozy like a mole in its hole. We take 2000 mg of vit D every day. The lab does a blood test every few months. It's our home now. We like it and what we're doing.'

'I don't mind too much either. Usually anyway. We're not going to find her. Are we? Katarina thinks the same. I was spinning in my chair and thinking this is a waste of time.'

'You don't seem yourself.'

'Nah, yeah, I don't know. I love this job. This is the first time, though, where everyone gets shot up. It was a relief when the doc from the base trauma center said they're all going to be okay. I guess I was thinking about how quickly things can change. For a while, my world was feeling relatively stable.'

'Solution is simple. You need a vacation.'

'You want to go?' asked Sheilla. 'Someplace warm and sunny. Not Mexico.'

'Far from Mexico.'

'Maybe even some European city,' said Sheilla wistfully.

'Maybe. We like it here, but we know we can't stay buried forever. Let's see if we can find Najma. When we do, let's talk about it.'

'Okay. You're right. The problem is, she's wounded. She might have crawled into a hole and died. We might never find her. Why don't I believe that? We're not rid of her. I feel it in my bones.'

'We have to keep up the search in any event, but I think you are right.'

'I better get back to work. I'm glad you're here and Vidya too.'

'I know. I feel the same.'

Sheilla walked by the technicians that were all staring at monitors. Fred shook his head to let her know nothing yet. She started down the hall past the computer banks and eventually past the labs. Then she sped up as she saw Nusmen. He was the last person she wanted to bump into.

After talking with Misa, she felt a little better. *I wonder if she would really go on a trip with me?*

Her phone rang.

'Sheilla, this is Martin Pearson, ah … from the CIA.'

'I recognize your voice, Martin from CIA. What's up?'

'Just touching base with you. Canada security is alerted, RCMP is alerted, and border patrol has sent two teams to the Okanagan border. How about you?'

'Zero. We haven't heard one suspicious thing. General Crystal is on his way back.'

'Yeah, he called. Take care, Sheilla.'

'Hey. Why did you call me on the phone? We've got twenty-four comms between you, me, and the FBI guy Shultz. I keep carrying around this clunky radio and no one is using it.'

'No excuse. Just felt like calling you on the phone. Talk later.'

Funny guy, she thought. *Nice voice.* She curled up on her sofa and soon dreams of palm trees and sandy beaches danced in her mind. A raucous dream bird morphed into a grating call on her radio comm.

'Sheilla.'

'It's Fred. We just tumbled to something. 'We logged the sheriff talking to his deputy a few minutes ago. He was telling him he was bored just sitting there all hours. The only car to pass was the veterinarian's, headed up the canyon to the ranch to fix a gunshot dog. The vet, Dr. Murray Lundqvist, was coming over the dirt road from the airport and passed the sheriff below the ranch, near Beaver Creek Road. We knew from an earlier call that the dog, Rosie, was being transported to Omak with Heather, so he wasn't needed at the ranch. Lundqvist hasn't been seen since, and he's not answering his phone.'

'That's got to be her. Thanks, Fred. Good work. Wait. What time did the truck pass the sheriff?'

'I called the sheriff. He said bout 1715.'

'Thanks.'

Sheilla looked at her watch. Over five hours ago. She pushed the button on her radio phone for a group call and relayed what Fred had said.

'One second,' said Jurgen. 'Okay. The vet didn't drive back or past the roadblock on Highway 20. That only leaves one direction. Beaver Creek Road turns into a dirt road just past Wolf Canyon Ranch. I'll get back to you.'

'Sheilla, please call me Martin. I'll notify the Canadians to focus on possible routes into and from that area. Over five hours. She could already be there.'

'Carter, Agent Shultz and I want your men near Conconully. As of 1715, we're pretty sure that the perp was headed north, away from Wolf Canyon Ranch, in a blue pickup belonging to the Twisp vet. Agent Shultz will send you the details. Najma has a five-hour head start and could be on dozens of roads by now. The FBI has people moving to all roads where she might have gone. Neilly's team is working their way behind her probable route to Conconully. Stay tight.'

The climate inside *The Barn* changed from lassitude to fervor. Orders were given. Assignments made. The goal: to get out in front of Najma. The problem was the slim odds of doing so. But while the FBI agent in charge sent dozens of people to the outer edge of the spider web, Najma had taken the direct route north around Conconully Lake's north side to Fish Lake into the Sinlahekin Wildlife area. The Sinlahekin Road wound past several lakes until it reached the small town of Loomis. The same road continued until eventually it crossed the Similkameen River to a junction where the road stopped at Nighthawk, a backroad into Canada.

Despite the multiple name changes, the distance was meager. Najma drove the thirty-five miles in a little over an hour. Except for the billions of stars illuminating the countryside and floodlights at the border, the night was black in the shadows.

Najma had researched this crossing looking for possible escape routes. The border was little used and closed at night. Only one U.S. Customs and Border Protection agent remained on-site. The Nighthawk-Chopaka crossing was known as a dead-end posting for U.S. personnel. An assignment for someone awaiting retirement. A stint for an officer transitioning to death.

Najma pulled off onto a little-used dirt track to a place known to the locals as Alkali Flat. She doused the headlights before she drove over the top of the flat. She continued over the top, flipping a lever that Murray had told her about. He'd used his truck for hunting and had not wanted to scare animals at night with his lights. Handily for her, he'd had a switch installed that allowed him to turn off the interior lights when he wanted. He said it also preserved his night vision. She pulled up and stepped out onto sterile soil. Sagebrush grew sparsely. The border crossing building stood a thousand feet due north.

Surveillance cameras became a part of her hastily developed plan as she approached the building. Through an open window, she spied an overweight man, seated with a large bucket of popcorn, laughing at his television. She tried the door. It opened.

The man turned to look. A pretty lady with dark hair and eyes. The same as on the FBI wanted poster he'd received earlier that afternoon. He started to push himself up. His pistol lay on a counter by the television.

'Don't bother to get up on my account.'

Bill Butler said, 'Don't mind me. I see nothing after sunset. Go on your way, girl. I'll close my eyes.'

'Not what I want, Mr. Border Patrol. What's your name?'

'Bill.'

'Well, Wild Bill. We're going to play a game. Not a long one, unfortunately, since I'm in a hurry.'

She picked up his pistol. A Beretta nine-millimeter. 'This is nice. A little noisy for my taste. May I keep it?'

She set the pistol down and with her left hand held the small .22. 'With subsonic ammunition, this gun is quiet. Of course, if I were to shoot in that big belly of yours, the lead might not get past all that fat.'

She moved toward him and casually fired a round into his stomach.

'What do you think? Did it get into your gut through all that blubber?'

The man stared ahead blankly until what she had just done sunk in. He started to groan.

'Be quiet or you'll force me to shoot you again. I don't want to.'

'Just go. You probably killed me. I ain't all that healthy.'

Najma walked closer with the double blade knife in her left hand. *How many have I killed with this?*

'Open your mouth.' She took a cloth lying on the table beside him and stuffed it inside. How would you like to fuck me, fatso? Could you? That little bitty piece of lead shouldn't keep a real man like you from taking advantage of a little woman like me.'

Bill shook his head sideways.

'Wrong answer, doofus.' She shot him in a shoulder. He shook his head up and down, his eyes wild with pain and fright. Najma smiled, moving closer.

'Let's see if I can find it under that belly of yours. I'm not sure. I think it might be too small.' She backed up and shot both his knees in rapid succession. The man was screaming into his gag.

'I would like to stay longer. Lately, though, I seem to be short of time.'

She put the small pistol behind her back and drew near. She held his gaze, watched the terror in his eyes, then plunged the knife into his larynx. His eyes lost their glisten to the sound of the Simpsons.

One more to go. Then I disappear.

She traversed the road to the Canadian border crossing building. She wanted to be seen by the cameras.

She saw a lone woman inside. A pretty girl on the

phone. *How long can she possibly talk?* Najma waited. The girl continued in animated conversation. As luck would have it, the girl hung up. Najma walked in, holding Bill's Beretta.

'Is it okay with you if I cross into your fine country?' Najma asked, peering into an adjacent room. 'You here all alone?'

The girl was on her first assignment. Americans posted people to this crossing as their last before retirement. Canadians posted people here as their first.

'What's your name?'

'Sally Yeats,' she stammered. 'Please don't hurt me.'

'Lay down on the floor. If you do what I tell you, I might not.'

Sally nearly fell to the floor.

'Turn over. Face up. Pull your shirt open.'

Sally was so traumatized she barely heard. Didn't care what she did. Wanted to live. In a daze, she unbuttoned her uniform. Najma straddled her, thinking about Heather and Jim. Someday, she would do the same to them.

Najma took hold of the girl's bra and cut it. She traced the point of the knife along one breast and then circled a nipple with the steel point. The nipple became hard.

'You like sex with a woman?'

Sally looked dumbfounded. Najma put the knife in front of her vocal cords and pushed it in. Not too deep but enough to stop her from screaming. Najma hated screamers. The girl struggled. Najma plunged the knife into her belly and twisted it. Sally knew she was dying. She screamed soundlessly as Najma watched her eyes.

'I'm sorry, but I need to get going. Once I heard someone say "shake a leg." Is that right?'

Najma let out a sigh as she pressed the blade into Sally's jugular. To avoid the pumping blood, Najma stood up. She searched the border crossing building for supplies. In a drawer, she found duct tape, and in a closet, several large plastic garbage bags. From a hook, she grabbed Sally's coat. Stepping in the pooling blood she said to herself, *I think they'll know I've been here.* As she moved to the door, she admired her bloody footprints. A pair of tall hiking boots had been set just inside the door. *It's the best I can do, and I didn't have to pry them off her feet.* Carrying her stash, she left the grisly scene and turned north into Canada.

CHAPTER 6

'Major Neilly, are you in a mood to work tonight?'

'What did you have in mind, Ms. McCarrick? Before you answer. How long have we known each other?'

'About two years.'

'Two years is a long time. Do you think you could start calling me Jasper?'

'Old habits die hard, Jasper,' said Sheilla. 'Shortly after 1700, the veterinarian, Murray Lundqvist, drove past the sheriff on Balky Hill Road. He was on his way up to the ranch to attend to the dog. He never made it and hasn't been heard from since. It's got to be Najma. There's only one direction they could go, without running into a roadblock.'

The rear of his all-wheel-drive Chevy van open, Neilly stood looking at his topo map on the van's floor.

'They have to go north. No turn-offs for four miles, and then dozens of forest service roads. Also, a road that goes back to Winthrop, presumably blocked.'

'Katarina and the CIA think she will head to Canada.'

'The FBI and local police have set up several roadblocks. One of them is on the road into Winthrop. There's been no sign of her at the roadblock or in the Winthrop area and no trace of the vet's blue pickup. Everyone knows his truck.'

'Fairly safe to assume she didn't go that way. We'll load up and start searching all the turn-offs. There are two houses not far past the ranch. Once we get past them, the search will take quite a while with all the forest service roads.'

'They all dead ends, right?'

'Looks so.'

'I'd suggest you stay on the main road that could get her to Canada. I'll have the planes search the spur roads in the morning. I told the FBI to get Carter and his crew to Conconully in the chopper. You could meet up with him there.'

'Okay. We'll be on the road in less than five.'

'Elias, my old friend. I've gotten to used to only talking to my Middle East or South America counterparts and don't get to call you often up in the northland.'

'That's okay by me. When the CIA calls, it always causes us trouble. Even so, it is nice to hear your voice. What's up, Martin?'

'New information for you,' said Martin. 'Najma is headed north toward Canada. Unless she hoofs it for thirty miles through the Pasayten Wilderness, she will try to get across closer to Chopaka. She was last seen in a 1988 blue Ford pickup registered to Murray Gerald Lundqvist, license number a Washington vanity plate: victor, echo, tango, the number 4, yankee, oscar, uniform. *Vet 4 You.*'

'Very proper of you, Martin. I've haven't heard the proper NATO names for as long as I can remember. You know, such as echo instead of "easy" or uniform instead of "ugly", eh.'

'I deal with a lot of NATO types, so I do know the difference. Just find her, will you? With all the roadblocks east of Highway 97, I think she'll try for the border near Nighthawk.'

'They're closed at night.'

'But you have people there, right?'

'Of course. And it might surprise you to know, you arrogant American ass, that we backward Canucks even have surveillance cameras up here in the wild north woods.'

'All right. All right,' said Martin. 'Don't let the moss grow in your toes. I'll stay in touch as we track her in case she slips by your cameras.'

'While you were palavering on, I looked this up: shift changes at Chopaka at 0800 tomorrow. They're four days on, three days off. A newbie officer, Sally Yeats, is there now. They are required to check in for the night at 1100. I'll get RCMP there now and, as soon as I can, scramble a CSIS team.'

Martin's phone rang two minutes after he hung up with Elias. 'No answer at the Chopaka crossing. The same for Nighthawk,' said Elias. 'I'll call you as soon as the RCMP get there.'

'Jurgen, Sheilla. My counterpart, Elias,' said Martin, 'at CSIS informed me there was no answer at the border crossing stations at either Chopaka or Nighthawk. RCMP will be there before a sheriff arrives at the U.S. side. Longer for the U.S. border patrol.'

'We've moved Carter there. He is five minutes out.'

'It's night and she's crossed into Canada, which makes us blind,' said Sheilla.

'Essentially,' said Martin. 'Carter, Neilly, and our SAD team all have night vision. She doesn't, unless she copped a set at the border crossing. It won't do anyone any good unless she is on foot.'

'We wait for verification,' said Shultz. 'I'll get a canine tracker team ready for sunup. What's our cooperation going to be with Canadian intelligence?'

'Reasonable,' said Martin.

'Back in a sec. I want to check out the border security cams,' said Sheilla. 'We should have them soon.'

'Carter has landed,' said Shultz.

'Sounds as though you are announcing his moon landing.'

'You are a smart ass. Carter said there was no sign of anyone as they flew in.'

'Old habit. I thought I'd left it behind,' said Martin, pissed with himself. *It's not who I am anymore. A joker. A smart ass.*

'Okay, I'm back,' said Sheilla. 'We're bringing up the U.S. security cams now. No doubt. It's her.'

Like Murray had with his truck, Neilly had wired the van's headlights so they could be turned off with the engine running. The interior lights also came with a kill switch to keep them off when the doors were opened. It was the only way they would equip vehicles. Their second one was similarly rigged. Neilly watched as it drove past the driveway.

Mac stopped the van a hundred yards from the driveway that led to the second residence. There was no sign that anyone had been to the first cabin. Five men and one woman jumped out of the Chevy van. Four men and one woman exited the silver Toyota Landcruiser parked on the other side of the driveway.

Neilly had worked out a search protocol. Two would stay with each vehicle. One inside and the other several yards away. Seven would approach the house. They would position on opposite sides of the house in front and in the woods. Three went up the drive first and disappeared into the trees.

'We're moving,' said Neilly. He advanced up one side of the gravel drive. 'Stay loose.'

'In position,' said Marilyn. 'Eyes on the house,' said Mac. 'Same,' said Jeff. 'No lights visible.'

Neilly approached the house, looked through one window and the next. He moved to the door. No sound. No motion. 'Night vision off.' He opened the door and stepped back. Nothing. He moved through the door and turned his NVG on. Roberta moved in behind him. They checked the house.

'Nothing here except for the resident mice.'

Roberta turned on a flashlight.

'Someone has been here. Mouse droppings and dust brushed off a table,' said Neilly.

Roberta squinted the table. 'There's a small amount of blood smear on the tabletop.'

'How old?' asked Sheilla over the comm.

'Dry. Not old, I'd guess. If it's her, and I assume it is, a couple of hours. Load up,' said Neilly.

They turned and jogged down the driveway. They received a clear from both vehicles.

'She's ahead of us. Call when you get to Nighthawk,' said Sheilla.

'You got it. She isn't going to wait around for us to catch her.'

Sheilla called Katarina. 'We've got our first verified sighting of Najma.'

'Good,' said Katarina, rubbing her eyes. That was faster than I thought it'd be. I figured I would get some sleep, so I'd be alert later.'

Sheilla filled her in on the vet's truck passing the road-block and disappearing. The vet's disappearing. On their way north, Dr. Lundquist and Najma had probably been at the abandoned house.

'Come to my office. I need to take a call from the FBI agent in charge. Then we can talk.'

'RCMP says the border protection woman is dead,' said Shultz. 'It's Hussein's MO. Knife in the throat.'

'Same situation on the Nighthawk side,' said Carter.

'Did she drive through?' asked Sheilla.

'The crossing is locked up for the night. I already asked the RCMP. They don't see any way she could have driven in,' said Shultz.

'So, she's on foot. Carter, spread out your men and see if you can find the vet or his car.'

'Or what's left of him,' said Carter.

'The director is contacting the RCMP. It will be a lot easier if my FBI guys can cross the border. We've done it before. It shouldn't be a problem under these circumstances. The forensic team should be there in less than a half-hour. The dog team will arrive at sunup. They'll be there before the RCMP can get a team from Kelowna. It will waste time if we can't cross the border.'

'The SF found evidence that someone was in an abandoned house not far from the roadblock near the ranch. Neilly said there was a spot of blood. Forensics should check it. Starting at sunup, I'll move the two search planes along the border.'

'No problem with them flying in Canadian airspace if they file a flight plan,' said Shultz. 'It's a long shot. It isn't going to produce much. Too many trees if she is on foot, useless she's commandeered another car. That said, you're still right to do the search. We do what we have been doing. Keep all avenues open.'

'Let's sum up,' said Sheilla. 'You're working on a cooperation agreement with the Canadians. Sending forensics to the border and the house. A canine unit to the border. Carter's on standby. Neilly to Omak. Planes start to search in the a.m.'

'Sorry to interrupt. My men found the vet's blue pickup truck,' said Carter.

'Along with the abandoned truck then,' continued Sheilla, 'the evidence suggests that she drove to the border, killed the guards, and is footloose somewhere in Canada. Our first encounter with her was after she came in from Canada to Seattle. Her cohorts were headed back to Canada. It makes sense she would have contacts there.'

'If the guards were dead, why didn't she drive the truck over?'

'Getting picked up by a contact?'

'Maybe. I'll take care of what we discussed,' said Shultz. 'I assume you will monitor CCTV cameras and communication in the area, including Canada. Someone might call about a missing person, or for help. Otherwise, we look at the evidence and choose our course of action.'

'Where do you want me?' asked Carter.

'Stay there and make sure you're fueled and ready to move,' said Shultz.

'More new information,' said Sheilla. 'You want a cup of java to wake up?'

'Maybe in a minute,' said Katarina. 'What new information?'

Sheilla told her what had been found. Katarina asked a few questions. When Sheilla had finished, Katarina sat silent for several minutes. Sheilla decided to let her think and not interrupt Katrina's neural transmitters. After a good five minutes of sitting, Sheilla wished she could spin in her chair but didn't want to disturb Katarina's thoughts.

'I don't buy it. The path is too obvious. She is leading us to Canada. Where she leads, we should look elsewhere. It's my general conclusion, based on what we have now. First, we need to get the forensic evidence, evaluate it, see if she shows her face anywhere else, and what the canine teams find … anything else new that comes up, like relevant communications. Let's go. Take a look at the footage from the border crossing in computing. They can do enhancements. I want to see what else might be in them.'

'They might have Canadian vids soon, too.'

'Tracks on the side of the road,' said Roberta.

'Don't stop. Sheilla wants us at the border.'

Roberta stopped despite what Neilly said. 'Pit stop, boss.'

'Yeah, okay. Anyone else?'

The side door opened. Four jumped out.

Out of curiosity, Roberta walked along the tracks. Off to the side of the little-used road, she stopped and pulled her pants down. If she had kept walking another few feet, she would have seen the tire tracks stop. She squatted, backed up a few feet for a better position, and touched something soft with her bare bottom.

'Grab a light and get out here. Follow the tracks until you get to me.'

'I'm supposing you are not looking for assistance?'

'It's a body, dumb-ass.'

Neilly and two others not designated to stay with the van jogged for fifteen seconds along the tracks.

'Put some light on his face. I'll send a pic back to BWC. Look in his pockets, Roberta.'

Roberta searched his pant pockets and found a wallet, a pocketknife, a bullet, six ibuprofens, quarters and pennies, and a cell phone. Neilly opened the wallet.

'Search his shirt and coat pockets. It's the vet, Lundqvist.'

Neilly called Sheila on his sat phone.

'We found the vet by accident. We'll send a photo and location. Najma's MO.'

'Things changed fast. From nothing to three dead in less than six hours.'

'Any word on the colonel and the major?'

'Both out of surgery and okay.'

'That news makes me happy. What does "okay" mean for the long term?'

'The doc said he was lucky. No long-term damage.'

'I can't say I expected to hear that about Colonel Johnson. He didn't look good when they loaded him out. How's the major and Techie Tom doing?'

'I heard good for both. They're going to call me with the details shortly. I'll let Agent Shultz know about the vet.'

'We'll get back on the road for Nighthawk?'

'Yep. Keep your eyes open. Katarina doesn't think Najma went into Canada. We're looking at the video now.'

'She might have a point. Later.'

'I'm more convinced than ever,' said Katarina. 'She marches right in front of the cams. She leaves us a bloody trail to Canada. "Come and get me," she taunts. Because that is what she wants us to do.'

'She's a killer,' said Fred. 'She kills for the fun of it. Perhaps this grand exit makes her feel better about her failure at Jim's ranch.'

'She doesn't have failures. It's hard for us to get our heads wrapped around a psycho's thinking. She has no emotion. As a group, they're narcissists. She sees herself as too good to fail. She's the best in her eyes. Failing is for others.'

Fred felt chagrined with his lack of knowledge. 'I see,' he responded.

'You're right, however. She kills. Except that psychopathic killers do not kill people out of rage or hate or passion. Their murders are planned. While she gets gratification from the feeling of control and power during the killing, Najma's motive at the border was, I think, part of her escape plan. It would have been more efficient to cross over out of sight and leave us wondering where she went. She wants us focused on the chase. And again, I think, she's leading us into Canada.'

'I see what you're saying,' said Sheilla. 'The border guards are premeditated killings. Not crimes of passion. So the question is why? The answer: part of a plan. What you say makes sense. I'll pass this along to Agent Shultz and Martin Pearson.'

CHAPTER 7

A pair of gray-blue eyes blinked open. A small smile appeared on Jim's face as Heather gazed at him. She smiled and then closed her eyes. 'Thank God!'

'Have you found faith while I've been out? And how long have I been out?'

'It's just an expression. You've been amongst the nearly departed only for part of today.'

'What about …'

'Don't worry, baby. I've done some hard thinking today. You can say her name. Najma is in the wind somewhere. Canada probably. More important for us, I feel that I really understand why you do what you do. I got a hint when you rescued us in Mexico. But not like I do now. She is evil. Sadly, I understand she isn't the only one in the world who is.'

Jim didn't say anything. He closed his eyes and reached out a hand to her.

'If it makes you feel any better, you apparently put two

bullets in her from that little pearl-handled pistol of yours. FBI said her blood was on the floor next to you.'

'I didn't put the pearl handles on it. It just came that way. It's the first time I've fired it at a person in the thirty years I've had it.'

He had to ask the next question. He was not sure if he wanted to hear the answer. 'Who else was injured?'

'I should have told you right off. Brush was and is fine. Both of you could have easily died if the bullets had been inches in another direction. No one was killed except for a lot of the Mexican cartel men. Tom, the one you call Techie, was injured and is okay.'

'Brush's magic seems to have worn off. If he gets shot many more times, he will catch up with me.'

'How many times is that, Jim? How many times have you been lucky?'

'I don't know, sweetie.'

'Yeah. If I were you, I'd be embarrassed to say, too. I'm starting to feel like an outsider. Glenda, Brush, and now Rosie. All shot.'

'Is she okay?'

'She's the pride of the hospital. I've never seen so many people standing around watching while they operated on her.'

'She's here? I mean I am supposing this is the Omak hospital?'

'Add one more question to that string and you'll sound like me. Partly in deference to the general, the hospital threw out all their rules and operated on her. The general had Rosie loaded on the helicopter that brought me over.'

'He can be magnanimous when he wants to be.'

'When he was wounded, he made quite a hit here. At

first, the staff were a little upset that he'd had a surgeon fly over from Fort Lewis.'

'They probably don't know that whoever it is comes from Madigan Medical Center, one of the army's most technically advanced.'

'Don't tell me the general has something to do with it. In case his boys get shot up!'

'I admit it's handy having it close. Madigan was set up long before the BWC. They train thousands of doctors in a three-year accredited program. It is designated as a level one facility.'

'The surgeon, a Lieutenant Colonel King, did win the other surgeons over. He caused a bit of a fluff when he reversed a procedure that the docs said is standard. You might not be lying here talking to me if he hadn't come over.'

She watched Jim. His eyes closed. His breathing soft. Heart rate fifty-six. Blood pressure 115 over 70. EKG normal. *I didn't get to tell him about Murray.*

'I'll arrive sooner than expected. We have strong tailwinds. ETA two hours and eleven minutes,' said General Crystal.

'The main reason I called,' said Martin, 'CSIS says we are welcome to send one or two people to work with them. Right now, there is nothing for the special ops teams to do, except stand by. If we actually encounter her, I don't want to be restricted.'

'I'll take care of it. Sheilla called just before you with an update. The BWC's psychological profiler, Katarina, makes a case that Najma is still in the U.S..'

'If it was any other perp, I would think she was desperate to get away and couldn't cover her trail. But she's not the desperate type. We have a lot of resources tracking her. Without the extra bodies, we probably wouldn't know about the veterinary. We would hear about the border guards, of course. Maybe she was being picked up at the border. Another reason for killing them?'

'It's not a binary choice,' said the general. 'Have you discussed this with Bertrand?'

'Yes, sir.'

'Meet you both in my office as soon as I land. I'm sure the world is not at a standstill while we look for Najma.'

'Colonel, I can't tell you how glad I am to hear your voice. Gee whiz, you've only been out of surgery a few hours.'

'I want you to keep me up-to-date. Where are we?'

Sheilla told him what she knew.

'I'm inclined to agree with Katarina's assessment. Maybe with a twist. She leaves an obvious trail to Canada. It could be to have us draw that conclusion until we realize she is calling the game and she really did go to Canada, but she didn't. It doesn't matter. The border is a political line, not a wall. She's somewhere.'

'You are right. The border doesn't matter.'

'I'll be in Omak for the night. Tomorrow, we'll be transported to Madigan Hospital at Fort Lewis.'

'You'll be the first to know anything. I'm gladwe are all gladyou're okay.'

'Ms. McCarrick, if there is anything I've learned over the years, it's to follow the evidence. I don't read into situations. Thinking too much obfuscates reality.'

'Reality can be what we think it to be,' answered Sheilla before she thought about what she was saying.

'Miss, you have become a rising star since leaving the FBI as a junior analyst. Leave the fieldwork to me.' Shultz immediately regretted blurting that back.

Sheilla diffused the jib. 'Special Agent Shultz, we have a job to do. We have resources that will be valuable to you. Let's just get the job done.' *What's this? Another misogynist?*

'Truthfully, I didn't mean to offend you. I'm on the ground here and you do have resources that will be useful. Being on the ground here might be what's leaving me out of sorts. We're here and the game has moved. I might as well be at our field office.'

'The one thing I realize about Najma Hussein is she never does the expected. She could be back in your lap by the time we disconnect. I wouldn't rule out that she will try to complete what she started. Colonel Johnson and the other two are being moved tomorrow to Fort Lewis. While they're still in your area, I wouldn't preclude that she'll try again. With anyone else, it would be the last thing I would expect. Not with her.'

'I'll try to consider those theories,' responded Shultz, still regretting what he had said earlier, 'while I stay focused on the reality that has always worked for me: evidence.'

'I'm going to leave Neilly on standby at Mid-Valley Hospital in Omak. Any objections?'

'You don't need them, and Carter is in Nighthawk. I've

got a high-profile FBI SWAT team on the way. Also, the CIA has sent one of their SAD teams.'

'With that group, you could probably conquer Canada,' said Sheilla.

'They spend most of their time playing with their … ah, sitting around waiting for some action. So, I guess they can handle just sitting around here with nothing to do. To answer your question. No objections to Neilly staying in Omak. I'm moving some agents to work with RCMP. I've called in another forensic team from Spokane. They are taking the abandoned house in Twisp and the veterinary. I want the main forensic team at the border. They're arriving shortly. I'm considering having the hounds start tonight.'

'Special Agent Shultz.'

'Let's get back on a different footing. Ms. McCarrick and Special Agent is too time-consuming.'

'Jurgen, then. I thought that the handlers were just as important in tracking as the dogs. If the handlers can't see, what's the point?'

'Okay, I won't rush it, Sheilla. I'll wait, as planned, until morning. We've found a construction outfit that was working at night on the highway in Oroville. Tonight, they've agreed to move their outdoor lightning for the forensic team. They should be setting them up soon. Forensics can get a head start tonight and be out of the way of the hounds in the morning.'

After they hung up, Sheilla wondered if Jurgen Shultz was making the right choice, hurrying things up. With that many people on-site, they couldn't help destroying evidence. *He might be right; every second counts,* she considered.

It's his call, she concluded, spinning in her chair.

Katarina understood that the FBI's job was to follow the trail and to deal with the evidence. They used psychological profilers for difficult cases, for serial killers who killed with no connection to their victims. Agent Shultz would have access to the profiles that Katarina and the FBI had compiled on Najma. *Would he look at them*, she wondered. Probably not. Many of the agents didn't see the need for the thinkers who strove to decipher criminal minds. The FBI would follow the trail left by Najma. Katarina would attempt to stay ahead of the trail by interpreting Najma and deducing the decisions she would make. Katarina typed her thoughts on a Word doc as she pondered.

Before Katarina's employment at BWC, the curly-headed blonde had studied both psychology and computers at Brigham Young University. She had been especially drawn to Unity Mitford, one of the British Mitford Sisters. Katarina's interest didn't parallel that of many historian psychologists. She was enthralled by the effect that Hitler, the pathological autocrat, had had on women, especially on Unity: Fascination for the Führer. A fascination that seemed to afflict women in particular.

For the same reason, Katarina was taken with the movie, *Almost Famous*. In the film, the co-star look-alike, Kate Hudson, had felt the same intense attraction for the leader of a rock band that Unity had felt for Hitler. Katarina knew that the better she understood the motivations of women like Unity Mitford or *Almost Famous'* Penny Lane, the better she would understand Najma's behavior as well as her insane obsession with the colonel.

We want to think that psychopathic personalities experience feelings of love and attraction, she said softly. But I have to get past that idea. Najma can't feel desire or affection for the colonel. She can't love. Her form of love is a mixed bag of non-emotional notions. What motivates a person without empathy? And how will those motivations affect her future behavior? *I have to straighten out my reasoning,* she thought before reverting to talking out loud to herself. What drives her? Well, first, she's a survivor. Second, she wants to prove her superiority to Colonel Johnson. And finally, she knows what causes pain in others, even though she can't feel it herself.

Najma's got a place to hide. This hideout will allow her to strike at Johnson when least expected. As in a movie script, she will set up a confrontation. Such staging will allow her control over the situation. In conclusion: she's not running away!

Now I'm getting somewhere, she reflected. Take the obvious. Najma has contact with the cartel. Does that mean she goes back to Mexico? No. She will hole up close by, so as to come for Jim Johnson when she is ready. For this reason, Najma probably won't go to Canada. The mistake was in thinking she was running. She wasn't. She will stay near her nemesis. In her script, both protagonist and antagonist will have a role. Phew, *I think I understand this.*

Carter's eyes blinked open to the sound of baying hounds. The pale gray sky on the eastern horizon marked the beginning of the sun's journey. There was just enough light for him to see men unloading dogs from a truck.

He stretched before strolling over to them. Two different

teams. One with bloodhounds and the other with German shepherds. One of the bloodhounds, a big male, moved into the light from the truck. Carter could not help laughing at the tan and brown floppy-eared dog. Tied around his neck was a red Texas paisley bandana, which signaled he was either the leader of the pack or the pride and joy of one of the handlers.

'Ready to start tracking?' asked Carter.

A man wearing an old army fatigue-style jacket said, 'As soon as it's light. A few minutes. Damn crows cawing all the time. I don't see how they survive eating all that dead shit off the road. You think they'd die of all sorts of diseases.'

'I dunno,' said Carter. 'They're a pretty smart bird.'

As they looked up, two crows were chasing another that had a small bit of white in its beak. They darted this way and that, eventually flying and fighting their way north up the road.

'Just like my kids. They always want what the other one has.'

'What's the plan?' asked Carter.

'The shepherds are going to follow the trail on the U.S. side. You FBI?'

'Attached to them as a special response team,' answered Carter.

'We've worked with you special ops guys before.'

He looked at the eastern horizon. A faint hint of pinkish orange touched the treetops. Carter looked up. The stars were dimming as the light increased. The handler said, 'Let's get moving.'

'Mind if I tag along?'

'Just stay behind us.'

The hounds were tugging at their leads. 'They already have her scent,' said Bill, the lead handler. For the humans working on the killings at the crossing, Najma had evaporated with the night. For the dogs, she remained very present.

Far up the road, on the Canada side, the lights of a Royal Canadian Mounted Police vehicle illuminated the trees. The faint glow softly blended with the dozens of other flashing red and yellow lights in a syncopated rhythm soon to be drowned by the morning sun.

'You're up, Bo,' said Bill. Bo's big head with its scent sweeping ears turned to Bill, let out a howl, and pulled fiercely on his lead. Bill was ready for him. He moved as best he could with Bo, only holding him back from a full run. Bo's nose moved within inches of the ground.

The other two dogs would be used later to confirm Bo's findings. Or in the case of a long track and chase, they would be used as relief.

At the front of the building, Bill walked Bo in circles. He knew Najma had been in the building. There was no reason to go inside. After circling the building, Bill nudged Bo onto the road where they made a straight track to the Canada border crossing building. Bill did the same thing there, walking Bo around the building. Seeing nothing, he looked at the Mountie while holding Bo against his will.

'Go ahead. You're cleared,' said an RCMP officer.

Tugging Bill, Bo leapt the few feet into Canada, where he let out his trademark howl. Nose nearly on the ground, ears acting as scent sweepers, Bo led his handler, the RCMP, and Carter north. Suddenly, the dog veered off the road and stopped at a small stream running along the edge. The stream went under the road. Bill walked Bo farther up the road. After a few hundred feet, Bo howled again and tugged Bill between the center of the road and the slow-moving ditch water.

'It looks like she came out of the water here. The typical way of trying to lose us, walking in the water, going through culverts. It never works; they all come out sometime. I'm going to go to the other side and see if she left her scent there. Then we'll head further up. She might have come out of the water and then gone back in. But I think she probably got in a car here.'

'Bill and Bo walked to the other side of the road. A crow pecking at the remains of a raccoon gave them an evil eye and reluctantly flew a few feet down the road toward the border where it busied itself pecking, waiting to get back to its meal. Looking for a further scent, Bill walked Bo back down the road. Bo lunged toward the bird. 'What are you doing? You don't chase birds.' Bo tugged, but Bill was the stronger and pulled him back to where they had lost the scent.

After several hours of following Bo for over two miles north of where Najma came out of the water, Bill said, 'Here's the way I see it. The lady walked up the road from the truck to the U.S. border building and from there to the Canada building. Killed her victims. Walked up the road into Canada. Went into the stream. Then back onto the road. My best guess is she was picked up by a vehicle on the road.'

'What do you mean by "best guess?"' asked Carter.

'Well, sir. It's the only logical explanation. I say "guess" because we never know for sure.'

'You'd better let the FBI know what you found.'

'First, we got more to do. These dogs can smell so good

they can get a scent off the road from a moving vehicle. Bo's the best and he deserves a rest. Kinda poetic, ain't I?'

'You should get yourself published,' said Carter.

'Yeah. Okay. Here's what we'll do. The other two dogs will start up the road with one on the other side of the water gulley. It's not likely, but she could have gone back in the water and walked further than we went. Bo and I will get in the back of a pickup and take a slow drive up the road for a few miles. That is, after I call the FBI.'

'What about the other dog team with the shepherds?' asked Carter.

'They are here in case we need to go in two directions. We don't. So, I'm going to send them further down the road a way on the U.S. side just to cover all tracks. Another couple of hours and we'll have this wrapped up, Bill gave a lopsided grin.

Carter nodded. 'Nice meeting you, Bill. I'm going to see how my team is doing. And nice meeting you too, Bo. I sure like the way he looks with that red bandana. I want to get a picture when you're finished.' He gave the big dog a scratch behind his ears.

The border guards, including supervisors, arrived from both sides of the border. It was a large group including the guards, the RCMP, and a few of the forensic team who were not busy.

'Who are those dudes? The ones who just got out of the black cars and are talking to the medical examiner?' asked one of the supervisors.

'Canadian intelligence,' answered another.

They turned back to their discussion.

'This woman is near the top of the FBI's wanted list. She's supposed to be cagey,' said a junior border patrol agent.

'Didn't seem too smart getting in the video and leaving evidence everywhere,' said the RCMP officer.

''She isn't caught, is she?' said Sally's female replacement. 'This woman might be smarter than you give her credit for.'

'Give us a break, will you?' said another RCMP officer.

'She's gone, and I'm lucky to be standing here. Sally traded days with me so I could take my kid fishing. I feel guilty that she's dead and that I'm not.'

'Maybe you'd been smart enough to take her down and then you wouldn't feel guilty,' said the officer.

'Screw you. I've got things to do.' She had made it a few feet away.

'Might screw you if you could handle something that big, eh?'

She turned around. 'I heard about that big thing of yours. Mary MacGregor. Remember her? You dated her until she dumped you. Mary said it was about the size of a sawed-off pencil.'

She turned away. He held up a middle finger at her back. She anticipated him and, without turning back, returned his gesture. Trying to regain his cool, he said, 'I don't think this terrorist is very smart. Look at her lame brain attempt to elude the dogs. Pretty amateur hour.'

'Officer, you might be right about the terrorist. But try to treat my border personnel with a little more respect.'

'I didn't start it.'

'You did, and she finished it.'

Their coffee cups were near empty, and the conversation had deteriorated. They started to go back to their jobs. Before they got more than a few feet apart, Bill's pickup truck screeched to a halt. Carter wondered what was up and jogged over.

Six bodies heading in different directions snapped back into a group.

'Get this,' said Bill. 'My dog's nose is so good, he picked up her scent off the side of the road four miles north while we were moving.'

'What'd he find?' asked Carter who, despite not knowing anyone other than Bill, had the air of someone in charge.

'Just her scent. Bo went nuts. She must've got out of the car. Well, maybe not. Maybe she chucked something out and then it blew away. It was on the right side of the road, assuming she was the passenger and going north.'

'Hell of nose he has,' said Carter. 'I'm not envious, though. I don't know if I'd want to smell everything that he does. You didn't see anything on the ground?'

'Nope, nothing. Only a few of her skin cells, I guess. That's all it takes.'

'Maybe she took a leak,' suggested one of the border supervisors.

'We would've seen that.'

'Looks like you were right about the car,' said the RCMP officer.

'Yep. Guess that proves the direction all right. And what we thought about her getting in a car. I'd best call the FBI operations center.'

Jurgen opened his direct channel to Sheilla and Martin. 'More new evidence she went north in a car. I assume that she has met a contact. It's going to make her hard to trace.'

'What new evidence?' asked Martin.

'The hound picked up her scent four miles north of the border. He said it was positive. She either got out of the car or threw something out the window with her scent on it.'

'Now you can add littering to her rap sheet,' said Sheilla.

'Focus on searching Canada,' said Shultz. 'I don't suppose they would like it much if they knew you were monitoring the RCMP along with civilian communications. I plan to catch the psycho. I'm relying on your support. Both of you.'

'Sheilla's computer group will be better at following local communications and video than mine. But combined with NSA, we can target national communication, Internet, and encrypted communications. I can put a specific alert out. We can target any past, known, or possible associates. Canada will be cooperative since it's part of the five eyes group with us.'

'The what?' asked Shultz.

'Us, the UK, Sweden, and Australia. We have a special sharing relationship. I'll start trying to find anything that can help.'

'No one wants to catch her more than I do,' said Sheilla. 'Unless it's Martin. He's the only one of us three who's had a painful in-person encounter with her.'

'Sure, I want to put an end to her,' responded Martin. 'She scared the hell out of me. I can only imagine how she makes her victims feel. It's getting old; one lone psycho always escaping us.'

'We'll monitor videos at convenience stores, weigh stations, or wherever they have them,' said Sheilla. 'If she gets to a high population area with several directional choices, it will exponentially increase the places to monitor. We'll do our best.' *Added to the fact that we will also monitor on the U.S. side of the border. I trust Katarina's instinct more than Shultz's,* she thought.

Sheilla thought it a waste of time to remind him of Katarina's hypothesis. Shultz was in charge of the search, and it was his call. Still, she planned to do what she could to track Najma on the U.S. side. And she was not going to rule out her going after the colonel in Omak either.

Neilly and his team should arrive in Omak soon. Colonel Johnson and Major McGuire would have the kind of protection the local authorities could not provide. That made her feel better. And Katarina had promised a detailed report concerning Najma's possible actions and where-abouts by noon.

'I don't want to scare the staff,' said Neilly. 'I'll make a quick pass by Colonel Johnson's room and see how he is. Then I'll let the hospital management know who we are.'

'I want to say hi to the colonel too,' said Marilyn.

'Me too,' said Roberta, immediately followed by JP.

'In due time. Check the entrances. Get a feel for the place. I'm not really expecting our twisted lady to visit. I'll be back in a few minutes and, if Jim is up for visitors, you can pay him a visit.'

'Can I make a suggestion, Rock? Three of us go in.

Check on McGuire, and I want to see how Techie is doing too.'

'Okay, Marilyn. Mac. Let's go in,' said Neilly. 'Marilyn, you check out the major and I suppose Glenda Rose is there too. Mac, you look in on Tom.'

'Major Neilly,' said Lt. Colonel King as he walked in

'Have we met, colonel?'

'Ms. McCarrick called and said you would be here.'

'How are they doing?'

'All good. Close call for Colonel Johnson. He lost a lot of blood. Two millimeters kept him from losing his liver. As it was, the bullet tore a section of his large intestine. We repaired it. Infection could still be an issue. Similar for the major except for the bleeding and the near miss. One .9 mm slug went clean through, missing most of the potential bleeders.'

'Tom?'

'He's going to have to do some physio. I think he'll regain most of the use of his arm.'

'Good news then.'

'Ask me in a couple of days when we get them back to Madigan.'

'Can I talk to the colonel? And these two standing behind me want to visit the other two.'

'No problem with that. Sixteen hundred. Chinook out front. See you there. I'm assisting the locals on a couple of surgeries. Good will and all that.'

'Surrounded by beauty. I could get used to getting shot up,' said Brush. 'How are you, girl?'

'I'm fine, boy. Better than you. When are you going to learn something about the new age of women?'

Glenda gave Marilyn a hug. 'My big guy's golden streak of avoiding bullets seems over.'

'From what that big hunk of a doc just said, the bullet sailed right on through, missing everything.'

'You see Jim?'

'Neilly's visiting now and Mac's in with Techie. We're all headed back together this afternoon. We've had our little excitement with guys again and have other places to be.'

'Glenda just talked to Sheilla. Between the CIA SAD team and the FBI SWAT, they can probably manage as long as things don't get too frisky, eh?'

'Yep. Second line teams should be okay now.'

'Where are you off to?' asked Glenda.

'Don't know other than it's North Africa. We haven't been briefed yet. Hey, it was nice seeing you. Bullets might not be missing you, but the important part is missing anything you can't live without.'

'There are those.' He winked at Glenda who gave him a look that said *mind your manners.*

'I'm going to give a hi to the other two. Then we're here to protect you since you don't seem able to handle it yourself.'

Brush threw a paperback book at her as she ducked out the door. Marilyn's head popped back around the corner and she blew him a kiss.

'She's good,' said Glenda.

'General says she's one of the best chopper pilots he's flown with.'

'Shoot,' said Glenda. 'She was injured in that crash at Tubutama. I meant to ask her how she is doing.'

'Roberta, Garcia, Aleski,' said Neilly. 'You have positions

staked out? I want to make sure the front entrance is covered from both sides.'

'We do. They are.'

'I'll call you in when we're loaded up.'

'Mac, put someone inside each of the four entrances. On the floor above and below. Three on our patient's floor. Jeff, put on some scrubs. Blend in.'

'I want to ask you a favor,' said Sheilla.

'I'm all ears,' said Martin.

'Katarina just gave me a multi-page report on what she thinks Najma will do. I'll send it to you. And I'm going to send it to Shultz, although he doesn't seem interested. In short, she thinks Najma led us to Canada but is still in the States. She has one proviso: unless Najma does really have Canadian contacts. Katarina doubts it.'

'Let me guess. You don't want to rule that out. You want the same surveillance for the U.S. as for Canada.'

'That's it. And Mexico too. I mean, she came here with the cartel. Surely there are lots of cartel members left in Washington state and California. If Guillermo sent her here, he could get her back to Mexico. The only connection to Canada is when she entered from there with Farasie's attack on the Space Needle. But that wasn't her choice. It was Farasie's gig. He would have arranged it.'

'My first take is to side with you.'

'Her having contacts in Canada is doubtful to me and to Katarina. Having them in the U.S. is all but certain.'

'Better if you … we, tell Shultz.'

'He'll say we're wasting resources.'

'NSA has them to spare.'

'Oh, yeah. Remember that she was on the Canada border when Farasie died. She could have gone over then. She didn't. She went back to Mexico. Those were Farasie's contacts. Not hers. Besides, as far as we know, when she went to Mexico, she didn't even know Guillermo.

'Anything else interesting in Katarina's report?'

'She says Najma is a killer, sure, but she's controlled. She stages her murder scenes. Like with the brothers in Mexico. She left one head sitting on the desk facing the entry door. A narcissist needs to broadcast "I was here." Katarina thinks Najma set the stage on the border for a reason.'

'Okay, so she's wounded. In her condition, it would be risky for her to fight. Easier to just go around the border crossing. Meet her contact and get away. The weak part of your scenario is that she might have a contact and she's throwing the double negative at you.'

'You could be right, Martin. Still, I do not want to look only at Canada.'

'I agree. Sometime soon, I'd like to put a person with your voice.'

'With all the NSA and company resources, you could probably dredge up a photo.'

'Not interested. Much nicer to be surprised.'

'I'm sure we will meet sometime or other. Thanks. I appreciate it,' said Sheilla.

CHAPTER 8

'Forensics hasn't found anything we didn't already know,' said Shultz. 'Najma Hussein is the culprit.'

'You have an in-depth group. The agency is doing everything we can,' said General Crystal. 'CSIS is cooperating fully. My question is, are you?'

'What do you mean, sir?'

'I'm looking at a brief by a very capable psychologist. You are dismissing what she says. You assumed the SF unit was not good. You are supposed to be a capable investigator. Those two opinions of yours tell me you aren't the right man to lead this.'

Jurgen Shultz knew he was at an inflection point in his career. His career was his life. If he said the wrong thing here, he might not have a life. 'General, I'm an old dog. I've solved many cases and tracked down dozens of villains. I formed habits, protocols. I let the evidence lead me. It's what I learned to be successful. Sometimes an old dog has to realize that there are new things to learn. Having you tell me that Neilly's team is good should be enough to clue me in that they are not screwups. Listening to another point of view coming from your representative is something I should not throw out. You're right. I need to investigate every avenue if we're going to catch this woman.'

Shultz wasn't just pandering to the general. He was starting to feel inept in this investigation. He decided that the general was right. *I need to change my ways,* he said to himself. *Or lose my career.*

'A long reflection on yourself, Special Agent Shultz. Do your job.'

~

"Roberta, Garcia, move up.'

'Catch you later, boss,' said Roberta.

'Aleski, I want you to secure our takeoff. It's not the lady's style to try to shoot us down, but let's not take any chances. You're a mile out. Fifty yards behind you there's room for us to touch down with our bird. Stay put until we pick you up.'

Aleski had been grid searching after he picked his position. He had seen nothing. He knew that Roberta on the opposite side had been doing the same. She was well concealed, but he had found her.

'Roger that,' he said as he looked through his scope at anyplace someone might conceal themselves to take out the oversized CH-47.

'What are we landing for?' asked Heather.

Aleski jumped in. Jim said, 'he left one of the watchers to make sure we got off safely.'

'Of course. She isn't going to give up, is she? You think she's out there?'

'In this case, it's just Neilly doing his job and being cautious. Don't give it too much thought.'

'Are you feeling okay, darling?'

'Always feel good in a chopper. Your sitting there fussing over me makes me feel good, and I always feel lucky to have you close.'

'I don't like to see you lying there with an IV line dripping into you,' said Heather as she squeezed his arm.

Jim knew he wouldn't exactly have chosen to be lying prone and headed to a hospital. Sometimes the circumstances dictated what one could do. *Laid up at the ranch in fall. Catching up on reading,* he thought. A stand-down that he had no choice in didn't sound all that bad. Besides, Lola was a good cook.

'I feel good too,' said Heather. 'We're going to have lots of time together. The aspens will be shaking yellow and the vine maples fire engine red. It's going to be a great fall for all of us. I'm going to try to write a serious poem. Pedro's looking forward to you getting back. Lola's in a tizzy trying to figure out what to cook. She says you need fattening up.'

The CH-47 wasn't quite full. There was not a lot of space left, however, after Neilly had loaded his special operations van. Bart King invited a surgeon and a nurse to accompany them.

The nurse had mentioned she had never flown over the mountains or been in a helicopter, and she was off work for the next two days. With only limited windows, the Chinook wasn't set up as a tourist helicopter. Marsha was able to sit right next to a porthole.

'What would you prefer to see?' asked Glenda. 'It's a clear day. Sit on the right side and you will be able to see Glacier Peak and Mt Baker. On the left, you'll have Mt Rainier.'

'I don't know. I've seen Mt Rainier from Seattle.'

'Tell you what. Sit on the north side and then hop over to the south side after you get a look at Glacier Peak. Most of the flight is over mountains. I'm sure Jean-Paul won't mind if you squeeze by him.'

'Not at all. Where are you from, Marsha?' asked JP.

'Right here, or at least not far, Nespelum. It's east on the Colville Indian Reservation.'

'You are Native American?'

'One hundred percent. My family originally was Nez Pierce. My mother is Sinkiuse and my father Nespelum.'

Jean-Paul was thinking this raven-haired, dark-eyed nurse was a near look-alike for Najma. Same tawny skin, but attractive in a wholesome way, differing from Najma, depending on if she was selling you on her sweet or killer side. Marsha had pretty eyes. Najma's were dead. Eyes that conveyed the cold darkness that was in her mind. Marsha had a sweet, sincere openness. One radiated outdoor health and allure. The other, a black widow spider.

Sensing JP's attraction, the young Omak doctor added, 'I've known Marsha for several months now. She is a dedicated nurse and a very capable lady. I watched an incredible event called the Suicide Race at the Omak Stampede this past summer. There was one woman riding in that race. You guessed it, Marsha. They come at a full gallop to a steep sand hill down to the river and literally fly over the edge. Many don't make it to the bottom on their horses. Some don't make it at all. If they get to the river and across it, they ride into the rodeo arena. Marsha didn't win; she was third into the arena. Considering that only about a third of the starters made it at all … I was pretty impressed.'

'I've heard about that race. Animal rights activists tried to stop it,' said Glenda as she sat on the side, holding onto Brush's gurney.'

'Why? Do the horses get hurt?' asked Brush.

'Sometimes, and so do the riders,' added Marsha.

'Why do you do it?' asked Glenda.

'It is a point of pride for my people. The winner is almost always a tribal member. The cowboys try. It's part of our culture.'

'I'd like to see it,' said JP. 'Are you riding it in again next year?'

'Yes.'

'Is Marsha your Native American name?' asked Glenda.

Marsha hesitated for a minute, knowing they would want to know what her name means after she said it. No, my real name is Sayen,' she answered feeling pride for her people.

'Does it have a meaning?' asked Jean-Paul, looking directly at her. Marsh had no idea that JP had an interest in words and meanings. She thought he was typical of whites growing up on westerns where Indian names always had a meaning. Without knowing, she sensed JP was not typical.

Marsha blushed, but met JP's eyes, and said, 'She who is sweet and lovely.'

'It is nice to have you back, General,' said Bertrand.

'Before we get to other world problems, I want to discuss Najma Hussein. What's new, Martin?'

'CSIS is offering carte blanche. They are focusing their efforts in British Columbia from the border crossing east into Alberta, west to Vancouver, and north to Edmonton. We are cooperating. Looking at all sorts of people, terrorist sympathizers, possible contacts, anyone who could help her get out of the country.'

'Did you get a brief on Shultz?'

'Yes. He's an old-line investigator with a track record of success. He comes with good marks. My worry is that he is not open-minded enough to catch up with Najma. Too traditional of an approach. She's not the typical criminal.'

'I agree,' said Will Crystal. 'We and BWC have to make up for his short comings.'

'He's not cleared to know about the BWC,' said Bertrand.

'I see no reason to let him know our resources. As far as he's concerned, Sheilla works here with Martin. Is there anything new with Najma?'

'No,' said Martin. 'Not a thing. Forensics provides us with all the evidence needed to say she is the killer. Dogs lost her scent about four miles north of the border. Shultz, the RCMP, and the CSIS all assume she was picked up by a contact. Or she could have accosted someone and taken their car. RCMP is searching the woods and off roads nearby for a body. BWC is monitoring news, missing person reports, police reports, anything that could suggest her involvement.'

'Last night we followed her. She was two hours ahead of us. Now she's disappeared again. What about the cartel?'

'We're monitoring them. DEA has been alerted. Siastra

Cartel has little business in Canada. They have extensive business in Washington State, however, especially in the orchard areas of the eastern part of the state.'

'If that's the case,' said Bertrand, 'it will be from the U.S. not Canada. I just read your BWC profiler's summary. She makes a good argument for Najma leading the search to Canada while staying in the U.S.. Simply put, she says: "Najma leaves a trail where she is not going and no trail where she isshe could be anywhere except Canada."

Najma walked half a mile when she saw what she was hoping for. Water running in a ditch under the road through a culvert large enough for her to get through. Coming from the north, the flow followed the road on the other side before being channeled under the road. She chose the southeast side to enter the stream, scrambled through the culvert, and out the other side.

She trudged 200 yards through the shallow water, climbed out, and walked over to the Nighthawk Road. She spread one bag out on the blacktop, and then sat on it in the middle of the deserted road, replacing her shoes with Sally's. Then she lay the remaining half dozen black plastic bags next to her. She cut two small holes in the bottom of one bag, pulled it over her legs, and then up to her waist. Using the duct tape, she sealed the bottom of the bag to Sally's boots.

Najma closed her eyes. *I can bear the pain,* she told herself. She lifted her heavy plaid shirt and the T-shirt underneath and squinted at the dressing covering her wounds. In the dark, she could only tell that the dressings were still in place. She carefully pulled the T-shirt and flannel shirt over the dressing. Her fingernail snagged a tiny amount of cotton. She shook it off.

After putting on Sally's coat, Najma pulled off a long piece of tape, securing the bag over the coat near her waist. She pulled a second equally long piece off the roll, wrapping it around her waist over the first piece, sticky side out. With short pieces of tape, she tacked it in place.

In a second bag, she used her double-bladed knife to cut two eyeholes. She put her shoes in another bag. Tied it tight. Pulling the bag over her head, she gathered it as tight as she could around her waist, sticking it, as best that she could, to the reversed duct tape. Where it wouldn't stick properly, she used a hand to gather it as tight as possible. She moved the other hand to her face to keep the bag away from her mouth and to keep the eyeholes positioned correctly for the long walk back to where she had first entered the road from where she parked Murray the veterinarian' truck.

Walking back toward the border, looking like a black marshmallow man, she struggled to see and breathe. The bag slipped and moved on her head.

This was not the most comfortable way to travel. Nevertheless, she hoped the plastic bags would prevent her skin cells from drifting to the ground. Her earlier ruse had been to walk in the water. A tracker team would see these ruses as the feeble attempts of a novice to throw off trackers and dogs. She knew, as they did, that these ignorant tricks would not work for either good trackers or experienced dogs. Najma wanted them to think she was ill-informed.

She walked back down the road to the border crossing building. Giving the bloody footprints a wide berth, she went around the back, avoiding the cameras that had recorded her going into Canada. Sally's boots, both their sole impressions and their scent, would seem normal. In this remote location, the border guards probably paid little attention to what side of the border they were on. Back in Washington State, on the same road -- the Nighthawk Road -- she struggled for nearly two miles to the point near where she had parked the vet's truck and entered the paved road. Her scent was already on the road. She didn't need to be careful any longer.

If the trackers were better than she hoped, they might also decide to track Sally. But why would she be this far over the border and stopping at the exact spot where Najma was. *They won't do it,* she thought. *I can't cover everything.*

Najma removed the bags. She switched back to her own shoes. She stuffed the bags, duct tape, and shoes together in a larger bag and hid it behind a sagebrush where she could hide if she needed to.

There would be little traffic on the Loomis Oroville Road. She had no choice but to wait. She positioned herself just over a small rise. East toward Oroville the road curved as it followed the Similkameen River. She was less interested in cars coming from that direction and would have plenty of time to hide in the brush if one approached, especially if she did not like the look of it. She preferred a car to come from the other direction. If none came, she would accept any car, kill the driver and passengers. She would have to dump them far away from here so as to not give away that she was on this side of the border.

The weakest part of her plan, she knew, was that there would be little reason for anyone to be driving this late at night in either direction. Kids parking, a rancher, an illegal hunter. Someone spending the night waiting for the crossing to open in the morning. Precious time lost. *Was the colonel dead or alive?*

The still, insect-free night moved slowly along its journey toward morning. An occasional moth fluttered by. Her eyes adjusted to the dark. Her shadow grew under the stars. White jewels stretched across the sky. The moon settled below the horizon. She couldn't get comfortable. Her shoulder ached. Her abdomen burned.

She waited for over two hours before a car's loud exhaust disturbed the silence. *Not a cop. I'll lie down in the road.* That ruse had worked with the vet. If the driver wasn't drunk, it might work again. To avoid getting run over in the dim light, she decided to lie near the side of the road.

The black car raced by, swerving, and then screeched to a halt before backing up. It's engine's exhaust throbbed and burbled. The driver pulled to the side of the road. Najma lay still, watching as the driver got out. A Mexican kid.

He walked over to her, kneeling. 'Señorita, está bien?'

Najma moaned, opening her eyes. 'No sé,' she said in her limited Spanish. While spending time in Tubutama with the cartel, she had picked up a few phrases. And then an image of Guillermo entered her thoughts. *He will die for trying to kill me.*

Najma turned over and glanced at the young male. He looked concerned.

'Are you injured? Can you get up?'

Najma struggled to move while the dark-haired teenager helped her. Gerardo Morales de León was older than she had at first thought. Early twenties. Ill-cut, ruffled hair. Thin, droopy moustache. He looked the quintessential Mexican movie bandito. The kind who'd wear an over-sized mariachi hat and a bandoleer. The image evaporated when, with a troubled voice, he asked her, 'What happened?'

'I was walking and passed out.'

Najma knew that, in the orchard areas, most of the pickers were illegals. She took a chance. 'I just came in across the border from Canada. I was running and scared. Maybe that is why I passed out.'

'I see many illegal Mexicans in the orchards. Never an illegal white woman from the north. We must go. I will take you to the valley, no? Are you going to Oroville? I can drop you off close to the main road. But my friends tell me there are roadblocks. I cannot go there. It is why I am driving this road.'

'You are here illegally too?'

'Sí.'

'I am going to Spokane,' she lied. 'And you?'

'I am joining more cousins to pick apples in near Wauconda.'

'I don't know where that is?'

'It is east forty miles, maybe.'

'What are the roadblocks for? Is that unusual?'

'Sí. I have never seen them before. Muy extraño.'

Najma hung her head. 'I have money, but we will be caught.' She wiped an imaginary tear away.

Gerardo stood silent for a few seconds wondering how much money she had. 'Señorita, I have little money. Perhaps just enough for gasolina. Do you have enough to buy some gas and maybe a little food?'

Najma looked at him sweetly. 'Al-hadh al-geed ho al-algham.' Feeling that she had struck gold with this boy and, a phrase from her Iraq childhood slipped from her tongue.

'What is that mean?'

'It is something I learned from my mother when we immigrated to Canada. It is in her language for, "Good fortune is mine." I have enough money to purchase fuel and food if we can ride together. What about the roadblocks?'

'My friends have told me where they are. I know how to avoid them. It is the reason I came this way.'

Gerardo felt that luck was his too. He would not have to spend any money to get to Wauconda. 'It would be my pleasure to take you as far as Wauconda, señorita. We need fuel soon. There is an orchard this side of Oroville. They will sell us some from the orchard tanks. It will be safer than going to a station. Can you walk to the car? We should not stay here longer. We are safer driving.'

'Un minuto, por favor. I need to get my bag from behind the bush.'

The black Nissan with its loud exhaust and stiff suspension carried them on their journey. It was jarring on her raw wounds. *Better than the stupid Viking vet's truck though*, she thought.

'Cómo se llamas?'

'It is Mary Williams,' she said smoothly. 'And yours?'

'Mary is a nice name. Mine is Gerardo. Gerardo Morales de León. It is only a few minutes to where we get fuel.'

CHAPTER 9

Sheilla stood over Fred as they looked at video from a gas station in Oroville.

'She wouldn't be foolish enough to show her face, would she?' asked Fred.

'No, but we have to check every possibility. I wanted to see the videos close to where we last placed her. I want to look at everything from Canada too. Right now, we're looking in all directions. If we can just spot her at one place, we'll know the direction she is heading in. We have nothing now.'

'You know I disagree,' said Katarina.

'Jeez. You startled me. I didn't hear you walk up,' said Sheilla.

'Sorry. I know it's just my opinion,' said Katarina. 'But I've never been more certain of anything in my life.'

'That's why we're looking in Washington State first,' said Sheilla. 'We still have to look in Canada as well. And, it's not only us. Shultz called a few minutes ago. All of a sudden, he seems to have changed his mind. He now accepts your hypothesis might have some merit. He still wants to focus on Canada.'

'Maybe you're more persuasive than you give yourself credit for,' said Fred.

The door to the Cave opened. They all looked up from Fred's monitor.

'I saw you out here,' said Misa, 'I wanted to say hi.'

'You have a hidden camera?' asked Fred.

'Of course. We've always had one.'

Fred sighed. 'Shoot. I can't even pick my nose without someone looking.'

'Don't worry, Fred,' said Misa. I'm surprised you haven't seen it. Look in the corner. Up there above the cabinet. See the red light on the bottom?'

'Yeah.'

'If it changes to blue, it's active. Otherwise, we can't spy on you. I only put it in so I could see who is out here. If either Vidya and I want to talk to you and you're not present, then it saves me a trip or calling you or dinging you on your computer and wasting time waiting for a response.'

Fred nodded. 'That makes me happier.'

'Well, I could always program the light to do the opposite. Hey, I'm kidding.'

'I was going to come out and see what you were up to. I saw Sheilla and wanted to say hi. Katarina, I feel like I both do and don't know you. You two want to have a cup of tea or coffee and discuss stuff?'

'Sure,' said Sheilla.

'Come on,' said Misa. 'We'll have a girls' conference in the Cave.'

'How're you ever going to get equal rights?' said Fred. 'I

can't call you girls, but you can. I have to say women. It's not fair.'

'Ponder it, Fred. You'll figure it out.' Misa motioned for Sheilla and Katarina to follow.

'Let's go to the kitchen. You can decide what you want to drink. There're cookies too.'

'You have a kitchen?"

'We sure do,' said Vidya, looking up from a monitor.

'We live here,' said Misa.

'I guess I never thought about it. Didn't know,' said Katarina.

'If you're going to talk about Katarina's report,' said Vidya, 'I'd like to sit in.'

'Give us a few minutes to talk, Vid. We'll be in the lounge.'

The two blondsKatarina with her curly tresses and Misa with her short bobwalked into the kitchen with auburn-haired Sheilla.

'Your hair is naturally curly?' asked Misa while they made hot water for tea.

'It's an affliction. Too much trouble. I used to iron it because I wanted straight hair.'

'I know what you mean. I used to dye mine and now I'm letting the gray come in.'

'You can hardly see the gray,' said Sheilla. 'I think it looks great.'

'It is what it is.'

'It blends in with the blond. I like it,' said Katarina.

'Thank you both.'

Misa opened a laptop. 'I want to ask you some questions about your report on Najma.'

Katarina felt pleased by Misa's interest. They had met

briefly at meetings. She also knew that the general and Sheilla held her in high regard.

'There is something on page two that I want to get your take on. Najma has almost always worked alone, as far as I know. So why did you mention that psychopaths frequently enlist someone else to work with them? Is it to cast blame elsewhere if they are caught?'

'I just want to cover all possibilities. I think it is more frequent with men, who tend to pick a woman. The woman has to have psychopathic tendencies. She also has to be someone the dominant person can easily control. It's possible that, if Najma met someone predisposed to psychopathic behavior, she might temporarily partner with them. As the dominant partner, Najma would undoubtedly choose a woman. It would be harder for her to join forces with a male.'

'So, we should consider it. What would we look for in this partner?'

'I'll have to think about it. No matter how remote a possibility, it was just something I thought we shouldn't overlook.'

Vidya knocked on the door. 'Do you mind if I listen in?'

'You can even talk if you have something worthwhile to add.'

'Thank you, Mikey.'

'I take it back. Just sit there and don't say a word.'

Vidya pulled his index finger over his lips.

'Okay,' continued Misa. 'You said that psychopaths are skillful liars. Until I read your report, I'd never thought much about sociopaths or psychopaths, their killer cousins.'

'Yes. They can manipulate others with their incredible charm and poise. Their cunning allows them to go unrecognized, even by many professionals. They often exploit people better than the rest of us by reading their emotions and feeding them what they need or want.'

'And, I take it, by hiding their true selves while faking charm?'

'They can con people. Najma can be a goody-two-shoes when she wants?'

'Absolutely. Most studies have concentrated on male psychopaths,' said Katarina.

'Big surprise,' said Sheilla.

'It's the obvious man's world issue. It might not be so strange that female psychos are better equipped to elude detection,' said Misa.

'They sometimes understand social rules better than we do. Then they prioritize their self-interest. Charisma, lies, and lack of remorse are their trademarks,' said Katarina

'You're convinced she did not go to Canada?'

'She's like a scriptwriter. She sets up the scene. It's her MO. I cited the brothers she killed for the cartel. She sends a message to the audience. Why bother at the border in Canada? Sure, she could get gratification in her disturbed over-the-edge state. She is also rational. Time was not on her side. In my opinion, this was a calculated scene to mislead us. Otherwise it makes no sense.'

'Then she did it to dupe us?' asked Misa.

'Exactly.'

'She's smart, right?'

'She is. As are most psychopaths.'

'What if it's some sort of double switch. She realizes we know who she is and how she operates. She leaves a trail to Canada. We assume she is therefore not going to Canada, when in fact she does go?'

'It's possible. We could go on with that ad infinitum,' added Vidya.

'Regardless, I think she is in the U.S.. She wants to stay close to her enemy, Colonel Johnson.'

'Look. We think psychopaths are nuts. They aren't. Just lacking empathy. Narcissists. However, in my opinion, Najma is crazy. Or, at least, severely delusional.'

'Explain about the colonel.'

'I touched on this in the report. But, since a lot is speculation on my part, I only hinted at it.'

'That's what I would like to hear,' said Misa, closing her laptop.

Katarina took a deep breath. 'Let's start with this. Najma is Jim's adversary. She presents a threat to him and, more importantly, to his family. She has proved to be an able and dangerous opponent. A person diametrically opposed to him. A true antagonist. She doesn't want to hide from him. She wants to play. To seek him out. To prove she is superior.'

'It's a competition for her?'

'And possibly for Colonel Johnson too. At least, in some ways.'

'You think so?' asked Sheilla.

'I don't know. It's possible.'

'Here is the part where I am stretching. I wouldn't want this to get back to the colonel.'

'Spit it out. Mum's the word,' said Misa.

'There are possibly several things mixed into this brew. Najma fits the devil archetype. A rampaging beast. Colonel Johnson represents the warrior-savior. Normally, Najma seeks out the weak for her cruelty. But she sees the colonel in a completely different light. For her, he symbolizes the ultimate conquest.'

'Ah! I get it. The battle of good versus evil? Dark versus light?' asked Misa.

'Yes, but there's more. Najma also acts as the perfect foil for Heather, Jim's lover and Pedro's mother. Heather's qualities -- passivity, helplessness, neediness, and vulnerability -- are the exact opposite of Najma's. Heather is pure and innocent. The delicate flower. The white-tail doe.'

'I don't quite understand,' said Vidya.

'I thought you were just listening,' said Misa.

'All right, Misa. You're even now. I won't repeat that nickname again. At least for now.'

'So, what's Heather got to do with this?'

'Jim exemplifies the protector, the defender of the weak, the conqueror of darkness. He embodies a demigod in her mind. Naturally, Najma finds Heather unworthy of him.'

'Are you going where I think you are with this?' asked Misa.

'Maybe. In her deranged mind, Najma feels part of a romantic triangle. She believes herself to be in love with the colonel.'

'Wow,' exclaimed Sheilla.

Jim woke and looked around his hospital room. His eyes settled on Heather, reading in a chair. Seeing her, he felt contented. Then an abdominal pain erased the feeling.

'What are you reading?'

Heather looked up and came over to him. 'Can I kiss you?'

'What do you think? Of course. I can think of only a

couple of things equal to your kiss. One, I might be slightly incapable of at the moment. The other is being able to see you when I open my eyes.'

Heather gave him a long, soft kiss. 'I love you, Jim. Don't you dare die on me. I don't know what I would do if you did.'

'Well, I'm still here! A book is sitting on the stand next to you, but I can't see what you are reading.'

'It's a book of poetry. I'm fascinated by it.'

'Who is the poem by?'

'It's a whole book of poems by Mary Oliver.'

'I want to understand better. Would you read me a few lines, so I can get a feel for what you like?'

Heather picked up the book. 'Oliver writes about nature in such a simple way. I love it. Okay, I'll read out loud the first few lines from the one I was reading, *The Chance to Love Everything:* "All summer I made friends with the creatures nearby—they flowed through the fields and under the tent walls, or padded through the door, grinning through their many teeth, looking for seeds, suet, sugar; muttering and humming ...." What do you think? You like it?'

'I see why you like it. It's smooth and descriptive. If you were writing it, I'd know why you put in humming. What do you think Oliver meant by humming?'

'I think it might be the humming of insects or simply the sounds of life.'

'Hmm. Interesting.'

'I want to write better, to improve. I'm going to. I want to write you a real poem. Not my usual train-of-thought gibberish.'

'You write well, and you've composed some good poems.'

'Thanks. Maybe one or two when I've been filled with emotion and let my mind roam.'

'I know you. If you set your mind to it, you will.'

'What's the other book? Would you mind if I looked at it?'

'I could let you read the Oliver poetry.' Heather raised her eyebrows. 'Not ready for that yet, I see.'

She retrieved the novel and handed it to him. 'It's an advance copy from my friend Beth. The one with the publisher in New York. She thought I would like it and wondered if I would write a review. It's due out in a month or so.'

'I'd like to put the back up so I can read a little. Do you see where the switch is for the bed elevation?'

'It's right here.' She took his hand and moved it to the side of the bed.

Jean-Paul walked out of Brush's room. He looked down the long, sterile hall. Marsha was chatting at the nurses' station. Now or never.

He cleared his throat.

'Can I help you?' asked the nurse behind the counter.

'Well, no. But thank you. Marsha, did you have dinner yet?'

'No. I was going to see if they have a cafeteria here. Would you like to join me?'

'I'd be happy to. We could go to the NCO club if you wanted.'

'The …'

'It's the Non-Commissioned O club, sweetie,' said the nurse. 'The food is okay there. Better than our cafeteria.'

'Okay. Lead the way,' said Marsha, her broad smile set in a face framed by black hair and golden skin.

I like this lady. Assertive and sweet.

The bar was crowded when they went through the door, but several tables remained open.

'How about over there, away from the bar?' suggested JP.

'Sure.'

They sat down and started to look at the menus when JP said, 'Uh-oh.'

'What is it?'

'Company.'

As they neared the table, Mac, Gaston, and Jeff said almost in unison, 'Buy you two a drink?'

'Suppose that would give you the right to join us?'

'Of course,' said Mac.

'He's just kidding. I'm Gaston. This is Mac. And Jeff, who I think you already met, is our team's medic.'

'Nice to meet you.'

'What are you drinking?'

'Diet Coke for me,' said Marsha.

'Same for me,' said JP.

'You got it. Have a good dinner. If you need some better conversation, we'll be over at the bar,' said Mac.

JP shook his head. 'Get lost, Mac.'

Mac is teasing,' said Gaston. 'Jean-Paul is the master of language. He's a hyperpolyglot. With that, we'll leave you two to your dinner. See you later, Caspar, Marsha.'

'They seem nice,' said Marsha.

'They can be when they are not being wiseacres.'

'What did they say you were? And who is Caspar?'

'Caspar is an old nickname. Cardinal Giuseppe Caspar Mezzofanti. He was a priest that spoke sixty languages.'

'What's the other thing they said?'

'I was born with an ability to pick up various languages quickly.'

'You speak sixty languages?'

'Unfortunately, no. The cardinal, Caspar in Mary Doria Russell's *The Sparrow*, spoke sixty languages.'

'How many do you speak?'

'I'm not sure. Could you say a few words in your native tongue?'

'Are you sure?'

'Please, Sayen. I would very much like to hear.'

Marsha thought for a few minutes. 'Long ago in the lake of the monsters. I will tell you a story …,' Sayen started in her upper Salishan language.

After a minute, she asked, 'Are you sure you want me to continue?'

'It is wonderful hearing you speak. It is very distinctive. There are few parallels to other languages. For instance, the word for moon—saka'am in your language —is dissimilar to even Asian languages. A language that I recently learned, spoken by the Shurar Indians in Ecuador, does not have a word for the number one. And it seems, from your story, neither does the Salish language.'

Marsha sat dumfounded. Her eyes big and questioning. Her mouth agape. After a few seconds, she pulled her lips together. 'You understood the story?'

'Parts of it,' said JP.

'How did you?'

'It's just something I was born with. Being able to put the structure and syntax of languages together.'

'You heard my story and can speak my language?' she asked, still not accepting that it was possible for anyone to do what it seemed he was doing.

'No. I wish. I only understood enough to have a general idea of your story.'

'But you could learn?'

'Yes.'

'I don't even speak the language. At least not very well. Hardly anyone does. I was told that story by my grandmother. She wanted me to memorize it so it would not be forgotten. I was showing off. Impressing you.'

'You told it beautifully,' said JP.

'Nothing,' said Shultz.

'What are you going to do?' asked Sheilla.

'We've lost her. I've put men at gas stations in a 150-mile radius. Fortunately, there are not many except at Oroville to the south and Osoyoos to the north.'

'CSIS is hitting their sources hard,' said Martin. 'We're checking everything we can through ours and monitoring news, police reports, cams, and communications.'

'RCMP is checking at rest stops, where a good Samaritan is passing out coffee. Also, they're checking at hospitals and clinics. Najma's been shot three times. I don't think she could get far in her condition. I think one of two things is probable. She has a contact and is long gone from this area. Or she hijacked a car and drove off into the mountains. RCMP is getting local police to check out deserted cottages.'

'Discouraging,' said Sheilla.

'We have to stay with it. If she's alive, she'll make a mistake,' said Jurgen.

~

There was a knock on the door and Glenda poked her head in. 'Everyone decent?'

'Come in,' said Heather.

'I'm not alone. I'm pushing this big lug around. He won't stay in bed.'

'I'm glad you are okay, Brush. Both of you,' said Heather. 'I think you are both berserk, but …'

'My reputation,' said Brush, 'of being impervious to lead projectiles is now history. But as a magnet for lead, you, buddy, haven't been diminished at all.'

'What can I say? The shooter always aims first at the most able opponent,' said Jim.

'Just shows you why we are still amongst the living. Ignorance runs rampant amongst the bad guys. And gals,' said Brush, looking at Glenda.

'You keep this up,' said Heather, 'and you will both run out of luck. It scares me. This is crazy. I'm sitting here looking at the three of you. All of you with one thing in common: you've been scarred by Najma. What is she? Some sort of a supernatural demon?'

CHAPTER 10

The chassis of the black Datsun creaked as Gerardo turned it into a two-track dirt road. Najma almost groaned out loud as the stiffly sprung twenty-year-old car jolted over protruding rocks that had been too large to dislodge when the track was bulldozed many years ago.

They drove to a small wood house that had once been white. It sat surrounded by tractors with attached wagons. Some were full of aluminum ladders. Others were empty, waiting to be filled with the mottled Gala apples the orchard was famous for. As they approached, an older man opened the door to the house. A porch light above him showed a man in his sixties who had spent many years in the sun and dust.

Gerardo stopped the car several dozen yards away. Najma stayed low in the seat. He walked toward the older man standing on the two-meter square porch. 'Buenos días, señor.' The man nodded. 'I was told I could buy gasolina from you?'

The old man nodded. He pointed to a large, rusted silver drum. 'Then come back. My wife will start our breakfast soon. You can join us.'

Gerardo drove the car to the tank and turned to Najma: 'How much should I put in?'

'Why would you not fill it up?'

'It is a question of money.'

'Fill it up. We won't have to stop again.'

'Sí. Gracias.' *I wonder how much money she has*, he thought.

The old man turned and walked inside. Gerardo filled the Datsun's tank, asked Najma for the money, and walked back to the porch. He knocked. The old man came to the door. 'You owe twenty-eight dollars and sixteen cents.'

Gerardo handed the man thirty dollars while reaching into his pockets, hoping to find the change. 'How did you know the cost?'

'There is a meter inside. It is my job. Do you want breakfast?'

'Muchas gracias. If you have something I could take, I would like to leave. The sky is getting light. I hear there are police everywhere.'

'Maria, did you hear?'

A faint 'sí' echoed back to them.

'Where do you go, señor?'

'To the orchards in Wauconda.'

An old woman came out of the house and handed Gerardo a paper bag. 'There are two huevos in bread for your trip.'

'Estoy agradecido.'

'Por nada, señor.'

'Do not go on the main road. Stay on this road through

Oroville. Turn left on Cherry Street, on over the bridge, then right on Chesaw Road. You should avoid the police that way. Buena suerte.'

Gerardo smiled, bowing slightly. He felt very lucky. The trip was costing him nothing, and he would be with his cousins soon.

He had no trouble following the old man's directions. He turned left on Cherry Street. Ahead at a bridge, he saw a flashing light reflected in the misty morning sky. Gerardo pulled the car to the side of the road.

'Mierda. Cops at the bridge.'

He pulled out a worn, stained map from under his seat. 'We will have to find another way over the river.' Najma squirmed on the floor, trying to find a comfortable position. It was too risky for her to show herself in the town, and she did not want to be seen with the kid.

The flashing lights at the bridge didn't make Gerardo nervous. He had been an illegal in the U.S. for several years. He knew the ropes. He knew how to avoid the cops and the immigration officers frequenting the picking areas. Some, including the local sheriff, were paid to look the other way. The orchards needed pickers, and the orchards drove the local economy. It was a more or less comfortable coexistence. Gerardo did not know that his passenger had been the reason for the cops' unusual stake-out.

Najma shifted her head and looked to the east. The sky was dark gray with a hint of lavender. There were a few stars still visible. Mist hovered low on the horizon above the Okanagan River.

'We cannot go across the bridge. La policía es un problema,' said Gerardo.

Despite her pain, Najma felt strangely content. Her

captors were only blocks away, but so far she had been successful in avoiding them. She felt that this was the last obstacle to her permanent escape. 'What are the alternate routes?'

'We can try the next bridge south. We have to pass over the river and there are few safe crossings.'

Held captive by the morning mist, the police lights' intensity increased. A siren sounded close. The police car sped by, heading toward the center of Oroville. An Arab woman had been spotted in the downtown area. Instead of maintaining their roadblocks, the local police jumped at the chance to catch an Arab terrorist in flowing robes and head-cover. Only a chase on horseback would be more satisfying, fantasized Sam, the cop who had just driven past the real Arab terrorist.

'We will drive a little closer to the bridge to see if any of the cops are still there,' said Gerardo. He drove just under the thirty-five-mile-per-hour speed limit. He learned long ago that, in trying to keep to the speed limit, illegals drove too slowly, signaling an illegal was at the wheel. Gerardo didn't speed. Neither did he go too slowly. But his old Datsun shouted "poor Mexican illegal." It was tough trying to earn a living in the land of plenty.

Heather stood at the window of Jim's room. He was still asleep. She stretched. Rolled her shoulders to get out the kinks from her all-night vigil in the green vinyl chair. She held her arms palms up. A conductor orchestrating the beginning of the day. The sky grew lighter. She smiled as she slowly raised her arms.

It was peaceful outside. A bird sailed across the parking lot. The gray turned pastel pink. She looked past the lot to a field of pubescent wheat swaying softly in the light morning breeze. The lavender-gray disappeared into the day as the edge of the sun breached the horizon. Peaches and gold. The sun's fiery surface far away belied its peaceful rise. Her palms lifted, willing the sun into the blue morning sky.

The pulsating wheat field eagerly awaited the sun's rays.

Gerardo drove the car to within a block of the bridge. He slipped into the parking strip on the side of Cherry Street several feet behind a silver Chevrolet pickup truck. Looking down the street and watching the traffic, he decided it was safe to cross the bridge. *They must be looking for her,* he thought. Haphazardly, he covered Najma with an old rucksack and frayed coat. To a casual observer, it appeared he was driving by himself and had simply thrown his belongings on the floor and seat.

From the opposite direction, a semi-truck passed them. From their cabs, truck drivers could look into cars. They would see nothing of Najma. Once over the bridge, Gerardo relaxed. 'Don't move. There are several trucks coming from the other direction.'

Najma groaned, pushing the old coat off her. She put a

hand on the dash and another on the seat. Closing her eyes and focusing on overcoming her pain, she pulled herself up onto the seat. Another large truck came toward them. She slouched in the seat and pulled the coat over her head.

'With no more stopping, we will be in Wauconda in less than an hour,' said Gerardo.

Najma was thinking about what she'd do after Wauconda. She could not stop on her way east. She might be spotted or caught on a security video. They had not yet eaten the egg sandwiches the woman had given Gerardo. 'You have been so kind, Gerardo. I would like to stop to buy more food. I want to have extra provisions to take with me when you drop me off. I will give you the money.'

Gerardo smiled. He had struck gold with this woman. Then he wondered again just how much money she had. 'There's a food bank before Wauconda, where this road joins Highway 20. And at Chesaw, there is another larger store with many items for sale.'

Strange, thought Najma. *Back to the same stupid Twisp road.*

'There are several roads from Highway 20 that will take you to Spokane. Truckers will stop for you. No problema.'

Najma was not afraid of truckers. After Farasie's attack in Seattle, many months ago, she had used a trucker to escape to the Mexican border. *My first encounter with the colonel,* she remembered. Thinking of him distracted her from the ever-increasing pain she felt in her gut.

'I want a warm coat too,' said Najma.

'Then stopping at the mercantile store in Chesaw is best.' Gerardo wondered if she was so rich that she might buy him a new coat. Then he had another idea. One that had been fermenting in his mind all along. One that he was uncertain of. He would have to decide soon.

The mercantile was well stocked. With Najma's never-ending supply of money, Gerardo purchased a large ruck-sack, bread, pepperoni, cheese, water, Coke, several candy bars, and a blue coat. He had slipped it on and liked the color. Just right for him. A little large for her, perhaps.

When he returned to the car, Najma was under his old coat, soundly sleeping. She hadn't slept for two days. He put the new items on the back seat. Pulling out a pepperoni stick, a Butterfinger, and a Coke, he put her change in his pocket. It felt nice there.

Gerardo watched her. Or, rather, he watched the coat covering her. She did not move when he started the car. He was happy. Money in his pocket, food, and a new coat. Soon he would be with his cousins.

He looked at his old coat as he drove past Bodie to the Torada Creek Road that led to Wauconda. His mind was racing. He decided to drive past Wauconda to Highway 20. He had never been east of Wauconda. He didn't want to be on the busier road for long or be seen as he drove through Wauconda. It will be better that way, he reasoned.

Gerardo was not wise, but his street smarts had kept him going for a long time in the United States. He changed from a naïve teenager to a savvy young adult. Most Mexicans were decent and, like in all cultures, some not so decent. His cousins were in the latter group. They worked hard, but they took what they could, stealing and cheating when it benefited them.

Wauconda was waking up. He drove through town and then exited onto Highway 20. He glanced every few seconds at his rich passenger. Najma remained still. Just past a bend in the road, he spotted a small dirt track. As he slowed, he nervously watched the coat. Not even any sign of her breathing. For a second he wondered if she could be dead. He proceeded up the rutted track for several hundred yards, where he spotted another little-used track. Still, no movement from his passenger.

On the right was a jumble of trees mixed in with boulders. Watching the coat, he stopped and turned off the ignition. He opened his door and pursed his lips as the hinge made a screeching noise loud enough to wake the forest. Reaching under his seat, he removed a socket wrench handle he kept for breakdowns. Biting his lip, walking lightly, he moved to her side of the car. He pushed the handle, slowly opening the door.

The grating sound woke Najma. For a moment, she didn't know where she was. Through a small gap in the coat, she could see trees close by. The last thing she remembered was stopping at the store to get food supplies. Her door opened. From the folds of the old tattered coat, her eyes peered out. She realized that something was amiss. Gerardo reached toward the coat; in his other hand, he held a metal rod.

Najma's position left her incapable of defending herself. Gingerly, she reached her hand toward his and gently caressed it, pulling it toward her. She opened her mouth and sucked seductively on his fingers.

Gerardo was transfixed. The exotic-looking gringo sent shivers through his body. Najma readied herself and bit as hard as she could on the two fingers in her mouth. As Najma had hoped he would, Gerardo yelped and jumped back. He would have won the fight right then if he had ignored his pain and attacked her.

Najma managed to get herself up and out of the car while Gerardo bent over, moaning. She pulled out her knife and moved unsteadily toward him.

'Puta,' he yelled as he swung the wrench handle at her. Weaker than usual, she didn't move fast enough. The wrench grazed her head, causing her to stagger. She turned sideways, and Gerardo hit her again as hard as he could in her wounded side. Najma collapsed to the dusty ground. Searing pain raced through her. Gerardo dropped on top of her, hitting her unhealed abdomen with his knee.

'I only wanted your money. Now I want to kill you, bitch.' Najma had held on to her knife. Gerardo rose up on his knees, the wrench ready to deliver a fatal blow to her head. He raised it high over his head. With his torso exposed, Najma drove her small double-sided knife into his groin. He dropped the wrench handle, clutching his stomach he slumped to the ground. Twice, Gerardo had reacted to pain. This time, his reflexive reaction would cost him his life.

Ignoring her burning wound, Najma rolled on top of him. He was holding his groin in his left hand. His bloodied right hand lay near his side. Najma placed her knee on top of that hand and pushed down hard. Gerardo screamed, striking at her with his other hand. He managed to hit her on her wounded shoulder.

She moved past the pain to attack, and not to retreat as he had done. She drove the small knife toward his throat. Gerardo's thrashing caused her to miss his larynx. The knife went through his cheek into his mouth. This time the pain caused him to pass out.

Najma was too weak to wait for him to revive. Angry with herself for allowing this kid to hurt her, she pushed the blade through his closed eye and into his brain, killing him. She collapsed by his side and lay still.

After several minutes, she examined her side. Sticky blood stained her shirt. Her shoulder throbbed. She willed herself to stand, stumbling to the car. Crawling into the seat, she lost consciousness.

CHAPTER 11

'God damn it,' said Jurgen Shultz. No one said anything in the Barn. 'She's not a ghost. She's there, hiding or moving. I want ideas.'

A hand rose. 'Beth.'

'Sir, we've all been wracking our brains. She's not a ghost, but we've got no leads. Nothing. Every hour puts her potentially further away. Twelve hours of nothing. With the resources we have, we would have found her by now if we were going to.'

'That's where we are. But aren't we still missing something?' responded Shultz.

No one spoke. 'All right. I'm going to get some rest. Let's go to shifts. We've been at this hundred percent focus long enough. I want you to be fresh if any leads come in.'

Jurgen picked up his sat phone and called Sheilla. 'Any leads?'

'Afraid not. Martin neither. I just finished talking to him.'

'Nothing to do then except keep at it and see what happens.'

Jurgen badly wanted to close his eyes. His fatigue stemmed partly from lack of sleep and also from the growing sense that he would fail. He had to call his boss in DC.

'Good timing, Jurgen. I just got off the phone with the DCI Crystal.'

Jurgen wondered what else could go wrong. *The general is asking for my head.*

'We've decided that the FBI is going to start a new unit. One to track terrorists both in and out of the U.S.. We've agreed that you will head it.'

'I thought he would want me grounded or fired.'

'Just the opposite.' *Well, sort of,* he thought.

Jurgen sat down.

'It will be a division under the National Security Branch. We're going to beef up all the operations in that branch. It's been under discussion for some time. You've got a sterling investigative record. You're tenacious and that's what we need to get it started. It might be a big plus if you could push your current operation into the history books with a success.'

'We've got zip at the moment. My personal feeling is that she had help when she was picked up at the border. She could be anywhere by now.'

'You know how things work.'

'Why does politics have to get into everything?'

Davidson ignored Shultz's comment. 'The new division is going to be important in the future. General Crystal had some reservations, but in the end, both the general and the executive assistant director for Security Branch agreed. The division is yours. You'll need the best tech people to complement your investigative skills. The plan will call for you to coordinate with CIA.'

'Worldwide is out of our mandate?'

'It was. This is a different world. You'll need to fully cooperate with the CIA.'

'Cooperation is not in their mandate.'

'It will take a few years. Then this division will be able to stand on its own. You have the blessing from above. Don't screw it up.'

'Meaning, the role is mine if I capture Najma Hussein?'

Thoughts tumbled through Jim's mind. The book by Barbara Kingsolver lay in his lap, his fingers marking page 121, the last page read. The back of his hospital bed was still elevated. He turned to Heather, sitting in the chair with her poetry book, mouth open, sound asleep.

He wanted to be home. He thought about waking Heather and checking himself out. He knew that Dr. King would not endorse him leaving. How many days would the doctor feel it necessary to keep him? His eyes drifted to the EKG monitor. He looked at his heart rate. Sixty-eight. Focusing, he willed the number to drop. Sixty-six. He sat motionless keeping his mind blank. At sixty-two, he blinked and looked at his index finger, wiggling it up and down.

Moving a finger or a hand seemed normal. No thought required. Reducing his heart rate didn't either. However, he didn't understand how it worked. Maybe it was no different from having any part of his body respond to his commands.

Where is she? Jim knew Najma would not quit. A temporary moratorium was the best he could expect. She needed to heal before the deadly jousting could continue. *Or did she?* Expecting the expected was a dangerous game to play with her. It was why yesterday he had asked Neilly to give him two pistols, a small .32 caliber and a standard army issue .45.

I'm not the only target, he thought. She wants to cause me anguish. Anyone I care about is fair game to her. He put together a mental list: Heather, Pedro, Brush, Glenda, Shuskin, Lola, the general. Possibly even Ben and Roy. The BWC was too well protected even for her to assault. Except when they went home. How many would she be able to identify? Misa and Vidya had been her captives in Mexico. With their monastic lifestyle, however, they were relatively safe.

Jim knew Heather would never allow guards on the ranch. And he did not want to alarm her with his concern. At his request, Sheilla sent one member of Carter's BWC team to the ranch posing as Roy's visiting brother. Roy liked the ploy. It would give him time off from tending ranch animals twenty-four hours a day. Even with Ben's and the old man's help, he remained responsible for all the chores.

Roy tried to remember what he had ever told Heather about his family. He couldn't remember that he had. His new brother was anointed Mike. He would arrive today. Roy hoped he had at least some ranching experience.

Jim liked the Kingsolver book. The novel wove a tapestry of

nature and personal relationships whose parallels to Heather and the ranch hit him solidly. The jacket flap's synopsis caught his interest as did the first pages in which Lusa, a bookish city girl turned farmer's wife, struggles to adapt to her new home on an Appalachian farm. Jim resolved that, during his convalescence, he would favor books about women as well as those written by women authors. His old nightmare memory from Vietnam flashed through his mind. The local woman's two daughters riddled with bullets. What had that mother felt as her children lay dying? What did Heather feel? His only answer: they must feel differently from the way he would feel. And then there was Najma who felt nothing.

For that matter, had he even considered what Heather liked and felt? He knew she loved poetry. But his view of it had always been one of willed tolerance. *How can I understand her if I don't understand what she likes?* Animals had been their currency. Love and lust their glue. Now they had a family. Had Heather wanted one? How would it change her?

She was a botanist. His botanical vocabulary amounted to a handful of words he had picked up as she had dropped them through the years. I'm a scientist by training. Why am I not more curious about plants? Compared to reading poetry, learning plant names gave him a good feeling. *Do what I have always done. Migrate to learning what I know the least about.* He sighed. Maybe there was something to be liked in poetry. Something he had missed. Heather told him once that no poem was like another. Just like music. Some people liked Bach and others preferred Eric Clapton. That thought had resonated with him.

He would have the time. The general would not want

him back until he had fully recovered. *At least I can be there to protect Heather and Pedro.*

The door swung open and Bart King burst through the door. He didn't duck as he entered, even though his dark hair nearly grazed to the top of the doorframe. He glanced at the monitors and turned to Jim. 'If you give me any problems about leaving before I'm ready to release you, I'll declare you insane and have you restrained to the bed.'

Jim smiled. 'For the moment, it is nice to be lying here. I feel good. So I suspect you are pumping narcotics into me?'

'If you would prefer to practice pain management, I'd be more than happy to oblige. I'd rather you just forgot about what I am doing. The pain meds will be tapered down through tomorrow. I plan to replace them with self-regulated morphine. I'm sure you know how to operate it.'

'How's Brush and Tom doing this morning?'

'I'm sure they are fine, or I would have been alerted immediately. I've been in surgery. You're my first visit.'

'Have you heard anything about our dog?' asked Heather.

'Rosie O Twisp. An interesting name. I hear that she is getting lots of TLC back at your ranch. She'll be fine. She has less damage than you do.'

'What do you mean?' asked Heather sitting up in her chair.

'The colonel's wounds are serious. Make no mistake. He does what I tell him, and he'll be fine. Your dog, Rosie, will be up and about in a few days. You won't, Colonel, if you're smart. I know you're going to be one of the toughest guys I have ever met. And I've met some pretty resilient patients in my time. Your record of hospitalizations is, to say the least, educational. I know you want out of here now. I'll accommodate you. You're also one of the most educated soldiers I've treated. You're intelligent. Now trust me.'

'You've convinced me, Dr. King.'

'It's Bart to you unless I have to call you sir, Colonel?'

'Jim will do just fine.'

'Any questions? If not, I'll stop back after I see my other patients.'

After Bart King walked out the door, Heather started to laugh. 'It looks like you've met your match. You're not going to boss that guy around.'

'Hmm' was all Jim said.

'Are you hungry?' asked Heather as she stretched, leaned over the bed rail, and gave him a lingering kiss. She ran her tongue over his lips. 'Hmm is right. I want you back in action as soon as possible. Bed action. Not missions.'

'Me too. I'm happy to say you have the effect on me that you always do, beautiful.'

'I'm glad,' said Heather. 'Maybe tomorrow, I'll put a "Do Not Disturb" sign on the door.'

Najma awoke, cold and shivering, atop Gerardo's old coat. Her legs hung outside the car. She pulled the coat off the seat and struggled into it. Lifting her left arm, she gasped. Through the pain and the foggy mists of sleep, she finally pieced together what had happened. She squinted at the dark woods. A sliver of light from the crescent moon slipped through the trees. *Where am I?*

As her mind cleared, she remembered a fight. Gerardo had attacked her. The supposedly kind young Mexican kid might have killed her. *I must have been out for hours. It wasn't even noon at the store.* She went to the driver's side and started the car. Fortunately, the interior light did not work. Otherwise, she might have run the battery down. She maneuvered the car until its headlights found Gerardo's crumpled corpse. *I need to hide the creep's body.*

In her present condition, she saw no way she could hoist the kid. There was nothing in the trunk. Two tires, old dirty clothes, and some trash. No rope that she could pull him with. She looked in the back seat. Nothing but more discarded items. All worthless. Under the front seat, she found a dull machete in a green plastic case. *I can't leave his body there,* she thought. But just as she concluded she had no choice but to abandon his corpse, an idea formed.

The car's parking lights illuminated Gerardo in a yellow glow. An hour later, she loaded the plastic bag containing Sally's boots into the trunk. Slipping behind the steering wheel, she almost gave out. The dry branches flamed up as she drove off. Najma had no clue where she was, but the car tracks had come from the way she was going now. It wasn't long before she found another slightly larger dirt path. Since Gerardo, no one else had driven on the roads. Once again, she followed the tracks until she joined a paved road. The stars were out in profusion. With the North Star on her left, she drove toward Idaho.

Fires here were illegal as the countryside was tinder dry. Najma drove past a sign that said, "No fires until further notice." And another below it: "Leave No Trace." 'Exactly my plan,' she declared to the cop car driving past on the main road. *Fortunately headed in the opposite direction,* she thought.

The effort she had expended might just accomplish what the sign said. *Not the fires.* Luckily, Gerardo was in a shallow depression. Najma moved a circle of rocks around him. Afterwards, she added smaller branches and pine needles over him. Searching the area, she managed to find several larger branches. She formed them into a tepee over his body. Then, she placed the largest ones she could find along the bottom edge. Her idea was that the fire would burn his body, its flames would destroy evidence of her DNA, and its ashes would cover what remained. If he cooked enough, she hoped no smell of his decaying flesh would remain. Perhaps campers would build a fire on top of the ashes, further obscuring what was beneath.

Even if someone discovered his charred flesh, he could not be easily identified. The authorities would probably assume a Mexican illegal. It would not be worth investigating. She had emptied his pockets. Then, she'd cut off his hands so there would be no possibility of fingerprints. Her final gesture had taken some time and effort. Cutting through flesh and bone, she had severed his head. Hands and head were tucked safely into the bag with the shoes in the trunk.

Najma didn't want to drive late at night. She would be less conspicuous in the daylight or evening with more cars on the road. A side road appeared. She drove several dozen yards down the gravel lane and stopped.

CHAPTER 12

'Rise and shine, pal,' said Brush from his wheelchair. He wore a lightweight black polar fleece jacket and jeans.

Jim lowered his brows.

'Our doc said that, with our base house less than a mile from here, I can check out if I stay in the wheelchair 'til I get home. Oh. And one more condition. I can go, but only if you stay.'

'I could start to dislike Bart King,' said Jim.

'He knows we both want out of here, but he is going to come to the house and check on me. He can't if you go back to the ranch. He said he's looking at maybe three days for you. I told him that was pushing it. He scowled and said maybe two days.'

'How you doing?'

'No complaints,' said Brush, 'but then I've got some morphine tabs for the next several days. Doc told me to wean myself. Doesn't want me getting hooked.'

'I forgot my coat,' said Glenda. 'Back in a minute.'

'I'll go with you,' said Heather.

Out in the hall, Heather stopped. 'Do you think Najma is a worry?'

'The wicked witch will always be a worry. She's wounded. And there's a lot of people on her tail. Probably nothing to worry about for the near-term. I'm sure everyone will be trying to anticipate her moves. Then again, she might not even be alive.'

'Think she cut out to Canada?' asked Brush.

'Sort of doubt it. Sheilla is coming out into the light and will pay me a visit today. She's bringing Katarina's write-up. Sheilla says that Katarina thinks Najma will hang close and try again.'

'Sounds about right to me,' said Brush.

'Sooner the better,' said Jim.

'Third time's a charm, buddy. The hunters got the advantage. But she's used up her luck. Any plans?'

'One of Carter's reserves is coming to the ranch, posing as Roy's brother.'

'That's a start. I'll try to get back here before you leave.'

'Phone's good. Stay at home with Glenda while you can. Maybe you both can come over to the ranch in a few weeks.'

'Sounds like a plan. Later, buddy.'

Glenda and Heather glided back in arm and arm.

'Ready, ya big lug? I want to get you home.' Glenda winked at him.

Najma awoke to motor noises. A dust plume obscured her view. As it settled, she could make out a logging truck racing down the road. *I gotta move.* She started the car. Before she could turn into the road, another empty logging truck roared past with metal banging against metal. Only feet from where she was parked, another logging truck rumbled past. The dust settled. Najma turned into the road, backed up, and started toward the highway. At the junction, another empty truck slowed, readying for the turn. She felt dwarfed as the ten-foot-tall chrome grille with a bulldog on top turned in as she drove out onto Highway 20. The Datsun lurched and backfired as she stepped on the accelerator.

Najma pulled her collar up. *I need a hat and sunglasses.* She pulled the car over and walked back to the trunk. She remembered seeing a filthy baseball hat sticking out under two old tires. She banged the hat on the car. It was covered with dirt and oil stains.

As she got back on the road, a sheriff's car passed from the opposite direction. She watched it in the mirror. The car's lights started flashing as the car did a U-turn, racing back up behind her.

'Screw off. Tozz Feek.' She started to slow, looking for a side road. Swear words from her past life in Iraq surfaced one after the other. 'Ya ibn el sharmouta.' She could see it was a woman. 'Y'a shar-moo-ta – you bitch.' Her pursuer suddenly stopped and made another U-turn. Najma could see the woman talking into a mic. The car raised a small cloud of dust as it spun its tires, heading back down the road, siren blaring.

Najma eased the car back onto the road. A sign read "Republic 5 miles." *I need a map.* Najma had a plan of where she would go. She knew it was in Idaho, not far north of Coeur d'Alene. She slowed to the speed limit at the outskirts of Republic. A sign read "Highway 21 South." Najma decided that until she figured out how to get to Hayden, she would continue east and hopefully end up in Idaho.

She thought back to her days in Tubutama with Guillermo. His name caused her to spit toward the passenger side floor. *I'm going to take my time with that dickhead.* She couldn't remember much of the conversation she had overheard. A name, Colbert, maybe, and something about light. Guillermo had not been happy with the man when he refused to do something or other with drugs. The name "Bright Light" arose from her memory. *A good omen, I think.*

'Hey, my man. I saw your wounds yesterday when Dr. King removed the dressing. I think putting a "Do Not Disturb" sign out is going to have to wait a while.'

'Hate to admit it. But probably right,' said Jim. 'We've waited a lot in our lives. A little more won't hurt.'

Heather smiled. 'Perhaps this will be the last time.'

Jim didn't smile back. He wasn't ready to become a stay-at-home partner yet. For one thing, he needed to be sure Najma would no longer be a threat. For another, he just wasn't ready to be what Heather wanted. He changed the subject.

'Brush looked good, didn't he?'

'You are quite a pair,' said Heather, scrunching up her lips.

'Everything turned out okay,' said Jim.

'Look at yourself. A needle in your arm. EKG tabs all

over you. A mess of an abdomen. A head bandage. But you're here. So that is good. But it's a matter of perspective.'

'Pedro is happy. The animals are good. I imagine Rosie is getting the royal treatment. We'll have weeks and months together on the ranch. You're zeroing in on your best poem ever.'

'I know, sweetie. And it's a beautiful time of the year. The aspens will be turning yellow and trembling in the autumn light. Red vine maples. A month before deer hunting starts. And we have a family now. It's strange, and as much as I have always liked Lola, now it's different. I feel like she has really become part of the family.'

'Yep.' Jim nodded. 'It will be a special fall.'

'If you are up to it and there's an Indian summer still in November, maybe we could hike into the Pasayten.'

'I'd like that. If Rosie is healed, I'd like her to go too.'

'Oh, Jim. Yes. Let's go. It's only six miles into Horseshoe Basin from the trailhead. It'll be beautiful and high hunt will be over later in October. No hikers or horses. Just us, the llamas, and Rosie.' Tears started to stream down Heather's cheeks. 'I love you, Jim. I'm glad you're still with me.'

CHAPTER 13

'Another day gone by. And nothing. The lady's a ghost. In the wind,' said Shultz to those assembled in the op center. 'We're spinning our wheels. Another day and night, and we'll reduce to a skeleton crew. Ed, have a list of who stays tomorrow morning. Everyone, back to work.'

'Sheilla, Martin. We've come up dry here. I'm going to reduce the crew tomorrow. Keep the rest for a few days longer. After, we can do just as much from our home base as we can here.'

'It's the same for us,' said Martin. 'Najma is either one lucky lady or dead.'

'This is one of the biggest manhunts I've been involved with,' said Jurgen. 'I'm guessing she faked us out and died someplace in the woods. With all of our resources, we should have gotten a lead. If she was running, she would have made a mistake. You would have picked her up on cams. Something.'

'What do you mean, faked us out?' asked Martin.

'I don't know. One strange thing. A woman here, Beth,

studied all the evidence. She thought it strange that Sally, the Canuck border officer, didn't have shoes on and that there were none in the building.'

'Conclusion,' said Sheilla. 'Najma took them. What would she do with them?'

'Beth suggested she put them on in the middle of the road to throw off the dogs. I called the trackers, and they said no way. The dogs aren't chasing scent from shoes, but from skin particles that drop off the perp.'

'Never thought about that before,' said Martin. 'They must have some noses.'

'Bill, the lead tracker, said something about thousands of times better snoots than us.'

'So, what's that mean?' asked Sheilla.

'It means it doesn't make sense. None of it makes sense. How'd her scent disappear in the middle of the road unless she got into a car? Then there was the scent several miles north. Why haven't we tumbled to any verifiable leads?'

'I gotta go,' said Martin.

'Later,' said Sheilla.

Heather looked up at the sound of several voices in the hall. The door opened a sliver. Heather caught sight of red hair and thought that Glenda had come back. They had talked about having lunch before Jim was discharged.

'Sheilla, come in,' said Jim.

Sheilla pushed the door open. She walked to the bed, followed by a troop.

'When I said I was coming to see you, everyone wanted to come too.'

Jim looked around at the faces surrounding his bed: Dr. Milton, Fred, and Katarina. Heather had jumped up and was hugging Misa. Behind them, Vidya waved to Jim. Last through the door, someone whom Jim would never have expected. A shock of wild uncombed hair. Nusmen.

Sheilla handed Jim a small box. 'Go on, open it.'

Jim pulled off the paper to find a brown ribbon wrapped around a brown box. Inside were twelve round cookies, all with different exotic decorations on top.

'I let it leak out that you liked both chocolate and cookies,' said Sheilla. 'Fred mentioned these cookies from New Jersey. We ordered them from the store.'

Jim extracted a chocolate-covered cookie with nuts on top and took a small bite. 'One request,' he said as he chewed. 'And this is a direct order. You each get one and join me.'

'Jim, they're for you,' said Sheilla.

'You heard me. Not allowed to disobey a direct order from your boss.'

'You still have three left,' said Sheilla laughing, as she extracted another box from a small rucksack and passed it to Jim. 'Just in case you started ordering us around, boss. We brought a backup.'

Jim smiled. He searched Sheilla's, Heather's, and the others' faces. 'Besides having the world's best partner, what more could a man ask for than to have a team and friends like you? You're all the best. And it's a big surprise to see all of you out at once in the daylight. Thanks for being here.'

⁓

Najma continued to follow Highway 20 over the Colombia River into Kettle Falls and then Colville. She shifted constantly in the seat, trying to find a position to make the pain tolerable. Nothing worked. The car made little popping noises as it continued through the towns of Tiger and Blueslide. From the sun's position, she could tell she was heading south. 'I don't want south,' she mumbled.

There was a green sign up ahead. As she neared, she could make out "Highway 211 to Spokane." Then another that had a left arrow with "Spirit Lake 47 miles" above it. And below, "Post Falls 67 miles." And below that, "Coeur d' Alene 74 miles." *From Coeur d'Alene, I will find this town of Hayden. The name finally came to her: Colbert.* According to Guillermo, Colbert was a survivalist who hated the government. If he didn't help her, she would kill him and find someone else.

'The loss of her scent in the road poses a riddle,' said Sheilla.

'She sits down, puts the border woman's shoes on, pulls her hands into the sleeves of her coat, and makes a dash for the creek,' said Fred.

'Maybe that would obfuscate her scent,' said Vidya.

'Makes sense. Or maybe a breeze blew away the few skin pieces,' added Sheilla.

'What do you think, Misa?' asked Vidya.

'I don't know. It's possible. Katarina, you don't look sold.'

'It explains how the dogs got her scent way up the road,' answered Katarina. 'Shultz says she got into a car and then threw out something or stopped to pee. The tracker says they would have found where she peed. Why would she stop at all, if she were in a car? I can't shake the idea that she both needs and wants to be close for another chance at the colonel.'

'Anyone for a cookie?' asked Sheilla.

'You devil, you,' said Katarina.

'I bought three boxes. They looked awfully good in the picture.'

'Let's start with a new question. If she wants to stay in the U.S., what story can we create that explains the evidence?'

Sheilla's phone chirped. 'Hi, Martin.'

'Hi.'

'We were just having a discussion, trying to think up explanations for Najma's scent disappearing in the middle of the road.'

'Why don't I do the same? For creating stories, Bertrand here is first-rate. They're puzzles to him. He gets off on them. You want me to have him give it a go?'

'Sure. I know he's exceptional. We're considering she put on Sally, the guard's shoes ... no wait. Let him start from scratch with the evidence. Skip giving him our ideas. See what he comes up with on his own.'

'I'll do it. FBI is going to be winding down. With no leads, Shultz can't justify keeping an operation center running for much longer. We'll keep up our monitoring, naturally, and I assume you will too.'

'As long as she's out there, we won't stop.'

'The other alternative is what the FBI is concluding: that she's dead.'

'That's one theory, of course. I'm keeping an open mind,' said Sheilla.

'Let me know what your boss comes up with. There's got to be a narrative that makes sense.'

Najma came to another junction. The signs read "Highway 2, Priest River," "Highway 41 to Spirit Lake," "Post Falls," and "Coeur d'Alene." Past the road signs, a large billboard read "Welcome to Idaho, The Gem State." *What kind of gems?* wondered Najma. Then she closed her eyes against the increasing discomfort. The dipshit kid must have ruptured something or opened what the vet fixed. The sound of gravel caused her to open her eyes. She had driven off the road onto the shoulder. Luckily for her, the shoulder was wide and flat. She steered back onto the blacktop.

Less than an hour. I can make it. She was feeling faint. Then nauseous. A small park with three picnic tables on her left. *I have to stop.* She drove onto the dirt road past a play area and swing before stopping at the remotest picnic table. A small wooden sign at the end of the road blocked anyone from driving further. She struggled with the pronunciation: "Pend Oreille River Park, Maintained by Newport Kiwanis."' *In America, signs are always saying don't do something.* "Dangerous River Currents. No Swimming." It was the last thing she remembered.

It was still light when she woke up to excruciating pain. She started to open the door to vomit, but she was too late. Vomit dripped from the door panel. She felt a little relief.

Maybe the food was bad, she thought. An hour to Coeur d'Alene. *Then how do I find this man, Colbert?*

Suddenly, she remembered the bag in the trunk with the Mexican kid's head and hands. Najma opened the door, got the bag out, and walked to the river's edge. *If I dump them out, will they float or sink?* She decided to drop some rocks in the bag and tied the top. Then she poked several small holes in it with her knife. Tossing the bag as far out as she could, she almost stumbled into the river.

Forty minutes later, she became nauseous again and couldn't concentrate. She nearly drove past a road to the left with a sign that read "Hayden Lake." Several sloppily painted wood signs nailed to trees read "NO HUNT." She wondered why anyone would put up something that made the person seem illiterate. Then a larger one commanded "No Trespassing." Several feet beyond the sign was a drive with a metal gate. Through blurry eyes, she saw the sign for Bright Light Compound.

She pressed hard on the brakes, almost heaving the Datsun into the ditch. A small pop and the car shut down. She wiped the steering wheel with her sleeve. She was too weak to do more. Najma managed to climb the gate and started down the road. She couldn't see the end. There were no buildings in sight. There were no more signs. Only the forest.

CHAPTER 14

'We have several tests scheduled for today,' said Bart King. 'You're healing nicely. If everything looks okay, I'll release you tomorrow.'

Heather walked in just as Bart King finished saying "release you tomorrow." 'Are you sure that's a good idea? You're not getting any pressure from my man? Or the general, or anyone else, are you?'

Jim started laughing, trying without success to keep his diaphragm motionless.

'I give. What's so funny?' asked Bart.

'It's an inside joke. There are too many things to list as to why I like Heather. Some people have habits and quirks that upset you. Heather has some unique habits, all of which I love. One of those is to never ask a single question. Often three strung together.'

'No pressure from anyone. Purely my own opinion. I do have some conditions. I don't think you will object to trading this bed for the one at your home. Somebody or other said it had a magnificent view. Maybe you'll invite me some time.'

'What are your conditions?' asked Heather.

'To start with, they are immutable until I say so. I call all the shots. Agreed?'

'Sure,' answered Heather.

'Let's hear them. Then maybe I'll agree,' said Jim.

'Tough guys never quit, do they? Never mind. Don't answer that. I think you will agree. Everything is arranged if you do.'

'What are they?' said Heather.

'First, I want to see some test results and blood work before I release you. Second, you'll transport back to your ranch in the way I have set up. And last, when you get there, I want the EKG and intravenous hooked up for as long as I say. Probably less than a week. I want blood samples sent to our lab. Peritoneal infection is likely. Should be out of the woods with that one in two to three days. You keep up with the antibiotic regime for another ten days.'

Jim looked at Heather, who did not say or ask anything. 'Sounds reasonable, Bart,' he said.

'It does, but how're we going to move him without that big helicopter?'

'Ah. Your guardian angels are going with you and you will have a mighty fine female pilot from what I hear.'

'Marilyn?' asked Jim.

'Major Neilly said, and I quote, "I want to see the ranch without Mexicans and a devil jumping all over it." He will bring six with him, including the pilot. One is a medic, and they are going to cart you right to your very own bed. We'll roll you out in this bed and onto the helicopter. They carry you to your bed without disconnecting a thing.'

'Colonel King, I like you,' said Heather.

'In the presence of a full bird colonel,' said Bart, 'Lt. Colonel might be more appropriate.'

'I hope I don't see you here again soon. But if I do, I'll know I'm in good hands.'

'You two take care.'

'I can't believe he's going to so much trouble,' said Heather.

'He's a good doc and probably treats all his patients this way.'

Jim didn't want to tell Heather, even though he knew he should, that there was more to it than concern and kindness. Neilly wanted to hang close for a few days in case Najma hadn't stood down. *Another thing I need to add to my reading list,* thought Jim. *Psychopathic personalities.*

Two male nurses walked in. 'You are going to be busy for a few hours. MRI, ultrasound, echo, and a few more. You won't have a secret body spot left.'

'Why the echocardiogram?' asked Heather.

'Ask the doc. Probably wants to check his output fraction and compare with his oxygen levels.'

Being thorough, I guess, thought Heather.

'Roll up nice and easy.' They slipped a board under Jim, rolled him back flat, and slid him onto a gurney.

'I'm glad you brought me this, Martin,' said Bertrand. 'A puzzle that needs a story.'

'Maybe we can find her if you can come up with the answer.'

'She went poof in the middle of the road. Either picked up by a car, truck, helicopter, or a winged finger.'

'A what?'

'Greek for pterodactylus. A pterodactyl. A prehistoric flying reptile. Hmm. Since flying extinct reptiles are not a good possibility, we are left with two reasonable choices. She rode off or walked away.'

'What about the scent down the road?'

'It certainly suggests what seems to have been arrived at by the FBI and trackers. That she left in some form of transport. How else could the scent get there? Two relevant questions. First, how did the scent get miles down the road? Second, why did the scent stop in the middle of the road? The two problems, as I see it. It's a two-lane highway, not that wide. If she were picked up in a car, why would she be in the middle of the road?'

'Can I see the pictures?'

'Note that there are no tire tracks off to the side. We eliminate the car pickup along with the flying reptiles. The scent down the road is the real problem. The trackers say that the scent was only in one spot. She did not walk from the road to that spot, or they would have picked it up.'

'Same problem for the scent in the middle of the road,' said Martin.

'That one is solved.'

'Huh?'

'Let's start with why she did not simply drive up to the crossing, kill the guards, and proceed into Canada. No one would know until morning. Why not sneak across and avoid the hassle? Until the truck was found and tracker hounds were brought in, she would be on foot, but with a big head start. No, the general's profiler is mostly correct. She staged this to look like she was going into Canada. The question remains, why? That's where the profiler could be wrong. She sets this up so any intelligent person will think she stayed in the U.S.. Of course it's possible, but she could be playing a con and going to Canada.'

'Doesn't sound too wise, as the task force put most of their effort in looking for her in Canada,' said Martin.

'Which brings us back to the middle of the road. Without flying, the only way would be to stop the skin cells from leaving her body and falling on the ground.'

'She covers up with something. Seals her body in.'

'I think you got that part figured out, Martin.'

'She's not in a vehicle.'

'A motorcycle?'

'Not bad. Get a hold of the tracker and ask if the dogs would still get a scent of someone on a motorcycle?'

'Okay, I'll be back.'

When Martin returned, Bertrand was sitting back, reading another file.

'What did they say?'

'That they would have picked up a scent in the road unless someone was covered with clothes, helmet, gloves, and traveling fast.'

'The way most would be dressed. We can't ignore that possibility,' said Bertrand.

'Are you going to work on this later?' asked Martin.

'No need. There are only two reasonable choices. She covered up and rode into Canada. Or she covered up and backtracked into Washington State.'

'Could have walked into the woods?'

'Not smart. Then what would she do?'

'What about the scent down the road?'

'Think about it. It didn't make sense to the tracker either.

Only one way that I can see. She dropped or discarded something, and something picked it up.'

'Fucking A. Right on. A bird.'

'Crow, raven, magpie. The only explanation that fits the facts.'

'So, which way did she go? North or south?'

'We can't tell from the evidence. My money is on the profiler at BWC. She's looking at getting into Hussein's head to answer that question. We can't tell for certain from the evidence. Combining it with the psychological data, Najma is probably remaining relatively close to her rival, the colonel. Not far into Canada or in the U.S. west somewhere. That's the best story we can construct until there are more clues. If she is moving, we might get one. I've got other things to do. Let me know if anything new comes in.'

Martin called Sheilla. 'Bertrand, the deputy director, loves challenges. I gave him the reports, and it isn't much help. His conclusion is she is probably close. He thought Katarina's report was good.'

'I know who Bertrand is,' said Sheilla. 'Besides us, Kat hasn't gotten much respect for her report. She'll be happy to hear that.'

Martin proceeded to tell Sheilla what Bertrand had said, saving the bird solution to the end and prodding Sheilla much as Bertrand had prodded him.

'Wow. That adds clarity. You're right. It doesn't help us find her. It does make the whole thing seem simpler. What sort of effect does all this have on you after your encounter with her?'

'I push it to the back of my mind. The woman is scary. I was pretty lucky to get off as easy as I did.'

'I'm not sure I would think having my thumb cut off as easy, Martin.'

'It wasn't any fun at the time. This might be hard for anyone to figure, but it has sort of become an asset for me in the agency. More importantly, the experience helped me grow up some. Nice talking. You know how to get me if you need anything.'

Sheilla started a slow spin. Martin certainly wasn't a typical male. Admitting what he just did in such an easy, forthright way was almost shocking to Sheilla. Besides his honest assessment of himself, he seemed kind and sensitive.

CHAPTER 15

'Y ou're good to go, Colonel,' said Lt. Colonel King. 'Don't push yourself. You're lucky to be amongst the living. Value it.' He looked at Heather. 'You have a lot to be thankful for.'

Jim's room was crowded. Glenda had come to visit and have breakfast with Heather. Brush remained at their base house, lying happily in bed, his mind wandering to her soft pale skin, delicious strawberry blond hair, firm currant-like nipples. Glenda had ordered him to stay there, saying he had had enough exertion and would see Jim soon enough. He was happy to obey her, not only because he was feeling worn out, but because she was right. It wouldn't serve any purpose to visit his old pal now.

Neilly moved aside. As they had done the day before, two male nurses shifted Jim onto a gurney. Dr. King touched Jim on the shoulder. 'I'd like to come and visit you sometime. Just don't come back here to visit me again soon.'

'You can count on that,' said Heather.

One of the nurses secured the drip bag to the gurney.

The EKG lead was unplugged from the machine and placed on the gurney. The procession started down the hall. Nurse, gurney, nurse, followed by Heather and Neilly. Mac brought up the rear, pushing a cart with the EKG machine, an insulated box with drugs, and bags.

From the cockpit of the Blackhawk, Marilyn watched the group file toward the helipad. Jim gave her a thumbs up. Fleur, Jeff, Roberta, and Aleski waited alongside. The two nurses turned Jim and the gurney over to members of the Special Forces.

'That group doesn't look like regular army,' said one of the nurses.

'Woman pilot too. It's an army bird. Must be some sort of special operations.'

'And special treatment for the colonel too.'

Mac flew co-pilot. In minutes, the Blackhawk reached Lake Washington, gaining altitude to cross the mountains.

'Trees are starting to turn yellow,' said Mac. 'They'll drop their leaves soon.'

Marilyn looked at Mac. They're conifers, doofus. Larches. Needles, not leaves. You've never seen one before?'

'Wrong climate zone from where I've spent my life.'

'You're forgiven. Beautiful, aren't they? And colorful. The yellow nestled in strips creeping up the mountain toward the snow.'

'It's a different scene from the swamps and deserts where we spend most of our time.'

Marilyn landed below the house. They had plenty of manpower to carry Jim to his room. Heather felt at peace. The aspens clung to their green leaves, trembling in the breeze that moved up the canyon. Heather could sense the change in them. That they were less pliable, slightly more brittle, almost yellow.

Pedro sprinted from the small aspen grove below the house to the helicopter. 'Dad. Dad. I take care of you.'

Heather looked up and said, 'I'm taking a deep breath. It feels like life entering my body.' She looked up from Jim's blue eyes to the sky. She spun around once, taking in Wolf Mountain, Coyote Ridge, and the river of aspens flowing down the canyon. The white-tipped Cascades rose high above the descending canyon. 'Life is wonderful.'

The Blackhawk's blades were nearly still. Mac and Roberta eased the gurney into the waiting hands of Jeff and Aleski. Neilly grabbed the EKG unit. Before taking his headphones off, he said: 'Nice landing. Felt like a feather touching down. The drug container is still in back. Bring it when you get the bird shut down.'

'Can do. See you in a minute.'

'Where's Lola?' asked Heather.

'She is inside,' said Pedro, 'keeping Rosie from getting up. Rosie is very happy. She is full, from Lola's food.'

'I'll bet she is,' said Heather. 'The bed's upstairs. Go around the front and up the steps. I'll meet you up there to open the door.'

The gurney just fit through the door. Jim could not help but grin. Lola sat next to Rosie, whose tail was beating the floor. Rosie started to get up. Lola held her shoulder firm. 'Push me closer?' asked Jim. He reached over the side, just barely reaching Rosie's large head.

'I swear that dog is smiling,' said Roberta.

'She eat all our food. I no have enough to feed army.'

Heather bent down and scratched Rosie's neck. 'We'll get plenty in town later. No worries.' Then she engulfed

Lola in a hug. 'I'm glad you are here. Happy we are all here.'

'Why you cry if happy?'

Marilyn came through the door with the drug container. Heather pulled down the sheets. In a few minutes, Jim was propped up in his bed, looking through the wall of windows at the mountains.

'A touch comfier than the hospital,' said Roberta. 'And just as good if not better care. I should get injured. Oops.'

'You tried that already,' said Mac.

'Not with this view when I was recovering.'

'You had us for company.'

'Some family we make.' It was said in jest, but to all six, it was true. They were a family. Roberta looked at Jim, letting him know that he was now part of it too.

'And I thought the views couldn't beat those from the air,' said Marilyn.

'It's the perspective that makes it special,' added Heather. 'Coyote Ridge and then No Name Ridge on the right, descending to Beaver Creek Road. The winding aspens disappearing down the canyon. The bump of Balky Hill and the Cascades rising into the western sky.'

'The north hills are dry,' said Fleur.

'Covered in balsam flowers in the spring. The bluebunch grass turns brown in late summer,' said Heather.

'Then cold and snowy. I go to kitchen. Pedro, you keep dog down. She get up and hurt self.'

'Pedro, I thought you were going to teach Lo to speak properly when I was gone. Instead, it seems she's been teaching you.'

'I am sorry, Mama.'

'Come here, little big man. I like you just as you are.'

Fleur fussed over Jim, making sure that everything was hooked up and operating correctly. She put a new drip bag on the stand and connected the EKG. You're all set, Colonel. You need me, I'll be downstairs.'

'Heather, you want to get some groceries?' asked Neilly.

'We need them. The cars or trucks aren't here. They're at the airport.'

'I'll fly you down,' said Marilyn.

Heather grimaced. 'I have had all the flying I can take for this year.'

'You want to get food, or should maybe Mac and Neilly get some?'

'Yeah, I'm fond of Frosted Flakes,' said Mac.

'Hmm. I guess I'd better supervise the shopping,' said Heather.

'Does that mean you don't like sugar-coated flakes?'

'Not in this house. Okay, you convinced me. One more flight won't kill me, will it? I hope not,' said Heather puckering her lip.

Neilly nodded at Roberta and Aleski. Heather noticed. She thought he was saying goodbye. What Neilly really wanted was for them to scope out positions to monitor the canyon. The trick was for them to find viewpoints that Najma would not expect if she were to rear her head again.

As Jim dozed, Rosie gazed at him with her bright golden eyes. Then her large head settled onto the bed of blankets Lola had made for her, and she dozed off as well. Fleur took a blood sample and stored it in the fridge. The shoppers returned. Marilyn left the chopper at the airport. Lola cooked a feast. It was warm enough for them to eat on the deck. Heather took two plates and climbed into bed next to Jim.

'I don't suppose with this crowd we could put a "Do Not Disturb" sign out.'

Heather turned toward Jim with a glint in her green eyes. 'You need a few days, big boy. You need to get better.'

Jim raised an eyebrow as if to suggest that snuggling might help. 'You're a good cook, but I can't believe what Lo puts together.'

'She's good. Too much salt, sugar, and fat for my taste. Tomorrow, I'll start working with her. At least get her to fix healthier food for you. I want you to get better.'

Jim didn't respond. He knew it was hopeless to discuss the merits of sugar with her. He liked Lola's cooking. He knew he should be saying what he thought to Heather. Be truthful. But not right now. Not in this moment. The view, Rosie, and Heather beside him were too nice to spoil.

Roberta and Aleski spent hours walking the ranch and marveling at the scenery. Over the top of Coyote Ridge toward Highway 20, the country undulated with bumps circled by mini valleys. The bushes and grasses were turning a dusky orange, punctuated with small splats of yellow and red.

'This is as pretty as it gets,' said Aleski.

'Yeah. It's beautiful all right. And lots of cover for someone to hide in, too. Lots of perfect position for us. Yep, dozens,' said Roberta.

'Let's walk around down there. I want to see how someone would approach from that side.'

Roberta pointed to a series of knolls. 'Around those would be my choice.'

'Let's go, and then we can walk No Name Ridge. I like that steep hill between it and Wolf Mountain. It's high above the house. Not on the ridge. Not likely to have any surprise visitors. Much taller than the ridges and without trees to obscure the house.'

Thirty minutes later. 'You smell what I'm smelling?' asked Roberta.

The distinctive stench of decaying human flesh grew stronger as they homed in on its source. 'Neilly.'

'What's up?'

'Remnants of a male Caucasian a half klick east of Coyote Ridge. Darker-skinned. I don't think Latin. More Mediterranean. Hard to tell. Birds have been at the remains. Probable entry wounds in the head and torso. Small caliber.'

'Two bodies you've stumbled onto in as many days. Get the coordinates and mark the location. I'll talk to Sheilla. She can probably get one of Shultz's forensic teams, or one of the military's that returned to Fairchild a couple of days ago.'

'We'll get back to our business then, boss.'

'Let's get over to No Name,' said Aleski. 'You think she would try to get through here at night?'

'Not unless her night vision in a new moon is better than mine. Pretty hard getting through here in the dark without NVGs.'

'Probably she doesn't have them, but that's a maybe. I don't expect her to try unless she does. I would say she is going to lie low, heal, and bide her time, maybe for months depending on how bad she is wounded. Doesn't mean I'm right. I like the colonel. I'd hate to be the one who screwed up and got him killed.'

'Let's check with Rock at dinner. I agree. No need for us both to pull an all-nighter.' They walked down the old cow path together.

'Some tree cover along this trail,' said Roberta.

They neared the house and started up the hill behind it. Roberta's radio beeped. 'Rock wants a parley. He'll be here in a minute.'

When Neilly arrived, they discussed what they were going to do.

'I don't want to take any chances, but I don't see her coming at night either. You two pick a spot for tomorrow, sack out, and leave before first light. The rest of us will pull two-hour shifts tonight. We're out of here day after tomorrow. Sheilla said the SAD team will replace us for a few days and Carter's team for a week. By then, the colonel should be up. There's a friendly from BWC's quick response team, posing as Roy's brother. The drone is sitting idle. Sheilla's going to fly it while we're here. Dinner's ready so get back as soon as.'

CHAPTER 16

Guillermo sat on the balcony overlooking his vineyards north of Avignon, France. In the distance were fields of lavender. His vines were heavy with red grapes that would soon go through the production rituals ending in the wine he liked so much, Chateauneuf-du-Pape. The reason he had purchased the vineyard.

While he enjoyed the softness and civility of the French countryside along with its wine, his primary reason for being here now was to stay out of the clutches of the U.S. government.

Colonel Johnson and General Crystal had caused his organization severe damage on two past occasions. After their attack on his Tubutama home he had decided to eliminate the colonel and the general. Sending Najma to Washington State to kill Colonel Johnson on his ranch and the general at Fort Lewis had been well-planned: it had turned into a fiasco.

After the Guillermo orchestrated his attack on Wolf Canyon Ranch, the U.S. authorities had pressured the

Mexican government to target his cartel. The CIA along with the DEA had been relentless, exposing his operations, stealing his drugs. He assumed the assault on his and the other cartels would last only a few days. It hadn't.

His failed plan resulted in the CIA placing a bounty on his head. Guillermo decided it was safer to be in France than in Mexico. He had taken great pains to devise a method of travel, which he felt confident would evade the authorities, and perhaps his ex-assassin, Najma. In many ways, after he tried to have her killed, she was the biggest danger for him. Prudence dictated he leave Mexico without delay. Two days later he was sipping wine on his French estate.

While the failed revenge operation against the colonel had cost Guillermo millions, he accepted the loss. However he was still pouring money into finding Najma before she found him. He also accepted that his arrogance and lapse of judgment had not only cost him money but had caused him to lose the position he had once enjoyed with the other cartels and the Mexican authorities. The aggressive U.S. approach had harmed the other cartels. And they directly blamed him. It would be only a matter of time before they turned against him. His removal would end the intense pressure his miscalculation was bringing to all the other cartels' drug running operations.

His drug operations in Washington State had almost ceased. Another cartel had muscled their way in. The Israeli assassin he had paid to terminate Najma after the operation on the ranch had disappeared. Najma had disappeared. Had the assassin joined Najma? With all his contacts, he had been unable to find either of them.

If the woman his men called "El Diabla" was not found,

if she were alive, he was certain she would come for him. He was not afraid. He had his skills. However, she was an exceptional adversary in killing, torture, and disappearing. She had an uncanny ability to do what she set out to do with the exception of Colonel Johnson. As the hours and days passed, urgency replaced his complacency. If she were not located soon, his chances of finding her would become nil. He learned through his contacts in the U.S. that the FBI was close to abandoning their active search for her. They assumed she died of wounds, somewhere in the wilderness, or had left the continent. The Royal Canadian Mounted Police concluded the same.

The CIA, working with their Canadian equivalent, the Security Intelligence Service, continued to search though the CSIS favored the FBI's theory that she had crossed into Canada and had died of her wounds. The CIA and BWC, he had found out, were looking on both sides of the border. Their working hypothesis was that Najma had not traveled far away, nor was she dead. They continued to focus most of their efforts in the northwest. They didn't, however, eliminate looking for clues to her whereabouts throughout the world. Guillermo had little doubt that his nemesis, General Will Crystal's organizations, were correct. Najma was alive, biding her time, waiting to strike.

Guillermo rehashed the events. It was a plausible theory. She drove to the remote Nighthawk border crossing in northern Washington, abandoned her car, and killed two border crossing officers. The FBI had concluded she was severely wounded in Twisp with her battle with Colonel Johnson. They assumed she stayed alive long enough to get to the border crossing and then disappeared in British Columbia where she died.

Tracker dogs had followed her scent north of the border where the scent ended in the middle of the road. The conclusion: someone on the Canadian side of the border had met her. She needed medical attention. Her wounds were thought to be serious. The investigation therefore had focused on her need for medical attention, but they found no trace of her seeking any medical help.

The American authorities and Canadian authorities did not think a lone female could evade them. In their overconfidence, the conclusion was simple. She had died, and was dead and decaying as his assassin Alva was.

In his search for the devil lady, Guillermo's representatives had contacted his old contact at Bright Light in Hayden. The leader, Colbert, assured them that she was not at his compound nor had she contacted him.

Differing from the FBI, his search focused on the U.S. where most of his contacts were located. He didn't know Najma well, however well enough to know that she did the unexpected. He felt certain she had killed the border guard as a false trail. Why abandon her car while wounded?

It made no sense to him. Still, he had not found her any more than some of the world's most powerful agencies had. Unbeknownst to Guillermo, the body of his Israeli assassin, Alva, lay east of Wolf Canyon Ranch. That is, what was left of him. Insects, beetles, eagles, and coyotes had all helped to distribute his remains. Soon the winter's snow would cover Alva's remains. In the spring the balsamroot, the bluebunch grasses, and other plants would gain nourishment from his decaying body. Bleached bones would remain for years before disintegrating, eventually being recycled into their primary earth elements.

Guillermo's thoughts and investigations flowed from

dead end to dead end. The probability of finding her diminished as each hour passed. His contacts were of a different nature than the government's. Still, they had found nothing of her. By the third day following the disastrous attack on Wolf Canyon Ranch, Guillermo concluded, differing from Shultz that she had found a haven much as she had done at his hacienda in Tubutama, Mexico.

CHAPTER 17

Jim lay in his bed. The thirty-two-foot-wide double-decker window wall spread before him. The sky was blue. The mountains crystal clear. Oval Peak topped the horizon. He looked at his watch: noon. A shadow appeared over the house. The wind picked up. Soon the aspen trees were dancing. The house was buffeted with heavy gusts. A low rumble. Then lightning on Coyote Ridge. It had been warm, hot for this time of year. He looked at the weather gauge. The barometer had dropped over two points to a fraction above twenty-eight. The house shook. Lightning crackled directly overhead. Hail pelted the house followed by the staccato of raindrops hitting the metal roof. Clouds of rain mixed with leaves torn from their branches blew sideways. The barometer dropped another fraction.

Heather ran up the stairs and jumped in bed beside Jim. She snuggled under the puffy duvet. 'Cool huh.'

'Cool is right. The temperature has dropped almost ten degrees in as many minutes. If the rain keeps up, it will rush down the hills into the canyon, causing another big washout. Remember when we were hiding out of the rain at Shuskin's cabin? The water coming off No Name had a wave in front.'

'I can't forget that,' said Heather. 'It was incredible. My hope now is that all our army visitors get washed out into the Colombia, never to return.'

'They all mean well,' said Jim defending them.

'If someone has to be here, it's too bad that tomorrow we trade Neilly's group for twelve new ones. I like everyone in Rock Solid's team. Quite a nickname, huh? Marilyn's a kick. I just found out today that Jeff's father was a poet. A published poet. I want to talk to him before he leaves.'

'Shouldn't be hard. He's taking one more blood test to send to Bart King. The last one, I think. He will be here in a couple of hours. Around four.'

'I travel a hundred miles to see what is right out in front of our window.' Heather jumped up, looking down at the ground. 'I can't believe what I'm seeing. It's a coyote, crouched against our front window. He's drenched. Poor little guy.'

'You better check on Rosie before she sees him or her,' warned Jim, as Heather hurried away.

Heather had finally managed to collar Jeff. She had been desperate to talk to him as soon as she heard his father was a poet.

'Jeff, I wanted to catch you before you left. I heard your father was a poet?'

'True. I grew up hearing poems as early as I can remember. Are you interested in poetry?'

'Yes and no. I try to write them, but I'm not very good,' answered Heather.

'I'm not fanatical like my father was. But I still enjoy them when I've got a chance to sit and read. That's not too often.'

'Who's your favorite?'

'Hard question. Sometimes one from one poet and another poem from another writer. If I had to blurt one out it would be Walt Whitman. I'm not personally fond of rhymes or limericks. But sometimes I like Shakespeare's sonnets.'

'What do you like about Whitman? So, you have a favorite Shakespeare play? Or sonnet?'

'Hmm. Let me start with the first one. I'm not religious. Whitman, though, makes me feel something spiritual about nature and life. Does that make any sense?'

'I think so. It's the feeling you get from his words.'

'That's right. Your second question. I like lyrical poetry and metaphorical poetry. A very difficult question to only have one favorite. The ending of Twelfth Night with the "Wind and the Rain." It seems appropriate after that little black cloud erupted today and I remember the line always, "When that I was and a little tiny boy." The song is haunting about the harshness of life.'

'That's one of the few plays I've seen. I thought the music was moving,' agreed Heather.

'Do you have a poem you would like to show me?'

'I'm not really very good at it. I just like to fool with writing them. I make notes in my diary about everyday observations and sometimes I try to create a poem.

Jeff sensed she wanted to show him something. 'If you show me something, I promise not to mention it to anyone else, ever.'

Heather squirmed. 'Honestly, I have never written anything worth your reading. I'd been reading Mary Oliver's poems during the day. Maybe they influenced me. The other night in the hospital as the sun was coming up, I looked at Jim and something happened. I sort of lost my mind. I wrote a poem for Jim. I don't want to show it to him, maybe ever. I want it to be perfect.'

'I'd be honored if you would let me read it.'

Heather tentatively lifted her notebook. After a few seconds, she handed it to him. 'The bookmark with the green tassel. It's titled "Amor Fati". I'm all pins and needles. Please, keep it to yourself and just tell me if you think it could be good. Should I work on it? Or just throw it out? I really want to know.'

'I promise to keep it to myself. Thank you for trusting me.' Jeff opened the notebook and read the poem several times. When he looked at Heather, she was looking down the canyon at the distant hills smattered with llamas. 'Heather. This is as good as anything I've ever read.'

'You think so? You really liked it?'

'Yes. I don't think you should change a word. I'm rather astonished. Impressed. This is very, very good. Amor Fati"Love of one's fate"sometimes it takes a shock for us to lose our mind, as you said. It allows something to be created deep within us. Our conscious minds very often prevent that beauty from escaping. It was probably your worry about losing Jim and seeing the good in your life. The sunrise. Emotions and feelings overwhelmed you.'

'It did just flow onto the page. I wasn't thinking. You're not just humoring me? Are you? Tell me the truth?'

'No, I'm not humoring you. It's only a shame that no one else can see it. It could win a prize if you submitted it. I understand, though, it's for someone special. Not the public. Show it to Jim. I'm sure he will feel what you felt when you wrote it.'

Jim's thoughts were never far from thinking about where La diabla was. Where had she disappeared to? Najma's thoughts, now a mere 200 miles east were even more fixated on him. He preoccupied her mind. It was as if he was sharing her mind. Thoughts of him, killing him, possessing him, haunted her.

Her string of luck, starting with the Mexican kid, had taken her to the Bright Light compound. Would her luck hold? She was too weak to care. She couldn't see any buildings or signs of life. Stumbling forward. She felt the forest began to spin. She reached out for her colonel. Instead of him, her hand touched gravel.

Najma listened before she opened her eyes. There were no sounds other than leaves rustling on the breeze and puffed small breaths through the wall of pine boards. She opened her eyes. The room had mismatched furniture. An old, light pine, five-drawer chest. To the chest's left, a closet made out of newer pine boards had been added into the room. The aged vertical tongue and groove boards on the walls were dark with thick shiny varnish. On her left was a mahogany china cabinet that housed books behind its glass doors. The curtains were made of heavy material with a tan and green leaf pattern. They appeared even more ancient than the walls.

Memories flooded into her head. The big vet, the border. Driving. Roadblocks. The car popping and backfiring. The Mexican who had tried to steal her money. Or maybe kill her. Colonel Johnson lying on the hangar floor. Squeezing into the helicopter's baggage compartment. Killing the Israeli man. Guillermo's betrayal. The ghoulish "No Hunt" signs. The endless road ahead. The last thing she remembered.

The door opened. A tall fit man with a military bearing said, 'You're awake.' Najma gazed steadily at him with bituminous eyes. He moved closer. She tensed. Jason Colbert could feel her tensing. 'I'm not going to hurt you. You're wounded and safe.'

'Safe where?'

'The road you were walking up is my place. It's called Bright Light. I'm Colbert. Yours?'

'Najma.'

'Get some rest. I have some business. I'll be back after Phil takes a better look at your wounds.'

Najma peered out the small window near her bed. All she could see were tree needles and sky. An occasional puff of wind penetrated the knotty pine planks. She ached everywhere. Colbert had given her some pills that took away the edge from her injuries. Another man, Phil, inspected her wounds. He cleaned them up. Replaced several stitches that the bastard Mexican kid had torn when he hit her. Her head had a wound. Phil said it didn't need any attention other than some antiseptic cream. He left and said he would check back in later in the afternoon. Her abdomen was stained rust-red with the iodine that Phil had poured over the area. A silly woman named Bambi with curly brown hair, wearing a long linen dress and brightly colored scarf had come in making small talk. She seemed to flow as she moved, each step purposely touched down so as not to disturb what she walked on.

Najma had dozed for several hours.

There was a soft knock on the door. Phil peeked around the corner, smiled and asked, 'Is it okay if I come in?'

'Sure,' she said as friendly as she could.

'How are you feeling?'

'Not too bad. Where is the bathroom?'

Phil laughed. 'I think you just want to get up and walk around. You'll be up in a few days. If you really have to go, I'll help you. Oh, ah, Bambi said she would bring you a brush, toothbrush, and toothpaste. You're traveling pretty light. Take my hand and stand up slowly? I don't want you getting dizzy.'

She smiled at him.

Colbert looked into the room as Phil was helping Najma out of bed. 'Phil, let me escort her. I want to talk with her.'

'Sure.'

Najma smiled coyly.

Najma knew Jason Colbert was attracted to her from the way he looked at her during their first conversation. *I need to find out more about this place and the people,* she thought.

She squeezed his arm on the way to the bathroom. They

walked out the door and around a brown metal furnace. A small kitchen was on the right, across from the bathroom. She looked up at him, 'Thank you, Jason. Is it okay to call you Jason?' she asked sweetly.

'Please.'

Thank you for letting me be here. I'll be well soon and able to leave.'

'No hurry. You're welcome here.'

Najma sat on the toilet thinking fate was on her side. She even considered she was pleased that the colonel had survived. She would have another chance at him. Guillermo would be hers to toy with, too.

Colbert walked with her back to her bed. The only other room in the pine cabin was a small living room.

Colbert guessed what she was thinking. 'This is a cottage that's been used for many things. We have a main house. It's quieter here.'

Najma debated whether she should or shouldn't tell him that Bright Light was the place she had been looking for. She decided, and said, 'I was looking for this place. I heard from the Mexican drug cartel you were not their friend. Their leader was upset with you. I am running from them. They tried to kill me. They shot me.'

Through his contacts with the Guillermo's cartel, Colbert had heard of a dark-haired assassin they called "La Serpiente." 'What is your connection with the cartel?' he asked, keeping suspicion out of his voice.

Najma hesitated, 'I did different jobs for them.'

'Generalizations do not contain information. What exactly were those jobs?'

Najma decided it was best to stick to the truth as much

as seemed reasonable. 'I killed people for them.' She watched him intently. He conveyed nothing.

Colbert knew her reputation. This did not deter him. He had known many killers in his life, both in and out of the army. It was what they had been trained to do. Some took to the killing more than others, but Najma was the first psychopath he had ever encountered. He failed to grasp that she had no empathy. She read and understood his wants and needs much as a well-programed robot might. He started to think that she found him as attractive as he did her.

'Guillermo Vasquez called me.'

Najma wondered if fate would turn against her. She wondered where her knife and gun were.

'He was looking for you.'

Najma waited.

'I didn't tell him you were here. I don't deal with him anymore. He does not need me for arms supplies, and I don't want to be involved in the drug trade.'

Najma relaxed. 'Thank you, Jason. Come and sit by me and tell me about this place?'

Jason told her a little about himself and the area. Najma listened attentively. *The more I know, the better I can plan.* Her first goal would be to make sure Jason Colbert stayed on her side. He was the leader here. She needed him. *He likes me. I can feel it,* she considered. She reached out and touched his hand. 'I'm glad to have stumbled up your road.'

'I'm glad you did too. You're safe here.' Najma felt nothing but loathing. Colbert felt his skin tingle at her touch.

A woman wearing a print dress, beads, and Indian slippers, walked in, with a toothbrush, toothpaste, and a hairbrush.

'I'll leave this for you. I'm Bambi. You can keep them. If you need anything, just let me know. Would you like some makeup?'

Najma shook her head no.

'You'll fit right in here. Most of us have no use for it. Jason doesn't like it. I like seeing myself in the mirror. Most of the time anyway.'

Najma was trying not to appear impatient about the interruption. 'Thank you, Bambi.'

'I'll come a calling later and we can have a little girl talk. Bye for now.'

Bambi could feel that Colbert liked the new visitor. Bambi was not the airhead that she sometimes appeared. She sensed there was something not quite right about Najma. *There's something odd about her. I can feel it.*

CHAPTER 18

Najma thought back to when she had first heard about the survivalists from members of the drug cartel. They were a small anti-government group, survivalists who had come to be called 'preppers'. They had never been directly connected to the cartel but had had some overlapping business years ago.

Bright Light, she would later find out, was an odd collection of people from hippies to ex-military. Weak and strong, all under the influence of their charismatic leader, Colbert, this man who was attracted to her. The Idaho preppers were a diverse lot. Some held extreme anti-government beliefs. Others supported themselves with underground firearm sales and drug distribution. A few were law-abiding families, preparing for Armageddon. The last group was different, with the nuclear catastrophists on one side and on the other a smaller faction who believed in a supernatural end to their world.

The one thing the majority of Hayden Idaho's residents shared was their survival preparations. While Idaho had its share of survivalists and individualists, Hayden was unique. It even had a large prepper store that the locals enjoyed as their local social club.

The survivalists believed in their preparations for many reasons. Some based them on religious beliefs. The apocalypse of the Bible. Others were certain that the world as they knew it, would end in a nuclear holocaust. Others, like most of those at Bright Light, didn't understand the more off-the-wall motivations. Nevertheless, they did understand the others' disdain of government. They shared a reclusive nature and a wish to be self-dependent. A few had a desire to be part of a community and to live an alternative lifestyle where they joined with like-minded societal rejects who spurned the trivialities of society.

Colbert didn't fit any mold. He had been a traditional patriot and still considered himself more patriotic than the government in Washington. He had volunteered for the army, was accepted to Special Forces, and trained at Fort Bragg. Before joining, he had watched *The Green Berets* starring John Wayne. He loved the idea of the army's "Special" Forces and the myths that surrounded them.

He was one of five members of his Special Forces A-team, based out of Fort Campbell, Kentucky, who trained to speak Farsi. His first station was in Iraq, near the Syrian border. Their missions were often intertwined with the CIA. At first, he believed he was there to help defend America. It did not take long for him to become disenchanted with the entire enterprise. His belief dissolved in the desert dust.

His team was moved to Afghanistan, where he formed a dislike for the Taliban and their treatment of people who were not aligned with their rigid beliefs. As time went on, he began to question his own convictions. Was what he was doing any different from what the enemy was doing? Women, children, and average hard-working people were caught in the middle. The CIA had ordered him to eliminate a small village, said to be an enemy stronghold. He had directed airstrikes. His team had then entered the village to secure evidence against the Taliban.

They found none. They found no evidence that the Taliban had operated there. Instead, they found families incinerated in their homes. A small school with massacred children. Having heard the explosions, a young man raced into the village. His wife, the schoolteacher, his mother, his three children, all dead. He was a shepherd, not a soldier. He had screamed hysterically for hours and tried to kill himself with a large block of rubble. The team's medic gave him a tranquilizer. Eventually, they were able to interrogate him.

It soon became obvious the villagers were not Taliban sympathizers. They were nothing more than families trying to live. Born into a war-torn country, they had had no choice, no means to move. They'd worked hard and hoped for a better life for their children. Imran, the sole survivor of his village and family, had lost everything. He didn't want to live. The team guessed he would end his life as soon as they left.

Word leaked back to Colbert's team that an army patrol passing the bombed-out village had reported seeing burned bodies and one male hanging from a lone stone door-arch. The door-arch was the only part of the village not destroyed in the attack.

The suicide didn't surprise Colbert and his team. What had surprised them was the knowledge that the extermination of that community had been nothing more than the

CIA's objective to remove all villages in the district. It was easier to blow up a village than to relocate its villagers.

After similar events, Colbert the patriot evolved from questioning his government to disliking and, eventually, to loathing it. Bureaucrats held forth from on high, never getting their hands dirty. They hatched plans they thought were winning strategies. People like him carried out their flawed schemes. American military became partners with the Taliban in destruction and terror and ended up leaving little of value in the country it had come to liberate.

Colbert and three of his Special Forces team resigned and moved to Idaho. They lived with an older couple that had built the compound from scratch. Sometime later, the couple died, after having willed the property to Colbert.

Originally, there was a large old farmhouse. The couple had added to it many security features and an underground bunker. The bunker was primitive at best, and not likely to keep radiation out in a nuclear attack. Colbert, along with his three buddies, set out in earnest not only to build secure underground bunkers but also a ground-level compound that could be defended if attacked.

Except for purchasing necessities, they shied away from the nearby town. Over the years, however, they would meet like-minded people at the ranch store and market. The number of inhabitants grew, a slow accrual of men and women approved by Jason Colbert and then accepted by his three Special Forces pals, acting as an informal tribunal.

Altogether, the compound comprised twenty-eight people. Fourteen men, eight women, and six children.

They were not polygamous. They didn't practice religion or go to church, although some still called themselves Baptist, Methodist or, in one case, Catholic. A few secretly prayed. Jason Colbert, forty-six years old, had never married. His ex-lover was an Iraq veteran and a retired army captain. She shared his beliefs and distrust of government, but they were both too strong-willed to share a relationship.

Bright Light's preppers expected the end to come from the federal government, from a Chinese invasion or, more likely, from a nuclear attack. They acquired explosives, guns, and every sort of protective military gear. Prepared to defend themselves at all costs, they had amassed claymores, grenade launchers, machine guns, and night vision goggles. Their three underground bunkers were connected by tunnels, each sealed by lead-lined doors. An escape tunnel led into the woods.

To support their chosen path, Colbert had acted as an occasional conduit for drugs for Guillermo's cartel. Colbert's motivation was not wealth. It was subsistence. When their store of money grew sufficient, Colbert refused further drug dealings with the cartel. Cutting ties with Guillermo was not something most could pull off. The cartel owned you and counted on your allegiance. The preppers' military training, self-defensive capabilities, and reclusive nature meant they were neither an easy target nor an inherent danger. Guillermo let them exist in their retreat, safe from him and the world. In the future, he could still use them as a conduit for anything other than drugs.

Using a backhoe, Colbert had excavated the whole of the underground compound and connecting tunnels. He had then reinforced the spider web of tunnels and, before covering them with dirt, had built sturdy covers reinforced with rebar-rich concrete.

With solar power and a water turbine that generated

power from a stream, multiple generators, large stores of food consisting of canned goods, rice, pasta, and cases of canned and bottled drinks, they were largely self-sufficient. They possessed two thousand gallons of diesel fuel and over 600 gallons of drinking water spread throughout Bright Light.

Above all, Colbert was concerned about radiation from an imminent nuclear attack. His military experience had shown him the government cared little for people's lives, whether those of the so-called enemy or those at home whom it had sworn to protect.

Two issues were paramount. First, immediate survival. Second, protection from the long radioactive half-lives in the outside environment. Bright Light's preppers were prepared to survive an initial attack. They had a deep-water source that fed through pipes to one of the bunkers. Eventually, the groundwater would be contaminated, and they would have to rely on stored water. Following instructions from a well-known Austrian survivalist, Colbert had also built an air-filtration system.

He had not yet solved the problem of their long-term survival outside the bunkers. He had purchased several surplus radioactive suits. He had not, however, figured out how to de-contaminate the suits so as to re-enter the compound safely.

Jason Colbert did not think of himself as a cult leader. Others would disagree. He was stubbornly resolute but revered. The others in the compound did not challenge his authority. They believed, as he did, that their time was limited, and a reckoning was inevitable. The government was falling apart. Politicians were passing ever more laws and finding ever-increasing ways to tax citizens, without giving equal measure back. Nuclear war was inevitable.

The survivalists were not alone in their beliefs; many of the local inhabitants shared their fears. Yet Bright Light's inhabitants trusted no one and mixed with no one outside their compound.

Those preppers who had migrated to the northwestparticularly Bright Light's community carved out of the woodsall embraced similar anti-government and anti-tax philosophies. Nevertheless, they varied substantially in their degree of commitment to the cause. In this, Jason Colbert approached the extreme end of the spectrum. He had seen what his government had stood for in Afghanistan. He had seen firsthand the wanton destruction of the weak. He vowed not to let the devastation he had witnessed abroad happen to his compound. For this reason, he had surrounded himself with like-minded men and women.

Unfortunately, Najma Hussein would prove to be a liability.

CHAPTER 19

Jim could hear Heather and Lola in the kitchen. The two were quite a pair. A continuous stream of Spanish words of drifted up to the loft. He turned to the shelf behind the bed. It served both as a headboard and a separation from the steps. Brush had talked about visiting Alaska and seeing the Tepuis in Venezuela. Jim, on the other hand, had always wanted to visit an island in the middle of the Mediterranean, a place his job would not likely take him. Perhaps that was the attraction. He had kept the travel book on the shelf above the bed. A DK guide to mountainous Corsica. *It would be good to have Pedro see Europe. The three of us should go hiking there,* he thought.

He shifted his thoughts to the book he was reading. The Barbara Kingsolver. He liked it. He would save it for late-night reading. Heather had collected several books from downstairs and brought them up. He'd requested women authors. Although she didn't say anything, she had wondered why he wanted them and thought it must be because of Najma. She decided she didn't want to talk or think about her. Biting her lip, she decided to keep quiet.

Jim separated the books into five groups on the bed. One was a tall stack of seven that looked interesting. He had earlier scanned *Sexual Personae* by Camille Paglia and had admired it. Eager to understand the thought processes of women, Jim would read it completely through this time. He almost eliminated Jean Auel's *The Clan of the Cave Bear*. On second thought, he picked it up, read the jacket flap, and put it back in the must-read pile of novels. Ayla, the woman protagonist, struggles with her clan. It was exactly what he wanted: to understand the more primitive motivations of women.

Besides The Clan, he had chosen eight novels he thought might give him the insight he desired: Julia Alvarez' *In the Time of the Butterflies*, Arundhati Roy's *The God of Small Things*, Beryl Markham's *West with the Night*. The last interested him because it was the autobiography of an exceptional woman and pilot. There was also a Daphne Du Maurier novel called *Mary Anne*, Margaret Atwood's *Alias Grace*, Patricia Cornwell's *All the Remains* and, finally, an author he revered for her philosophy and offbeat moral code, Iris Murdoch's in *The Message to the Planet*. Jim made a mental note to ask Heather to look for yet another iconic book when she was in town: Ayn Rand's *The Fountainhead*. He had read it and *Atlas Shrugged* a long time ago. He didn't embrace Rand's philosophy, so the shorter book would be the better choice.

Jim only planned to read a partial section of Lynn Margulis' *Kingdom Plantae*. He hoped it might help him to understand more about botany, Heather's profession and passion. He would give it pride of place. Not because he was eager to read it. Rather, he felt he *must* read it.

Heather interrupted his thoughts. Jim hadn't heard her come up the stairs. 'Anything I can get you?'

'I'm okay, but I would like it if you could find *The Fountainhead*.'

Heather could barely keep her mouth shut. *That freaking Najma is going to haunt me, she grumbled to herself.*

'I just thought of another, *Madame Bovary*. I know we have it. It's interesting that a cigar-smoking user of prostitutes could write sensitively about a woman.'

Jim sensed Heather was disturbed about something. 'Sweetie, other than you, I feel I have spent most of my life with men and missions. For some reason, men seem simple for me to understand. While I have to lie here, I want to figure out what makes women tick. I want to understand you.'

Heather ran to the bed with tears in her eyes and grabbed hold of him.

'What's the matter?'

'I love you, Dr. Johnson. I thought … never mind.' *What's wrong with me? Najma is dominating my thoughts.* 'I'll find those books for you, darling.'

Jim shook his head, wondering what he had missed.

Heather bounded back up the stairs, carrying two books. The Flaubert he had requested, and another. Heather handed it to him. 'I don't think you've read this. *Paradise* by Toni Morrison. It's great. I'll get *The Fountainhead* in town even if I think her objectivist philosophy sucks. I gave our copy to Vidya when he visited.

'That gives me plenty to study.'

'I almost brought up Brontë and some others, but your pile does look pretty grand. What's first?'

He held up *How to Read a Poem and Fall in Love with Poetry.*

'I know you. Start with the least favorite, eh,' as Brush would say.

'Maybe, but also maybe the most important.'

'I gotta get back down to Lola. We're cooking up a feast. Will you discuss Edward Hirsch's poetry book with me?'

'I will and all of these, too, if you want.'

Najma was tired of being confined to bed. There was nothing in this room except for three books on the night table. The top one: *The Flame Trees of Thika* by Elspeth Huxley. Najma scowled. A kid's story from the looks of the cover. The next: a backhoe mechanic's manual. Worthless. The bottom one: a small paperback titled *The Kama Sutra of Vatsyayana.* Its chapter titles disgusted her.

She soon realized that Bambi was leery of her. If there were other women here, she would struggle to win them over too. To secure acceptance here, her best chance was to seduce the leader. The thought repulsed her.

She threw *The Kama Sutra* on the bed. She stared at the wallboards. She could flirt with Colbert and feign injuries. Keep him wanting her. *I can do that for so long. Eventually, I will have to fuck him,* she thought. Looking at the ceiling, she said out loud, 'There is only one person I want inside me. His seed in me. I'll have his son.'

'Do you have a phone?' asked Bambi. 'I heard you talking.'

'I was saying a prayer about how grateful I am to be here,' she easily lied.

She doesn't seem like the praying type, thought Bambi. *But then Brenda doesn't look like a witchcraft and devil believer either.*

'Where did you come from?'

Najma had not thought through what she should say. This was as good a time as any to make up a story.

'I don't even like to think about it. The U.S. government put me into a prison in Cuba. I hadn't done anything. For them, being from the Middle East is enough. They said I had no rights. The jailers raped and tortured me. There was a prison break since someone there was high up in the Mexican cartel. I got out with them and ended up even worse off in a Mexican compound belonging to a drug king who used me as he would a whore.'

Bambi was skeptical. Still, she felt sympathy for Najma. Women's routine subservience to men had always bothered her. Yet Bambi liked men and never wanted to give it all much thought. 'Then how did you get here?'

'I was taken by a lieutenant in the cartel to this place in Washington State called Omak. I escaped from them. I hitchhiked, and this man tried to rape me. I hit him and he shot me.' Najma looked down, doing her best to look ashamed. She tried to cry but couldn't. 'I hit him with a rock and took his car. I heard about this place from the cartel. I didn't know where it was, exactly. I remembered the name and that the cartel leader was angry with Colbert. Will I be safe here?'

'You're safe here.'

The story sounded plausible to Bambi. Perhaps the woman had been so brutalized that she had become hard, maybe that is what she was sensing.

'Can you tell me more about this place? Are there others besides you, Jason, and Phil? And are you … do you … with one of them?'

'I don't have anyone. The rest is a long story. There are twenty-eight here now. It started with Jason, Phil, Gab, and Rob. They were all in the army together. Little by little, others were brought in. A collection of strays. Are you religious?'

Najma did not know what to say. She decided that religious nuts always wanted to convert you, so she was safe saying, 'My parents were. The world seems cruel to me. It's hard to believe there is a God. I don't know.' She watched Bambi, looking for a reaction. One that could give her direction in how to respond.

'Nah. We're not really. One of the men was some sort of ex-preacher. He says he lost his way and was traveling around trying to find it. He says he never did. He's been here for two years. Then there's Brenda who thinks there are witches, and that she is one. Does some weird ceremonies, but basically she's harmless.'

'Sorry to break this up,' said Colbert, walking straight into the room this time. 'I'd like to talk to our guest.'

'You're insatiable,' said Glenda Rose.

'Don't blame that on me. Look at you. If I took a pin-up photo, you'd be on every guy's locker in the army. They would throw all the other Playboy pin-ups into the trash.'

'I thought you were a Canuck, eh? Now you're sounding like an Irishman.'

Brush put on a fake scowl. 'How do you know what an Irishman sounds like, eh babe?'

'In America, we have books and movies. You think they would want a pin-up of an old woman with three bullet hole scars?'

'You're not old.'

'I'm not twenty.'

'The scars are erotic. Give you character. I've said that before as I remember.'

Brush did what he loved doing. He circled his index finger slowly around her nipple, never quite touching it. Just a light *brush* every three or four times. Glenda's nipple grew hard.

'Are you planning on seducing me again, big guy?' Glenda felt something and reached down. 'You are amazing. How can you get hard again so fast?'

'You never listen. It's not me. It's you.'

'I know, my guy. It's the same for me.'

Brush moved his hand down to his other favorite spot. The thin reddish hairs covering what he thought was the finest mound he had ever seen. He loved its feel. If he'd been a teenager, he would have lost it just looking at her.

'It's a wonderful life that we got this lucky, eh?'

A stretched out soft 'Uh-huh,' was the only answer he got.

CHAPTER 20

The days passed uneventfully. The security teams came and went. The green aspen leaves showed their first glint of yellow. It was as if the night had rained golden stardust on the canyon's trees. The moon was almost full. Shuskin went into hiding. Roy's pretend brother had taken over his duties.

Jim understood, as did Heather, that with the presence of so many armed men and some women, Shuskin chose to do what he had always done. Escape. This time in his cabin. Pedro visited the old man. More recently, Jim had called on him. Heather was always welcome. Lola sent home-cooked meals. Shuskin was cloaked by the cabin walls, but not alone or starving.

Heather finally put her foot down. 'I want our home, our lives back. I'm no longer afraid. You are able to help protect me now. No more troops destroying the peace,' she told Jim with determination.

Jim's strength increased with each passing day. He was strong enough for walking on the canyon floor. Soon he planned to hike up the traversing cow path to Coyote Ridge. The balsam roots' leaves were lifeless and brown. The bluebunch grass was no longer filled with chlorophyll. The crisp air and golden fairy dust in the tree leaves, along with the occasional burst of red vine maple, provided a different visual punctuation. The season's change was not only represented by the temperature change and the length of the day; he plants and their colors displayed their own story.

The FBI had closed the op center in Winthrop. Special Agent Jurgen Shultz was forced into early retirement. Command of the terrorist task force dangled in front of him and predicated on Najma's capture, never materialized. He had failed and was out.

The constant movement of people on the ranch did not bother Jim. They were his friends. After Neilly, Jeff, Roberta, Aleski, Mac, and Marilyn left, the house became the private domain of Heather, Jim, Pedro, Lola, and Rosie.

Jim finished several of the novels. Kingsolver's *Prodigal Summer* had been special. To say he liked the book would be an understatement. Two of the female protagonists shared traits with Heather. The reclusive wildlife biologist more than the bookish city-girl become farmer. As he turned each page, a realization came to him. He had always prided himself on accepting and respecting women; in some ways, he thought them superior to men.

On average, men were physically stronger. For exceptional abilities, one needed to look no further than Glenda Rose Stuart, Marilyn, or Roberta. Heather had none of their skills or experience. Why did he love her? What is love anyway? Something more than lust. He liked her. Her quirky interests and thoughts. Her picking up bugs and toads. Her unabated love of most animals. Her insistence on adding Lola, Pedro, and Shuskin to their home. He knew it was the right thing to do, but on his own, he would not have invited Lola or Shuskin to the ranch. Still, he was glad they were here. Heather had pushed him and now the blustering stout, Yaqui Mexican and the old transient were part of his life. Their life.

Jim planned to read Hirsch's poetry book straight through, but found he couldn't. Instead he read section by section. He learned things he had never thought about. But still, it was a struggle. Now that he was out of bed, he only read at night. He had decided to read *Sexual Personae* at the same time. A few pages of each, and then he opened one of the novels.

His thoughts wandered to JP. Heather had been urging Lola to learn proper English. How must it feel to be coerced into speaking American English while no thought was given to Heather's learning Lola's Uto-Aztecan tongue? The woman had been forced to learn Spanish, forced by the cartel into servitude. *Are we forcing her to learn English? Forcing her into servitude?* Jim didn't think so, but how could he be sure?

His overriding question remained. How do women's thoughts differ from men's? At times, he felt he was close to understanding. Could he picture himself a high school cheerleader? Even the idea upset him, although many of the girls in school relished it. Why? Then there were men who did, too. Men with a developed feminine side, perhaps? The thoughts and the questions confused him. He could not penetrate his ignorance and find the insight he sought. He remained trapped in a transition zone, unable to escape into enlightenment.

I love her, but I don't understand what motivates her. It's right there in front of me. *Why can't I grasp it?* Why did she love him when half his life was spent away from her? She wanted him here. He needed her, too, but not more than his work and his newly adopted Special Forces family. Was that fair? He certainly needed her affection. He thought back to this morning: her sitting astride him, moving seductively, still careful of his healing wounds. Her glazed eyes alternating between closed and open, looking into his.

He was certain his lust was inexorably intertwined with his liking. The combination emerged as love. It was why he had never indulged in prostitutes. To do so mystified him. Why spend money on a physical act when the same result could be achieved so much more simply in private. What was the attraction? Was it because it was forbidden? And why did such men not see they were readily participating in the degradation of women? Was that even always true? Some disputed whether it was or wasn't. *I'm wandering,* he thought. *Stay on track.*

Jim moved his thinking to resolving the two primary issues. First, to understand fully the love of his life. And second, to understand his nemesis. Where was Najma? What was she thinking? He wondered if it would be easier to enter Heather's mind or that of his psychopathic antagonist. In some ways, he better understood Najma. Jim was empathic for the weak, but not for power hungry, cruel types. This quality provided some insight into Najma. His insensitive half was the totality for her. She had no empathy for anyone. She was strictly motivated, so it seemed, by revenge, dominance, and hate … And that is where he started to lose the understanding, he thought he'd achieved. *Without emotion, how could she hate?* He wondered.

Jim was in tune with Brush, with Neilly, and Will Crystal. It simplified life. The long relationships with men he felt he fully understood. And here he was grasping for knowledge of the two women in his life. Both of them different and equally incomprehensible. Someday he would address the third woman: Lola.

After Jim was well enough to leave the house, he held talks with Will, Sheilla, and Martin Pearson. Katarina often participated in his conference calls with Sheilla. Having agreed that Najma was probably alive, they discussed ways to protect everyone at Wolf Canyon. The ranch's inhabitants remained vulnerable targets on the ranch. The only certain way to defend them would be to move them to the base at Fort Lewis until Najma was either captured or killed. After her robust opposition to having their domain invaded, Heather evolved to an even more dogged intransigence. The subject was therefore never raised with her. She would not be moved. She had become nearly fanatic in her refusal of a protector other than Jim.

In some ways, Jim was sympathetic. He too, wished for the blissful days they had once enjoyed together with their animals and nature. What differentiated him from Heather was that he was a realist. If Najma were still alive, she would surely come for him, eliminating anyone in her path. The problem was when and how?

Heather asked Jim to teach her how to properly shoot her PPK 380 pistol. She had learned the basics by shooting at cans and targets. But Jim knew that shooting while being shot at was something he could not teach her. Heather felt a certain sense of accomplishment in that she could now hit the target. Unfortunately, this was as far as her interest in self-defense had gone. Ben and Pedro, on the other hand, had begged for continuous instruction from the Canyon's protectors. They were delighted that some of the most highly trained men and women had offered snippets of self-defense.

Heather's cell phone played its song.

'Maria, how are you? See anything of Nusmen?'

'Good. Nope, fortunately he's out of my orbit. And how's our colonel?'

'He's doing fine, and the good part is he's here. I hope he'll stay.'

'Heather, try not to fall into the same trap again. He'll get well. He has another side to him. Embrace both sides or you won't be happy.'

'I know, and sometimes I think I understand. Jim and I are two sides of the same penny. We come together on the fine edge of the coin. Our competing world views separate, but also join us.'

'That's progress.'

'At times, I feel as though I can fully embrace my fate. I wish I could all the time. Allowing the other to thrive, explore, and dream — freely and without restraint. Feeling together when most separate.'

'You are sounding a bit poetic. Are you getting this all down in your journal?'

'Sorry, Maria. It's just that I think about this all the time. Even when he's here. I'm happy when he is. The longer he is, the more nervous I get. I know it will end.'

'I understand. When things are going especially well, I start to get on edge. We both know life is half one thing and half the other. It never is only the good parts.'

'What are you up to?'

'Mostly training. Nothing going on at the moment. It

won't last either, but then maybe something exciting will happen'

'Are you sailing much?'

'I wish. In two weeks, if the weather's nice, I can take a week off. I might try to make it to Friday Harbor.'

'Ben goes on and on about your boat.'

'I'd like him to go again. Maybe you and Pedro, too?'

'It would be nice to get together. Hey, Jim will be better in a couple of weeks. What about coming over here? Maybe some others like Misa and Vidya. What do you think? I know you want to go sailing, but you could come over here for the week. Maybe the weather will be terrible.'

'Bad weather will drive me east to you. It's a promise.'

'I'm going to invite the others anyway.'

'A good idea.'

'Maybe just us girls: Sheilla, Katarina, Misa, you, and me. A party, just like we used to throw at uni,' said Heather.

'I don't think that would be such a good idea,' said Maria.

'We were a little wild, weren't we?'

'I don't think I could ever do what we did back then again. I don't think we ever got tired. An endless party. How'd we get through school?'

'Don't ever go and get old on me, Maria,' said Heather.

CHAPTER 21

Najma's days passed slowly. Her pain lessened. The pills Colbert and Phil provided her helped. She felt different. Less on edge. Jason Colbert was besotted with her. She knew what he wanted and what she would have to do. At first, she feigned pain and weakness. Then she acted demure, pretending inexperience. Which was, in fact, true. Except for the teenage rapes of her father and his friends, she had had no real sexual experience.

Once when she and Colbert had been kissing, she'd felt a tingle. She tried to make it happen again. Najma reasoned if she could feel pleasure, doing what she knew she would have to do might be tolerable. But pleasure was nowhere to be found. She steeled herself to enduring his gross hairy body on top of her. His hard penis inside her. The thought made her nauseous. *For this, he will pay. I'll cut it off and stuff it in his mouth.* The vision made her feel better. It is what I will think about when he enters me.

Out of eight women in the compound, only two came to visit her. Bambi was boring. Full of questions. The other,

Brenda, was the only woman who attracted her. Najma was glad Brenda would be visiting this afternoon. It kept Colbert away, and she liked hearing her weird tales and beliefs.

Brenda said she could prove that aliens had abducted her. When Najma asked her how, Brenda told her they'd hypnotized her. Then, she had recounted in detail things only someone who had been with the aliens would know. Or so she said.

Before entering the knotty pine cabin, Brenda stood on the porch for a minute. She had a covered bowl of spaghetti Bolognese with lots of extra meat. Najma had previously told her she liked meat.

Brenda handed Najma the container. 'You can eat while we talk if you want. I've eaten already.'

Najma smiled while taking the lid off the ceramic bowl. 'You said just before you left last night that you were a witch and we could do a ceremony.'

'It's so nice to have someone else as a believer here. I was going nuts. There are sweet people at Bright Light, but they have a problem with the supernatural. They just don't understand. Wait. I am going to lock the front door. I don't want anyone sneaking in and eavesdropping.'

Najma found all this to be humorous She smiled again at Brenda when she came back into the bedroom.

'I'll tell you about the ceremony I do. A ritual. I set up my altar. I keep my things hidden. I've a statue of a naked goddess and one of a male. I have a red candle, incense, salt, water, my toasting drink, and a pentacle. I put on soft music and start to meditate. I imagine roots growing from me into the ground.'

Brenda's ceremony reminded Najma of some Muslim

rituals she had watched her father perform on his rug after he had raped her. She tried to look interested instead of disgusted. She swallowed.

'Then I recite chants. I bless the salt. I bless the flame candle: "I cleanse and consecrate thee, candle flame. May your essence bless us and bring your passion to our circle."' As she chanted, Brenda looked at Najma and smiled with her eyes.

'So, what happens then?'

'That's only the start. I have to conjure up the circle of power, a boundary between two worlds. I invoke the deities and eventually toast them. You'd be welcome to attend when you can get around better. I have a secret place. It's a ways walking.'

Conjuring "power" interested Najma. 'Do any of these deities or witches show themselves?'

'I think there are two in this compound.'

'Who?' Najma thought this lady was nuts, but she was at least more interesting than ex-hippie Bambi and the men with their brains in their pants. Brenda didn't answer.

'Come on, Brenda. Who?'

'You have to promise not to tell anyone. They already know I am a witch but not what kind.'

Najma's mouth was open. 'What do you mean what kind and who is the other one?

'The other one is you.'

Najma stared at her.

'I think you are a witch. Maybe even a high priestess. Perhaps even more. I overheard you were called La diabla. Others thought you were.'

Najma rarely laughed. Few things were funny to her.

But this time, she was trying really hard not to laugh out loud. 'So, I'm a witch, a devil. What kind are you?'

'You promise not to tell anyone?'

'Cross my throat and hope to die.'

'I'm a succubus.'

'A what?'

'It's why, without a coven, my powers don't dwindle. We could have a coven together. We would be very powerful.'

'I don't understand.'

Being a succubus gives me more power than I would have just as any old witch who needs a coven.

'What's a succabus?'

'It's succubus with a "u." A female demon.'

Najma looked at her without saying anything, 'Explain better.'

'I go into a trance at night and prey on men. I have sex with them when they are asleep.'

'What about when they are awake.'

'As much as I can. Three of the men in the compound, as much as they are able. But they are getting weak and sick. It is what happens with repeated sex with a succubus. I have to please myself all the time too.' Brenda moved closer to Najma.

'Sex with a high priestess would strengthen me. Both of us.'

'You want to have sex with me?'

Brenda nodded with a slight smile.

'I've never had sex with a woman … nor a man.'

'I thought you were seducing Jason.'

'I haven't.'

'If you do, you will own him. Control him. It's the way it

works. You could get him into our coven.'

The thought of power and control over men, or even over one man, interested Najma.

Brenda said, 'Wait. You're a virgin? That's scary.' Brenda moved back a little.

'Why are you scared?'

'Virgins are especially dangerous.'

'Thanks to my father, I'm not a virgin.' She spit on the floor. 'I didn't have sex with them. They forced me.' She spit again, remembering the trucker she had seduced to get to Mexico. Then she smiled as she remembered killing him.

'Your father was a warlock and the others must have been in his coven. You need to be purified. I can help you.'

'Anything new?' asked the general.

'I'm afraid nothing,' said Sheilla. 'We're doing everything we can think of. How long can we keep a drone flying over Wolf Canyon?'

'The day we give up will be the day she shows up. But we have to stop sometime. You monitor and search for her using anything that makes sense with your computers. The FBI is doing the same from their offices. We have other work. Don't drop it. Don't emphasize it.'

'Mirrors my thoughts. Heather doesn't want any more guards on the ranch. Should I call Carter's team back or leave them?'

'When Jim's up and about. He is capable of protecting himself.'

'I have an idea, sir. Heather mentioned that maybe Misa,

Maria, me, and a few others would like to come to the ranch for a party.'

'When? I'm flying back in three days.'

'No date yet. I was thinking that, of course, Brush and Glenda would want to come. Maybe they could stay on at the ranch. Heather wouldn't mind that. She liked Glenda.'

'I see. If Jim and Heather are okay with it, I'll keep Glenda off the active role for a while longer. It's a good idea having three of them. Set up the party and let's have at least a section of Carter's team patrolling.'

'It would make me feel safer. I'm not sure Misa would go otherwise. Both she and Vidya remember Mexico all too well. I'm surprised they would go at all with Najma still on the loose.'

CHAPTER 22

Najma was in a quandary. She knew she would eventually have to sleep with Colbert. After all, she was the one seducing him. Controlling him. The thought of Colbert's touch made Najma angry.

She sensed Brenda wanted something. She didn't know what, but she wanted to keep Brenda as an ally. So far, Najma had not tried to ingratiate herself with the other women. She played along with Phil, Colbert's second in command, and Gab his army buddy. She was savvy enough to want to keep selected people on her side. *I have to play along with those three. Between them and Colbert, it is enough.*

Brenda was due any minute.

'I can't stay and chat,' said Brenda. 'We're having some kind of group meeting. I have to go.'

'I want to talk to you.'

'Later. How far can you walk?'

'As far as I want.'

'I'll come and get you at 9:30 tonight.'

Najma didn't know what she was getting herself into.

With someone like Brenda, it couldn't be too bad. *She's a head full of air,* Najma thought shaking her head in disgust. Najma had never thought one way or the other about how women looked. With her long light brown hair, brown eyes, and slender figure, *Brenda would be on the pretty side,* she thought. *I wonder where we'll walk to.*

Heather was excited. With the men gone, she was able to bury Najma deep inside her mind. She refused to let her drift into her conscious thoughts. Jim was the opposite. He kept wondering where Najma had gone and when she would return. Using Carter as a courier, Katarina had sent Jim material a week ago. Along with her annotated write-up, she had included a thick stack of papers from Sheilla and Barbara, some to sign, others letting Jim know the current state of research in the lab as well as any issues Sheilla thought he should be apprised of. When Heather was not there, he read up on psychopathic personalities.

His biggest takeaway was that psychos were, as a group, efficient and utterly ruthless. They were good planners. This made them difficult to counter. It was like a chess match where two contenders imagined the future moves of an opponent. Najma would envision what Jim needed to do to protect himself and his family. She would find a way around those plans. Alternately, Jim tried to guess what her plans might be. He tried to get into Najma's mind and to ask himself the questions she would ask. *How would I take me out if I was her?* he wondered. His conclusion was not reassuring. His demise would be far too easy. They were vulnerable on the ranch. Jim was not used to safeguarding a position. Normally, he was the hunter. He tried to think back to how he had defeated others in this situation. There were too many choices. The only thing that could save them from an attack would be luck.

With no solutions, Jim's thoughts turned away and to his books. Women authors writing about women. But what he discovered was more about himself than about Heather. Through Katarina's analyses, he also felt he now knew more about Najma. He understood the cool calculations of the psychopath. He wondered which of the two he had the most in common with.

Beryl Markham's memoir caused him to reflect on what made him happy. She wrote about giving up flying. Leaving the plane and walking away. Forgetting about emergency landings, sick guests, inclement weather, and engine failures. She said, "You can never look at the plane again. You may become a very happy person, so why don't you? (But) It's going to be boring."'

Is that what I fear? Being bored? Is the ranch and Heather boring? Does Najma feel boredom the same way I would?

Camille Paglia challenged his traditional thought, as he saw it now, of men visiting prostitutes. "… striving to keep sex free from emotion …," she said. *What's the point?* wondered Jim. *Is it like pornography in the flesh?* With all the risks, Jim again wondered why bother. Risks to family, self, society. Or did risks themselves defeat boredom?

Unbeknownst to Jim, Najma was also asking herself questions about sex. She had always assumed that her disgust for copulation came from her experiences with her father. The association seemed valid; however, it wasn't sex alone that disturbed her. Rather, it was the association of sex with men. She had known nothing beyond her childhood experiences, except for the one crude truck driver that got her to Mexico. The only pleasure she derived from that man was killing him.

Najma and Brenda stepped through the forest toward Brenda's secret place. The special place where she performed her ceremonies as well as the new home of Bright Light's coven. The two night-fairies flitted out of the shadows into the starlight and then into a meadow which had years ago been cleared for the homesteader's cabin.

Najma had taken two of the pills. Something she had never done before. They would help her pain if they walked far. The pills made her feel sleepy when she was in bed. When she was up and walking, on the other hand, she felt light and dreamy.

'Are you not afraid to be here alone in the darkness with a witch?' asked Brenda.

'I haven't thought about it one way or the other. Do you mean to harm me?'

'I mean to find out who you are.'

The small cabin listed to one side. Its interior tendered a single room about ten by twelve feet, containing only a chest and a large black metal saucer with kindling. Brenda busied herself with statues, candles, salt, water, and other items. After spreading a heavy blanket, she kneeled on it, arranging the other articles on the floor's crude wooden planks. Before turning to Najma, she lit the kindling; then she lit several candles on a chest. She was wearing a long, dark oiled coat, similar to an Australian outback duster. She faced Najma and unbuttoned the coat, letting it drop to the floor. The candlelight flickered over her naked body.

'Do you think you might get cold?' asked Najma.

'I hope neither of us will. We have to do the first ritual of our coven without clothes. It is the proper way to do it.'

Najma shrugged, taking off her plaid shirt, T-shirt, and pants. Standing naked with Brenda, she felt nothing. Brenda reached out and took her arm. 'Kneel next to me.'

There it was again. The feeling she had felt once with Colbert. However, this time a more intense tingle. She looked down as if she would be able to see it. They knelt on the heavy blanket and Brenda said, 'First, we meditate. Let your mind go. Relax. Close your eyes.'

Najma felt a light touch, accompanied by more of the same elusive feeling.

'You said you hadn't had sex, willingly. I have already, once this morning, with myself. It is never enough for me.'

'What do you do?' asked Najma.

Brenda hadn't been sure about Najma before. She realized now Najma was probably as inexperienced as she had said. 'Lie down on your back.'

Brenda curled up close and turned Najma's head to her. She kissed her lightly and then more forcefully. Najma's nipples were hard. She had never felt like this. 'What's next?'

Brenda was taken back. *She's obviously as excited*, she thought, *as she is mentally uninvolved*. She swallowed. Her courage returned, overcome by the urge to reach an orgasm. 'Touch me here like I am touching you.'

Najma focused on the shadows dancing on the ceiling. The feelings intensified. She thought of sitting atop Jim. Then imagined sitting atop Heather. She felt something very strange. Her pelvis was throbbing. She pushed the knife into Jim's throat. Then Heather's. She tensed and was overcome by a chemical rush.

As the feelings waned, she wanted them back. 'I want to do this again.'

'I'd like that. I want to come here again with you too.'

'Now. Not later.'

'Where have you been all these past years?' asked Brenda. 'I had to finish myself off. You stopped. I want another too.'

'Me first,' demanded Najma, 'then show me what to do to you.'

Najma didn't care about pleasing Brenda. She couldn't care less about Brenda's feelings. Najma had to learn the motions and sounds of pleasure to convince Colbert he was pleasing her. The thought of him angered her and nearly took her focus away from the physical feelings that Brenda was giving her.

CHAPTER 23

Colbert walked into Najma's room. He sat on the bed's edge, giving her a kiss. 'Good morning, beautiful.'

'Good morning, my man,' she parroted back.

'I am going to town this morning for supplies. We're going to have a birthday dinner tomorrow for Bambi and one of the children. Would you like anything special?'

Najma was relieved that he would not try to take her now. She realized, however, that she could not string him along much longer. She steeled her mind and said, 'Only that you come back to me.' She looked at him with the same longing expression that he wore for her.

'I'll get something special for tonight.'

After he closed the door, Najma's face reverted to expressionless. She reached down and hesitantly touched herself. Ever since her father, she had had an aversion to touching her genitals. The feeling immediately reappeared. The one first caused by Brenda. Her mind turned to what she would have to do this evening. The sensual feelings abruptly left.

Another knock on her door. 'Can I come in?' asked Phil.

In Najma's eyes, Phil resembled her colonel. 'Yes, please.' Two affirming words, she had learned, that could generate trust.

'I'd like to check on your wounds.'

'I'm fine. There is no need.'

'Since you've started to go outside, I thought you might be up for a tour of the compound. Jason asked me to show you around when you were able.'

'When?'

'Now, if you like.'

'I'll be out in a minute.'

Najma had wanted to see more. The only things she knew about the compound were her cottage, the outside of the main house, a couple of other buildings, and a Quonset hut. She needed to know details. She slipped her knife into its black leather holder and clipped it on her belt. She was pleased to have it back. Colbert must have taken it when she arrived. One morning, it was sitting on the bedside table.

Phil introduced her to several people as they walked around the compound. Brenda walked out of the main house, wearing a long dress, beads, tall deerskin moccasins, and a canvas bag slung over one shoulder.

She smiled at Najma in a way that left little doubt about how she felt about her. Najma returned the greeting, trying to provide Brenda with the response she needed while not giving anything away to Phil.

'I'm going to collect mushrooms. Do you want to come along?'

Najma looked at Phil. 'I'm giving her the full Bright Light tour.'

'Maybe later,' said Najma.

Brenda skipped down the road past the metal-topped Quonset hut.

'You've made a friend,' said Phil. 'I saw you stroll by last night with Brenda. I'd be ....'

'Be what?'

'I don't know. Never mind.'

'What's in that building?' asked Najma, ignoring Phil's statement.

'Trucks, equipment, and that sort of thing. Jason's baby too.'

'His what?'

'His backhoe.'

Inside the main house, Phil walked to a door. He opened it and pushed the hanging clothes to the side. At the back of the closet was another door. He opened it and started down the stairs. 'This is what makes our compound special.'

Both doors were wood. However, a heavy metal door stood open at the top of the steps. At the bottom of the steps, Phil and Najma continued through a tunnel for several yards. Eventually, the tunnel gave way to a spacious storeroom packed with supplies.

'Impressive, isn't it?' asked Phil.

'It's a lot of supplies,' said Najma. 'There's no room for people?'

Phil opened a connecting door. Another heavy metal door was open against the wall. 'We only close the radiation and security doors if there is a threat.' They moved through the tunnel for two yards. Phil opened another door. Bunk beds lined one wall. There were several tables. Through another door was a kitchen. Another door concealed two composting toilets.

He directed her down another longer hall to a third room. Najma smiled at the sight of several dozen weapons on one wall. There was a worktable. On the opposite side, behind a heavy plastic curtain, was a small tool shop. On one of the side walls were two hospital beds with cabinets behind.

'How do you shower?' asked Najma.

'We don't. Strictly towel baths here. Water is precious. We have a well that comes directly to the bunkers. Until we solve the problem of groundwater contaminated with radioactive particles migrating through the soil to our source, we have Geiger counters and radiation contamination detectors.'

Najma was going to ask about air and electricity and how the composting toilets worked. But she didn't want to hear any long-winded explanations. Instead, she asked, 'Can I handle some of these weapons?'

'Sure. Try not to touch the metal.'

Najma scowled at him.

'Sorry.'

Najma picked up a strange-looking plastic weapon. It looked sort of like a fat rifle, half as tall as it was long. 'You going to tell me what this is?'

'You don't know, huh?'

'Spill it, jive blow.'

Phil laughed. 'You said it backwards. It's blow jive.'

'So what? I've heard that said before. I like it that way. Well, Mr. Blow Jive?'

Phil said with some pride, 'It's a blinding laser weapon. They're illegal now. We had some experimental ones in the army.'

Najma spent some time quizzing Phil about how it worked. She carefully looked over the other weapons.

'I'm ready to go up top,' said Phil.

He decided not to show Najma the third exit into the woods. He had perhaps shown her too much already.

'How many acres do you have here?'

'One hundred sixty deeded.'

'Deeded meaning?'

'Bright Light owns them outright. We have 600 acres leased adjacent to the compound. All trees and meadows. No farming. The milking cow, sheep, goats, and chickens only take up an acre. Most of the rest of the land behind us is forest service. Your car is buried there.'

'Buried?'

'Colbert dug a big old hole with his backhoe and pushed it in.'

Jim looked up at Coyote Ridge. It would be his first long walk to the ridgetop since returning from Madigan Hospital. He looked forward to resuming his old life and way of doing things. He wasn't fully recovered and was still weak. It bothered him, feeling that way. He was eager to regain his strength.

He walked down the rear drive and across a flat area before arriving at an old water-worn gulch. The gully had not seen heavy runoff for dozens of years. Bushes and trees invaded it. With the intense storm they had just had, Jim wondered why there was no water draining from the hills into it. Filling it would probably require the melting of the heavy snow cover combined with torrential rains.

Knowing that, to form the ditch, a similar scenario must have happened in the past, he wondered if a similar gusher might occur in the future above the big barn. *Did I build it high enough to avoid a gully-wash flood?*

As he climbed through the ditch, it struck him that maybe it was not caused by a heavy flood as he had just surmised, but rather had been formed from a wetter time when an artesian well had flowed near the upper part of the canyon, carving the ditch over many years. *I'll see if I can find such a source someday.*

Past the ditch, an oddly secluded flat area nestled between the head of the aspen grove and the base of the ridge. Not as secret as his and Heather's Secret Glade, it nevertheless felt as though one could sit here unnoticed from most parts of the ranch. Several scraggly aspens emerged between the flat area and the main grove. *Implies insufficient water,* he thought. *Is there still a small amount of underground water source from up the canyon?*

Jim couldn't know the historical hydrology that had formed the mystery he was trying to solve. During a wetter time, an underground river might have flowed, much like the one supporting the aspens that still followed the water flow down Wolf Canyon to Beaver Creek. The flow had diminished over the last hundred years to a point where only a few of the scraggly aspens remained where larger trees had once thrived. The fallen giants' skeletal remains had years ago been digested by beetles or consumed by fungus.

As Jim approached the base of the ridge, he turned to look up the canyon. A flash hit his thoughts. The remnants of the homesteader's cabin belonged to the irregularly shaped 160 acres at the top of the canyon. It had been staked out by a homesteader to follow the contours of the upper canyon. The settler would have had no use for hillsides. The cabin would have been built for easy access to water. Without it, the land was useless. The stead had been abandoned when the water disappeared. The water must have gone dry not long after they staked out their claim.

With the mystery of the gully solved, Jim felt ebullient as he traversed the old cattle trail up Coyote Ridge. The walk was easy. It was an optical illusion. One didn't climb the ridge, rather the ridge descended along with the canyon. The trail appeared to climb as it traversed the ridge. An illusion. It was nearly flat. The cattle knew this. It was an easy way to get to the bunch grasses on the other side. Go up without climbing. He was happy with just this amount of walking on his first outdoor excursion.

He planned to sit atop the ridge and take in the mountains, the canyon, and the sky. After school, Jim had promised to visit the barn and see the animals with Pedro.

He gained the ridgetop. To the east, a series of mounds where the remains of the unidentified Middle Eastern man had been found. His death would be a mystery harder to solve than that of the gully. The man must have been part of the cartel's attack. Forensics had said that his death, while difficult to say with certainty, fit Najma's pattern. *Why would she kill him?* Both Katarina at BWC and Bertrand at the CIA had been charged with coming up with a story that fit the facts.

Jim found his favorite spot and lounged back. His feet straddled an oversized fall-brown bluebunch wheatgrass. The toe of one boot sighted at No Name Ridge. The other toward the house and the upper canyon. To his left, the aspen grove, sprinkled with dots of yellow, wound its way down, while Oval Peak and the Cascades rose into the intense blue of the fall sky.

The browns and the yellows, punctuated with an occasional red from a vine maple, enhanced the pigment saturated sky. Jim was forever grateful to have some understanding of why the autumn sky was so blue. His long years at the University of Washington provided many happy memories, but also the wherewithal to understand the world around him. The deep blue was a result, he knew, of a lower sun angle which resulted in Rayleigh scattering, directing bluer color toward his eyes. Lower humidity acted as a minor contributor to the effect.

Science told him the why. But it couldn't completely explain the source of his pleasure. Life was good. He had the ranch, the love of his life, a child whom he adored, and two odd characters who gave the ranch a special flavor.

Then Najma entered his thoughts. Where was she? What was she doing? When would she come for him? His three questions caused him to smile. In this moment and time, Heather was here. Najma was not.

There were no clouds. Just the endless blue. The llamas were in the fields below. The horses grazed on the side of No Name Ridge. A long caw from one of the peacocks drifted up the ridge. From his cabin, the old man walked up the road toward the main barn. A diminutive figure no larger than the beetle that had just flown past Jim.

Pedro had learned some self-defense moves from the ranch's guardians. As much as anything, they provided him with a perceptible air of self-confidence. At school, the larger, older tormentor types sensed he was no longer as vulnerable. And all but one had become accustomed to his brown skin. Because of his bulk and slightly older age, Butch remained the dominant bully and Pedro's nemesis. Unfortunately, Butch had acquired prejudices from home, where his father degraded ethnic minorities, ranchers, and educated "Coasties." Butch felt it his duty to harass Pedro every chance he got.

Pedro struggled less with his new language. He was absorbing new words every day, and Heather had quit correcting him. Along with his skin color, his home-acquired vocabulary set him apart from most of the rancher boys.

The visiting Special Forces teams understood his wish to protect himself. They shared his desire to learn to defend himself. And they delighted in giving him fighting pointers. Pedro also learned from them not to start a fight. If one started, however, the rules called for him to finish it fast without getting hurt. He was also told that school skirmishes generally produced no winners. Although Pedro had gained confidence, he still gave the bigger, wide-faced, butch-cut bully a wide berth.

Jim planned to return to the house and resume reading. As much as he was enjoying rereading the novels, he had not yet come to the understanding he sought. He still struggled to grasp poetry. The few things he had learned were illuminating, such as poetry was not all the same. As with music and novels, poems were all different and appreciated by people with varying tastes. He had learned that there could be beauty in words, as in art and nature. That metaphors were widely used. That the message conveyed by the poet often lurked below the surface to be discovered by the reader. Jim still, however, had not learned to love poetry.

He found a line or two that expressed what he felt about the world, but never a complete poem he could admire. "Anyone who planned to enjoy the world is not faced with a hopeless task. Stupidity isn't funny. Wisdom is gay. Hope isn't that young girl anymore ..." These were words Clare Cavanagh had used. Simple words that mirrored Jim's feelings.

Jim was straightforward. He didn't embellish. A realist, he sought simple truths. He wondered whether Najma liked poetry. The question caused him to think of the world he had seen. Its cruelty. Its unfairness. *Had he become hard?* It worried him that perhaps he understood Najma better than he did Heather.

Still, he loved Heather. She was everything that Najma was not. *I live in two worlds*, he concluded. *I embrace the one and understand the other.*

The home he shared with Heather, Pedro, and Lola seemed warm after the crisp fall air. He came in quietly so that Lo would not hear him. He wasn't even sure whether she knew he had gone out. Kitchen sounds told him lunch would be ready soon.

CHAPTER 24

'Do you think we would become bored with domesticity?' asked Glenda.

'Not me. It feels more like I have you right where I want you.'

'I don't mean sex.'

'You mean washing dishes and clothes and that sort of thing?' asked Brush.

'You're hopeless. I'm being serious here.'

'I thought that was a serious question I just asked.'

'I think you need to look up the meaning of domesticity.'

'I don't need to. You're not getting bored, are you?' asked Brush.

'I'm never bored with you, big boy. I am thinking ahead. Do you think you would ever want kids?'

~

Colbert would return soon. Najma knew she couldn't postpone this any longer. She turned up the heat on the propane stove, took off her clothes, and climbed under the sheets. *I need to survive. I need to embed myself here. I need to keep Colbert's support*, bracing herself for what she would have to endure. Colbert wasn't ugly like the truck driver she had had to endure. But they had the same fault: men were repulsive to her bar one. She grimaced as she turned over. Pains still clawed at her from inside. Then she opened the drawer of the small bedside table. She removed the lid of a plastic container and swallowed another pill.

She let her eyes play on the ceiling. It was covered with square ceiling tiles. The pain in her gut melted away. She remembered the rickety cabin, the candles dancing shadows, and Brenda. Two hours later, a noise entered her dream. The foggy sense between dream and reality cleared. An image of Jim formed and faded. She opened her eyes. Colbert was standing looking at her.

He reached down and pulled the quilt over her exposed breast. The cabin was warm. Najma took his wrist and pulled him to her.

The door closed. 'I'm home,' said Heather.

'Many things,' answered Lola. 'I take to kitchen.'

'I'll take them. There's more in the wheelbarrow outside the door.'

Lola looked out the door's window. 'Many bags?'

'They're for the party.'

'You no tell me you make party.'

Heather laughed. 'I forgot. Lo siento, Lo.' That made her laugh even more. 'Yes, we make a party this weekend.'

'Okay, I get. You leave bags here. No put away. I do it.'

Heather bent over and kissed Lola on the forehead. 'It's your kitchen now. I want to see how Jim is doing.'

'He very quiet. Maybe asleep. No eat lunch. You take up to him.'

'Pedro,' called Heather. 'Where are you? Lo needs your help,' just as Pedro came through the door.

'I saw a snake.'

'What kind?'

'I don't know. It was brown.'

'Probably a bull snake. No patterns or diamonds? No rattles? asked Heather.

'All brown. Let's find it.'

'It will be long gone now.'

'Snake no good.'

'Lola, they are very good. They eat mice. Without the coyotes, snakes, and birds, we would be overrun with mice. They help keep nature in balance.'

'Snakes. Parties. I have to put stuff away.'

'Pedro, help Lo.'

'Dad said he would go to the barn with me.'

'He will, but I want to spend some time with him first.'

'Oh, Mom.'

Heather gave him a look and headed up the steps.

'How're you feeling? Learn anything new?'

'Not for want of trying,' said Jim. 'I did manage a walk up to Coyote Ridge.'

'Wow, you are feeling better.'

'It's not that difficult. I like it up there.'

'You're halfway through Hirsch's book, and he has not

made you fall in love with poetry yet? Haven't you seen anything you like?'

'Most of it seems like a foreign language. I like what you write.'

'Besides just being nice to me, why do you like what I write?'

'It seems simple. Direct.'

'I'm not sure if that's a compliment. So, give me one thing you like in Hirsch's book.'

'None, really. Sometimes there is a part that I like, but it seems never the whole poem. Even short ones.'

'I have a better idea if you will play along and humor me?'

Jim nodded. He wasn't sure where she was going with this, but ....

'You like it on top of Coyote Ridge, right? So, what do you like? What makes it special?'

'It feels like the top of the world.'

'Okay, that's a start. What is it about the feeling you have when you are up there? The colors? The mountains?'

'I was thinking more about the sky's color and the dry plants.'

'What happened to you sitting there? Besides what you saw? What did you feel or hear?'

'I was sitting in my favorite spot thinking about the bluebunch grasses turning brown. And how they rustled in the autumn wind.'

'So, the bunchgrass rustled in the autumn wind. What else?'

'I was thinking about the long summer leaving the soil dry. And then I thought about the fall sky's color. And that it would soon be winter. Then spring.'

'I know this is hard going,' said Heather. 'But try, darling. Put what you just said into simple sentences.'

Jim exhaled air, causing his lips to vibrate. He took a deep breath and said, 'The bunch grass rustled in the autumn wind. The dry soil of summer past and the thick blue sky portends of winter to come. The melting snow will make the dried grass blue-green again.'

'That, my dear, is the making of a poem. That's great.'

'Now you are humoring me, special.'

Heather smiled at him. 'Let's continue. What does it mean to you?'

'Just what I said. What I thought about.'

'Think, baby. Is it about the seasons, or love lost and found again? Did the words mirror your thoughts? Think about your feelings. A poet paints with words. Maybe we can do this again.'

Heather settled on the floor against the wall. She pulled out a notebook and started writing furiously. Jim settled back against the pillows, wondering if he would ever care about poetry. He had hoped to make a breakthrough. To see, to find what he had missed. He wondered if it would ever happen.

'Dad, can we go?'

'I'll be down in a minute.'

When Jim returned to the house, he needed to rest. It had been special sitting on the ridge and spending time with Pedro. Lying on the bed was a notebook. It did not have dog-eared corners. It was a new volume. A note stuck to the top said, 'I'm glad we talked. I'm glad you're alive. I'm glad you are here. This is how I feel. How I've felt. Also, a poem that says what I feel that I copied once and have read often when you are gone. I hope that one day I will be able to write a good one for you. I'm on the plateau above the house. Come to me. Be with me. Stay awhile.'

You're here for now. I hope for a long while. Still, I'm readying myself for your leaving. When you go, no clinging. Rather a cooling off. I will have control. No abandonment for me! So, I go through the motions, remembering how it felt when we were one. Pretending I'm not chilled in our shared bath. Pretending I am not wholly Heather again.

When you're away, you keep me in your mind's small satchel, sequestered and hidden. I keep you, too, in my tiny pocket. At times, I pull you out to finger and observe. A sharp, crystalline stone. Black obsidian.

Jim wondered why she referred to black obsidian. Was it a metaphor for his emotions? Was it part of poetry or writing where the author didn't say in simple terms what they meant? Or did they leave a word puzzle? Was there ever only one answer, or was it up to the reader to supply their own?

Kestrel

Small falcon, speak to me.
   You hover in the air, head to the wind.
   Swift. Agile. Long wings pointed.
   Last night, you flew too far for me to see.

Although lovers, we live in separate
   buildings, shed and barn.
   You visit me sometimes from your oneness;
   taste my supplicant's meat.

• • •

I write of your feathers, of your hooked beak.
> You circle to hear my odes, my yearning,
> knowing I'll never hold you,
> knowing no one in this world can be held.

Maybe I am learning, Jim thought. "Oneness," my own self, not us. "I write of your feathers," I think she is just describing what she sees and telling the reader what that is. The last part was clear enough. She can't control me or who I am. She accepts her fate. He looked back at her journal page and continued to read.

At least with all these forced separations, we can't bore each other. The fire still smolders, waiting to flame up once more in our Secret Glade. Senses stay keen. Sex stays new. My body still tingles at the thought of you.

If only we could make a child! If only he would engender a being within me! A part of him to cherish. To have and to hold.

Abstinence spawns longing. A honing of desire.

Jim's chin dropped to his chest. He reopened his eyes. The walks, the talking left him content but sleepy. He settled onto the pillow and lifted the journal. Before reading another word, his eyes closed again.

He was still dreaming as his mind moved to a conscious state. Najma knocked on the door to the house. Then she pounded. The noise forced him to wake. He listened. There was no pounding. Jim opened his eyes. The journal lay open on his lap. From the corner of his eye, he sensed a person.

'It's been a big day for you,' said Heather. 'You're still healing. It will take some time before you regain your stamina.'

'I...'

'Shush. I understand. Heather reached over and gave him a light kiss. Their lips tingled. They both felt it. For an instant, they both marveled at the sensations as they touched. Jim rolled toward Heather. He reached to her hair and stroked it. Heather closed her eyes. They both stopped thinking, losing themselves in their feelings. Several minutes later, Heather said, 'A really big day for you. A wonderful one for me.'

'Me too. I feel close to you.'

'Me too.' Then they both laughed.

'I didn't finish what you wrote. I understood the poem, at least I think I did.'

'You finish it when you want. I'm going to start getting things ready for the party.'

Jim lifted the journal. He glanced at the poem again and started reading from where he had left off.

Each time he returns, I feel like a virgin. Shy, but eager. As he prepares to take off yet again for a lengthy mission, I am becoming a nun. Resigned to chastity.

Intimacy. Why do you fear it? Lover, why do you flee me to save the world?

For a fraction of a second, Jim thought, they had just been intimate. He didn't flee. Then it became clear, it wasn't a moment's intimacy. She meant their life together. *It is not all that obscure,* he thought. *I'm beginning to understand better what she means.* The words started to flow.

When you are foreign and far away, I am foreign too. I watch the changing days like an orphan awaiting affection. But after a while, I divorce myself from you and your dimming memory because it hurts too much to have been relinquished.

I am important: the one he returns to. And insignificant: the one he chooses to leave.

I am the type of woman who remains behind. The kind who hovers, waiting. Passivity is an ugly form of love.

Now she's lost me again. "An ugly form of love?" *I missed the keyword, "passivity."*

This morning before you woke, I walked out to feed the llamas, bringing sweet molasses as a treat. Sharifa and Benji were there as well, munching tender grass and stalky alfalfa. Tall firm wooly-tan single humps stood above the llamas. In the transition to daylight, they turned their haloed heads toward me in greeting. Until Pedro arrived, these had been my children.

I am afraid. These missions are a taste of the future. A future headed toward loss. Inevitably, the watermelon snow will melt. Our hidden bower will be overrun with weeds. A dull ache pulses in my chest when you are gone. Oh, Jim! Take care! I don't want to lose you forever!

CHAPTER 25

Najma forced herself to moan, pretending to have an orgasm with Colbert. The small kernel of excitement she had felt when he kissed her days ago didn't reoccur. As Colbert entered her, she could only think of her father. With him, or his coven, as Brenda had referred to them, she had never shown any emotion. She had lain still, trying to take her mind elsewhere while they humped and groaned on top of her. When they hit her, she forced herself to remain impassive.

Except for the outward pretense at enjoyment, it was the same now. She thought of Brenda. She thought of her colonel. She thought of killing the hairy pig on top of her.

Colbert gave one last disgusting groan. He slumped to her side. His filthy seed leaked from her. She thought of climbing on top of him and thrusting her knife into his throat.

Colbert said, 'A shame, I have to get back to the main house. You stay and rest.'

Najma was relieved he'd had to leave. His staying in

bed would have been too much. She watched him go through the door. She waited until the outside door closed, then she jumped up and went to the bathroom. At the sink, she splashed hot water on herself. She worked water up inside her to cleanse his slime from her body.

Colbert didn't know if he was in love. He was pleased. He felt something, a burning attraction for Najma. Beyond the physical attraction, something drew him to her. Why he felt so attracted perplexed him. Perhaps he saw something in her that he saw in himself. They both had seen the harder side of life. What Colbert failed to see was Najma's true personality. He decided to set the question aside and enjoy her body and her apparent affection for him. *She does seem to be taken with me,* he thought.

Brenda was closer to understanding Najma than was Colbert. She recognized Najma's lack of emotion. That lack had not prevented her, however, from having physical enjoyment. Brenda knew nothing of psychopathic personalities. If she had, she might have embraced Najma even more. Brenda knew that the devil could be either gender or could appear in many forms. It thrilled her to think that perhaps Najma was the devil, or Satan, or Beelzebub. Any demon was always welcome in her ceremonies. *Maybe my prayers have been answered,* she thought.

While the thought excited her for the present, Brenda mostly cared that she had a new body to give her pleasure. Long before Brenda embraced the occult, she had been hypersexual. Her sexual desires preceded her spiritual beliefs. Brenda never gave it much thought. She didn't care who Najma was, only what she needed from her. Bright Light had similarly accepted Brenda, a person, a woman, and left her to her own beliefs.

Her addiction brought her pleasure every day. At night, she was a succubus who preyed on men in their sleep. Most days, she masturbated. When she could seduce one of the men, she had sex, when she could, more than once a day. Najma raised a new level of desire in Brenda. Sex with a woman was as new to Brenda as to Najma.

❧

'I'll meet you in the hangar,' said Sheilla.

'It is scaring me a little leaving here. Maybe I have become an agoraphobic,' said Misa.

'Have you ever had panic attacks?' asked Sheilla.

'No.'

'Have you ever had an encounter with Najma?'

'Unfortunately. You know we have.'

'Conclusion,' said Sheilla. 'You're not agoraphobic. I started to wonder about myself spending so much time below ground. I looked it up. It's about the fear of getting involved in embarrassing situations. Fear of having a panic attack in public. You're a strong, smart woman. I think you only have one fear: Najma. She's still out there, and I don't blame you. The good news is she is that she's injured and recovering somewhere, or dead. She's in no condition to do us any harm.'

'I hope you're right. But the recovering sounds ominous.'

'If it makes you feel better, I kept one drone at the Methow State Airport in case we needed it. I plan to give it some exercise when we are in Eastern Washington. And Carter's full squad is already patrolling the ridges above the ranch. Eyes from the air and eyes on the ground.'

'Why is it, that I don't think a twelve-member, specially trained military unit is a match for her?'

'Even if they aren't, remember you are going to visit the colonel who bested her in Mexico. This time there is also Glenda and Brush. Not to mention the general.'

'Okay, you convinced me. Time to feel the sun. I wonder if I will still like seeing trees and mountains in a different reality?'

'What reality?'

'We can see any place in the world we want on our computer screens. And Vidya's been experimenting with alternate reality goggles.'

'Really.'

'Ha. Yes, really. We're not taking a computer. That's pretty scary. I feel as though I'm leaving our children behind.'

'I'll be up in a minute. The general and I have to talk to Captain Kramer and Nusmen. Kramer's the duty officer while we are away having fun, and Nusmen is in charge of the labs.'

'As long as I've been in America,' said Misa, 'the word "while" never sounds right to me. We Brits speak English, but it isn't the same.'

Sheilla smiled and said, 'Take the lift up. Whilst you wait for me, try not to be nervous up top.'

'Love ya, Sheilla. Let's go to England sometime. You'll fit right in.'

The partygoers assembled alongside the general's new replacement Huey in the hangar.

'Sheilla, you want to act as co-pilot?'

'It's a beautiful day and you let me before. Maybe someone else should. Any takers?' asked Sheilla. 'Katarina,

I think you should. You told me you were looking forward to flying over in a helicopter.'

Katarina looked at the others. Maria and Barbara both nodded at her. 'Okay. What do I have to do?'

'The co-pilot has to fly, of course, while I nap,' said the general.

'Go on with you.'

'I'll take her around and get her strapped in,' said Glenda.

'Let's load up then,' said Will.

Brush looked in the cockpit as the general got into the left seat. 'Couldn't get an older one, eh?'

'Tells you something about our age. They're all moth-balled in the museum. The 1H is all I could requisition. The day there're no Hueys left and I have to fly a Sikorsky, or a Blackhawk is the day I retire.'

'This one has a better engine than the older ones, eh? Otherwise, looks about the same.'

Glenda walked around the nose. 'Kat's settled in.'

The massive hangar door slid sideways. The general started the engine. The blades started their slow turn. 'Got enough headsets back there?' asked the general.

'Looks like,' said Brush.

The general's "new" fifteen-year-old UH-1H rose above the shiny gray painted concrete. Stable at five feet above the concrete, he moved through the opening.

Brush, Glenda, and Sheilla stayed in the middle while the other five crowded toward the windows. Maria wanted to be on the west side to look at the sound and her sailboat. 'I'll stay over with you, Maria,' said Barbara. 'I've seen that peak most of my life.'

Their headsets channeled their constant chatter. 'I sure

haven't,' said Misa. 'The mountains never cease to amaze me. Nothing like Mt. Rainier in the south of England.'

'Anyone know any songs?' asked Vidya.

'If you start to belt out the Simpsons, I'm ripping your mic out,' said Misa.

Vidya held up both hands as a peace offering.

'What's with the Simpsons?' asked Maria.

'Vidya watched *Planes, Trains, and Automobiles*. John Candy sang the Simpsons' theme song to a busload of people. Vid seems to have been taken with it.'

'Oh. I've not heard that song.'

'You are lucky. It's stupid,' said Misa.

'It makes me happy, Mikey,' said Vidya.

'Now you're going to get it. Didn't they used to throw people out of helicopters in Vietnam, major?'

Brush reached over and grabbed Vidya in a bear hug. 'Open the door. I'll throw him out.'

Everyone laughed, except Vidya. 'I'm being crushed by this King Kong.'

'Squeeze tighter, will you, Major McGuire,' said Misa.

'I think I'll let him live for now. We'd be one short for the reunion.'

'Thanks for that, major,' said Vidya.

'Ms. Jensen, you can turn that bunch in back off, if you want,' said Will Crystal. 'Flip that switch on this panel. It's there to cut out the passengers while pilots are talking or when I need to talk to air traffic control.'

'It sounds like they're having fun back there, sir. My god, the scenery is wonderful.'

'You said you hadn't flown over before? Can I call you Katarina?'

'Yes, please. Only in a commercial jet, way up high. This is different, general.'

'You are an important staff member at BWC. When we're out of the office, please call me Will.'

'Thank you, general. I will.' She smiled at Will.

The general cracked a small smile. 'The chopper leaves you feeling in touch with the environment. You want to fly.'

'No. Really. I can?'

'Hold the cyclic. Like this.' He took his right hand away and took hold again.

Katarina gingerly wrapped her fingers around the stick.

'Put your feet on the pedals in front. Feel what I am doing. He moved the cyclic slightly and pushed the pedals first left and then right. When I say, "You have the controls," you say, "I have the controls," and it's all yours.'

'It sounds scary.'

'You will be fine. Ready. You have the controls.'

'Nothing is happening.'

'Don't forget to say, "I have the controls." It's important.'

'Sorry, sir, Will. It seems so easy.'

'That is the way it should be. Now, push the cyclic to the left slowly about an inch or two.'

'It's turning.'

'Now right, then up and down a little.'

'Amazing.'

'When we do our approach below the house, you can hold on and follow what I do. Flying straight and level is one thing. Hovering and landing are a little more difficult. I have the controls.'

'You have the controls,' she responded smiling at him.

He took it slow as he flew up the canyon. An aerial tour

of Wolf Canyon Ranch. As he approached the house, a tiny figure jumped up and down, waving its arms in great arches.

'That would be Pedro,' said Will. 'The boy loves helicopters.'

'I had a brother that loved trucks when he was little. He grew up to be a diplomat.'

'I think Pedro might want to join the army. Well, he might defect to the marines or air force, but I'd wager he is going to fly. Unbuckle and bring Pedro over. I'll take him for a ride now, or he'll be bugging me for the rest of the day.'

Jim watched the general's replacement Huey fly down the canyon, turn toward Coyote Ridge, pick up speed, and disappear over the top. *The general, Pedro, and myself. All in love with flying choppers.*

Jim heard the familiar voices as they entered the house, gay boisterous talking even without the addition of the general's booming voice. His best buddy: Brush. The others had become friends through their more recent experiences: Glenda, Sheilla, Misa, and Vidya. Maria, he had worked with in many places throughout the world. Barbara and he shared many years in the lab. He admired how capable both had always been. He liked them. Maria was Heather's old school friend from Reed College. Jim and Maria had never had the time to get to know each other well. Their duties kept them from social discourse.

He had known Maria longer than some of the others, especially Misa and Vidya. While he and Maria had worked together in stressful situations, surviving the deadly battle in Mexico with Misa and Vidya brought them immediately closer. Concerned that it would upset them he hadn't talked much to Misa, Vidya, or even Heather about what they had endured after they had been held captive by Najma and the cartel near Nogales. After two days of captivity, lifelong bonds inevitably formed for the three captives. Vidya, who disdained guns and violence, had shot a man. Misa and Heather carried shared scars from watching Najma torture and kill, while the cartel men raped and murdered one of their companions. Jim's solo rescue cemented the group's friendship in a way that only the direst situations can.

Here they all were. He started toward the stairs, just as Heather bounded up.

'How are you?'

'Okay.'

'Hmm, you look tired. You don't feel well, do you? Did you get enough sleep? You don't have any pain, do you?'

'It's typical. One day feeling fine and the next less so.'

'Lie down. I'll explain. Everyone will understand.'

'No. Let's go down. I'll be okay.'

'Are you sure? Never mind that I said that.'

The enthusiasm that greeted them when they touched their feet to the slate floor flushed away his weariness.

'Let's go sit. It's a bit early for drinks, but if anyone wants a drink now, Lola has enough sitting ready to intoxicate an army.'

'Caution to the wind,' said Glenda. 'I'll have a white wine.'

'Beer for me,' said Brush.

'What the heck,' said Misa. 'Me too.'

'Lola, bring in a bottle, make that two bottles, of white wine,' said Heather. 'I'll get the nuts and chips.'

Thirty minutes later the group had forgotten about the rest

of the world, Najma, Mexico, viruses, and the cartel. Their ebullience permeated the house. The mountain views were forgotten. No one paid attention when the helicopter thumped its way up the canyon. Jim relaxed, watching, observing, thriving on the comradery. Heather looked his way several times. She was in high spirits, flushed with excitement.

The seven women over-powered the three men with their talking. When the general came in with his excited sidekick, even his booming voice was no match for them. They had moved into a parallel universe. Duties, worries, Najma, and responsibilities had evaporated. Seven of the eleven had been touched directly by Najma's cruelty. Katarina and Sheilla indirectly. Maria and Barbara only from hearing stories about La serpiente, La diabla.

Jim felt a small twinge. What an opportunity Najma would have if she could know that this group was assembled here. How could she? An answer invaded his thoughts. The cartel had the means. Could Guillermo have assembled a new and better computer team, one that could penetrate all of BWC's firewalls? Was he determined enough to try again this soon? *It'll never end until they're terminated,* he thought.

'Whatcha thinking, eh?'

Jim didn't answer.

Brush knew Jim, through their long years, so well he hadn't needed to ask the question. 'Best choice is not to say her name out loud. That is, even if they would hear you. It's a nice group that's been assembled at the BWC.'

'Nice to see them interacting like this.'

'I'm a few days ahead of you recovering. You still having up and down days?'

'About it. Normal. Wasted today, better tomorrow. How are you on the home front?'

'I don't recognize my old self. It's hard to imagine liking someone this much. And knowing Glenda feels the same.'

Pedro ran over to them. Brush reached out and grabbed Pedro, holding him up in the air. 'You're getting hefty, big man.'

'I like it up in the air.'

'You're going to be a pilot,' said Will.

'I want to be a pilot. We flew all the way down to the airport and fueled the chopper. I helped land it.'

'He did a good job too. I can hardly hear myself think in here. Is it too cool for lunch outside?'

'Nope. That's a plan,' said Jim. 'Pedro, can you get my coat and bring it out?'

'Sure, Dad.'

They went out the double door and down the steps to the deck. More aspen leaves were turning gold, the wild rose leaves were a dusty mauve. The day was warm with the crisp feel of fall.

'Dad, look. Down by "Spooky Meadow." It's the bear with her twins.' The mama bear stood, resting her front paws on the small tree trunk. 'Oh. Oh. She's eating Mama's loganberries.'

'This is an amazing place,' said Vidya. 'I feel in tune with that bear. Soon she'll be in her cave for the winter and Misa and I will be in ours. Both safe and sound.'

'Notice that you didn't bring a laptop with you?' asked Jim.

'We said it would be an experiment not being connected for the weekend. I didn't realize how big of a toll it would take on me. It's like part of my life is missing.'

Colbert nodded at Brenda. She went around the corner and returned with two huge bowls of ice cream, each with sprinkles and chocolate, and topped with a candle. Six kids started to jump up and down. Ice cream was a rarity at Bright Light. It was frequently asked for and not provided.

Colbert started to sing happy birthday to Bambi and Matt. Najma couldn't believe what she was hearing. Everyone singing this silly song. One of the women looked at Najma. Najma smiled before joining in the singing. The woman continued to look at her. She didn't like what Najma's lifeless eyes told her.

'Blow it out,' said Colbert. 'It might melt.'

Brenda brought in a tray with several bowls of ice cream, followed by two more trays loaded. Matt was digging into his large bowl. Colbert slid a package down the table. Several others followed his example, sliding brightly wrapped packages toward Matt.

The benefit of an extended family meant lots of presents.

Colbert looked at Bambi.

'Please don't sing for me,' she said before she was drowned out with the song.

In the end, everyone pulled out a package and slide it toward her, including Matt. Bambi was his favorite, and he'd worked hard on making her a wood carving.

'Everyone ready for dinner?' asked Colbert.

'I don't want any,' said Gab. 'But I'll have some ice cream. I've forgotten how good it is.'

'Everyone suit yourselves. I know the ice cream was backwards and should have been after dinner, but,' … his voice was drowned out now just like Bambi's had been by shouts of 'not true.'

'It was the right way. Dessert first from now on,' said Gab.

'It's a new rule,' yelled Matt.

The days moved into fall. In mid-October snow sifted across Bright Light. It didn't stay long. The leaves turned a furious orange. The night temperature dropped in the thirties. Najma learned everything she needed to about the compound. Sex with Colbert was a duty that had little effect on her now. Sex with Brenda was a different story. The more orgasms she had, the more she wanted. Colbert heard rumors about Najma and Brenda. They could not keep their affections hidden. He shrugged, not minding his lover being involved with a woman.

He didn't know why it didn't bother him. If Najma had slept with a man, it would have driven him crazy. His thoughts eventually evolved to seeing the two women together and finally the two of them being with him.

He was aware of the old ramshackle cabin in the woods but had no idea that was where Brenda performed rituals, both for her beliefs and on Najma. Colbert followed them one night. He peered through one of the many knotholes in the cabin. His face flushed. His body didn't feel that it belonged to him any longer. He moved to the door and stepped inside. Brenda and Najma didn't stop. They looked at him and Brenda extended her hand. Jason Colbert couldn't resist.

Brenda knew it would only be a matter of time before Najma brought Colbert to their coven. It was inevitable. She doubted anyone would be able to resist the two witches.

Colbert was both embarrassed and at the same time unable to resist the ménage à trois.

Phil was Bright Light's resident techie. Najma wanted to acquire items that were not available to her. Phil told her about the *Secret Web* and she knew she had to know more. Phil said, 'It's was developed to keep censorship and government surveillance out of our hair.'

'I've never heard of it.'

'Most haven't, but it's been around for a long time. Our government basically started it thirty years ago. Lots of funny stories. Like the Stanford students engaging in selling marijuana to MIT students early on. You can get anything you want now from fake passports to bombs to any sort of drug. It's where we got our Semtex. I get my music free from it.'

'Will you show me? I am curious.'

Najma's life had taken several new turns. One box had closed, and another had opened. Sex at night. The dark web during the day.

CHAPTER 26

'We've had this conversation before,' said Sheilla. 'Here is the question again. How does someone disappear without leaving a trace?'

'It's not uncommon,' said Kramer. 'We usually trace missing persons through their friends or extended family. Najma has neither. No ties. She could be walking around Olympia or Seattle right now. The only thing we have is her appearance, her fingerprints, and her MO.'

'She has the cartel,' said Fred.

'The Siastra Cartel has never received so much attention. They're monitored up the gazoo by us, DEA, CIA, the Huachuca boys, comms, computer communication. You name it,' said Sheilla.

'We know where she isn't and who she is not contacting. The question remains the same: if she's not dead, and I don't think she is, where and how did she disappear? People rarely disappear when they die. Bodies are almost always found. I can't think of any that weren't,' said Fred.

'Well, lots of examples of that, too,' said Captain Kramer. 'Jimmy Hoffa. No trace of him.'

'Yeah, okay. But that's not my question. Let's put ourselves in her shoes. What would you do?' asked Fred.

'Getting away took luck,' said Katarina. 'Kramer said she could be in the big city. Possible, but not her style. No deaths with her MO that we know of. She's out of sight like she was in Tubutama. Sequestered somewhere. The question then becomes, what sort of place would serve that purpose?'

'We know where she started from,' said Sheilla. 'It doesn't matter if she is in Canada or the U.S.. Are there any cults or groups that restrict outside interference?'

'I have an idea,' said Fred. 'My uncle built a bomb shelter. My cousins think their dad is a nut case. They say he is being brainwashed by survivalists that he socials with.'

'We've considered that. There are those types all over the West. Mostly Idaho, Oregon, Utah. Misa, Vidya, and the Huachuca pups have looked and kept track of every place they can think of.'

'Sheilla, they've not found any evidence Najma is with them. It does not mean she isn't. These are closed, secretive groups. The FBI monitors them all the time. They know a little about their members but not a whole lot. They use the deep web to buy and sell.'

'Wait.' Sheilla picked up the phone. 'Misa, have you guys, or Jake, or Jason monitored the deep web?'

'Sure. It's part of our job description. If you're asking about whether we've tumbled into any psychos or not, the answer is yes. Hundreds. Maybe thousands. But not our evil lady. Unless that's not your question.'

'How come you never talk about it?' asked Sheilla.

'Probably because we haven't seen anything interesting. Like bioterrorists selling anthrax. The deep web has been around for a long time. It didn't become useful until this year with the release of Freenet.'

'Just an idea. I'm feeling a little ignorant. Let's set up a meeting. I think I need an education about it.'

'Stop in anytime. You're always welcome in our Cave.'

'Maybe tomorrow morning around ten.'

'See you then.'

'It's not a dead-end,' said Sheilla. 'Doesn't the FBI monitor these groups? They must have informers?'

'It's worth checking out. If they have undercover people among the survivalists, they are looking for something different than we are. They might know of something that will help us that was no interest to them,' said Kramer. 'Typical intelligence problem. One arm doesn't know what the other needs to know.'

'Okay.' Said Sheilla. 'We've touched on some new ideas. Kramer, pursue the FBI angle. Katarina, can you get profiles from both the FBI and CIA on these groups? Maybe some of them have connections with the cartels.'

'Sheilla, that's brilliant. That is a new idea,' said Katarina. 'It leaves me wondering how many ideas there are we haven't yet touched on.'

Jim had recovered. Nerve sensations were the only reminder. Not particularly painful, just a sign that a foreign substance had torn through his body. He hadn't learned a great deal about poetry. He'd finished the Hirsch book, but he hadn't fallen in love as the title suggested he might. He decided that he had other strong points. Let the poets and Neilly's Special Forces polyglot, JP, deal with language. *Language has never been my forte,* he rationalized.

Jim and Heather had grown closer. After he returned from school, Pedro would spend his time with Old Man Shuskin and Ben. Shuskin was old enough to be Pedro's grandfather. He became more to Pedro, a friend. Ben bridged the gap between the two. The two boys still practised what they had learned from the Special Forces: play fighting with each other daily. Nearly grown Ben's childish side diminished daily, He could still be a young boy, however, when the circumstances required.

Day to day, the ranch moved from September to November. The golden leaves had lost their grip on branches. Aged, dry, and brown, they littered the forest floor, insulation against the impending icy white.

Phil was proud of his protégée, and Colbert was delighted to have an aspiring computer expert. The special supplies that the compound needed were only available on the dark web. There was talk of a new protocol that would be completely secure from prying eyes.

Brenda put both hands on Najma's shoulders as she sat at the computer. 'What's so intriguing? You spend all your time looking at that screen.' She moved her hands down to Najma's breasts and rolled her nipples in her fingers.

Najma felt the electric sensation she had learned to need. 'I'm busy. Maybe this afternoon.'

'You promise?'

'Yes, I promise.'

'The sky is blue. And it's warm. An Indian summer, I guess. I'll fix us some lunch, and we can have a picnic. I know a small meadow a little way up the road.'

'Sure, okay,' said Najma, wanting Brenda to leave her.

Brenda sensed Najma's irritation. 'What's so bloody important?'

Najma sighed. 'It's an idea I have. A surprise. It's complicated.'

'You're sweet. I'll come by your cabin at noon.'

Najma shook her head as Brenda skipped out of the small computer room. *Simple-minded fool,* thought Najma. *She thinks the surprise is for her.* The computer was both boring and exciting. Boring because frequently she had to wait minutes to get a result. Exciting when she retrieved data she wanted. Phil tried to explain the ins and outs of the Internet. How the deep web worked. Najma wasn't interested. She cared about only one thing: acquiring information to carry out her plan.

As the BWC went about its normal business, the mystery of Najma's disappearance hung over some like an ominous cloud. Sheilla twirled in her chair. The computer group followed new ideas, all of which ended in exasperation. No hint of Najma was found. Could she be dead?

Martin Pearson continued to push the small group at the CIA to investigate. At first, his days started with hope and ended with vexation, until the frustration mellowed into the expected.

Heather stood at the kitchen counter listening to Jim's silence as he held the phone. She knew he was listening to the weather. *He's going to fly.* Jim took a deep breath and nodded his head. 'Heather, I have an idea. Do you have a minute?'

Shit. 'Sure, Jim.'

'I just checked in with NOAA. There's a unique weather pattern setting up.'

'So, you're going to fly to the BWC?' she said before clamping her teeth together.

Jim saw her tense stance and chuckled. 'Come here, sweetie.'

Heather went over reluctantly. He reached up and took her hand. 'The weather's going to be unseasonably warm. An Indian summer. There's always a chance of snow higher up, but I think we could get away with … '

Before he could finish, Heather burst into tears and wrapped her arms around him. "I was afraid you were going to fly away.'

'I didn't mean to scare you.' He stroked her long hair as she relaxed, looking into his eyes.

'You know I want to go. Pedro wants to go. I want to take Rosie. Where do you think would be good? Pasayten? Washington Pass, maybe?'

'You pick. I'll be happy wherever you choose.'

'Are you sure you're recovered enough?'

'I'm doing fine around here. So yes, I'm healed enough. It'll be fine.'

Heather thought about his past wounds, about the llamas, the mountains, the jarring road to the trailhead that led to Horseshoe Basin, the possibility of the weather changing in the mountains, and snow. She stared out the window toward Oval Peak, thinking about Oval Lakes. It would be their last hike of the season. *How healed up is he really,* she wondered.

'What about Hart's Pass and Windy Peak? We haven't been there for a long time and there probably won't be anyone else around.'

'I think I'm healed up enough to go there. That's an easy trail. Driving the road is the hard part.'

'I hear you, Jim. Six thousand feet trailhead, the scariest road I've ever been on. If snow came in before we got out, it would be a treacherous drive. I was thinking about the truck doing the climbing and not you. Where's a better place, do you think? What about Oval Lakes? Or … I got it, Easy Pass Trail?'

'It's a good choice. I like it,' said Jim. 'In fact, it's perfect.'

'It will be beautiful and maybe the larches will still be golden-yellow, and the peaks will have snow dusting them. Maybe even more important, it's not an easy hike, which will make you feel better. Ha-ha. Just kidding.'

'But it is a good one. Not too high. Trailhead is just off Highway 20. On the off chance it snows, we won't have much trouble even with the two-wheel drive Ford.'

'What if they close the highway? It's really late to still be open.'

Jim picked up his phone. A minute later he announced, 'It's open for the next two weeks unless there's a heavy snow.'

'We're good to go. No time to waste.' Heather turned her head, 'Lo, you want to go llama packing? It will be beautiful.'

'La idea es completamente loca. No good. You stay home. Muy peligroso!'

'We're going for sure. It will be special. You're part of the family. I want you to come. It's safe out there. No danger.'

Lola turned back and went into the kitchen. Spanish mutterings were all they could hear. Jim raised an eyebrow.

'Okay, Lo,' said Heather as she smiled at Jim. 'You stay and take care of Tom. Ben likes your food too.'

Silence from the kitchen. Heather continued to look at Jim for a few seconds before she leaned her forehead toward him. They touched, their eyes open while they slowly moved their heads back and forth.

A pan clanked; dishes rattled. The silence ended. 'Big eaters. You right. I can no go away. The old fool needs me. Boy still growing. I stay. I still be scared with you no here, señor.'

CHAPTER 27

D r. Milton stopped as she walked around the corner of the long lab bench. Standing over the bench fifteen feet from her, Nusmen stood motionless, hands on the counter, head bent slightly forward. His untamed hair didn't seem in as wild a tangle as it used to be. *I've gotten used to his eccentric appearance.*

I wonder what he is in so deep in thought about. His oversized Adam's apple moved up and down as he swallowed. Not wanting to disturb him and not wanting to stand spying on him, she decided to close the distance. He would hear her coming. She had a meeting later in the morning up top with a pharmaceutical representative and was sporting three-inch pumps for the occasion. She tapped her way toward Nusmen. Halfway there, she saw his head straighten up and his Adam's apple bob as he turned to her with glazed eyes and mouth slightly open.

As she neared, he still did not say anything or materially change his expression. Her blue eyes met his brown eyes.

Although he was three inches taller than she, her heels made her five-foot-nine height equal to his.

Nusmen opened his eyes wide. *He almost looks as though he's afraid,* she thought. She decided not to be the first to break the silence. In the few seconds they looked at each other, Barbara marveled at her evolution: Nusmen almost seemed normal to her. His comic book looks almost appeared ordinary. She was glad that the general had recognized his brilliance and had forced her to accept him in the lab, at first under house arrest and later as her equal. At least equal in title. No one disputed who the lab's director was. Just as no one disputed, any longer, Nusmen's zeal and second sight into all things microbial.

Others mixed work in the underground with lives in the sun. Nusmen lived only for his work. Fully committed day and night. There was no other love in his life.

'What are you thinking about, Nus?'

Just as Barbara had grown accustomed to Nusmen's looks, Nusmen had grown to accept and like Barbara. She was older by several years than he. Thin-boned. Hair tinged with gray at the temples. He had acquaintances in the lab, some at least who tolerated him. Barbara and he were becoming friends.

Nusmen sighed, lowering his eyes, and said, 'Same problem. VRSA. I can't solve it. Several times, I thought I had. And poof. Nothing. And I still feel bad.'

'If there is anything in this world that I believe, it is that you will find a way. There is something in the *Staph's* genetic code. With the upgraded equipment we keep receiving, it's only a matter of time before you solve it.'

'But the people I hurt,' he said, looking back into her eyes.

He wants forgiveness, she thought. 'Under all the delightful chaos you bring to the lab, there's empathy in that brain of yours. When you first got here, I wouldn't have believed it.'

'Am I that bad?'

Barbara laughed and wanted to answer yes. But it was not what he needed. 'You've never been bad. Just a wild crazy guy like the comedian that wears an arrow on his head.'

'You mean Steve Martin?'

'Yep. That's him. Look, Nus. I know you won't believe me, but we all do things we wish we could undo.'

'You never have. You're ah—you're ah, perfect.'

'Hah. If you only knew. When I was a kid, I used to do things like put Tabasco sauce on my father's hamburger.'

'So?'

'He couldn't stand spicy things. I mean, I put a half bottle in a hamburger once. I think it just about killed him.'

'I did kill people. Even little kids.'

'Your antibiotic-resistant *Staphylococcus* aureus did. Think about it like this. Do you think Henry Ford is responsible for all the people killed by cars?'

'That's illogical.'

'I'm making a point. What about the Manhattan Project?'

'Yeah, maybe.'

'When I was doing my Ph.D., I had a history class in twentieth-century doctors. They didn't know what bacteria or viruses were. But several solved problems, not with understanding the cause but with seeing the result.'

'I don't understand, Barb.'

'One guy didn't know that microbes existed. But when

he had doctors with their hands in lye, the death rate went down in the hospital. Here's one I remember by name. Dr. Coley. Same first name as you: William. He had a cancer patient that got strep throat and recovered. He decided to start injecting cancer patients with bacteria. It stimulated their immune systems. He could be considered the father of immunology. In the process, he killed several people.'

A tear trickled down Nusmen's cheek. Barbara said, 'You'll find a cure for the VRSA and it will save a lot of people.' Barbara gave Nusmen a hug and said, 'Come on. We've got lives to save.'

'I wish I were a falcon. Wouldn't it be wonderful to glide down the canyon? I feel like I'm flying, Jim. I'm so happy. I'm going to start packing right now. Pedro is down with the llamas. He's excited too. We'll start loading the truck.'

'I've got a few things to do. After, I'll come down and help.'

'You stay here. Take it easy. I want you raring to go first thing in the morning. It will be a big day getting the llamas loaded and to the trailhead. Don't look at me like that. I mean it. We don't need that much. I'm thinking five llamas and that is overdoing it for the three of us. You think?'

'Four is probably enough and, in case the weather changes, we can be faster packing up.'

'All righty. Shasta, Coco, Pipey, and who else? How about Cinnabar?'

'I like Cinnabar. This might be Coco's last trip. His pasterns are getting worse.'

'I know. I wish things could stay the same. You here.

Coco Motion as he used to be. Give me a hug before I fly off to the big barn.'

~

Najma closed the door to the computer room. She sat down at the desk, sent the message "Here," and waited for Hari to answer. He had demanded, and Najma, alias Mary Fairy to Hari, had agreed, to five email exchanges. In them, she would describe her body to him, touch herself, and narrate in detail what she was doing. After each session, Hari would send more information about how to wire an explosive vest. Najma had also agreed to meet Hari at some future time. He would travel from his home in Venice Beach, California. But Najma knew he was all talk and would never come to meet her. She wished he would. She would like to kill the peckerhead, an expression Phil used often. Hari had what she wanted and needed but he made her go to all this time-wasting effort to get it.

She typed into her computer that she was rolling her left nipple between her index finger and thumb. 'I'm slow typing,' she wrote. 'It feels so good. I'm going to stop typing. It feels wonderful,' she rolled her eyes and sat back in the chair, hands behind her head. *What an idiot*, she thought. After a few minutes, she typed, 'Tell me what you are doing. It will turn me on.' For some strange reason, she wanted to type "on turn." *I like doing things different than they are supposed to be.*

'I'm jerking off,' he said.

'Me too, now. Oh. Oh,' she typed, as she took a sip of cold coffee. 'Heh, Mister Venice Beach. Where's my first installment? I could do this again right now if you want?'

No answer. 'You there?'

'I need a minute. I made a mess.'

Najma rolled her eyes again. *What a fool.* She turned her thoughts to the colonel. What she would do to him? *Hold him at knifepoint and kill him. No! First, I want his seed to grow in me. I want a son.*

'You need these things first.' A list of several items followed, including wire, tools, tape. Nothing that Najma couldn't find in the compound. Then he added, 'You need something to put the explosive in. A down vest would work. A butt bag would be okay. Mary, be here tomorrow at 3:00 p.m.'

Phil opened the door. 'What's the big secret with the door closed?'

'Mind your own business, dick head. I'd say head dick, but I'm tired of you always correcting me.'

'It's beautiful out. There's nothing anywhere on earth like this. Clear sky. Clean, fresh air. The llamas are so happy to go that they're lying down in back, chewing their cud.'

Pedro was holding on to the steering wheel with Jim. 'If I can fly a helicopter, I can drive too, yes?'

'I'll teach you when we're back at the ranch,' said Heather. 'You have to promise me something first. Lots of young men drive tractors and work with farm equipment. There are also lots of missing fingers, arms, and legs. You have to promise to be really, really careful.'

'I promise.'

'I don't want to lose you, and you can't fly helicopters missing your phalanges.'

'What does that mean?'

'Your toes and fingers,' answered Heather.

Jim pulled onto a side road that led to a parking area. Heather got out and directed Jim to the loading ramp. The llamas jumped up off the floor. Pedro ran onto the loading ramp and started to untie some of Heather's knots. He hadn't made much progress when Jim and Heather joined him.

'Let's put the saddles on in the truck then tie them outside.'

'I'll climb over and get started untying the storage rack,' said Jim.

'I know you think I tie way too many knots.'

'Better safe than sorry,' said Jim. He did think she tied three or four times as many knots as were needed. Untying them made extra work. A minor price to pay and she was right in her thinking, anyway. Not securing the back gate and the equipment could cause a lot of damage to the animals. Jim remembered the one time that Darby had kicked open the rear door to the van and jumped out the back before Jim could stop. Rocky also jumped out before Jim could run around and close the door. The only thing that kept Bobby Sox and Tulip in the van was that they'd slid forward when Jim hit the brakes. Jim smiled as he remembered the sweltering temperatures at UC Davis' campus and the two llamas running off down a four-lane highway. He had cornered them after several hours. It had been his first introduction to llamas after having just purchased the four from an Arabian horse farm. The incident happened nearly twenty years ago. Only the first of hundreds of adventures with the ranch animals.

Would he have been content to stay on the ranch? He

didn't have to dig very deep to conclude that he wouldn't have been. The ranch could never replace the job and his adventures with Brush and the general. *I'm content with my life. Will Heather ever be?* he questioned.

It didn't take them long to get loaded. Pedro had learned how to saddle Pipestone. As always, Pipey would carry the two blue plastic coolers containing the food they wanted to keep cold. When they hiked back, he would carry the trash that could not be burned or buried. With only the three of them, it was light duty.

Pedro cinched up the belly strap and carefully lifted Pipestone's tail to hook the butt strap as Heather had taught him.

'You take that side of the cooler and we'll both lift it in place.'

'Okay, Mama.'

Heather checked to see how tight the strap was as she moved to the other side. She didn't want Pedro to see her checking on his work. 'Nice job, Pedro. You're getting to be an expert at so many things.'

Pedro jumped in the air, threw his arms up, and raced over to his dad. 'Let me help.'

'Nothing left to do. Who do you want to lead?'

'I want Meteor.'

'That means you will be leading with your mother.'

'I know.'

Jim looked at Pedro. 'You're getting pretty wise.'

Pedro giggled again as Heather walked over holding Meteor's lead.

'I'm up front with you.'

'Good choice.'

'Dust-free and better view, being in the lead,' said Pedro.

Jim tied Coco Motion's lead to Meteor's saddle and tied Shasta at the end, behind Coco. He would lead Pipestone since Shasta would spit at any llama tied behind him. Jim wondered about the thoughts going on inside the llamas' heads. If tied to Shasta, Pipestone would close the gap and bump into Shasta, egging him on. Shasta would spit vigorously, but he couldn't turn his head back to aim at Pipey while constrained by his lead.

Pipestone seemed to delight in teasing Shasta. Jim often considered the limits of human intelligence, supposedly at the top of the pecking order among animals and yet we struggle to communicate with dolphins, whales, and other primates. Some progress, while limited, had been achieved by Lilly's early work with dolphins. And others successfully taught chimpanzees sign language. *But here I am, having only the weakest of intuitions about what is going on in Pipey's mind.*

'We're off to see the wizard,' said Heather. As she and Pedro headed up the trail, Jim could hear her animated explanation to Pedro about the "Wonderful Wizard of Oz." Jim settled well back from Shasta, who kept tugging and pulling, turning around to warn Jim he better not get too close. Jim thought, *how can I ever understand what is going on in Pipestone's mind while I am still struggling with the full machinations of Heather's.*

~

Najma had made many trips to the bunkers. No one paid attention to her anymore. She was careful not to disturb anything. She lifted several of the weapons, feeling their individual heft. She suspected that, at first, Gab and perhaps Phil had spied on her and checked the supplies after her visits. Soon, she would need to remove the Semtex and detonators for the vest.

The trail led through the forest for several miles. By mid-afternoon, they arrived at the edge of the small lake and started to set up camp. With the sun streaking through the trees, the late fall day felt almost balmy. When the sun set, the temperature would drop to below freezing, with the forecasted clear skies, perhaps way below freezing. They all had brought heavy down coats. As much as Jim preferred not to have a fire, he knew Pedro would like it and it would provide warmth and cheer while they ate and talked. It was good to have just the three of them.

The ever-vigilant Jim knew that, at any moment, serenity could erupt into chaos. He had not mentioned to Heather his concerns about Najma. He didn't expect the woman to attack out here. That is, if she was healed or alive. He still could not rule it out. He carried his small, .25 caliber pistol on his ankle and, in his butt bag, a smaller thirty-two. The latter was not his first choice. His Beretta, however, was too large for the small waist pack. *She's alive,* he thought as he looked into the shadows. *She'll come for me, but it won't be here. It will be when I least expect it.*

CHAPTER 28

Najma was one step away from having what she needed to make the bomb vest. One more silly session with Hari. She would receive the last of the instructions tomorrow. As stupid as she thought the man was, his instructions were clear and precise. Najma was gaining confidence in her plan. She wanted to begin her trip before the heavy snows of winter covered the roads. First, she must make the vest and then convince Colbert she had to leave. Would he trust her? Would he allow it? She needed a backup plan in case he didn't.

The morning sun streaked through the window. Najma and Colbert acted like a couple, living together in his room in the main house. The other preppers grudgingly accepted their romance, while Brenda thoroughly reveled in it, and in her new coven. Having the leader of the compound involved in her ceremonies and in a threesome, insulated the two women from excessive criticism. Her next move was to enlist additional participants, and then, perhaps, to use Najma's old cabin as the coven's home. The cabin was perfectly situated. Separate from the main house and yet not so far away as her hut.

Najma paced, waiting for the appointed time with Hari. She was getting anxious to see the eyes of her nemesis. To embrace him. To observe his pain.

She had a routine now with Hari. She encouraged him to get excited as fast as possible. She told him how much she looked forward to feeling him inside her. Najma imagined meeting him in the future. She had convinced him that one of her fantasies was to tie him up and do to him things he had never imagined. Hari's idea of unimaginable things and Najma's were quite different. Every time they had talked, she envisioned squeezing Hari's testicles over and over until permanently relieving him of his agony.

The computer exchange ended. Hari fulfilled his promise and was confident that Najma would be in his future. The thought would keep him happy for many lonely nights.

Najma had found a plastic beer cooler large enough to hold her bomb-making supplies. She hid it in the woods several hundred meters behind the house. The last instructions included the final connections. She found a torn and discarded child's vest in the trash. She pulled out fluffy handfuls of the down stuffing. Except for the detonator and plastic explosive, she had everything she needed.

I'll leave it here until I return with my son, she thought. *I can't afford to have anyone see that it's missing until the colonel has entered my web.* Najma moved off into the woods, heading this way and that, and positioning herself to spot anyone pursuing her. After an hour, confident she was by herself, she pulled the last of the instructions from her pocket and removed the forest litter from the top of the red cooler. She attached the wires as instructed, leaving only those that would attach to batteries and allowing the detonator to dangle loose. She returned to the compound using the same cautious zigzagging and watching that she had used to go to the hidden cooler.

Daylight ended before dinner. Colbert was not going to join them until later. It was early evening when Brenda and Najma entered the hut. Brenda turned her head toward Najma and said, 'You're going to come back, aren't you?' Najma nodded, but didn't say anything.

'I love you, you know. I've always looked for and never found what we have. What I feel for you.'

Najma liked the physical feeling she got from Brenda. She felt nothing else. She didn't even know or care about the love Brenda professed. The indifference only made Brenda care more. Najma had become more important to Brenda than the coven and her other sexual relations. As for Colbert, he hadn't begun to understand his feelings. He was entranced by the evenings spent with Najma and Brenda. Although he wanted to, he couldn't pull away. The forbidden sex they experienced became an addiction from which he couldn't break free.

Najma had easily persuaded Colbert to let her take a vehicle for personal business. She didn't care which vehicle as long as it was reliable. Najma had deflected when he asked her why she needed to go and where. When he persisted, she had raised the temperature of her response, daring him to press her further. He backed down and let her have her way. He assumed she was moving her possessions to Bright Light. That she would remain at the compound excited him but also gave him cause for concern. He knew he couldn't break his addiction with her here. He had always been in control. He thought of the many in the army who had been addicted to drugs. He'd never understood why a man could let a substance control his future. For the first time, Jason Colbert sympathized with an addict's powerlessness to break free.

The massive effort to capture Najma declined. From intense manpower, it had dwindled to wanted photos on walls and bits of information in computers. CIA and the BWC both maintained their dedicated groups. BWC's Najma dedicated staff was reduced to Cynthia. Each day, Fred spent a few minutes with her, checking on the systems he, Misa, and Vidya had installed. They'd put in a program that would automatically search the news wires, police reports, and any mention of Najma's known contacts. Misa frequently made small improvements to the search protocol code. Sheilla called Fred daily to be sure the search stayed active. Everyone except Katarina started to wonder if Najma might be dead. As the days passed, even Sheilla's resolve lessened.

Despite General Crystal's leadership, apathy at the CIA permeated the remaining specialists whose fruitless efforts resulted in deep discouragement.

The FBI's position switched to "probable" deceased. They distributed posters. Najma became a picture on post office walls.

At the BWC, working with pathogens once again became paramount. Fortunately, with the colonel and Major McGuire recovering, there had been no demand for their special brand of field operations. Microbes continued their natural mutations. Viruses jumped from one species to another before reaching an existential dead end. Circumventing the hypothetical creations of terrorist labs once again became the Biological Warfare Lab's primary role.

A nefarious plot to spread Creutzfeldt-Jacob disease came to the lab's attention and, consequently, Nusmen became obsessed with prions. He set aside his other projects and dived full-time into understanding the pathogenic protein. The general, Barbara, and Jim encouraged his single-mindedness.

Through conversations with Barbara and Sheilla, Jim had become involved anew with the lab's day-to-day activities. After the daily adverse reports about Najma had been transmitted, discussion turned to the only terrorist news that had recently come to their attention: the prion responsible for mad cow disease in humans: CJD.

The lack of a cure for the disease as well as years between infection and symptoms made the prion a unique entity for terrorists with a long-term horizon. It had been several years since bovine spongiform encephalopathy or BSE had made the news in Britain in the late '80s. For a while, prions had remained under the radar.

A blue light flashed through the door window in one of the level three work areas. Barbara pressed the intercom. She couldn't enter when the red light showed, freezing the entry keypad's function. The flashing light stopped. Nusmen raised the face shield that had partially obscured the mass of uncombed hair protruding below his headband. His eyes looked glazed. His mind was elsewhere.

Dr. Milton's voice penetrated his thoughts. 'What's with the UV light?'

A blank look preceded Nusmen's, 'Huh?'

'What are you working on? Can you open the door?' asked Barbara.

'Ah. Yeah. I'm finished,' he said before turning his eyes back to the UV light apparatus.

'Anytime will do, Nusmen. You're interesting to look at through this window, but I would rather talk face to face.'

'Ah, sorry.'

Nusmen moved toward the small window and Barbara heard a click. As she walked in, Nusmen removed his shield and set it on the counter. 'I can't find a way to kill it.'

'I presume you mean the prion?'

'Of course. That's what I'm working on.'

'I've been studying up on it. It's a strange thing. No cure, long latency period, hard to kill and, unlike anything we know, no DNA,' said Barbara.

'I never thought much about that before,' said Nusmen. 'It makes me wonder about life. A prion's kinda zombie-like in the way it makes other proteins bend to its image.'

'What kind of defense can we ever have against it? It's scary,' added Barbara.

Nusmen looked back at the UV light container with prion protein inside. 'I don't even have any ideas. Just a regular protein string of amino acids turned into a nightmare. There's a million, a bazillion ways for proteins to fold, and this is just one of them. What if there are billions of preeeeeeons that could form?' He puckered his lips, stretching out the name to emphasize their vast numbers.

'What's your plan?'

'Don't know. Maybe if it can bend other proteins to be like it, I guess, to find out how to change the shape back into something that doesn't affect brains. The whole thing is weird.'

A blanket of cold air settled into the llama camp. Molecules of sun-warmed air jittered their way toward the speckled night's sky. Pedro's teeth started to chatter. He sat as close to the fire as he could. Dressed in a heavy down coat with sweaters and a vest underneath, he looked like a puffball.

'It's getting pretty chilly,' said Jim.

'Amazing how cold it can get when we are just sitting. I think it's sleeping bag time for you, my child.'

'For all of us. I'll check the llamas' stakeouts,' said Jim.

'I'll get Pedro tucked in and the kitchen ready for the night.'

Jim moved two of the llamas closer to their tent. He shortened the lines from their halters to the metal screw-in stakes. He left Pipestone tied to a stake. Jim was afraid Pipey would try to roll in the dying embers and catch his wool on fire.

There was a light breeze moving the nylon tarp above their four-man backpacking tent. Heather spread a tarp over the kitchen and weighted the edges down with stones and wood. There would not be much wind in their forest camp, no matter how the weather changed. A heavy dew would condense by morning. Blue skies were in the forecast for the next several days. *This is my heaven, out here with Jim and Pedro.*

Colbert looked at Najma. For a few seconds, he struggled with whether he should let her take his pride and joy: the blue Bronco. It pleased him to think about. Neither dark or light blue. A vivid cobalt blue. While he had a strong attachment to his backhoe, it paled in comparison to the passion he felt for his blue metal box. He had purchased it as a teenager. Kept it stored and cared for throughout his army time.

In recent years, he'd driven it little. Just looking at it gave him joy. Knowing it was close at hand in the Quonset hut relaxed him. Loaning it to Najma would be perhaps the most altruistic step he had ever taken in his life. As much as anything, he sought to prove to himself that he loved her and could place his unblemished inanimate object on the altar of that love. Deep down, though, he knew he didn't believe in what he was doing. Neither did he believe in his affair with Brenda and Najma. In both instances, he was acting against his better instincts.

He took a deep breath and set the keys to the Bronco on the table. 'I thought you needed the truck and trailer?'

'I do. I have some things to load in them. While they're parked, I want something to drive.'

'You can unhitch the trailer and drive the truck. It's easy. I'll show you how. Or I could come with you?'

Najma didn't like the way the conversation was heading. She had at first thought that asking for the truck and trailer would back up her excuse of moving her belongings to Bright Light. She didn't really need the trailer, and the Blue Bronco would be a lot easier to drive. But she couldn't pull the trailer with the Bronco. 'The Bronco will fit in the trailer, won't it?'

'Yeah. But I don't understand.'

'You can't come with me,' she said. 'What if I take the Bronco in the trailer? I have my reasons. You trust me, don't you?'

Colbert didn't trust her at all. Nevertheless, he knew he had to say yes. And maybe having the Bronco in the trailer would be safer.

The whole argument became moot as Phil poked his head around the corner. 'I wasn't eavesdropping, but I heard you mention the trailer as I walked up. I just received a message that our supplies are arriving in two weeks. We'll need the trailer.'

Najma didn't need to leave at any special time, but she didn't want to wait till the roads became clogged with snow. 'I could go now and be back before you need it.'

'Too risky. We know about when to expect the flight. It could be a week on either side. We have to park the truck and trailer at the airport so they're there when the shipment arrives. I get notified when they're loaded. Then we pick it up.'

Najma became curious. Not usual for her. 'What are you receiving?'

Phil looked at Jason, who gave a slight sideways nod. 'Some military supplies,' he said, not knowing what else he could say.

Colbert didn't want to tell her he was doing one last deal with her old boss: Guillermo.

'Can you make do with the Bronco?' asked Colbert.

Phil turned wide-eyed and then decided it was time to make his exit.

Najma's idea of using the blue Bronco as bait and then hiding it in the trailer before returning it to Bright Light, vanished in a flash. *What do I care if he gets his hunk of metal back, anyway? My plan is the same. Now I'll just dump his blue piece of junk car and get another.*

'I guess it will have to do. I promise to take good care of

it,' she said. 'I know how much it means to you,' added Najma sweetly. She was getting used to saying what Colbert wanted and needed to hear. She even started to enjoy the way she could manipulate him.

Colbert refrained from adding, *I hope so.* His self-deception left him with a knot in the pit of his stomach, wondering if he would ever see either one of them again.

However, a tiny sense of calm crept in as he thought of her absence. The separation would provide a forced halt of their nightly threesome. He knew he didn't have the resolve to stop it himself. Maybe the break and the sacrifice of the Bronco would allow him to regain what he had lost of himself. Then Najma said, 'I'll miss you, sweetie, but Brenda will be here for you.'

His mind ground to a halt. It hadn't occurred to him that he could be with only Brenda. *Is that what I want? What I need?* he wondered. Brenda's addiction was as strong as his own, and he had sometimes wondered which of the two women he would rather be with. Brenda seemed only to care about the physical aspects of their relationship, but maybe there was more. Deep down, Jason knew that she was real while Najma only pretended authenticity. He wouldn't admit to himself that he knew who she was: a killer, a warrior. *We have that in common,* he thought. He understood that part of her. She left him guessing. She intrigued him. She was a riddle. It left him confused. Perhaps being with Brenda would be simpler, more relaxing.

Then he laughed at the absurdity. *Brenda! Relaxing?* Ha, he thought. *She was a physical beast.* She left no doubt about what she wanted. Her single-minded pursuit of orgasms was easy to understand. There was no mystery to Brenda.

Maybe that was all he needed. Maybe he didn't need love. Maybe desire was enough.

Suddenly clarity penetrated his thoughts. He wanted Najma to leave. He was starting to wonder who he was. Who he had become. He had been refusing to allow the truth to surface. Maybe sacrificing the Blue Bronco was a fair exchange. Then he frowned.

'I'm hot,' said Pedro, pulling back the top of the down sleeping bag.

'I think it is warmer,' said Heather. 'Hard to figure with the clear skies how it could be.' She looked at Jim. 'You think?'

Jim unzipped the side panel and they all peered at the pure white landscape. The tall trees disappeared into the murmuration of snowflakes swirling and twirling before settling silently to the forest floor.

'Wow,' shouted Pedro.

'You think we should get out of here?' suggested Heather, knowing it was not the right thing to do.

'Weather called for a high-pressure system. This is probably a fluke low that dipped in from the north. We should just stay as we are.' He craned his head out and counted four white lumps in the meadow. 'Llamas are fine. Let's just lie here and enjoy it for a while. What do you think, Rosie?' With Jim, Heather, Rosie, and Pedro inside the four-man tent, they didn't have much room left for personal gear. Rosie's huge head lifted toward Jim. He could see what she intended. He turned his head to the side. Her big tongue, as rough as his morning stubble, pulled across his cheek. Jim scratched her ears. 'You need to go out, girl?' Rosie laid her head down on top of Jim's chest. 'Guess you want to stay in out of the snow.'

'If it doesn't stop, I'll bring the pack with the food and a stove over here where we have some shelter. The kitchen will be impossible. I never expected this,' said Heather.

Jim wasn't worried. However, the snowstorm was unexpected and snows this late in the season had a habit of only getting worse as the days crept toward the harsh cold mountain winter. 'If it keeps up after breakfast, Pedro and I can string the tarp over the kitchen. It'll be more or less snow-free under the llama packs.'

'Can we build a snowman?' asked Pedro.

'Sure we can,' said Heather.

'Now, please?'

Heather looked at Jim and smiled, thinking about what else they might be doing if Pedro was not here. *Pleasurable sacrifices.* The thought made her laugh.

'What's so funny?' asked Jim, smiling.

'I'll tell you later,' she said, raising her eyebrows.

Jim turned and kissed her. 'You help Pedro build a snowman and I'll see if I can get a tarp strung. Then we can decide where to eat breakfast.'

'The tarp should work over the kitchen. There were plenty of trees and branches to tie it off,' said Heather.

Pedro was out of his bag and climbing over Jim and Rosie to get outside. Rosie reluctantly stood. None of them had removed their clothes, or heavy coats, hats, or gloves before getting into their sleeping bags. Heather squirmed out of hers, climbed over Jim, straddled him, and gave him a beaming smile and a kiss. Pedro was already lacing his boots in the small snow-free place next to the tent that had been protected by the tarp.

'Come on, Mama,' shouted Pedro as he jumped around in the snow, batting at the large snowflakes.

Thirty minutes later, Jim watched from under the newly strung tarp as Pedro poked a hole in the snowman's head for a mouth. Jim had found a small pinecone and carved a hole. He pushed a stick into it, making a rudimentary pipe and tossed it by the snowman. Heather dug it out of the snow and pushed the stick into the snowman's mouth. 'Whatcha think?'

'I think he's beautiful,' said Pedro.

'What about you, Rosie?'

Rosie stood with her coarse tan coat turning white. Her head was only slightly beneath Pedro's. She shook the snow off. Her eyes vibrant gold in the white.

Pedro put his arm over her shoulder. 'She thinks so too.'

'Handsome he is,' said Heather as she looked around at the snow-covered forest. 'Our snowman is. Everything is beautiful.'

Heather lay down in the snow, moving her arms and legs back and forth. 'Come on, son. My angel needs a companion.'

Jim rummaged through a pannier to retrieve green Lexan plates and cups.

'Let's get some resin from that old pine tree,' said Heather.

She grabbed Pedro's hand and walked to a gnarly old pine. 'You have your knife?'

'Yes,' he said with pride.

'Be careful. It's hard and a little brittle but see if you can pry some off the tree like this.' Heather cut underneath a piece of the translucent yellow resin and plucked it off.

'It's the same color as Rosie's eyes.'

'That's what made me think of it.'

'What's it for, Mama?'

'It's a trick for starting fires when it's wet out. There'll be enough dry twigs on the lower pine branches. We put some wood under the tarp last night, but this will make the fire really easy to start.'

The two angels were still visible but quickly filling in with snow as they walked back to the kitchen carrying their golden treasure.

Jim packed their lightweight titanium pan with melting snow and placed it on the two-burner propane cook stove. Next to it, their coffee pot spouted a fine trail of vapor as it began to bubble.

'It's beautiful, isn't it,' said Heather. 'Pure and soft. All the ways the world isn't.'

'What do you mean, Mama?'

'Let's scoop the snow off the top of where we had a fire last night. It could still be hot underneath. Then we can build a tepee with sticks over our pine resin.'

'Why isn't the world beautiful?'

'It is beautiful. What I mean is that, in our minds, the sins of the world disappear and are cleansed under all this white. At least, for us here. Not everywhere.'

Pedro's eyebrows pinched down over his eyes.

'Hmm,' said Heather. 'Not making much sense, am I?'

Pedro continued to look into her eyes. 'The snow is clean,' he said. 'Not everything in the world is?'

'You're very perceptive. I'm very happy that you are my boy.'

Najma and Jason drove up the two-track road past the Quonset hut, across a meadow, and toward hills visible a mile past the meadow.

'It's an automatic,' said Colbert, putting it in park. 'The oil's fresh, so it shouldn't give you any trouble.' He took a tissue out of his pocket and wiped a small amount of dust off the chrome casing around the odometer.

Najma rolled her eyes. *An automatic.*

'It's very nice,' said Najma. 'I'll take good care of it.'

'There aren't many of them still around. Rare to see one nowadays.'

Colbert's blue Bronco would be easy to spot. In fact, it would be downright conspicuous. Perfect! A conspicuous ride would fit her plan. Another piece of the puzzle solved.

CHAPTER 29

The crystalline flakes continued to settle and swirl through the trees making their world an opaque blanket of white. The early morning gray lightened to day. The shroud thinned, turning opalescent. The flakes grew larger as if to make up for the increasing distance between them. The lacy shapes high above changed to wispy vapor as if a magic wand had been waved. The sky turned blue first in the west, the veil above wafted east, and the morning sun streamed through the trees.

All three sat mesmerized by the stillness, squinting at bright strips of sunlight through the tall trees, each with their own thoughts. Rosie lay on her side with her head on Pedro's legs. He rubbed her ears, his hand moving slowly in tune with the changing scene and his body far away from the cactus and bitterbrush of his Mexican home. In his mind, he saw his parents and his old yellow dog, Rojizo. A tear trailed cool down his cheek as he looked into Rosie's amber eyes.

Heather felt cleansed by the purity of the snow and the

sheer beauty of the towering trees. Green needles first against a gray-white sky, then blue. Scaly brown bark rooted in over two feet of snow.

Jim sensed Heather's contentment. She was whole and alive in the mountains. Their isolation and the snow made them safe. He wished he could keep her in this moment forever.

'I hear you are leaving,' said Bambi.

'In a few weeks,' answered Najma, wondering why the curly-haired Bambi had decided to break her silence.

'Oh,' was all she could say, disappointed. Bambi clearly wanted to make small talk with Najma, but Najma had nothing to say. Just as she had changed Colbert's innate temperament, Najma had changed that of Bright Light itself. While Bambi and Jason had been nothing more than comfortable friends, they might have been a couple. That is until the arrival of Miss Hussein. Their able leader became diminished rather than strengthened by Najma. Everyone knew about the threesome. The previously ever-present Colbert had become detached from the extended family of the compound.

Bambi turned wordlessly and left. Najma watched her delicate walk. The light swishing movement made her appear to have no muscle strength. *She's wearing moccasins,* Najma sneered at the woman's weakness.

Najma waited until Bambi was gone. It was time. It was a custom at Bright Light for the group to eat together. Najma rarely joined in. While they were busy she planned to go to the bunker and procure ammunition. She needed nine-millimeter bullets for her Glock and 380 for her PPK. She hoped to find some .22-caliber short for the silent, plastic-encased rifle and for her pistol. When she first stumbled up Bright Light's road, she had kept the .22 in her coat pocket along with her double-sided knife. The other guns she had left in a plastic bag hidden several yards off the road. She had secreted the bag under a large deadfall and covered it with leaf litter. She had been barely conscious at the time and hoped no water had been able to get into the bag. Fortunately, she had a clear memory of the large leaning birch tree alongside the road. She felt certain she would be able to recover her weapons. She needed ammunition and hoped that Phil and Gab would not miss what she'd removed.

She had spent hours each day searching in vain on the compound's computer for news of the colonel. There was nothing. No mention of the Biological Warfare Center, the general, or the major. The only thing she had found was a short article about Heather in the local Twisp paper. The Methow Valley Times had written a story about the mystery man of the mountains getting new teeth and a home at Wolf Canyon Ranch.

If I leave between Christmas and New Year's, they will all be at home. Not a good idea, she thought. *The colonel will expect me when others won't.* She wondered what sort of security there would be at the ranch. Could she safely spy from the same ridge she had before? *No,* she concluded. The plan had to be different. Not having any information bothered her. She was adaptable but walking in blind against the colonel would be foolhardy. *I'll continue searching the news for information, get my supplies, and make a decision before*

Christmas. There was nothing more to do. It was time to go to the bunker.

Sheilla, Katarina, and the full computer staff, including Misa and Vidya, sat in the conference room. Brush and Glenda were asked to join the BWC group. On their new LCD screens, members of the CIA's search team appeared in one square, the FBI in another, minus Shultz who, not by his own choice, had taken early retirement. There was a small NSA team in the third square.

Sheilla was delighted to see Martin. The meeting was intended to find whether the multi-agency group could arrive at a way forward in their search for Najma. Despite the FBI's conclusion that she was probably dead, the CIA and the BWC both still thought she was in hiding. Much of their opinion was due to Katarina, who staunchly maintained she was close by and underground. Her theory made sense in that they all agreed that the further Najma traveled, the more likely they would find a trace of her.

Jim and Katarina had discussed possible scenarios. 'She'll appear when we least expect it. How long before we become complacent?' Katarina had asked.

She remembered Jim's answer, 'Could be anytime.'

A voice interrupted her musings. 'Assuming you are correct,' said Martin, 'what is your prediction of when she will strike?'

Katarina thought back to the answer she had given the colonel. 'A year or more might be a good guess. However, I don't think she has that sort of patience.'

'So, we have failed to find her, and I'm not suggesting

we stop searching, but the chances of success have narrowed,' said Sheilla. 'We know who she will come after. We need to start focusing on how to protect Colonel Johnson.'

'I agree,' said Katarina, 'with one exception: she'll want to punish the colonel. That means she will just as likely come after his family and friends.'

'Colonel Johnson will be able to protect them,' suggested Vidya. 'He was very capable in Mexico when he rescued us.'

'Not likely,' said Brush. 'The hunter has too big of an advantage. Thousands of ways to attack. No one can watch their back all the time. Add others into the mix, and it's impossible.'

'The only way is to get them on base here,' said Glenda. 'Jim wouldn't do it for himself, but he will for Heather and Pedro. He knows the odds. I think the bigger problem would be Heather.'

'If anyone can convince him, it will be you, Brush,' said Katarina. 'But I agree. Heather is the one that needs convincing. Glenda?'

'I think you're right,' said Glenda. 'I also think that you should join us, Katarina. With you, we'll have a sounder psych approach.'

'Shall we break up the meeting?' interjected Martin. 'The FBI doesn't need to stay on this call. I'm going to let my people get back to work too, but I'll stay with you while you work on a plan.'

Martin did want to be involved, but his main interest had changed: he couldn't take his eyes off Sheilla.

'Thank you, everyone,' said Sheilla. 'I'm always available if any of you find even a scant hint of Najma.'

'Best plan would be not for us to go over to the ranch, but rather to get Heather here,' said Katarina. 'Prove to her that this would be a comfortable place. Get her involved in a project. Even more important: we've had a lull, but things could change, and the colonel could get called out. Surely we can convince Heather that the safety of her child warrants staying on the base?'

'You just had the right idea,' said Glenda. 'I know her well enough that a project that will interest her is the way to approach this.'

'Jim will go along,' said Brush. 'He knows the odds. Heather, though, has a mind of her own.'

Warm temperatures started to melt the sun-exposed snow. Heavy blobs fell from the trees. Branches covered with slices of angel food cake started to drip. Patches of snow disappeared in the open where grass and rocks transferred their warmth to the surrounding snow. The snow-free patches widened as the morning went on.

Heather trudged out of the kitchen to check on the llamas and untie Pipestone. Jim went with Pedro a little way into the forest. 'I forgot tissue,' said Pedro.

'That's a problem. What are you going to do?'

'Run. Get me some.'

'Surprise, son.' Jim tossed him a small roll of toilet paper.

'You teased me, Dad.' Pedro hitched his pants up, bent over, grabbed a handful of snow, packed it into a ball, and threw it at his dad. Jim easily turned, and the snowball missed. Pedro bent over to get snow for another. When he stood, a large glob of snow landed squarely on his chest.

'You tricked me.' He threw another at Jim who decided to let it hit him.

'We're even. You take care of your business and then we'll go see how your mom is doing.'

They walked back into the open area where the llamas were staked. Pipestone jumped in the air and did a twist before rolling on the wet ground. He stood and shook off clinging snow and dead needles.

While Pedro watched Pipestone, a snowball hit him in the shoulder. 'Mom ambushed us.' They both laughed.

As suddenly as the storm had come, the brown understory appeared. The white retreated to the shadows. The sky turned a dusky blue. Heather moved the llamas to a small meadow dense with fescue, to wet oat grasses striving to regain their stature, and to the llamas' favorite and the reason the animals eagerly carried packs into the mountains: sedges.

Heather sat with her journal on her lap and her back resting against a tree. Her mind cleared. Her eyes opened to the forest and to an erratic, a boulder dropped by a passing glacier long ago. She wrote, 'A fluke storm turned to Indian summer.' Then she changed the title to 'A blizzard turned to Indian summer.' Her eyes focused on Jim and Pedro walking back toward the camp with an armload of dry kindling. *Could life be any better? This is where I belong,* she thought.

CHAPTER 30

'I want to sit up front with Dad,' said Pedro.

Heather bit her lip, letting Pedro know she was serious.

'Please, Mama.'

'Let's make a deal. We study for your test in the back and when we get to Leavenworth, we'll stop and get an ice cream cone. Then you can sit up in front the rest of the way through the mountains.'

Pedro needed to study American history, his weakest subject at school. 'I don't like it. They cheated the Indians.'

Heather thought for a few seconds, wondering what to say. She knew the textbook and the teacher were spouting the same outdated Pilgrim stories she'd been taught years ago. She made a decision. She didn't want Pedro to go to class and start an argument with his teacher. She doubted that Mr. Thomas had read or studied anything new since he'd first learned history in grammar school. It wasn't even his topic. Shop was what he understood and felt at home with. The Twisp school had been short of teachers for years, and Brad Thomas had been given the task of teaching history. He'd approached the assignment by going through the motions and reciting what he remembered from grade school.

Heather said, 'There is always more than one side to anything. History is no different. It's subject to interpretation. I'll make you another deal. You ready? This is a good one. One you will like. You learn what your teacher is teaching you—she wanted to say, 'forcing down your throat'—then we'll do our own study, okay?'

'Okay,' Pedro answered, wondering why it would be a good deal.

What Heather had in mind was the short nonfiction book that had enlightened her thinking about the field: Howard Zinn's *A People's History of the United States.* 'We'll have fun. I promise. It's important to see all sides to something and then make a decision.'

While they talked about textbook history, Jim drove alongside the wide expanse of the Columbia River before turning west and climbing into the mountains. An hour and a half later, to Pedro's relief, a sign said "Leavenworth."

Pedro looked out the window at the Bavarian buildings brightly lit with multi-colored Christmas lights. A twenty-foot tree twinkled next to a sleigh pulled by reindeer. A large sign read "Now, Dasher! Now, Dancer! Now, Prancer and Vixen! On, Comet! On, Cupid! On, Donner and Blitzen!"

'Are those all girls' names?'

'Confusing, isn't it? What do you think?'

'You said Rudi was about to lose his antlers in a few

days. All those reindeer have theirs for Christmas. You said only females still have antlers by Christmas.'

'It's a long, hard job pulling that heavy sleigh all over the world. The females are stronger with more endurance, but they had to call some of them males' names.'

Pedro didn't respond for several seconds. 'You're making a joke. Someone messed up when they had them all have antlers, right?'

'You are very astute.'

'Does that mean I am bad?'

'No, sweetie. That's a good word that means you are becoming very smart and perceptive.'

'Ice cream!'

'After our cones, you can explain to me how history and myth differs from reality. It will be a good exercise.'

'Oh, Mom.'

Jim pulled into the German Bakery. A long neon sign with a wreath around it announced "Forty-Nine Flavors of Ice Cream."

'Get me a single vanilla yogurt,' said Heather. 'Pedro?'

'Two scoops butter pecan.'

'That's my favorite too,' said Jim, ruffling Pedro's hair.

'I know, Dad.'

A short while after pulling out of Leavenworth, the mountains came into view. A dusting of snow on the trees, but the road was clear and dry.

'What d'you buy, Mama?'

'Two dozen gingerbread cookies.'

'Can I have one?'

'You may, as soon as we find out if there are enough for the BWC folks.'

Maria Dakine waited at the front of the first-floor offices of the BWC. Jim called and let her know that they were twenty minutes away. The black Suburban pulled up in front. Pedro jumped down and saluted Maria. An MP, who stood just beyond her, smartly saluted him back. Maria and Heather gave each other a long hug.

'It's been far too many months,' said Maria. 'I don't want to lose touch with you.' She let go of Heather's shoulders. 'Pedro, we have an exciting few hours. First, I'll show you your army quarters for tonight. An MP is going to give us the full base tour, and then we'll have a snack on my sailboat.'

'Can we go out in the boat?'

'Not today, but you can start the engine and I'll show you how the sails work.'

'Thank you, Maria,' said Jim. 'Shall we meet at our home and then go out to dinner? Say about 1700?'

'You got it. You ready, Pedro?'

'Behave with Maria,' said Heather. 'She's my best friend ever.'

'Oh, Mom.'

Maria and Pedro drove off in Maria's white Toyota Corolla. Heather waved. As she lowered her hand, her cell phone rang. 'Really. Okay. He's not worried? I'll come straight back. Thank you, Roy.'

Jim looked at Heather, waiting for her to explain. 'Sharifa is on the verge of having her baby.'

'Is there something wrong?'

'I don't know. Roy called over the new vet from Omak.

The new guy said that she was ready and needed a cesarean. I don't trust him. Roy is going to stay with her until I get back.'

Jim raised an eyebrow. 'I can get a helicopter and fly you back?'

She handed Jim the bag of gingerbread cookies.

'It will be quicker,' said Jim.

'I'd rather drive. It wouldn't be that much quicker if I get on the road now, and the weather looks kinda skunky for flying.'

Jim weighed everything in his mind. The weather. The reason they were here. To convince Heather and Pedro to stay at the base. He pursed his lips as he thought, *Foolish idea with the animals. She'll never leave them.*

'I'm going to drive.' Jim handed her the keys and said, 'We'll hitch a ride and come back over first thing in the morning.'

'Don't take any risks with Pedro on the base.'

Jim felt a knot in the pit of his stomach. He was convinced Heather wouldn't come to stay on the base. Najma was nowhere to be found. He watched the Suburban drive away. Heather put her arm out the window and waved.

Jim took the elevator down and entered Sheilla's office.

'Where's Heather?'

'She had to go back. Let's figure out what we can do to secure the ranch. She's never going to agree to stay here.'

Sheilla picked up the phone and called Katarina. 'Jim and I will be in the computer room in a couple of minutes. Heather's left. Call Brush and Glenda Rose for me and have Fred get Misa.'

'Unlucky. But it's the reality of the problem,' said Katarina.

'Best-laid plans,' answered Sheilla as they entered the computer room.

'How about using drones?' asked Fred.

'Hard to justify them for personal protection,' said Jim.

'Training exercise?' suggested Katarina.

Brush and Glenda opened the door. 'Hey, Jim,' said Glenda. 'What'd we miss? We headed over as soon as Katarina called.'

'We were discussing drones and more generally if there was any way to protect the ranch. Jim doubts Heather can be persuaded to stay on the base,' said Sheilla.

'The best argument is Pedro,' said Misa. 'She won't want to put him at risk, will she?'

'I know Heather well enough to know she's no risk-taker,' said Glenda. 'But, and a big but, she is stubborn and won't want to let Najma dictate how to live her life. Not to mention that Heather won't leave the animals and the ranch.'

'But that leaves Pedro and the others all in danger too, including Colonel Johnson,' said Katarina. 'I agree with Misa. That should be a strong enough rationale to sway her. This isn't just about her.'

'We could think of her as bait and set a trap,' said Fred. 'Sorry, Colonel. Then we would be justified in using government resources to capture Najma.'

'It's okay, Fred. We can't have extra bodies all over. It would only alert Najma, and Heather won't put up with it.'

'Jim's right. What about cameras?' suggested Brush.

'The best idea,' said Vidya. 'Misa, Fred, and I will work that out. We should have done it months ago.'

'The problem will be transmission of the data. We'll need repeaters and either electricity or solar power. It will be hard to camouflage them,' said Misa.

'Dad, I like the boat.'

'As much as helicopters?'

Pedro moved his lips back and forth. Then he exhaled, causing them to vibrate.

Maria laughed. 'We used to call that a raspberry.'

'No sé.'

'No sé to the question or the raspberry?'

'No sé.' And they all burst out laughing blowing raspberries at each other.

'Let's go to the commissary and get some things,' suggested Jim.

'What's that?' asked Pedro.

'It's an army store.'

'Do they have games?'

'We'll see. Then we'll go home. Afterwards, we'll take Maria out to dinner at the Officer's Club.'

The staff sergeant looked around before talking softly to Jim. 'A buddy just flew from Japan and brought a new game for his boy. He brought an extra. You'll need to buy the Nintendo game console.'

'Okay. One Nintendo it is. What's the game?'

'It's called "Super Mario." His kid said it was really good. Guess my friend couldn't wait to give it to him for Christmas.'

'Sergeant, I thank you. It looks like this one will be well used before Christmas too.'

Pedro's eyes became enormous as he stared at the colorful game cover. 'Thank you, sir.'

'Never wanted to be a sir, little guy.'

Pedro looked at Jim. 'Sergeant Gillespie prefers to be called Sergeant, Pedro.'

'Thank you, Sergeant. Thank you, Dad.'

'Much appreciated, sergeant. Come on. Let's go home.'

Maria had bought a large bag of items. The three walked out, happy with their purchases.

'I'll follow you, Jim, and leave my car at your place.'

After dinner, Pedro tore the packaging open and in no time was glued to the TV.

'Night, night, Pedro. Come back so we can go sailing. And enjoy your helicopter ride tomorrow,' Maria said as she left.

'Bye,' he said, barely looking up from the screen.

The next morning, Jim had to pry Pedro away from Super Mario so they could fly to the ranch. As soon as they landed at the house, Pedro raced inside and hooked the Nintendo up to the TV.

'It's supposed to be clear skies for a few days, so it won't hurt leaving the Huey outside below the house. And the general's in Washington, so he won't be needing it,' said Jim.

'Nice of him to let you use it,' said Heather.

'I won't ask often. Surprised he even said okay. It's the closest thing he's got to a son.'

Heather contemplated Jim. 'Besides you,' she added.

Jim pulled out his cell phone and, after a couple of

words, returned it to his jacket pocket. 'Spoke too soon. The general is on his way back.'

'Does that mean you can't stay?'

'He said he'd call me tomorrow.'

'I hope he doesn't want you back pronto. Pedro's riveted to that game. Whoever said kids don't have an attention span?'

'Guess history lessons can't compete with Super Mario.'

'Hmm.'

'Any change with Sharifa?'

'Nope. False alarm, I guess. She wasn't due for another three weeks. Maybe it will be a Christmas baby. The new vet is good with the ultrasound. You want to know what her baby is?'

'Yep. Okay.'

'It's a boy.'

'Another little Benji. But you wanted a girl, didn't you?'

'If it had been a girl, we couldn't breed her to her dad when she grew up. So, a boy is good. How'd things go at the base?'

'Pedro had a good time. Maria said to say hi. The game Pedro is playing is from Japan and isn't released here yet. The commissary sergeant was nice enough to give it to Pedro.'

'I really wanted to tour the labs with you. Do you think we can try again soon?'

'Anytime. You could ride back with me. I heard Nusmen had something to show you.'

'I'd like to go before Sharifa has her baby, maybe two weeks from now.'

Jim raised an eyebrow.

'The Omak vet doesn't have a brain. She wasn't due.

He's a nincompoop. Two more llama babies are due about the same time. I need to stay for a few days. And I want to help Pedro prepare for his test. Then let's try the tour again. What'd you do over there?'

'We had a meeting and talked about the ranch and Najma.'

Heather jerked her head up. 'I've forgotten about that bitch.'

'She might be dead, but my guess is not. As time goes on, the probability of her reappearing increases.'

'I don't want to hear about it. I don't want to think about her ever again.' Heather stomped her foot on the floor. 'I mean never. Please, Jim.'

Jim squinted into the sky as he walked to the general's helicopter. Heather's obstinance worried him. With every passing day, it was more likely Najma would return. *If she's alive*, he thought.

Jim and Sheilla had decided that, when Jim returned to the BWC, they would review their new security plan for the ranch. Six members of Captain Carter's quick response team arrived yesterday. Besides watching out for the ranch's inhabitants, their overriding priority was to remain unobserved by Heather. Two were hidden as snipers while the others roamed. The remaining six of their twelve-member team would arrive tomorrow to rotate surveillance duty. Except for refueling, a drone would fly twenty-four hours a day until a final protection plan was arranged.

The Huey's blades started their slow turn. Pedro waved, surprising Jim that he could pry himself away from the game. Jim waved back, lifted the UH-1H off the brittle December turf, and thundered down the valley. The helicopter was a hundred feet above the big barn when Jim spotted Shuskin standing outside. Jim smiled as the old man ducked into the barn.

Cynthia had a list on her computer screen. 'This is everything we've planned so far. The general gave his approval this morning. I think giving special consideration for Pedro is correct. We didn't think guards standing around at school would help much. Too obvious. So, everyone is undercover. We had to pay the bus driver to relinquish her position.'

'Cynthia, thank you. I have a meeting.' Fred had assigned Cynthia from his computer crew to oversee the protection plan.

Sheilla briefed Jim about the issue of the Ecuadoran president's missing daughter. The colonel assumed that was what the general wanted to discuss. He also assumed that, with the general present and the multi-people meetings, as soon as they had some indication of the whereabouts of Angélica Noboa Perez and her captors, he would be on a plane to South America.

'We have a two-fold mission here,' said the general. 'To capture Miss Hussein, and to ensure the safety of your family.'

'I know you will do whatever you can. I still don't like to leave.'

'We both know,' said General Crystal, 'that you could only do so much if you were here. We don't have any idea if she will rear her psycho head today, or six months from now, or ever. We're ramping up CIA's efforts to locate her. Our team here is doing everything they can. Let's hope she makes a mistake.'

'Not her style to make a mistake.'

'Sergeant Williston has everything organized for your flight. When we get some idea where the young woman is, Miss Perez, it'll probably be a go. Neilly's team has arrived at an old CIA training base in Ecuador. It will be your staging area.'

'The usual,' said Heather when Jim called her from Fort Lewis. 'Rudolph is sick. I think the females were picking on him since he dropped his antlers. Not sure why he got sick, though. Maybe stress, but I'm trying something new. The reindeer don't seem to be able to handle antibiotics. I think it kills their stomach flora. So, I am intubating him with yogurt every few hours to replace the good stomach bugs. What's up with you? When will you be back?'

'Not sure. I might have to go away for a few days. Later tomorrow or the next day.'

Heather's stomach tightened. She bit her lip and managed to get out, 'A mission?'

'Yes.'

'I want to see you. I was going to ask if I could come to the labs tomorrow. Remember you said you would give me a tour since I have clearance, and I want to know more about what you do. I asked Ben if he would ride over with me. Maria Dakine is going to take him sailing.'

'Winter sailing?'

'It's supposed to be sunny tomorrow, and it would only be for a few hours.'

'What about Pedro?'

'He'll be fine with Shuskin and Lo.'

'What about feeding the reindeer?'

'If you can believe this, Shuskin is turning into a pretty good hand. But he won't have anything to do with vet stuff, like sticking a tube down Rudi's throat. He's capable of taking care of the feeding and seems to like it. I think he feels more comfortable with animals than most people. I don't ask him to do anything. He seems to want to.'

'If you're sure he'll do it. That is a bit of luck, having him to back us and Ben up when needed. But what about intubating Rudolph?'

'This one will really floor you . . . Pedro.'

Jim thought that, with Heather gone, Carter's team could focus on Pedro. They still had to watch out for Shuskin and Lola, but it would be one fewer person. The school and bus were well covered. They had enough cars to follow Heather's and Pedro's bus without their knowing.

'Pedro liked the boat so much, I thought I'd bring Ben and let Maria take them both out. I talked to her and she said she would.'

'What time are you going to drive over?'

'Pretty early. Around six or seven.'

'I'll talk to the general.'

'He said it was okay before and said, since you were in charge of the labs now anyway, it was up to you.'

'True. See you tomorrow around midday. I have a meeting at noon, so I'll have Doctor Milton or Nusmen meet you if you get here before I'm out. Drive safe.'

'Love you, Jim Johnson. Thanks for this.' Heather's eyes

crinkled at the thought of Jim giving her a tour. It was about time she found find out more about the labs. It's a part of his life that they could share. Then her mind flipped to his leaving. Going away again. *A mission? No doubt. Dangerous? No doubt. Shit,* she thought. *I have to come to terms with this. I have to. He's letting me in. I have to accept being in his life.*

CHAPTER 31

Heather walked out onto the fresh dusting of snow. She started the Volvo. Starlight bounded off the whiteness. The air was crisp. It would be dawn soon. *It's beautiful. I hate to leave.* But then she thought about seeing Jim. She was finally going to get a tour of the labs. She had always heard about them without having a clue what they were like.

As they walked together toward the full planning meeting, Jim turned to the general. 'I promised Heather a tour of the labs. You still okay with her having access?'

'After Mexico, she got a clearance that allows it. Your call.'

After the meeting, they talked again. 'Now that we have some idea where the president's daughter is, you should be able to get in and out without much trouble. Because her father was the old school chum of our VP, we've put on an almost excessive amount of equipment, birds, and people.'

'Sounds easy. A straightforward rescue mission.'

'I know what you're thinking. Even after all our best planning, nothing is ever simple or goes the way we think.'

'The way it always is. I'll check on Williston's supplies tonight.'

After the briefing, Jim and Brush headed to Jim's office. Brush smiled. 'Sounds like fun: rebels, miners, mountains, jungle, a nutsy rich eco-girl, head-shrinking natives, two countries' armies, and we can't drink the water 'cause it's full of lead, arsenic, and mercury.'

'We couldn't drink it anyway. Full of bugs we can do without,' added Jim.

'Bacteria and parasites are your department. All in all, a piece of cake, eh?'

'Truth is, Brush, I'm looking forward to it. It's been a while since we've been in the field. After the admin around here and sitting at home, it will be a relief. I'll reassure Heather when she gets here that we'll get back way before Christmas for sure. I don't want her to worry about that, and I don't want to miss Christmas with everyone, especially Pedro.'

'You feel like the situation is covered at the ranch?'

'About the same as our mission. Lots of bodies and equipment.'

'Think it's overdone, eh?'

'Overdone, yes. But for the best.'

'Time's passing. The odds of the lady showing up are increasing.'

'Hmm,' said Jim.

Maria's boat, the North Star, churned away from the dock. Ben had flipped out over the sailboat. Meanwhile, Heather felt a prick of excitement as she set out toward Jim and the Biological Warfare Center.

Upon her arrival, Jim strode toward the burgundy Volvo. In a starched and pressed uniform, an MP saluted at the door.

Inside, there was a front counter with a long wall. The wall separated a large open desk area with several halls behind that led into the building's depths. Jim's workplace was not at all as she'd imagined. *I guess secret agents still need to have an office somewhere. But where is "Q" and all his special gadgets?* she wondered.

'This is a large office but not quite what I expected, Jim,' she said.

Jim smiled, looking forward to her surprise when she saw the full extent of the BWC.

'Either you have very tall ceilings, or we are going down more than one floor. And what's with that mirror?'

'We're going to level minus four where my office is and the main labs. The mirror has a video camera with facial recognition.'

Okay, this is getting interesting. I've never heard of facial recognition.'

The elevator door opened. Heather gasped. 'Oh, my. I

had no idea. This is gihugeic. Two floors tall and the offices above. Wait. You said floor minus four?'

'There are five underground floors. The offices up top we use, of course, but they are there as cover for what we really do and so people don't wonder about staff coming and going. We have hundreds of people, and we need cover for them. Behind the offices is the hangar. Let's take a short look at the whole place so you can get your bearings. It will take a few minutes. Each floor is about 500,000 square feet. About sixty acres total. Then there are annexes to HazMat. Your friend, Doctor Dakine, is headquartered there.'

'You got to be kidding. I never imagined that any laboratory could be this big. Holy cow. Sixty acres!'

'Let's look around the labs here first. The secure level labs are below. There's no reason to go in them. We have up to level four security for the dangerous bugs.'

'I guess I should have known. You mean like MRSA, Ebola, and that sort?'

'Yep, and including most everything you can think of. Nusmen is working on prions.'

'Jeez. I thought CDC did all that? It's dangerous, isn't it? Why do you have them?'

'We need to understand how to counter them if a population becomes exposed.'

They walked past endless blinking equipment lights, lab benches, and banks of computers. 'Jesus, Jim. How much computing power do you have?'

'Let me introduce you to our resident IT types. Heather, meet Fred. He's in charge of computing.'

'I'm pleased to finally meet you,' said Fred. 'I know all about you, of course, from the Arizona-Mexico, ah, problem. I know it turned out well for most of us. Just not all.'

'Nope, it didn't turn out well for everyone,' said Heather as she remembered her friend murdered and raped in front of her at the hands of Najma and the Mexican cartel.

Heather skipped down the hall to meet Nusmen. Even with Jim's departure looming, she felt closer to him. He wouldn't be gone long. Life was good.

Unfortunately, the Ecuadoran assignment would become more complicated than expected. The original mission to rescue one woman from a small band of guerrillas, which had at first appeared relatively straightforward, turned out to be anything but. Simply saving Angélica Perez, however, morphed into a series of operations that threatened Jim's return in time for Christmas.

CHAPTER 32

'I f you're ready, let's go,' said Colbert, wondering why he felt so "up" with his woman leaving him. But he did understand, he just didn't want to face it. He felt as though a dark cloud was lifting. Then he looked longingly at his blue Bronco as Najma climbed into the driver's seat. He shrugged as he climbed into the seat of the Chevy pickup. He started the truck and pressed the brake. He saw Phil give him a thumbs-up in the rear-view mirror. Colbert turned the right blinker on and then the left. Phil waved. Colbert was an expert at hauling trailers. Even so, he watched the path of the trailer's tires in the outside mirror as he made his first turn. It was an unnecessary habit he had learned to enjoy. As the trailer straightened, the Bronco came into view. He turned his eyes to Bright Light's entry road. He fondly remembered his first foray up the drive to the old couple's house.

Minutes later, he pulled the trailer into the airport parking lot. He put the key under the floor mat on the passenger's side, closed the door, and got into the Bronco.

Najma stopped at the entry gate. Najma pulled through and Colbert closed it. He would have left it open since she would be leaving soon, but he couldn't break the habit of securing the compound.

Nearly everyone in the compound stood outside as they pulled up. Colbert gave Najma a kiss before joining the others. As Najma drove away, neither Brenda nor Bambi stood waving goodbye with the others.

Jason Colbert felt a sense of relief that was shared by nearly everyone as they dispersed to their daily chores. Most hoped never to see her again. Most knew, just as Jason did, that it was inevitable they would. Najma felt nothing as she waved without looking back.

Najma's recent experiences with Brenda had changed her. She felt aroused as she drove west toward the colonel. She daydreamed every day about confronting her nemesis. Over the months, she had decided she would have to collect information before she could formulate an attack. She felt certain the ranch would be watched, even monitored. She planned to take one of the forest service roads near the Loup Loup Ski Bowl. When she found an observation point, she would survey the skies for any sign of a drone. Then she planned to drive toward the Methow State Airport and up Balky Hill Road toward the ranch. It could be risky as she might be sighted, but she had to survey the airport for signs of military. She could observe the airfield from Balky Hill before driving over the top to observe the entrance to Wolf Canyon Ranch and the lower ranch house.

Najma knew the pitfalls of driving. However, she was

confident that the blue Bronco, while noteworthy to some, would also look like a redneck's toy. She had pulled her hair up under an old brown baseball cap with a faded yellow "Case" label. Phil had loaned it to her on one of their walks and later told her to keep it.

Najma pulled into the airport, parked by Colbert's truck and trailer, and painted her face with makeup she had borrowed from Brenda. She applied thick blue eye shadow, heavy black mascara, red blush, and purple lipstick. She changed into a pink and blue top with a large ruffled edge. She left a button undone, exposing cleavage.

She would only have to stop to add fuel from the five-gallon cans in the back, Najma had brought along plenty of food and warm clothes. The makeup and hat would disguise her from cameras along her route. The tarty clothes were added to distract people from looking at her face. She had studied the map repeatedly, pondering her trip. Part of her wanted to waste no time arriving at her destination. Another part wondered whether back roads might be safer. The main roads could provide cover. The Bronco would be somewhat undetected among the heavier traffic. She made her final decision based on curiosity about Gerardo's remains. She would drive north toward the Pend Oreille River and then northwest to Kettle Falls, Republic, and Wauconda.

At Newport, her road, Highway 2, joined with Highway 20 at a busy intersection. A white car with a light bar on top pulled out of a McDonald's parking lot. A cop. Najma looked down as much as she dare. The traffic was slow. The policeman passed her, going in the opposite direction. The state patrol officer stared. Najma's hand moved to her pistol. He gave her a thumbs-up. She nodded. He hadn't been looking at her. It was the car. The classic blue Bronco. She smirked, and whispered, 'Camouflaged in plain sight. His pet car was a good choice.'

Dust swirled softly behind the Bronco. There was no one at the gravel road where logging trucks had been months ago. She continued up the path to where she had baked Gerardo's corpse in her makeshift fire-pit oven. Besides morbid curiosity, she wanted to know whether her pursuers had accidentally stumbled on his charred carcass. If he had been found, she would have to be more alert. She would have to assume the authorities could attribute his death to her. All they would probably deduce is the route they had taken. That is, unless they connected Gerardo to the car and found film of its license plate on a video camera. She doubted his mutilated cadaver had been discovered, however. She doubted they could trace anything back to her. If he were found without his head and hands, how could they identify him? Would they think she had anything to do with his death? *Not likely,* she thought.

Najma stood beside the fire pit. Along its edge, several blackened branches remained charred but unburned. The fine materials in its center looked like cement. Rain and snow had bonded the soot. Sealed under lampblack, Gerardo had not been discovered.

The sun was overhead as she drove through Wauconda. The two-lane road weaved along a stream west toward Tonasket. There were few cars. No cops. Najma looked at the fuel gauge and shook her head. Thirty years ago, the Bronco's fuel mileage had been acceptable for the times. She pulled off from black asphalt onto a narrow dirt road. A small sign said "Willow Ranch." The road snaked into the rolling hills with no sign of anything other than sage and scattered pine trees.

She filled the tank with the first of the five-gallon plastic containers Colbert had put in the back. The second container consumed, she threw it and its companion onto the stark but previously litter-free countryside. The gauge said three-quarters full. She turned left toward Tonasket. The road streamed south, following a river that fed the endless apple orchards. More traffic. She pulled her hat bill down and sat low in the seat. A pickup tooted. Another flashed its lights. The blue Bronco: the star of the road.

Riverside-Cherokee-Omak-Okanogan. The road turned west and flowed seamlessly up hills, which were more like mini mountains. Had she been like anyone else, Najma would have felt excitement. Her destiny was close. She drove past the Loup Loup Ski Bowl parking lot, did a U-turn and pulled off to the side of Highway 20. She could see the ski hill, which lacked enough snow to cover the ground plants. Seeing no activity in the unopened ski area's parking area, she turned in. The Bronco was at home, churning through the unblemished snow. She stopped in an open area pointing west toward the ranch and settled back into the seat, watching the late afternoon sky.

Except for the contrail from a high jet, the sky was empty. The truck shook. A loud crack jolted her. A fighter jet skimmed the treetops. It was so low she barely saw it rushing past. It had been going faster than the speed of sound, the reason why she had not heard it approach. Were they looking for her?

She waited, wondering whether the jet had seen her and whether pursuers might surround her at the empty ski area, closed because of insufficient snow. She scanned the parking area and searched the sky. No sign of small planes or drones. She drove back onto Highway 20 and headed downhill past Beaver Creek Road almost to Twisp, where she turned right on the Eastside Road. She drove slowly past Methow State Airport, looking for signs of the military but the airport appeared deserted.

She made a hard right turn up Balky Hill Road, bumping over the washboard curves. The Bronco's suspension creaked. As she accelerated the tires slipped and lurched up the hill. Najma did not want to get out and manually lock the hubs unless she had no choice. The snow was hard packed from the few cars and pickups that drove the road. No vehicles appeared. She crested the hill, descending slowly down the slippery surface that led to Wolf Canyon's lower ranch house, stopping as soon as she saw the ranch entrance. Waiting as long as she felt prudent, seeing no sign of people, she continued down the hill and drove past the driveway to the house and still saw no one.

Inside the house, Roy set his coffee cup down and pulled on his coat. Heather and Pedro would be along soon. He needed to saddle the horses for their ride up Pipestone Canyon.

Captain Carter reported that Heather and Pedro were walking down the canyon road toward Beaver Creek Road. 'How long before the Air Force low altitude zone is cleared so the drone can get back on-site? With Heather and Pedro settled in for the night, the drone surveillance would be adequate. And he could get out of the cold.

'We're expecting clearance at 1700,' said Sheilla. 'I'm here with Cynthia, waiting for word from Fairchild.'

'Just like a war zone. F'ing jet floating in silently and

then bang, hits you with a sonic boom, nearly blew me off the ridge it was so low,' said Carter.

'Probably why they call it a low altitude fighter jet training area,' added Cynthia, who was on speaker phone with Sheilla.

'When we get back to BWC, I'm not sure if I want to box your ears or take you to dinner,' said Carter.

'Neither, Captain. I've got a boyfriend, and I was in the Martial Arts Club in college.'

'Just checking,' said Carter, a little disappointed. He had started to grow fond of Cynthia's voice.

'Business, Carter,' said Sheilla. 'We're without our eye in the sky for almost three hours. Heather should arrive at the lower ranch at about 1445. I don't like these gaps.'

Thirty minutes later, the main-gate surveillance camera showed Heather and Pedro as they passed through the main gate.

Najma sat in a pull-out to the side of Beaver Creek Road about 400 feet west of the ranch entrance. She remembered the spot from last September when the Viking vet had driven past it. She carefully scanned the hills and road. On the upper ranch side of the road, the hill was nearly vertical. It would be a tough climb with the snow. She got out and looked up. It would be a good vantage point high above the entry gate.

Najma climbed up the slope using small trees and vines as handholds to pull herself up. A half hour later she crested the top with a hot body and cold hands. While she climbed, Heather and Pedro walked onto Beaver Creek Road before turning left onto Balky Hill Road. Neither aware of how close they were to each other.

There were two entry gates, separated by the stream, a

hundred feet apart on opposite sides of the eroded 'u' where the ranch road met Beaver Creek Road. The original entry alongside the sand hill and next to the stream rose steeply for twenty feet where it met Beaver Creek Road. The other entry road that Jim had added was flat but had to cross the stream. He had built the wooden plank bridge to cross it. The new entry road also passed next to a hundred-year-old homesteader's apple tree. Seeing the stream and the old tree, as the planks rattled when they drove over the bridge brought unexpected pleasure to Jim and Heather.

The original steep road was only used in the summer for heavy trucks or tractors that were heavy for the bridge. The roads were not visible from each other as dense trees and brush grew alongside the stream.

The hill Najma had climbed was formed of sand deposits left from the large river that once flowed through the Methow Valley. Without Heather's Douglas firs seeding themselves and securing the sand, the hill would have disappeared.

Najma had accidentally selected a great spot to spy. In all the years he had owned the ranch, not even Jim had had the enthusiasm to climb the sand hill. The cows avoided it. Why would anyone in their right mind scale that hill when only a few feet away they could easily enter the canyon? On top of the hill, the descent to the ranch road toward the old homesteader's apple tree was more gradual.

The ranch seemed unguarded. She was pleased to see no surveillance aircraft, drones, or cameras. Atop the hill would be a good place to start her stakeout. After the climb, she used her boots to clear a small spot to sit. She found sand under the crusted snow, brushed a top layer away, and sat down. Behind her, the large conifers stood like sentries.

Below her, the entry road forged a furrow toward the ranch. The aspen grove wound its way up the canyon to where she expected to find the colonel.

Between the big trees behind her, she could see snippets of the lower ranch house, Balky Hill Road, and open fields. A movement. She adjusted her position for a better view. Three riders on horseback crossed Balky Hill Road into a field. The rider on a short black horse was small. After a few minutes, the riders disappeared behind a hill. The canyon was still. Nothing moved. The late afternoon skies dimmed and the temperature dropped as the sun set over the western mountains. Najma looked back toward where the riders had disappeared. A sudden motion. A black horse galloped across the field toward Balky Hill Road and vanished behind the ranch house.

Several minutes later, two horses emerged. One carried the small person and the other an adult. The horses sauntered toward the ranch as day turned to twilight. Stars pricked the sky. The minutes passed. Night set in, and the stars multiplied, coalescing into a brilliant band of light. Balky Hill Road became a bright-lit ribbon. The snow crystals surrounding her sparkled under the intense starlight.

The riders out of sight, Najma thought it time to descend to the blue Bronco. Before she stood, two shadows moved on the gleaming gray of Balky Hill Road. Two shapes—one larger and one smaller—tramped toward the entrance gate of the ranch.

CHAPTER 33

The purity of the stars and snow excited Heather. She was still feeling the after effects of adrenaline from when the cougar had killed the doe with a young fawn at her side while they were riding in Pipestone Canyon

Her mind drifted back to the narrow canyon that had allowed Roy to rope the youngster as it ran away. Pedro jumping from Blacky to rescue the fawn. The mare seeing only a darkening canyon and a killer cougar, turned and sprinted away to the safety of her home.

Heather let out a raspberry, causing Pedro to look up. She smiled at him, pulling him close. *We've had quite an experience,* she thought.

'It's beautiful out, isn't it? Let's hope we can hear the hoot owl. Shuskin is going to build a fire in the barn. The office stove will warm us up.'

Heather felt at peace. At one with night and canyon. Her son beside her. A new family and Jim soon to be home.

They clumped over the small wooden bridge. Heather looked up fondly at the old abandoned road that led toward Jim's and her Secret Glade. *He'll be back soon. Christmas will be special,* she thought.

A small crunch of snow. A voice said, 'Walk straight ahead.' A sharp prick as Najma pressed steel against Heather's neck.

Najma was elated at her luck. She had expected to spend days looking for an opportunity to get to the colonel and presto, she didn't need to find him. She had what she needed to make the colonel come to her. Heather started to shake. Najma smirked. 'Boy, walk with this woman who thinks she is your mother.'

Fear of this loathsome creature paralyzed Pedro. He was able to eke out one word, 'Mama.'

'Shut up, boy. She is not your mama.'

The little brat needs to learn, she thought. *I will teach him to be a man.* Najma backhanded him.

'That's right, baby boy. Cry one last time. You will soon learn to have no use for whimpering. Move it, woman. Walk, I said. Up the unused road I saw from above.'

Heather thought, *that's stupid,* it would take hours to get to the house through the crusty snow that covered the old road. She was too weak with fear to talk and nearly too weak to walk.

'Move in there, through the bushes,' said Najma. From high up on the sand hill, she had seen the small, enclosed area.

The Secret Glade brought her a momentary sense of calm. *Our place of love and togetherness.* The cooling trickle of blood from the knifepoint cleared her mind. *Not here. Please, God. No,* she pleaded silently.

They pushed their way into the small secret area. 'Lay down, woman.' Heather dropped to the ground. 'No, woman. On your back. You, boy. Move over there.' She pointed to a tree a few feet away.

Najma straddled Heather, looking into her green eyes. She heard Pedro's feet crunch as he lunged toward her. 'He is brave, no?' Najma backhanded him hard just before he got to her. Pedro stumbled backward, hitting his head on the tree.

Najma pressed her small double-edged blade into Heather's throat. Blood seeped into the surrounding snow. Heather's head listed to the side, and she saw the red-stained snow. Her favorite red algae-colored snow. Her watermelon snow. She smiled.

Najma scowled. The green eyes, the blood-red snow, the look of happiness. She stood straddling Heather. She spit. She gave Pedro a hard kick in the shin.

'Get up, boy. I said, get up.'

Pedro managed to stand. Through half-conscious eyes, he saw his mother lying dead in the snow. Najma pulled his arm hard. 'Keep up, unless you want the same.'

'Cold night for a walk,' said Carter. 'I've had my fill of this sitting out in the cold. My next assignment better be in the tropics.'

'The drone will be back on station in a few minutes,' said Cynthia. 'It should be able to spot Heather and Pedro as they walk up the road to the barn.'

'Good,' said Carter. 'Cause with the full moon, the stars, and the snow, our night vision is no better than binocs.'

'We're starting to get an infrared signature near the barn

road. Not too clear as the drone is still over Beaver Creek Road.'

'I have a figure in sight. Looks like she is carrying the boy. They've entered the barn.'

'The drone is overhead now. We've got an infrared increase from the barn.'

'Yeah, I can see a faint glow from the stovepipe. They must have started a fire.'

While the drone approached the upper ranch, Shuskin had left the cabin, after finishing his dinner. He cuddled the baby llama close to his chest as he walked back to the barn. Under the stars he thought about how good it made him feel to have the big-eyed newborn lie on his bed while he ate, its feet tucked under its body, neck straight and tall, big adoring eyes watching.

He opened the door into the barn and passed through another door into the office. *Got to get a fire going for Heather and Pedro.* He set the brown and white baby on the sofa as he lit the kindling he had placed in the wood stove earlier. The fire caught, and he put in two pieces of wood, closed the stove door, adjusted the damper, scooped up the baby, and went to the vet room. *So soft and fragile,* he thought, rubbing her coat.

Shuskin couldn't think of any place he would rather be. He gave the baby girl the small bottle filled with cow's colostrum. She sucked on it vigorously. He waited ten minutes, stood the baby up on its four legs, and rubbed its behind as Heather had showed him. The baby girl spread her hind legs a little and out popped some ill-formed pellets. Shuskin thought it was amazing that he could produce this effect on the little one. He grinned. *She thinks I'm her mother,* he thought.

Shuskin attached Velcro fasteners on the down coat around the baby. He snuggled into his sleeping bag, adjusted his pillow, and pulled the small cria next to him. The pleasure he felt contrasted to the fear that had permeated his being when he'd slept on the street. He silently said a prayer of thanks.

Najma was unaware there was a video camera at the main gate. The other entry road and the one she took had no tire tracks and tall trees along the stream, shielding her and Pedro from the drone when it passed high overhead. From her earlier vantage point on the hill, Najma had noticed the two entrances. The main car gate was less steep. A hundred feet north of the more level entrance was a little-used gate. Since it was the quickest way back to the blue Bronco, Najma chose it, luckily for her, preventing the video camera on the main gate for seeing her.

She had parked the Bronco facing north on Beaver Creek Road and decided to take the same road Murray the Viking vet had taken toward Conconully and again unknowingly avoided the surveillance camera.

The Bronco would be fine on the snow-covered road the vet and Najma had traveled in September. She continued to be lucky. Driving north, the tall sandhill shielded her from the drone's searching camera. She had driven two miles to where the county road ended. The road ahead was not plowed. Najma had little experience driving in snow but decided that was what this vehicle was made for. She drove twenty feet into the unplowed snow and stopped. She put the Bronco in reverse and backed up to the cleared road.

She got out and, as Colbert had showed her, turned the four-wheel drive locking mechanism on the front wheels.

The Bronco charged through the blanket of crusted snow with little difficulty. She was confident she would make it to the other side of the low hills that separated Beaver Creek and the Okanogan Valley apple orchards. From there, her path back to Bright Light would be snow-free. The going was slow but steady. She reached the places that had been stripped of trees by loggers and remembered what the vet had said about Heather and clear cutting; she grinned. With the road unprotected from the wind by trees, the snow had whisked away the snow leaving the road was almost clear. Najma sped up. She hadn't gone far when the headlights lit the snow-covered road ahead. She saw no reason to lower her sped. The Bronco abruptly came to a stop in the deep snow drift. Najma pushed the accelerator, and one wheel after another lurched and spun.

'Ayreh Feek,' Najma shouted. Pedro rose from the floor and said, 'Where are we?' Through sleepy eyes, he looked at Najma and started to shake.

'Shut up, boy,' she yelled, taking her frustration out on him. Pedro cowered in the seat as far away from her as he could get.

'Ayreh Feek,' she shouted again, raising her hand to hit him. 'Screw you, Colbert. Fucking stupid car. She opened the door forcing it back and forth, pushing snow aside. With her overconfidence and lack of winter driving experience, Najma had driven into a three-foot deep snowdrift. She pulled the door closed and tried to back up. The tires spun uselessly on the high-centered Bronco. She managed to push the snow away that blocked her door and got out. She sank up to her waist in the snow.

She tried to crawl on the crusty surface. After only a few feet, her chest and head fell through into the powdery snow underneath.

She made it back to the car. The crystal-clear night disappeared. Flakes started to fall. Back in the warm car, she reached over and cuffed Pedro. *I'm a sitting duck*, she thought. What she didn't know was how few traveled this road in winter. It could be days or even weeks before someone came along.

Najma crawled into the back seat. She had brought a down sleeping bag in case she needed to camp while scouting out the ranch. She wanted Pedro alive or she might have just let him freeze. 'Get back here.'

Pedro crawled between the seats. 'Get in here with me.' Pedro could think of nothing worse than to be close to the devil woman. He wanted to kill her.

'Don't make me say it again, boy. Get in here.'

The feeling of nausea abated as Pedro, mentally fatigued from the day, fell asleep. Najma remained angry for an hour before she fell asleep.

Clanging motor noise woke her. The Bronco's windows were covered with condensation inside. Outside, six inches of new snow covered the vehicle. Even so, bright lights lit the inside of the Bronco.

Najma scrambled out of the sleeping bag. 'Stay there and don't make a sound.'

The clatter, engine noise, and lights moved past the Bronco. Najma climbed into the front seat and managed to open the door part way. She looked toward the noise and lights. It was a large truck, plowing through the snow. *It drives through the snow. Why can't I? Colbert's stupid piece of shit car ....* As she watched, the truck stopped. A man got out and walked through the cleared area toward the snow-covered Bronco.

He tapped on the passenger side window. Najma crawled into the passenger seat, holding her Glock pistol. She rolled the window down. A man with a beard stared at her.

'You're lucky to be alive, lady.'

Najma smiled sweetly. 'I am. Can you get me out of here?'

'Think it's best to pull you backwards. You're high-centered. Put the car in neutral. I'll hook up a chain.'

Minutes later, the Bronco started to move backwards. When it stopped, Najma opened the door and stepped out. She looked at the truck. Its two back wheels on each side had chains on them. Its flatbed was loaded with cement blocks. A row of lights on the cab made the road blaze. Najma put her hand in her coat as the bearded man walked toward her.

'You can drive now if you stay in the plowed part. The road's clear, but take it slow for a couple of miles. No snow past where I came from in Conconully. Start her up. I want to make sure you're on your way before I leave.'

'Alhazu,' said Najma.

'What'd you say?'

'It's just my way of saying good fortune. How can I thank you?'

'You're darn lucky, all right. I'm only here 'cause we're having a snowmobile gathering in a couple of hours. Yesterday, it didn't need no clearing. Then, this freak snowstorm in the night. I gotta plow all the way to where the county pavement ends on Beaver Creek Road and then get back to my home. Glad I could help. Let's get the snow off the windows and get you going. The rest will blow off when you're moving.'

Several minutes later, Najma saw the man waving as she drove away. The sky ahead was lightening. She looked at her watch. It was almost eight. They would find Heather soon if they hadn't already. She pressed the accelerator. *Alhazu. But, with the delay, maybe not so lucky.*

In planning for the past few months, Najma had thoroughly memorized the map. Forty-five minutes later, she drove around Conconully Lake, then through Omak, and toward Coulee Dam. She drove the speed limit. She was getting hungry for something hot. 'I'll get close to Wilbur, eat, and decide which way to drive,' she said.

'What?' asked Pedro.

'Shut up and lay down.'

'I'm hungry.'

'You learn to do what I say. Then I'll get you some food.'

It was two hours before Najma pulled into a side road. She poured ten more gallons of gas into the Bronco and threw the red-plastic containers into the grass. The one remaining container should provide enough fuel to get her to the compound. *Are they chasing me yet?* she wondered, climbing back in the driver's seat. She tossed a Saranwrapped sandwich into the back seat. 'Eat it and get into the sleeping bag.'

CHAPTER 34

A ftermath – December 22, 2000

As he had done hundreds of times, Jim descended, losing altitude rapidly past the edge of the Cascade Mountains into the narrow valley hemmed in on the east by lesser mountains. In the early morning light, the Twisp River looked like a silver ribbon. There was no sign of the sun as the north and east held lingering clouds from the snow-storm. *Lucky it stayed just north of here,* he thought before glancing east toward Wolf Canyon and home. He could only afford a quick look. Speed brakes up. One notch of flaps. Power reduced, he dropped into the white and gray valley. Snow-capped Oval Peak rose majestically on his left. Below, his winged shadow crossed the river. He flew above the town of Twisp and, speaking over the local radio frequency, announced his intent to land. No one answered.

He scanned the air, looking for a glint from anything

flying but saw none as he descended straight onto Methow Valley State Airport, Runway 31. Exiting onto the center taxiway, he drove the plane fast to a silver metal hangar, pulled in front, and pushed a remote door opener. The forty-four-foot-wide door creaked. As the door rose, its bottom half folded into its top half.

Jim climbed out onto the wing and jumped down. He loaded a shovel with sand from a metal washtub. He arched it out toward the front plane tire spreading along the path the front tire would take. A small motorized tow stood inside the door along the edge of the hangar. He flipped the choke lever and pulled the cord. Nothing. Once again, he pulled the cord, and after sputtering, the tow started. He left it idling while he took a scoop of coarse sand from a bucket and made a trail from the plane's front wheel into the hangar. He engaged the clutch and steered the single wheel machine out of the hangar to the plane, clamping it on the front nose-wheel. The tow's single tire slipped and lurched every few turns, but the sand allowed enough friction to pull the plane into the hangar. The plane weighed about the same as a small car. In an emergency, he could push it in by hand, but this way was quicker. He closed the hangar door and a few minutes later he was on his way. *Almost there,* he thought. *No journey is at an end until it is. Close is not there … Soon.*

He engaged all-wheel drive and took the most direct route over Balky Hill Road. Twenty minutes later, he drove the black Chevy Suburban through the main gate, up the snow-packed road, past the large old homesteader's apple tree, and over the small wood-planked bridge. Looking toward the old road, Jim saw foot tracks heading toward Secret Meadow: his and Heather's special place. It wasn't a meadow or glade as they sometimes referred to it. Rather, a few square meters of open area surrounded by a thick group of trees and bushes. To any who did not know its location, it remained their secret, hidden from view.

Tracks went in and out. *Heather making multiple visits just to look?* he wondered. She had always loved the place, probably more than he, if that was possible. They had found the sequestered site a long time ago while searching for a lost calf. They became enthralled with how concealed it was, yet so close to where they often walked. Upon an earlier homecoming, Heather had welcomed Jim by hanging candles in paper lanterns on the trees and bushes. She had made an exceptional picnic lunch. They had made love, pulling a few spiny prickles from their bottoms afterward. Then they had argued. He was dead tired. She was full of life. The two did not mesh that day. So much had happened since then. Now he couldn't wait to see her.

He continued straight up the canyon and across the speedway, a flatter area with a small rise at the end. Just over the rise and on the left, the main barn came into view with llamas in the snow-crusted fields, the scattered remains of their previous dinner carpeting the white snow with a dusting of green. Mounds of llama droppings, frozen until spring, also dotted the fields.

On his right stood the old homesteader's cabin where Old Man Shuskin now lived. He didn't see Shuskin and drove straight on up the road, past Spooky Meadow, toward the house. With a feeling of having arrived, he turned off the ignition. Lola was standing at the end of the covered walkway. Wrapped in a shawl, she was standing by herself.

'Bueno, you are back, señor. Heather no here,' she said in her clipped English.

Jim raised an inquisitive eyebrow.

Lola's language was still limited. Her ability to read his face was not. 'They camp at big barn last night and no come back up for breakfast.'

'I'll be back in a few minutes with them, and we can eat then. Nice to see you, Lola.' He turned quickly, wanting to get to Heather and Pedro as soon as he could.

He retraced the drive from only seconds ago, down the road to Shuskin's cabin where he turned right up to the big barn, with its office, vet room, and stalls. Heather and his son were probably there, caring for a new baby, raking or cleaning, or immersed in another project. There was never an end to projects on the ranch. Rosie stood in the drive, her heavy tail moving her rear quarter back and forth in the cold morning air. Shuskin appeared at the end of the barn under the covered drive-through, holding a fine-tine tooth fork, a newer variation of a pitchfork with several tines that worked for picking up the small llama droppings. In his other hand, he held a several-foot-wide aluminum flat-toothed dirt rake. But there was no sign of Heather or Pedro. They must be occupied with a birthing or with a baby llama, a cria. *That must be the reason they had stayed over last night.*

As he climbed out of the Suburban, Rosie ran to him, lifted her large body on hind legs, and put her paws on his shoulders, her head and eyes even with his. As Rosie ran forward, Shuskin took a step back. As usual, he was spooked seeing the colonel, a person who still frightened him. Shuskin was not the old man of the woods any longer; his fingernails were clean in comparison to what they had once been, and his teeth had been improved greatly by Heather's dentist friend. Shuskin, or Grankin as Pedro now called him, was a new man, with a new home, and a new life.

'Where's Heather and Pedro?' asked Jim as he rubbed Rosie O Twisp's neck. Their eyes peered blue into gold. Jim struggled to pet her while keeping her massive tongue away from his face. Shuskin shuffled back and forth with his head down.

'Dunno.'

Jim gently lifted Rosie's paws off his shoulders.

'What do you mean? They stayed here last night?'

'No, sir.'

'When did you last see them?'

'They walked down the road.'

'When?'

'Afternoon, late, yesterday.'

Jim pulled out his cell phone and called Roy.

'Hey, Jim. You want to come on down and retrieve the little guy?'

Jim relaxed. Pedro was with Roy.

'Sure would. I'll be right down.'

'I'll try to get a diaper or something on 'im, so he won't mess up your car.'

Jim hesitated.

'Who are you talking about?'

'The little deer fawn. Didn't Heather tell you about him and the cougar?'

'Better tell me what you are talking about, Roy. Heather isn't up here.'

'Last evening, she and Pedro walked up to the barn just about sunset.'

'Shit, Roy. They're not up here.'

The old man backed away as Jim's voice rose.

Jim rushed back to the Suburban, jumped in, spinning the tires as he backed up. He turned the selector to all-wheel drive and drove faster than was safe down the ranch road and around the curve, skidding around the bends until he accelerated, and the traction control kicked in. Around the field that surrounded a sub-irrigated grassy area below Shuskin's cabin, he recklessly stepped on it, over the small hump and down the speedway. Heading down the steeper hill that descended toward the lower ranch, he was forced to slow on the slippery packed snow. He pushed it, pumping the brakes, sliding and bounding his way down the road. The bridge boards rattled as he drove over them and lurched to a stop by the footprints that led in and out of Secret Meadow.

Jim had been and always would be a consummate realist. He wasn't sure, but his instinct, which assessed possibilities and probabilities, had made a prediction. His mouth went dry. His heart raced. Heather missing. Pedro missing. The multiple tracks. They had never found Najma and had grown complacent looking for her. Or worse: the cougar Roy had mentioned. The tracks in and out.

He processed other scenarios. A hungry bear that should have been hibernating. He looked more carefully at the tracks. More than one person. Two adult tracks going in and one coming back. Different shoes. He steeled himself. Then he called BWC.

'Sheilla, where did you last see Heather and Pedro?'

'They left the lower ranch and the drone had them going into the barn. Carter saw them from the ridge.'

Jim relaxed a little. *Maybe I'm wrong.*

Jim took a few quick, long strides through the snow, staying out of what was probably Heather's tracks, another adult, and the smaller imprints that belonged to Pedro. Two different adults going in. One adult coming out. Pedro's tracks led both in and out. Subconsciously, he assessed those tracks, something his conscious mind was unwilling to do. *I'm not wrong.* At the same time, he assessed his culpability. Najma was bound to come for revenge. It was her nature. He should have been prepared better. He should have protected his family better.

He stopped short of entering. The tracks all led in and out of the glade. He circled to the east. As hardened as he was to death, he knew he would not be up to this particular carnage. Everything important to him would be no more. The woman who made his life worthwhile, turned from living tissue into nothing more than rotting flesh, decomposing into its constituent chemicals, the process slowed by the cold winter nights. Never to love again or be loved again.

He took a deep breath and pushed his way through the brush and willows that obscured the small, secluded area.

CHAPTER 35

Christmas was normally a festive and peaceful time in the small ranching town of Twisp. This holiday, however, the residents had to contend with the invasion of dozens of FBI agents and technicians, mixed in with a smattering of local and State Patrol Officers. Other men and women scattered throughout the town and valley. They didn't advertise their affiliations by wearing suits and dark glasses or by flashing credentials as the FBI did. They didn't have the flat-brimmed Smokey Bear hats that State Patrol Officers wore. They didn't wear uniforms. Some were clean-shaven. Others sported beards or stubble. Even the women had a distinct look to them. They all had something in common, however. They looked fit and serious. Even the cowboys, some of whom were willing to challenge outsiders, avoided them. They sensed a difference. A seriousness of purpose. A confidence. Outnumbered, they choose to give them a wide berth.

Mostly, the locals consisted of conservative, church-going ranchers with families. They were gritty by nature and prided themselves on having a Puritan work ethic. Over donuts and coffee, they'd argue politics. One thing they never argued about, though, was the God-given right to own a gun. They hid their guns in their coats and noticed the invaders did the same. It was the only thing they had in common with one another.

The two adjoining towns of Twisp and Winthrop were popular with citizens from the west side of the mountains. The day-trippers sported the latest in REI hiking attire. The ranchers thought them intruders to their way of life and mockingly referred to them as "Coasties."

The more classically educated westerners were appalled to see the locals wearing sidearms on the hiking trails and displaying rifles on racks in the rear windows of their pickup trucks. Road vehicles held the same disparity as their clothes. Volvos, BMWs, sport-utes, and Subarus contrasted with pickup trucks. Ranch owners identified each other by the color of their pickup trucks, by tailgate on or off, by open back or camper top, and by make: Ford, Chevy, Dodge, and the increasingly popular, Toyota.

There was no love lost between the two groups. Nevertheless, the locals realized that they were getting more and more dependent on dollars the Coasties brought to the valley. The Wild West was dying and, while they would never say it aloud, the locals could foresee its inevitable demise.

Jim found Heather spread-eagled in the red-tinted snow, the blood snow of her last conscious thought. He tumbled through a cascade of uneasy images, bringing both despair and relief. It was immediately obvious to him who the killer was. A knife to the throat was Najma's distinctive modus operandi.

Anguish. He would never hold her again. The only woman he could truthfully say he had loved. It was only his practical nature that prevented him from ending his life and joining her. Relief that Pedro was not lying there too. He saw where Pedro had fallen or been knocked backward, leaving an indentation in the snow.

Jim could see through clouded eyes the scene as it had been. Little Pedro had come at Najma, and she had knocked him back. The small spot of blood, both in the snow and on the tree bark where his head hit, indicated that the boy, his boy, had been injured. Jim hoped the impact caused him to blackout as Najma killed his mother.

Najma had claimed many times that she was Pedro's mother. She was a cold rationale psychopath. But on the issue of Pedro, it was insanity to think she was his mother. Perhaps it was a delusion, or simple ownership, or even a fantasy that Pedro would eventually benefit her, as sons sometimes do. Many months ago, in Mexico, she had carried out her new employer's orders by viciously murdering Pedro's entire family including Rojizo, Pedro's old yellow dog. Najma had abducted Pedrothe sole survivorvowing to turn the small brown boy into a real man.

Having the family killed was nothing more than an object lesson ordered by Guillermo Vasquez, the head of the Siastra Cartel. Pedro's older brother had been attracted to the cartel leader's daughter. The cartel chief had entertained visions of moving to worldly Europe and of marrying his daughter to a titled suitor, not a Mexican peasant. The execution had served a dual purpose. Guillermo had fed the cruel desires of his assassin and, at the same time, had provided a warning to the young men of the village to steer clear of his daughter.

Najma took every opportunity to cause fear and to inflict pain. Her savagery was traceable to the treatment she had received as a child. Raped over and over by her father and his friends, Najma had become empty of empathy.

Eventually, Najma could take it no more. A knife lay on the table, her father's back to her. She picked it up and stabbed him just above the hip. He had turned and looked at her in astonishment. She plunged the knife into his over-sized thigh. He crumpled to the floor. She fell on him, stabbing him in the stomach over and over. Half his size, she straddled him, as he had so often straddled her. With her left hand, she grabbed his testicles and, with small fingers, squeezed as hard as she could.

He was mortally wounded. Weakened, but not yet dead. Searing pain caused him to grimace. He was too impaired to resist her. She moved her face closer to his and was surprised at how his suffering made her feel. Triumphant, she smiled at him as she slowly took the double-sided knife and pushed it into his throat.

Since that episode, she had treasured that knife, the author of her freedom. It had become her trademark weapon. Whenever she'd straddle a person and wield the knife, she remembered the day that had shaped the rest of her life. Since that day, she'd sought fear and pain in her victims' eyes, whose glimmer inevitably dulled in death.

Having killed her father, she stalked the other men and, when they were vulnerable or asleep, she killed them the same way. She found she enjoyed it. The method had become her modus operandi.

In Mexico, she had taken refuge with the cartel and become its leader's assassin. Her cruelty at first earned her the nickname, La serpiente, which and had later morphed into La diabla. The men of the cartel treated women with disdain but had never before feared them. But all feared the devil lady. La diabla was not a normal being. Comely, she presented a conundrum. Her dark brown, nearly black silky hair, black eyes, and a pretty face, was marred only by a raised scar like a small red starfish behind her right ear. Normally, they would have desired her, wanting to subjugate her to their will. After seeing and hearing her in action, however, they were no longer intrigued. Convinced she had the devil in her, they wanted nothing to do with her.

La diabla had come to kill Colonel Johnson. He was the only man she thought her equal. The only man she would bed for pleasure. Still, she knew she'd have to kill him. He would pursue her with a vengeance for having murdered the weak and ineffectual woman he'd thought he loved. A weakling was not right for him. Jim needed a match whom he could respect. An equal. She remembered Heather's inept marksmanship. After shooting Najma in the shoulder, Heather had not killed her, even though Najma had been restrained only feet away.

The colonel would come. While she waited for him, she would make the little Mexican boy a man to be reckoned with. Eventually, Jim would become her life partner. The ultimate object of her desire. But if Najma couldn't persuade him to be hers, she would reduce him to nothing. Gradually, she would push him bit by bit, piece by little piece, into oblivion. She would ravage his manhood, and he would expire in misery. But first, she would make him crave her.

CHAPTER 36

Jim hid his grief from the government investigators, but he couldn't hide his heartache from his long-term friends. He struggled for control. To his close associates, he was no longer the steady thinker who could execute a mission with beneficial outcomes. He was consumed by the desire to avenge Heather's murder, combined with a desperate need to find Pedro. His rancorous quest became an obsession. Terminate Najma. Liberate Pedro.

His rational side tried to push thoughts of Heather aside and to keep his mind focused on Pedro. The boy's resilience had always been incomprehensible to Jim. How had the happy, loving little boy been able to surmount Najma's massacre of his family? As a guiltless witness to her unthinkable depravity, could he yet again survive emotionally intact? Or would Najma ultimately root out the good inside him?

Jim had always been concerned with the effects Pedro's past trauma at the hands of Najma would have on him.

Impossible to assume it would not in some way taint his future well-being. The question was how much? Would being with Najma now alter his psyche? Before Jim could mourn Heather, he needed to find and save Pedro from as much psychological damage as possible. *I need to talk to Katarina.*

To say Jim was concerned would be an understatement. He reflected on the young boys and girls whom he had observed in various wars. Armies of children had been brutally brainwashed to maim and kill without compunction. Would Najma turn Pedro into a monster like herself? Or would good somehow prevail, allowing him to return to a meaningful life?

~

'He's a cute little guy.'

'He is, Ben. We shouldn't be doing this, though. Better that nature takes its course,' said Roy.

'You watched his mother get killed by the cougar?'

'Sure did.'

'You have to take care of him. He'd die out there for sure,' said Ben.

'Guess we've no choice.'

'Must have been somethin' seein' that cougar jump out of nowhere.'

'Lookie here, Ben. I'll keep him for the rest of the day. Then you think you can take him home in that old Jeep of yours?'

'Sure, Roy. Look at him. When you hold the little guy, he doesn't hardly move. You're right. He can't hurt Craig's old Jeep none.'

'He's still a wild one. Looks sleepy enough, but he could start jumping around in the car and cause an accident.'

'Nah, he's just a little fawn. He'll be okay, Roy.'

'You go on then. You got chores up top. That old man of the woods probably needs some talking to. He seemed mighty upset by Heather bein' gone and all.'

'Ya think Pedro's alive? Or d'ya think he's dead too?' asked Ben, a tear starting down his cheek.

'Jim's a certain he's alive. He'll find him. Even without the help running all over town. We'll sure miss her. Won't be the same around here with her gone. Not the same after Craig and them,' he stopped, glancing at Ben.

'You can say his name, Roy.'

'I know he was like a pa to you.'

Ben started to say the name and then stopped.

'I miss him, Roy.' He lifted his head. Standing erect with red eyes, he said, 'Duane. He was special. He was a dad to me.'

'It's a hard life sometimes. Now you lost Heather.'

'She was more like my mother than anyone,' said Ben.

'I know that, Ben. You get on now. Off with you.'

'I'll go.' But he didn't move. He didn't say anything. Then he wiped a tear away and said, 'What's with the dogs?'

'Them's tracker dogs.'

'Why? Doesn't make sense. The killer musta had a car. Can't track a car with dogs.'

'That's not what the FBI is doing. They're tracking her killer to the car with them dogs. Not where the car was a driving.'

'What good would that do?'

'The guy earlier explained that they have teams to look

at tire tracks. They can get some idea what kind of car. Said they could learn a lot. Maybe find out where the car's been from dirt left by the tire.'

'It's mostly frozen, ain't it?'

'Nah, lots of loose dust dancin' around on top. Snow tracks would work just as good, maybe better.'

'I get it. Guess there's lots of people to work on stuff like that. I ain't never seen so many people in this town, Roy.'

'There's dozens of them, all right.'

'Hundreds.'

'A lot, anyway. Go on. Them animals needs their breakfast.'

Jim sat between the sand hill and the entry gate not far from where Najma had sat watching Heather and Pedro. He looked down at the Secret Glade, now a place of grief and memories. A place Jim would never again willingly enter. Below him, men swished metal detectors over the snow-covered ground. Dozens of agents, some on hands and knees, covered every square inch of ground between where Heather had been murdered and where the getaway car had been parked. Small stakes with multicolored flags protruded from the snow.

Jim rocked back in a chair that was nothing more than two pieces of stiff foam encased in sturdy black nylon. The covering was formed of one piece that connected the two squares. Adjustable straps, attached to the outer corners, formed a hypotenuse, which kept the two sections at ninety degrees. One piece shielded his butt from the snow and the other piece supported his back. He dug his heels through the snow and into the fine sand below. He leaned back, his mind lost for a moment in the blue sky.

Several years ago, he had had the sand evaluated but had been told it was too fine to be of much use. His mind wandered to the Methow Valley, carved by a river over hundreds of thousands of years. Several hundred feet above the Twisp River where he now sat, sandbanks had been deposited along the valley sides. The primeval sandbank he sat on was at least a hundred feet deep and spread over several acres.

His eyes quit the sky. The agents below brought him back to reality.

Several were now walking along Beaver Creek Road, looking for any sign of the car's direction. Najma could have taken any of three routes: back toward the main highway, west over Balky Hill Road; or north down Beaver Creek Road, which eventually butts up to forest service roads. If you knew which forest service roads to take, you could end up in Twisp's sister town of Winthrop. An unlikely choice. With the North Cascades Highway closed until spring, Winthrop was a dead-end destination in winter. With Najma, however, the unlikely choice could not be rejected.

The FBI was the correct agency to be involved in a kidnapping. Homicide was not normally within their mandate unless the murder was part of a federal crime. Two unusual occurrences brought hundreds of agents and forensic specialists to the normally sleepy off-season towns of Twisp and Winthrop: an abduction and the escape of one of the most wanted terrorists on the FBI's list.

There were other reasons, of course. As head of the CIA, the general had a certain amount of influence. Najma was partly responsible for shooting down his favorite Huey and almost ending his life in the crash. Those might have been reasons enough for General Will Crystal to pursue her if, that is, he indulged in personal vendettas. His long-term friendship with Colonel Johnson, which for several years had included Heather, was justification enough. And, finally, Najma was a terrorist and a danger to the country.

It had not been necessary for General Will Crystal to use his position as CIA director to push the FBI beyond their customary response. Nevertheless, his involvement increased their response. The extra men and women added to the BWC teams and the FBI's special Hostage Rescue Team made for a formidable force.

The ground investigation was manpower intensive with agents searching for any clues and it paid off when, four hours later, they discovered the car's tire tracks. The tires' distinctive flaws gave it away. The car had pulled off the side of the road near the Loup Loup Ski Bowl.

While they searched, a technician identified the tire tread as belonging to a Goodyear Wrangler. Agents quickly determined its size and came up with a list of vehicles using that tire. A long list. One that, even with advanced computer programming, they could narrow only slightly. From the depth of the track and the compression of snow, the tire's weight could be gauged, and the car's identification narrowed.

Their assumption was that the vehicle had turned east on Highway 20 from Beaver Creek Road, gone up the hill to the pass, and pulled off to the side for some unknown reason. It was where Najma had made a U-turn and pulled to the side to observe the ski area's parking lot before pulling in. The FBI's conclusion was wrong. Their assumption, however, saved them countless hours as the search moved to the east into the Okanagan Valley. Najma had taken the long way to get to where the search was now centered.

'If she went the way they are saying, why didn't the cam at the front gate see her going by?' asked Katarina.

'Glenda asked the same,' said Cynthia. 'Glenda's having them search in the other directions too.'

'We're looking at every second of the entrance road recording for interruptions, but we won't likely find anything. She went the other way.'

After searching miles of the route Najma had driven, they'd discovered no further signs. Any tracks were lost with the traffic from the snowmobile gathering and the plow truck. They didn't know but surmised she had not gone that way.

The mistaken conclusion put the agents accidentally on the right track, Agents interviewed owners of gas stations, restaurants, and convenience stores, scrutinizing security videos whenever a store, station, or highway had them.

Again, they got lucky. Or was it the sheer determination of so many skilled investigators looking into every possibility? The truth was never black and white. This was a case of luck combined with skill.

Unbeknownst to the men and women of the FBI who handled domestic investigations, the CIA crossed over the line from its foreign mandate, interjecting itself into the domestic issue, using their formidable analytical tools. With the general's blessing, Bertrand Gupta charged Deputy Director of Intelligence Martin Pearson to form a team composed of however many technical experts he needed to get the job done. The goal: to locate and capture the missing woman and to rescue the child.

Martin assembled many of the same staff who had worked with the FBI and BWC when Najma had escaped to Canada. With all their resources, including the BWC's computer staff, the team felt embarrassed that Najma had escaped them before. That is unless, as Jurgen Shultz of the FBI had written in his report, Najma was wounded, died in the wilderness, and would someday be found by a hiker or logger. With Heather's murder and Pedro's kidnapping Shultz's theory retired to the dustbin.

Martin Pearson had his own reasons for wanting to find Najma. He had been tortured and humiliated by the terrorist, and although the experience had in some ways made him a kind of hero and a better person, no one apart from Jim, wanted to find her more than he did.

Many people harbored the hope that this would be the final chapter. Having allowed the dark-haired psychopath to escape from Guantanamo and to slip from their grasp more than once in Mexico, members of the agency needed to prove to themselves that they were able to apprehend this particular terrorist. The Biological Warfare Center had also been humbled. After the mostly failed attacks, both in Seattle and on Wolf Canyon Ranch, Najma had managed to escape.

Guillermo, as head of the Siastra Cartel had intended the attack on Jim's ranch to be both a show of strength and payback for the destruction of his villa at Tubutama But the ranch still stood and Guillermo's position had become tenuous. Najma herself had foundered and been captured by Neilly's Special Forces. Now she was like a hunted animal, determined to meet and subjugate her nemesis.

'There are several things that I need to ask you, Colonel,' said Sheilla.

'Save it. You take care of the decisions. Call the general or check with me if you need advice. You're in charge until this is over. Barbara will manage the lab.'

Oh, my God, she thought. *Not so long ago, I was a tech in the FBI.*

'Why not put Barbara in charge?'

'Think about it! Dr. Milton runs the labs with Nusmen. She has her hands full accomplishing that, and she doesn't know anything about field operations. You do. The general's occupied in D.C. Everyone else at BWC is a specialist. You're capable and good. You're it.'

'Yes, sir,' was all she could say, nearly in tears.

Monotone cars were going in every direction and were parked at every motel and store. There were more drab black cars than the town's residents thought existed back in the other Washington: Washington, D.C.

'Reminds me of a bunch of black ants swarming around looking for crumbs,' said Betty Lou.

'I hope they catch her for good,' said Loretta.

'They will. I'm sure of it.'

'I heard some call her a she-devil.'

Remembering, she burst into tears.

'She murdered my Craig. Now Heather, and she's taken Jim's new boy.'

'There, there, Loretta. You've got Ben to take care of. We've got each other.'

'More like, Ben takes care of us now. He's as much yours as mine.'

'He's growed up all right. A fine young man.'

Loretta wiped her eyes and busied herself accomplishing nothing, moving the groceries around in the cart.

'Let's go home.'

'You go to the checkout,' said Betty Lou. 'I'll meet you. I forgot I need some jam still.'

CHAPTER 37

Her skin was like a white peach. Strawberry red hair, nearly invisible eyebrows. That part of Glenda Rose Stuart was visible to everyone. The three ragged bullet scars on her abdomen and the three smaller exit wound scars on her back were not. Even when relaxing in public, she had moved to one-piece bathing suits to conceal from curious eyes the wrinkled marks that Najma had inflicted at the Seattle Space Needle.

Sometimes, she almost felt gratitude toward Najma. Her wounds had brought her together with Brush. Major McGuire had been the first to her side after the shooting, doing what he could until medical help arrived. Visits in the hospital followed, turning to longer visits, and eventually, the die-hard bachelor had fallen completely for her.

For her part, she was no easy catch. She was a competent woman, who had finally found in Major McGuire a worthy match. They both had discovered something they had observed in others but had never felt for themselves—a deep and confident love. They trusted what they felt. Brush had never told a woman he loved her before. He told Glenda often, and he meant it. For the first time in his adult life, he understood what it was to love someone.

Brush stirred and raised his head from Glenda's shoulder. Without moving, she opened her eyes and looked at him. The corners of her eyes crinkled as if to say that the sight of him always amazed her. His lips turned up. They watched each other for several moments, communicating without words. Then Brush mouthed while they held each other's gaze, 'I love you.'

'I know,' she whispered.

They didn't say anything more. Almost at the same time, they closed their eyes and drifted off to sleep again, comfortable in the knowledge that their life together was real.

They were staying at the Frontier Hotel in the center of Twisp, asleep in one of the several log cabins alongside the Twisp River. Brush and Glenda were catching a few winks, both still dressed. It was over twenty-three hours since they had rested, and they remained in their clothes so that they could leave at a moment's notice.

Glenda had been placed in charge of the investigative units. Jasper Neilly's Special Forces were preparing for a mission in another part of the world, but they remained ready to assist the operation if called.

A light glowed softly by their bed, which was still made up. They had fallen asleep on the sofa at three in the morning and expected to rejoin the teams at six. Glenda did not need to set an alarm. She was able to do something that she had become accustomed to, but that still amazed her. A time clock lodged in her brain allowed her to wake up to the second she intended. A biological mechanism that ticked along in the background, accurately, without conscious thought. What would have astonished her, even more, was that Jim could do the same. Just like her, he had always wondered about the mechanism in his brain that allowed him to do it. This strange gift had never come up in conversation. Each had tested their internal clocks by setting them not at simple times, such as 0500 or 0600, but also at more complicated times. Glenda had set her internal time clock at 0544 and thirty-two seconds before going to sleep less than three hours ago.

Her eyes opened wide, and even before looking at Brush, she looked at her watch. Five forty-four and thirty-five seconds. She reasoned it had taken her three seconds since opening her eyes for her mind to recall the experiment and look at her watch. The feat never stopped astounding her. Brush was equally happy to rely on Glenda to wake them when needed.

'Time to rise and shine, mister.'

Brush opened his eyes and looked at Glenda. 'You have a meeting.'

'Hopefully, there will be some new information.'

'Nobody woke us, so I'm assuming she is still on the loose.'

'Do you think it would be a good idea to check on Jim?'

'More like check-in, not check on. He doesn't want to be babysat. I'll bring him up to speed after your morning meetings.'

'You are right, big guy. He doesn't want anyone's sympathy. I know him well enough to know what he wants is information. I'm still having a hard time accepting that Heather's dead, and I can only imagine what Pedro is going through.'

'I know Jim. He has taken her death hard but sees no reason to share his grief. I think he feels it somehow diminishes her and his feelings if he shares his pain. He's a realist, though. He's seen his share of death. He knows how fragile our existence is. He understands how improbable it is that his or anyone's life will continue without disruption, either by a failed part on a helicopter or by an enemy's bullet. We delude ourselves into believing that we will last into the future. He knows it's not so. Pedro is still in the present, and he has to be his primary concern, not mourning the past. Not yet, anyway. There will be time for mourning.'

'I've never heard you talk like this,' said Glenda.

'Things are not often this personal. Sometimes I need to be reminded of how valuable the present is, and those in it.'

'And why I cherish every minute with you, mister.'

'I know,' said Brush, and they smiled at each other.

The black Suburban crested the rise that separated the snow-covered meadow from Shuskin's cabin. The pond was the only place not covered with snow. On the coldest days, it froze, but a supply of underground water added enough warmth to melt less stubborn ice. The old man gave an imperceptible shiver, knowing Jim was coming his way. Then he slunk back into the door frame as the colonel stopped on the road next to the cabin.

Jim had looked into Shuskin's cabin yesterday while the old man was working in the barn. With Heather gone, his attitude toward the old man had shifted. He trusted Heather's judgment, and Pedro's too. Maybe he had been wrong to distrust the old vagrant. In any event, he felt drawn to help the old man. He knew it would be something Heather would have wanted.

He also understood that Shuskin adored Pedro and that, while Shuskin had experienced loss before, it must have been extremely painful to have two people befriend him, as Pedro and Heather had, and then to lose them in an instant. Shuskin seemed to be reacting much as Jim to his loss: work, stay busy, and think only of the present.

Jim had kept himself busy this morning by going to the Twisp Feed store, which doubled as the hardware store in town. Yesterday he had noted items Shuskin might need in the one-room cabin. Jim remembered the many happy days he had spent in that cabin long ago. The time had been uniquely enjoyable, even if spent in the middle of a bitterly cold winter. The solitude. The beauty. The freezing trips to an old wooden outhouse. The stack of books read under nearly a foot of covers. The remnants of World War II newspapers, yellowed and crumbling, had been pasted many years ago on the wall behind the wood storage shelves. One announced the bombing of Pearl Harbor. Jim knew full well what Shuskin needed: the things Jim had gone without when he had stayed there.

Just after he stopped, a red pickup drove over the crest and pulled in behind him. Shuskin panicked. He closed the door. He was going to be transported back to his old life in a mission or on the street. He wanted to run, but there was only one door in and out of the cabin. He looked through a crack and then looked down and closed his eyes as Jim crunched through the snow and walked onto the narrow porch.

'Shuskin. Can I come in?'

No answer from inside. Jim slowly opened the door and

said, 'I have some things for you. Can I set them down inside?'

The old man raised his eyes without raising his head more than a fraction of an inch and saw that Jim was standing in the door with several packages. In his befuddled mind, a thought flashed. Heather had said how much Jim had liked the cabin. Maybe he was moving in. More panic spread through him.

'Take this,' said Jim, causing Shuskin to shake. 'It's a new comforter for you.'

Shuskin's mouth drooped and his face went blank. His lips involuntarily opened and closed. No words came out. His eyes opened wider as Jim passed him the over-sized paper-wrapped package that held a new down coverlet.

Jim could feel the old man's confusion. He put the Christmas box down on the bed and the rest of the packages on the spindly dining table that separated the bed from the woodstove. 'Go ahead. Open that big one on the bed. It's your Christmas present.'

Shuskin shuffled to the bed and timidly tore off the paper. A bright green comforter expanded when he liberated it from its wrapping. He looked at Jim, dumbfounded.

'Yes, it's for you. It can get cold in here.' Then Jim reached over and shifted several smaller packages onto the bed. 'Go on. Open them. I'll be outside helping Fred install some things on your cabin. We're putting up three solar panels. Normally the store wouldn't carry them. They were going to wait until spring to put them up on the hill to light their cross. Better use for them on your cabin than gathering dust.'

Shuskin could hear noises outside while Jim talked. Something heavy was placed on the porch. 'Those would be the batteries,' said Jim. 'We're going to hook up a light in here for you. The oil lanterns are none too safe.'

Shuskin was in a state of shock. This man was doing things for him that no one else had done before, with the exception maybe of Heather and Nusmen. Even while he grappled with what was happening—one simple four-letter word had not escaped him: "your." Could it be? Could it be that this was his home? Jim seemed to be telling him that it was. Heather had said so, but he had learned long ago not to have expectations. Not to trust what people said. Could what he was hearing be true?

The door pushed open and Fred, the assistant at the feed store, slid another oversized box through the door. 'New propane stove.' Fred let go of the box and reached out his hand to Shuskin. The old man just stood there.

'He's a little shy,' said Jim. 'Those packages are for you. Open them up if you want, while we get your old chair outside. I'll help Fred bring in your new lounge chair.' There it was again: the word "your." As the two went outside, Shuskin calmed down enough to open the rest of the packages. He had been told to open them, but he was still a little unsure. Warm gloves, socks, a new down coat, hats, scarves, a folding knife, a red radio, a CD combination player, and several discs. A mountain of new things stacked on the bed. He couldn't believe that the tall, blue-eyed man was giving him all this. Suddenly Jim's kindness, Heather's death, and Pedro's kidnapping overwhelmed him, and he started to shake again, but not from fear. His crying turned into a wail. He hadn't cried since he was a child.

Jim dropped the new chair and raced inside, thinking the old man had hurt himself. In front of the bed loaded with gifts, Shuskin stood heaving and howling. Then he did something that surprised them both. He turned to Jim and clutched him, sobbing.

Jim stood for a few seconds, not knowing exactly what he should do. Then he put his arm around the old man and said, 'Don't worry. You can stay here as long as you want, and soon Pedro will be back to keep you company. You belong here. This is now your home as long as you want it to be.'

The old man turned bright red eyes up to Jim. This was his final conversion from street vagrant to homesteader. The old man of the woods was now settled. Part of a place, part of a family. At some level, he understood that Jim and he felt the same about Heather and Pedro.

Shuskin arranged his new belongings on the bed, while Jim and Fred hooked up the new stove. They put the new brown recliner in front of the old storage shelves that had held wood for the old stove and would become shelves for Shuskin's new treasures. The stove would run from the batteries through the inverter. Jim only worried that, on temperate winter days, it would put out too much heat in the small space. But in the uninsulated cabin, the stove would keep Shuskin warm on bitterly cold days and nights. Jim remembered all too well just how feebly the old wood-stove had heated the cabin when it was freezing outside.

He motioned to the recliner that sat next to the new pellet stove. Shuskin sat down in the chair. Fred showed him how to move the recliner lever. Jim removed a couple of chinks of wood and set the red CD radio on the shelf. Fred strung an extension cord around the edge and plugged it into the small inverter. Jim pushed the eject button and inserted a CD. Heather's favorite: Rolling Stones' "Bridges to Babylon."

Shuskin sat with his feet up, listening to the slow beat of the Stones. He remembered hearing these tunes when she had played them in the Pasayten. He grinned. Jim nodded and looked at the old man. His teeth looked nothing like the stained and missing ones he'd had when he first arrived with Nusmen. Heather had done the right thing. And Jim felt as though he had just done the right thing for the old man, too. He had done it as much for Heather as for Shuskin. Returning Pipestone to Heather in the Pasayten had been Shuskin's good deed, thought Jim. This is mine. And, for a few minutes, Jim had been able to set aside thoughts of Heather and Pedro. He turned and went outside. A third vehicle was coming over the rise and around the morning's sun-drenched crystalline meadow.

Brush climbed out of the olive drab sedan.

'Surprised that thing made it up the road,' said Jim.

'Piece of cake. Just need a lot of momentum before the tires lose their grip. Then it's all wishing it up the rest of the slippery slope.'

Jim waited on the porch as his old friend and partner walked the few feet to him. 'Nothing new, I take it?'

'Glenda just finished the morning briefing. Nothing new, but I'll tell you what they are doing. They're busy. You got some coffee in the barn office? I'll follow you and get this car out of the road.'

'Just leave it where it sits. Fred can get around you when he leaves. Let's go up to the house. You had breakfast?'

'Donuts. Seems to be what the FBI lives on.'

'Lola will whip us up something. I think she wants to feel useful.'

'What are you doing with the cabin, pal? Trying to scare the old man with your presence?'

'Let's go,' said Jim, without answering Brush. He understood that his old friend was letting him know to go easy on the old guy.

Brush peeked inside and stepped back out of Shuskin's hearing and said, 'I see. You suddenly take a liking to Shuskin and are worried about Lola feeling useful?'

'Just get in the car.'

Jim started up toward the house and past the main llama field on the left. As usual, llamas rushed to the fence, jostling for space, hoping for some molasses corn, oats, and barley. *Maybe I'll bring them some sweet COB later,* thought Jim. Brush looked to his right through the window and out at Spooky Meadow with the six reindeer who ignored their passing. Then he heard a loud caw. A brightly colored peacock with over-sized tail feathers perched in a tree above the small meadow.

'That's Junior Junior,' said Jim.

'How do you know?'

'He's the head male. There is a female in the Peacock House next to Spooky Meadow. She's about to hatch her eggs. So, he is standing guard, flashing his colors and biding his time.'

'You keep her in there so he can't breed her, eh?'

'Nope. They breed when they want. The coyotes get them if they aren't contained. The chicks can't fly. The peahen will stay with them on the ground. I like the coyotes, but I'd rather they eat mice than peahens and chicks. The little ones will survive as soon as they can fly and roost in the trees.'

'Glenda mentioned a family.' As soon as Brush said it, he regretted that he had. Jim had just lost the biggest part of his family.

'What else has been found?' asked Jim.

'Car with Goodyear Wranglers was parked past the ranch gate. They're analyzing a minute amount of a soil sample. They had to send it off. Too small an amount to analyze here.'

'The mass specs at BWC might be the best place.'

'Didn't hear where they were sent.'

'Anything else?' asked Jim, hoping there was more.

'They found tire tracks facing east on the side of the road by the Loup Loup Ski Bowl.'

'Lots of Wrangler tires in this area.'

'Glenda said scars on the tires are like scars on people. They're sure it's the same car that was parked off Beaver Creek Road. They've been searching in all directions. The dirt road north of the ranch was plowed for some snowmobile get-together. They didn't find anything there.'

'Big thing here.'

'Plowing? Or you mean the snowmobiling, eh?'

Jim shook his head. 'You know which I meant.'

'Getting pretty active around here. There's a lot of activity at the Loup Loup. I guess the snowstorm got them excited about opening. Only a slight dusting south of the storm. Guess they're hoping it will change and they can start up soon,' said Brush.

'About that time of year,' said Jim. His mind drifted back to skiing there with Heather and Pedro and how Pedro had taken to the sport.

Brush watched, wondering where his buddy's thoughts were taking him. 'Besides the main roads, there're dozens of dirt roads off the main highway,' said Jim.

'Glenda mentioned that. She also said that, because of the tire tracks, it would be a good thing if Najma turned on one of the roads off Highway 20. Easier than finding her on a paved road unless they get her on camera. They're identifying the possible car types. Then they figure they'll have her cornered.'

'You think so?'

'I'm with you. Najma's wily and will be expecting them. Glenda will figure that too. She'll call if they tumble to anything else. The next move is to look for video in gas stations and stores over the other side of the pass.'

Jim looked and sounded fine. But Brush had known him for half their lives. He knew what Heather had meant to him. He knew Jim was hurting, and he also knew better than to say anything. Jim would handle it in his own way. As he had told Glenda earlier in the morning, his newly adopted son would remain Jim's priority.

They drove up the hill to the back of the house. At the end of the covered walkway, Lola huddled in her large blue shawl. Jim had never had time to pay much attention to Lo, as Heather had called her. He wondered why that was. After all, Lola had taken very good care of both Jim and Brush while their wounds were healing not so long ago. After all that had happened to them in Mexico at the hands of the cartel and Najma, both Lola and Pedro had been given a reason for living. For the first time, Jim felt real caring and concern for the stout mestiza. Lo and Shuskin were both special to Pedro too. Furthermore, they were what remained of his and Pedro's family. Jim would do willingly what Heather would have wanted. They would remain his link to the life that he and Heather had built.

Jim had not yet spoken to Ben. The havoc this woman has caused, killing Craig, then Duane, and now ... Jim sighed and stepped out of the car. Brush and Jim walked up to Lola. She had had a hard life but covered it up with a maternal bossiness. Jim had never seen her cry. But crying she was, as they approached her. First Shuskin and now Lola.

Jim walked straight to her and put his arms around the not quite five-foot-tall Yaqui Indian. She held him tight. Jim pulled his head back a little and looked down at her. 'Let's go inside, Lo.'

'Sí. Sí. Too cold. Warm inside.' Jim kept his arm around her shoulder as they walked to the first door, through the mudroom, and into the house. Lola turned to him and said, 'You find our little boy. I want him here.'

Jim nodded as he looked at her.

'You kill devil lady. No good jail. She get away and kill us.' She turned her nearly black eyes and looked up at his ice-blue eyes. 'You make promise. Heather would want. Pedro never be safe with the woman living.'

They heard noises from the kitchen. Brush had walked past them and was doing something that was about to get him into a lot of trouble. Lola's short wide body scurried down the hall.

'Shoo, shoo. Out. Out of kitchen. Go sit. No be in kitchen.'

Jim couldn't help but smile at her antics.

It was only days ago that he thought of his family as Heather and Pedro. Now it was old man Shuskin and Lola. Ben, too, in some ways. *Pedro is alive and we'll have him back again. We'll all make it somehow,* he assured himself.

CHAPTER 38

'I want to locate and look at every store security cam, at any video you can find from every location east leaving Highway 20,' said Glenda.

'You got it.'

Sheilla disconnected and within a second her phone chirped.

Jim said, 'Sheilla, do you have satellite yet?'

'No Colonel We're trying to divert coverage.'

'You said Misa and Vidya were trying to monitor all cell signals from the area?'

'They are. Along with Jake and Jason at Huachuca.'

'What about the second drone?'

'It's being airlifted and will arrive in the Methow Valley in about forty-six minutes. An hour to prep and get it in the air.'

'She's headed east. If we get satellite, have the drones concentrate east of us. I want to get out in front of her.'

'Glenda wants to check the dirt roads running off the main highway.'

'Discuss it with her. She's in charge.'

'Sure. Why are you so certain about her direction? She doesn't do the expected.'

'Tell me where you think I'm wrong,' said Jim. 'North is the border and harder to get across with Pedro. I don't think any of us believe she went across the border before. It was, as Katarina said, a fake-out. Doubling back west might be effective, but where to? Seattle? It makes no sense to me she would block herself in against the Pacific, especially with Pedro. He would likely cause her more trouble in a populated area.'

'She could still go south,' said Sheilla.

'Ask yourself, where has she been hiding out all this time?'

'Okay, it could be anyplace.'

'I don't think so. I think she needs someplace counter-culture where they don't like to interact with outsiders or the government. The only place that makes sense is with the survivalists in Idaho. It's the largest group, and they might have had contacts with the cartel.'

'That does sound plausible, but it could apply to other places in western rural areas.'

'It could.'

'We'll focus on Idaho.'

'Start researching the survivalists. Get the CIA to do the same. Look for hardcore rightwing groups. My bet is one of them. She can be inconspicuous with those types. My wager is she's with a right-winger in Idaho,' said Jim.

'Okey-dokey. Hope you're right, Colonel.'

'Me too. Call me with anything, no matter how insignificant.'

Najma expected that the government and the colonel would be after her soon. If she hadn't been marooned in the snow overnight, she could have made it back to Bright Light by now. *Even with the overnight holdup, they can't get a search up and running this fast. If the guy pushing snow on the road had covered my tracks, they might not even know my direction. Maybe they haven't even found the bitch yet. Or maybe they found her right after I left.*

She was confident they didn't know where she was or headed. When they did, she knew they would use overpowering force to capture her. Even so, the size of the force that had descended on Twisp would have surprised her. The FBI became immediately involved with Pedro's kidnapping. Furthermore, she was a wanted terrorist, and the general possessed nearly unlimited power. Within hours of Colonel Johnson's discovering Heather, planes and cars full of agents, along with more men from Carters' BWC response team, were dispatched to the sleepy mountain valley.

'Convenience store video outside of Grand Cooley. Blue Bronco, dark-haired woman, and Latin boy. She was wearing a baseball cap and kept her head down. The boy looked out the window. Positive ID.'

'Outstanding,' said Glenda. 'What time?'

'One minute after 0900 this morning.'

Glenda smiled to herself as she dialed Brush, thinking her and Jim's hunch about Najma heading east was correct.

'Brush. We have her and Pedro in a blue Bronco headed east from Grand Coulee Dam. No eye in the sky yet, but there are limited ways she can go.'

'Okay, sweet stuff. I'll see what Jim wants to do.'

Jim stood waiting as Brush clicked off his cell phone.

'They have her identified just east of Grand Coulee Dam. Pedro is with her. What do you want to do?'

Jim dialed a number on his phone, and said to the pilot, 'We're ready to go. We'll be below the house.'

'You're right about east.' said Brush.

'The chopper should be here in ten minutes. We'll try to get out in front of her. If we find her, we'll keep the feds back and look for an opening.'

'We talked about it this morning and Glenda knows if they swoop in,' he hesitated for a second, 'she will probably kill Pedro out of spite.'

'My guess too, so we watch and wait.'

Jim walked into the kitchen. 'We have to go. They spotted Pedro. He's still a captive, but okay. We'll be back as soon as we can.'

Lola's eyes misted over once again. Until the last few days, overt emotion was something she had never allowed herself. It still embarrassed her. She turned away from Jim and motioned for him to leave.

Jim grabbed his rucksack and started out the side door, followed by Brush. They walked down three stone steps and onto the octagonal deck. Jim turned toward the house. Lola's face was framed in the lower part of the kitchen window. She didn't smile or show any emotion. Her early years in Mexico had taught her that hope led to disappointment. Her life on the ranch with Heather left her confused. She felt something that seemed foreign to her. A small dose of hope swirled in her thoughts. She badly wanted the boy back. He was her bridge both to her country and to Heather. After losing her son to the cartel, she had thought of Pedro as her son, before relinquishing that position to Heather.

Pedro would need his Lola again. The colonel would bring him back. She allowed hope to push into the front of her mind. Hope that he would return. Hope that Jim would cause the devil lady excruciating pain. To lose Heather, who had become her mentor and friend, was cause enough for grief. To lose Heather and Pedro would devastate her. She wondered if she could survive.

Jim and Brush went down the remaining steps, through the leafless aspens to a flat area where Jim landed helicopters. They could hear the beat of the blades echoing up the canyon as the two choppers churned the morning air.

Brush stomped on the crusted snow, pushing his boot through the hard surface and into the fluffy snow beneath. 'About a foot. Shouldn't cause them any problem.'

The lead helicopter flared above the snow, settled down, and collapsed the crusted snow as though it did not exist. Jim and Brush had stood, heads lowered, past the outer circumference of the blades. The moment the chopper settled, they held their hats, jogging the few feet to the door that opened as they moved forward. Each grabbed an extended hand. The door closed, and they lifted off before they could sit, just as Jim had ordered the pilot to do the previous day. The pilot knew he was serious when the colonel had ordered him to ignore protocols, and said, 'Time and efficiency was the only concern.'

Jim plugged in the David Clark headset. 'Find a secure off-road location to set down, approximately a hundred miles plus to the east of her last known location. Even if our target diverts to an alternate road, I don't want her to see us. Confirm we are live comm with the FBI and the BWC.'

'Yes, sir,' said Warrant Officer Kara, flying directly at Coyote Ridge.

Along with Glenda the previous evening, Jim had discussed dozens of contingencies and protocols with the two pilots and co-pilots. Both helicopters had been outfitted at the BWC under the personal supervision of Master Sergeant Williston. The second helicopter had extensive communication gear and four of the BWC's special reaction team members.

'Comms check?'

'Loud and clear,' said Sheilla.

'Loud and clear here, too,' said one of Carter's men in the following helicopter.

'Same,' said Glenda.

Jim sat back. There was nothing to discuss until new information filtered in. They had agreed that intercepting Najma with agents was far too risky for Pedro. They planned to stay far out of sight but observe with satellites and drones. Several of the lead ground agents had pickups and older cars and were dressed like ranchers. Glenda had requested mixed gender, race, and ages for the first followers. She wanted to prevent the agents from detection.

While the plan was for them to remain behind Najma, she could also have turned around or have stopped, in which case their primary responsibility was to remain incognito. Anyone who encountered her would be removed from further surveillance. They needed physical verification through gas station cameras. Until they saw relevant footage, they could never be certain she was ahead of them.

The danger was that they would get in front of her, and she would spot them.

The elaborate precautions made sense on one level. On another, did anyone think Najma would not be expecting them? Glenda had considered that the only reason Najma would not be expecting them was if Heather's body had not yet been discovered. That remained a possibility, but she must know Pedro would be missed. She would be expecting a pursuit, it was only a matter of how soon.

Glenda assumed that, even with the civilian vehicles and casually dressed agents, Najma would have an advantage. She would regard anyone as a potential adversary. As soon as they had satellite and drone surveillance, the advantage would shift. Even so, the drones would position high and as far away as possible. Najma was smart enough to search the sky for them.

'Drone launch in forty minutes,' said Sheilla. 'Sat coverage will begin in twenty minutes.'

Jim studied his handheld GPS. The pilot Kara was doing what they had discussed. He was not tracking the road but angling miles south of Najma's last known position. They had climbed to 5,000 feet. Their current position put them four miles south of Grand Coulee Dam.

'Colonel, the terrain north looks strange. I've never flown in this part of Eastern Washington. Am I wrong? Do those features look like giant ripple marks?'

'You're right. Until airplanes were invented, no one had noticed these marks from the ground. Flooded maybe more than once and as far back as 18,000 years ago when an ice dam northeast of here ruptured, sending water rushing over this area. South of us, the exposed ancient basalt floodplains are called the Channeled Scablands. They were formed where the volume of water was so great that it washed the topsoil away, leaving the underlying basalt.'

'Jesus, Colonel. You sound like you know what you are saying.'

Brush chimed in. 'He's a colonel with a Ph.D., eh.'

'Where'd all the water go?' asked Kara.

The water took the easiest path around the mountains until it carved a path in a mountain gap that eventually became the state line between Oregon.'

'Son of a bitch. The Columbia River.'

'No further footage at stations,' said Glenda. 'But then, she probably doesn't need to stop for gas for a couple hundred miles. The Bronco doesn't have a very long range. We're plotting all likely stations where she might stop.'

Jim called Glenda. 'Another few minutes, and we'll look for a place to park.'

'My gut tells me,' said Glenda, 'the smart move is that she'll beat it to Idaho's border. Little value in wasting much manpower searching secondary roads. Still, we have to look at all possible route scenarios and guess her current location on any one of them. I have spotters arranged coming from Boise and Spokane. I'll put them out in front of her at stations where she might need to stop for fuel. Either the spotters or the air surveillance should see her or the Bronco. We're flying agents into Spokane and from other cities. We'll have plenty of manpower if we need them.'

Jim considered what a wise choice Brush had made with Glenda, a smart capable woman. *I hope we're both right about Najma's direction*, he thought.

Brush pushed the talk switch on his mic. 'Ms. Stuart, you, of course, said that in error—surely you didn't mean "man" power.'

'It's a phrase. Stay focused, Major.'

Brush chuckled. He had made his point. Two women directing the operation. Sheilla and Glenda, the two women in charge of hundreds of agents for this mission, were where they were because of their superior skill and expertise. *Jeez, I'm proud of her. How'd I get so lucky?*

While Brush bantered, Jim was focused on Najma. He knew he was capable, but so was she. He couldn't underestimate her. After all, it was she who had engineered what was now happening. This would not simply be a showdown as to who was superior. Or would it? How complicated was her mind? Or perhaps the better question, how simple?

People always expect others to reason as they do. To have comparable morals. To react in the same way. *Rarely the case.* It's almost impossible to get inside the head of one's opposite. How does one understand a psychopath? Why does one person save a moth while others squash it?

Jim had killed just as Najma had. What was the difference between them? He knew they were not alike. The precise question was, why not? He did not tolerate bullies or anyone, for that matter, who would persecute others. Jim felt drawn to gentle people who could not or would not protect themselves against the Najmas of the world. The former were vulnerable, and Jim felt compelled to help them.

He wondered if there was something in his and Najma's upbringing that made them who they were. He knew she'd been abused and raped as a young teenager. Such abuse could affect anyone, but was it that straightforward? Had she killed her father because she was inherently a fighter who stood up to his mistreatment? Or had she been born with psychopathic tendencies? Jim knew for certain that there were few black and white answers for anything, let alone human psychology.

He often placed behavior on a linear scale: psychopath at one end and full empath on the other. Most people fell somewhere along the middle of that line. Najma was an exception to the rule.

Where am I on that line? wondered Jim.

His thoughts were interrupted by the co-pilot, 'We're going to set down, with your approval, on that tabletop mountain to our four zero.'

'Looks perfect,' said Brush. 'Sort of like a little tepui I want to visit in Venezuela, only not as tall.'

Sheilla added, 'It's the best we could find. No roads and no ranch houses close. No one should see you landing. Unexposed as we could get.'

'Good choice,' said Jim. He wanted to ask Glenda if there was anything new but would just be wasting her time. She would let him know. He didn't need to ask.

Twenty-three miles southeast of Grand Coulee at the small eastern Washington town of Wilbur, Najma turned south on Highway 21. A few miles south of Wilbur, she pulled into a convenience store, purchased gas, two Cokes, an orange Fanta, and a large bag of potato chips. She wore a dark green baseball cap and made an effort to look down when she was at the register where the surveillance cameras were angled at the till.

The cameras recorded all customers on video for thirty days. They captured with clarity the occasional robber, but more important to the store's owners, the surveillance detected employee thefts. Since pay was low, the temptation to shortchange the till was great.

Najma stood in full view of the camera. However, her down-turned eyes and baseball cap prevented her face from being recorded. While she rarely smiled, she could not help a small upturn at the corners of her lips after she raised her head for a second, pretending to swat at an insect.

Back in the Bronco's front seat, Najma ground up another sleeping pill on a small piece of paper. She creased the paper and tapped it as the grains slid into the Fanta bottle. 'Wake up, kid. I have one of your fake orange drinks.' Pedro tugged himself from his drug-induced dreams. Blurry-eyed, he took the bottle as Najma drove out of the station. He looked out the window at the gas station as she drove past another surveillance camera mounted on the side of the building. Another idiot pickup driver blinked its lights and gave her a thumbs-up. Pedro drained the Fanta. His world turned hazy before he slumped on the seat.

CHAPTER 39

Pedro remained still as Najma continued driving south toward Odessa. She scrutinized the infrequent ranch houses along the way until she spotted one far off the highway. Atop a dented mailbox, a small address plaque jiggled beside the entry road. The dirt road was rutted. The barbed wire was broken in places and sagged between fence posts. The fields were overgrown and full of weeds.

Najma cruised past the long drive. She saw no one on the main road or in the fields ahead. She did a U-turn. No cars ahead. She searched her review mirror and, observing no cars behind her, turned up the bumpy drive.

On the front porch of the ranch house, a wizened man sat on a chair, holding a white mug. Deep facial creases showed under the bill of his frayed blue cap. A sun-bleached "Ford" embroidered on the cap attested to the owner's preference in tractors. Sweat stains bled outward from the hatband onto the hat's bill and migrated up its front, meeting the Ford label.

He didn't rise as Najma walked toward him.

'Good morning, missy.'

Najma judged him to be close to eighty. But the arduous life of a rancher, exposed to years of sun, dirt, and hard labor made it difficult to tell his age. In fact, the old man had turned seventy a week ago. Having had a cancerous lung removed, he knew his working days were behind him. Without a puff on his pipea pipe that now protruded unused from the pocket of his plaid shirtthe old man got little enjoyment from his mug of coffee.

A sturdy woman with frizzy white hair bustled out the screen door and nodded at Najma. She surveyed the younger woman and at first did not like what she saw. Then Martha Adams relaxed a little. The visitor's green baseball cap with a shock of black hair protruding from the back, spelled "friendly" in rancher speak.

'What can we help you with?' she bellowed, accustomed as she was to addressing Harry, her husband of fifty-one years. As with most ranchers, years of working with noisy equipment had caused his hearing to deteriorate. Their ranch, too, had been deteriorating for the last few years. It had been a good life, a hard one, and they had lost a son to it. Still, they carried on. They owned the land and the house and carried on.

'My boy is sick,' said Najma. 'I'm taking him to a hospital at Moses Lake, but my car's motor is starting to clank and misfire.'

'Sounded fine when you drove in,' said Harry.

'It does that. Sounds fine one minute and then almost quits the next. Can I use your phone to call a mechanic or do you know any close around?'

'Thought all you young folks had those new-fangled phones you carry in your pocket,' said Harry.

'Not me,' said Najma. 'I don't like them.'

'Harry, you up to driving the lady and her son? Can't sit there all day a doin' nothing,' said Martha. 'I might join you iffen you do. Could do some shopping in that new Moses Lake Walmart.'

'Car could use a bit of a run, I suppose. You okay with that, missy?'

'I'm much obliged to you.'

'Don't just sit there,' said Martha. 'Go'n git the car while I git the lady a mug of coffee. I'll fetch my hat and purse, and we'll have an outing while we help her and her son.'

Najma would have better understood their willingness to help if she had known that, years back, they had lost their only son, crushed under a tractor. Harry pushed himself up and stretched.

'Git moving, old man. Her boy needs a doctor.'

Harry struggled down the two steps and headed around the back of the house.

'Come on in. It's warmer inside. My name's Martha. What's yours?'

'Najma Peters.'

'I never heard anyone called Najima before. How d'you git it?

'My mother told me she saw it written somewhere and liked it.'

Najma didn't bother to correct the pronunciation. 'You live here alone?'

'Just the two of us. It's all we got: this place, memories, and each other.'

Harry opened a side door to a shed. He shuffled over to a hanging door. It swayed in and out with the light winter's breeze. He took a deep breath and leaned on the handle attached to the aged wood door. Through years of sun and weather, the door had worn and split. It creaked, making small resistant groans as the metal rollers turned in the corroded metal track.

He slid the barn door along and stepped to a thirty-year-old beige Buick Estate station wagon. The keys were inside the meticulously maintained car. He knew it would start right up. Hearing a slight pop in the distance, he shook his head.

He couldn't hear much and imagined all sorts of noises. Some were real, and some weren't, so he paid no attention to any of them. There was something to be said for not hearing all the clanging and banging, not to mention the racket from crying babies and over-talkative town folk.

He pulled the car up below the front steps and tooted. Then he remembered he needed to get his driver's license. He got out, leaving the car idling with the heat on high.

Najma stood in the kitchen, drinking coffee from a white mug. Martha liked the white ones, so she could tell they were spotlessly clean before hanging them on a hook under the cupboard.

'Gittin' my driver's license and we's ready to drive,' said Harry. Then he frowned. The woman, whose name he didn't even know, was holding a pistol pointed at him.

'You won't need a license where you're going,' said Najma. 'Get over here into the kitchen.'

Harry was dumbfounded but not afraid. Years ago, he would have taken that puny peashooter away from the woman. He had survived Korea, so no little gal was going to cause him trouble.

He walked around the kitchen counter and his heart sank. 'Marty' was all he said. Martha lay on the floor with a red hole in the middle of her forehead. His knees weakened, and he dropped to the floor beside her with a sob. Najma fired the pistol at his head, and Harry's thoughts stopped.

The slug entered his brain, tearing through his cerebrum, dendrites, and neurons until it encountered the inside edge of his cranium. Lacking enough force to punch through a second time, the bullet ricocheted, tunneling back to the other side, boring through the soft matter over and over until, its force expended, it came to rest.

The small caliber was her favorite for many reasons. It was not as noisy as larger calibers and, for close-up work, it had enough speed to penetrate the skull and enter the brain. The lead missile banged around for a while before brain tissue halted its momentum.

Harry slumped lifeless beside his wife.

Najma wasn't worried about a surprise interruption. From the looks of the place, the two old people had no friends or much life left. She reasoned she had done them a good turn. Still, time was short; she had pursuers. Her mission was to get Pedro to their final destination, not to toy with two withered relics.

Pleased with herself, Najma opened the blue Bronco's door and lifted Pedro out and into the Buick's back seat. She locked the door and walked back, retrieving her belongings and placing them in the wide front seat of their new car. Then she drove the Ford around back into the garage and closed the sliding door.

She didn't want to linger too long on the off chance that someone would drive up. Nevertheless, she walked back inside, found a large shopping bag, and began filling it with food supplies. She did a quick search and found an old Colt

.45 pistol and a handful of ammunition. On her way out, she grabbed several old hats off a hook and one coat. She locked the door.

She deposited the bag and coat on the Buick's floor in the front. Then she walked around and climbed behind the driver's wheel, adjusted the rear-view mirror, and steered the over-sized car onto the long driveway. At the road, she had planned to turn north back to Odessa, but with her new car, she decided it would be better to blend in on Highway 90, the main east-west interstate just a few miles to the south.

She reasoned that, if and when the video at the store south of Odessa was viewed, they would probably guess she was headed south. At the interstate her pursuers who would have to make another choice, which direction she had taken. They would probably assume she was still heading east. But her followers would have to consider she might be heading in any direction. In any event, they would continue searching for the blue Bronco not the older Buick. She had bought herself several hours. Maybe much more. Maybe enough to get back to Bright Light.

The fuel tank was almost full. The old guy had kept the car in top condition. She assumed the oil was topped off. With the food and gasoline she could make it all the way back without stopping.

There was little traffic. She held the steering wheel with both knees and guided it down the road. With both hands free, she pulled her hair up and managed to don one of the faded red baseball caps. She wanted her black hair hidden from view from any passing cars. A short distance before Highway 90, she pulled over.

The main interstate had a lot of truck traffic. From their

elevated position, the truck drivers could look down into the station wagon and see Pedro. She needed him out of sight. She looked both ways. No cars were coming. She did U-turn and drove back to a side road she had passed just a few moments ago. Pedro would wake up soon.

She stopped the car over to the side of the single-lane dirt road. Before taking out another orange Fanta from the food bag, she rummaged in her rucksack and found the bottle with the sleeping pills then got into the back seat with Pedro. He was still out. Shaking did not arouse him. She slapped him on the side of the head, but there was no response, so she leaned over the seat, got a water bottle out of the front, and poured some on his head. He stirred. It took another minute before a groggy Pedro murmured, 'Mama.'

'Yes, boy. I am your mama.'

He squinted at her. He was too dazed to grasp where he was or that it was Najma next to him. Her patience wore thin.

'You must be thirsty, boy. You want a soda?'

He nodded listlessly before his head fell to the side. She grabbed his face, a thumb on one side and an index finger on the other. His mouth opened. She pushed a white pill over his tongue toward his throat before tipping the bottle to his lips. Clamping his mouth closed, Pedro swallowed. Najma wanted him out of sight for the rest of the trip back to Bright Light. She pushed him onto the floor and placed a blue tarp over him that had been covering the carpet in the rear of the station wagon.

With Pedro secured and out of sight and with a new car and a different-colored hat, Najma felt confident she would not be spotted. *A few hours and I'll be back at the compound. It could be days before the old couple is discovered.* At some point, her pursuers would find the Bronco and trace it to Colbert and the compound. She would be ready for the colonel when they did. The soft suspension of the Buick rolled over the ruts and out onto the highway.

CHAPTER 40

'I like this, Misa,' said Sheilla.

'We whipped this up with the juniors in Huachuca.' Misa moved closer to Sheilla as they stood in the coffee room. 'You plug in the last known location and the map generates probable locations on all roads.'

'Wow. I have to get this to Glenda.'

Misa picked up her pager and typed in a short message, 'She'll have it in a minute.'

'Cool. Not sure how we ever got along without you two.'

'It isn't only us two. It's you, Glenda, Dakine, and me. We're now the squad, and we rule.'

'Yep! Females rule!'

'Yeah, worthy thought. But besides Vidya, there is Colonel Johnson, Major McGuire, and General Crystal, not to mention Fred and the other computer geeks,' added Misa.

'Four against them is a big enough advantage.'

'Not quite, Sheilla. You can't forget Nusmen,' said Misa,

trying desperately to keep a straight face. Sheilla's eyebrows lifted as her eyes opened wide, and she tried to keep her lips together. Both couldn't contain themselves any longer and simultaneously doubled over laughing. Fortunately, they were not standing too close to each other when the bending forward caused them to touch heads. The light bump only made them laugh more.

'There're no sightings and nothing on store videos. The drones are ready and launching. I've got agents parked in public areas on all routes,' said Glenda.

'We're going to sit tight,' said Jim.

'It's more complicated since we can't assume she won't double back, and there are roads in multiple directions. I still think she is headed east, but I could be wrong.'

'South or east. If she is headed east, and that's my guess too, then Highway 2 and 90 both converge in Spokane. All the country roads end up filtering to one of those two highways.'

'What worries me is that we could get ahead of her in checking store security camera tapes. Employees might be yapping about the FBI when she shows up, alerting her.'

'My guess is she will assume we are looking for her. Nice not to verify that fact for her. She could also be holed up and not moving.'

'You're right. I'm going to leave the agents stationed on routes. But get people checking every security camera. With the new computer plotter the BWC just sent, we can chart the position she could get to driving at the fastest speed she could be driving.'

'Like you said, now multiple routes. On our GPS, I count possible positions on fourteen routes and that will keep growing with time.'

'Let you know as soon as we get anything. Ciao.'

Glenda thought that they'd been lucky finding Najma near Grand Coulee. With every passing minute, however, they were losing any advantage they had gained. There were dirt strip airports where she could hide the car and then be hundreds of miles away while they were still watching roads. This wasn't a haphazard fleeing. Najma had time to plan. *What would I do? I've got all the resources in the world to find one lone woman and a boy.* Shit! That's not true. Najma could have joined with someone or several others or passed the boy to another person. Damn, damn, damn. *I've got to get my head wrapped around this, or we are going to lose her.* She ran her fingers through her hair while she concentrated on her options.

Jim slouched in the seat of the Huey. The side door was open a few inches. A cold breeze drifted over the mini tabletop mountain and slipped inside the chopper. The pilots chatted in the front. Jim stretched his long legs out. He mused again on what Najma might do. Going over and over the same information, hoping that a new insight would find its way into his thoughts. Katarina at the BWC and profilers at the FBI and the CIA were putting their conclusions into more formal write-ups. Jim would read them as they came through, hoping to find some useful notion of Najma's decision-making process.

It was a synthesis. Eliminating some of the analysts'

opinions, keeping others, adjusting some to fit his thoughts. She knew they would be tracking her, of that he was certain. She didn't know when they would start, or perhaps the extent of the manpower available for the search.

Locating her was the current ground game. In that, they might not succeed unless Najma was baiting them and setting a trap. Beyond the immediate chase, all the agencies had dozens of analysts working to see if they could find where she had been staying before her assault on Heather. Where had she been all these past months? How could she stay out of sight?

Reams of documents fed into Glenda's FBI command vehicle. They had been on the move for over two hours, heading east on Highway 2. The forty-five-foot-long, dark gray Prevost recreational vehicle looked like any other top-end snowbird bus. Close inspection, however, revealed myriad antennae and communication apparatus on the roof. For the most part, they were hidden in a recess that had been fabricated within the dome. Otherwise, the gray command bus would have looked like an alien ship on wheels. Thirty-seven navigation and communication devices lived in the recess cut by FBI engineers. The recess was cut so that semi-truck drivers in their lofty perches could not see the nest of antennae lurking on the roof. Still, the gear could not be obscured from higher vantage points, such as buildings, overpasses, airplanes, and helicopters.

The conversion had cost more than three million dollars. The vehicle was cumbersome and heavy. After they'd imported it from Quebec, the FBI had made extensive changes to the shell in order to accommodate the weight. Its 800-horsepower Volvo motor would not win any drag races. Nevertheless, the RV was no slouch on straight-aways. Unfortunately, the vehicle did not handle corners well, and its fuel economy was hopelessly inferior, requiring over-sized auxiliary tanks to function adding even more weight.

The Prevost had been christened many different names. The drivers called it the Titanic. The technicians who worked inside favored Battlestar. Glenda, for the time being, called it simply the Bus. There was a sleeping room with bunks that resembled a stack of pancakes. Claustro-phobic staff refused to squeeze into the bunks, preferring to sleep upright in their desk chairs.

Four technicians talking into mics caused an intermit-tent buzz. Faxes chattered. Cooling fans hummed in the background, as did the well-insulated diesel as it headed east and passed the town of Wilbur on Highway 2.

Having no information to support her thinking, Glenda nevertheless made a decision. A gamble. She flipped a switch, keyed her mic, and said, 'Let's fuel up at Fairchild Airbase.' She flipped another switch and said, 'Get the base commander to alert the MPs that we are going to station there.'

Glenda had decided to get inside Najma's head and to do the best she could to mirror the woman's thoughts. The profilers had provided extensive psychological data. Glenda accepted that the profilers were skilled. Najma was a linear thinker, disciplined and expedient. Nothing she did was random. Glenda decided, much as Jim had, that the killer would head directly to her destination. She would stay ahead of her chasers. She would not double back or choose circular routes. The question was, how would she get there? And where was there?

Glenda made several more assumptions. Although it couldn't be ruled out, Najma probably did not have the resources for helicopters. In that case, she would be restricted to roads or small planes. She would not stop to rest. Glenda decided the blue Ford Bronco was a ruse, and inevitably it would be dumped. She concluded that she needed cameras on the main roads. High enough definition for a positive identification.

Suddenly a new thought crossed her mind. With a small plane Najma could easily fly under the radar into Canada. *Shit. Why didn't I think of that before?* As she slammed her fist on the desktop.

Glenda turned to her right and pushed her chair back a couple of inches, waving at Brees to come to her station who was looking and wondering why Glenda hit the desk. Brees, her third in command, was at the small table near the back end of the bus that served as a place for meeting and eating. Brees was a black woman in her mid-forties, mid-height, mid-weight, and sharp as a thorn. Kitty was a slender woman with dark hair and skin that resembled Glenda's.

'Find out what cameras are on Highway 90 just past Spokane and before but east of where Highway 2 merges. I want a camera that is high enough definition for us to identify a face through the front window. If there isn't a traffic cam already in place that can do that, get one installed.'

She looked down at Mia's GPS program. Its red blips represented cars moving slowly out the network of roads. She estimated the time it would take a car to get to Spokane.

'You have two hours max. And I need you to research how the Border Patrol tracks small planes flying over the border, especially in remote areas.'

'Okay, but I need to borrow Chen to check on the traffic cams. Not much time. While she talks to the locals, I'm going to get our field office rolling on setting up a portable unit,' said Brees. 'That leaves Sept to check on the plane issue.'

'Good idea,' nodded Glenda.

Brees walked a couple yards back toward the table and tapped Chen on the shoulder. Chen took off her headset and turned her head up to Brees, twisting her lips up and around as she often did. Brees was intrigued by Chen's strangely endearing facial expressions.

'We got a job with less than two hours to accomplish. Glenda wants cameras that can identify drivers and front passengers in Spokane. Find out what traffic cameras they have, and I'll start trying to get a portable unit set up.'

Chen, the lead technician on the team, nodded as she puckered her lips, scrunched up her nose, and put her headphone back on. As Brees moved back to her station on the other side of Glenda, Chen was already talking into her mic.

Glenda had worked with Brees once before when the former had still been with the FBI. Glenda thought back to her old FBI days before the general had recruited her for her dream job. She had loved the idea of being an FBI agent. Then reality set in. Her male bosses had never accepted her as an equal. She thought it ridiculous that those biases still existed. Brees was a good example. It had taken her over twenty years to get promoted to special agent. Brees had always been an administrator. A personal assistant.

Someone bosses depended on to make operations successful.

Glenda mentally compared Brees to Sheilla. A black woman with a few extra pounds, forever smiling, and concerned about her friends and workers. Her medium-length dark hair and medium height were not that different from Sheilla's, but the deep black color contrasted with Sheilla's auburn hair. As efficient as Brees was, Glenda wondered if she would ever be given the chance to step up to the same high-caliber decision-making position to which Sheilla had been promoted. Brees was special, but Glenda had doubts that she could do what Sheilla did.

There were two other staff members in the command bus. Thin, tall Septimus, or Sept, as he preferred to be called. His medium brown hair was cut on the short side and neatly combed. A detail guy, not personable. He had similar antisocial issues as Nusmen, with a major difference. Sept wasn't totally wacko. A communications technician, he kept quiet when doing his job. He liked nothing better than to trace phone calls. He often sat head forward near his computer screens, endlessly staring at numbers and frequencies.

Sitting on Glenda's left side was Caitlin, aka Kitty, the last remaining member of the command team who, like Sept, disliked her given name and refused to even acknowledge it.

'The only traffic cams,' said Chen, 'are at two truck weigh stations west of Spokane and another past the Idaho border. We are hooked into both, and I have a tech team cleaning up the resolution. Still, not all that great. They are also trying to add facial recognition, but they say it is difficult through windows speeding along the highway.'

'It's a start,' said Brees. She turned to Glenda, 'If we're putting the effort into improving image quality on those two cams, I see no reason we should not begin monitoring more of them.'

'Agreed. Do it,' said Glenda.

'Our field unit is on its way to setting up portables on a pedestrian overpass on the east side of where Highway 2 and 90 merge. We should have a high-quality feed in about an hour.'

'Portables, plural?' asked Glenda

'Three as there are three freeway lanes.'

'Facial recognition?'

'They are going to live monitor the cameras. I'll get Chen to explain. She's talking to the field office and Bureau headquarters about the latest and greatest technologies.'

Chen proceeded to explain the technology to Glenda.

'Facial has not yet been very reliable, but the Bureau has been testing new systems constantly. It's getting better,' said Chen.

Glenda interrupted her and Chen compressed her mouth, producing fish lips. Then she raised her eyebrows, scrunched up her nose, and puckered her lips yet again. It was captivating to watch. Glenda resisted, trying to stay focused. 'What's the reliability percentage?'

'In recent tests, about eighty percent. But it will be less through car windows. Fortunately, the sun angle will be in our favor. After dark, we won't be able to get much with it.'

'Infrared?'

'Nope. Nothing that I can find that will help the three monitoring live images at night either. Doesn't help with the facial features.'

'Traveling at night is to her advantage.'

'Brees, check with the general to see if the CIA has any better facial recognition, they can send you. If we had more time, BWC might be able to suggest software improvements. Check with them anyway. Maybe we can use it before this is over with.'

'On it. Glad the weather is good for the next twenty-four hours. A cold front is moving in about this time tomorrow.'

CHAPTER 41

G lenda's monitor showed an incoming radio call from
Colonel Johnson.

'Hey, Jim"

'Hi. Anything?

'Nothing. No new sightings. I'll call you first if we do.'

'I know.'

Wait, hold on.' A few seconds passed and she came back
on. 'We have her just south of a town called Wilbur on
Highway 21.'

'How far south?'

'Not quite two miles. They're sending us copies of the
store's video.'

Glenda leaned forward and said to Chen, 'You're getting
a security video. Bring it up for all of us, including Colonel
Johnson.'

'Just far enough,' said Jim, 'to lend credibility to the
directional change.'

'Think it's a head fake?'

'No way to know.'

Glenda looked down at Chen, who nodded and shifted both upper and lower lips sideways, farther than it seemed they could go.

'Video's up,' she said.

They watched the video straight through.

When it was finished, Jim said, 'She looked up. She wanted to be seen.'

'Fast forward.'

Chen brought the video forward to where Najma walked up to the store's counter.

'Not too subtle,' said Glenda. 'Yep, she wants to be identified. There are trucks parked, and agents are asking whether anyone saw her or Pedro.'

Chen said, 'Another video from outside.'

They all watched. The video was intended to record cars and license numbers in case their owners left without paying. There was no sign of Pedro in the Bronco.

'We've got a trucker who said he remembers a blue Bronco. Here's the recording.'

'Sir, sorry to bother you. I'm from the old person's home in Wilbur. We have a dying woman and need to find her daughter and grandson. She's driving an older blue Ford Bronco. Have you seen her?'

'Maybe did. Admired that car. I didn't see who was driving, but man-oh-man one of the best off-road vehicles out there. Short wheelbase and tall clearance. Doesn't get high-centered.'

'Which way did she go?'

'South. Watched it all the way down the road.'

'You didn't see it come back north?'

'Nope, but I closed my eyes for a spell. Could have missed it if it did.'

When the recording stopped, Glenda said, 'She could still have doubled back.'

'South to the interstate is my guess, unless you get someone else noticing her going in another direction.'

'The drones are up now. I'll position one south where Highway 21 meets the main east-west freeway I 90. The GPS says she should be there in a few minutes. The agents interviewed him again, and the truck driver said she wasn't speeding. "Drivin' normal like," he said. We're heading to the airbase.'

'Probably a good idea,' agreed Jim.

'You think she will turn east?' asked Glenda, knowing it was a mindless confirmation to what both their guts were telling them.

'Thinking and knowing are two separate things. We will catch up with her because of the sheer manpower. We'll do it faster with lucky guesses.'

'You think we should cover the opposite directions?'

'No. We'll know we were wrong soon enough. If she doesn't go where we are predicting, we'll look in the other directions. Concentrate our efforts on disproving our existing hypothesis.'

'I don't want to make a mistake in judgment here, Jim.'

'We'll meet you there. What's your ETA?'

Glenda had gotten to know Jim well, especially during their weeks in South America where they'd worked closely in surroundings ranging from the Amazon to Rio. His saying he would meet her at the airbase was his way of agreeing with her that Najma was heading east.

'Fifteen hundred, assuming no interruptions. Tell the major to stay out of trouble.'

Jim clicked off. 'She says hi.'

'She didn't want to tell me herself?'

'She's busy.'

'My lady is very good, but she does have a lot to keep track of. Like a few hundred people.'

Jim didn't respond. His mind was working overtime. On the outside, he looked relaxed. Inside, his thoughts weighed possibilities and assessed probabilities. He tried to let his subconscious meld with Najma's. Run parallel to her synapses. Try to get inside her head. Hers was a brutally efficient single-minded psycho mind. How will she elude us? Straight up, I think. No hesitation. She'll stay ahead of us by not deviating and heading straight to her destination. With her wounds after our last shootout, she couldn't have gone far. Where?

Talking to Jim reminded Glenda of the past few weeks in Colombia, Rio, and the Amazon. The whirlwind events were still fresh in her mind. She started to recall how many skirmishes they had been in and immediately stopped. Focus, girl. You've got a job to do. Get your mind back to the present. You've a lot of resources at your disposal, more than I can remember anyone ever having. One lady. A psychopath with unique survival skills. She's escaped before. I can't let that happen again. She's my target, right? Should she be? Or should it be rescuing Pedro? The answer was simple. She declared out loud, 'Both. They're the same. Find one. Save the other.'

Glenda was back on point.

The helicopter blades started to turn. Jim pulled the door closed. It was a nice position. A good place for a house. He was always thinking about special living sites, both in the U.S. and in the rest of the world. Then he would return to Wolf Canyon Ranch. The same thought always gurgled up through the images of unique properties he occasionally found. None measured up to the ranch. *But can I remain there? Will Pedro be able to overcome the images of Heather's death?* As special as the ranch had been, they might eventually have to start fresh, somewhere without the nightmarish memories.

Jim would rescue Pedro. They would stay on at the ranch until they were both ready to clear their minds with a trip to Colombia and the Amazon. *Pedro will need that change as much as I will,* he thought.

He looked at the plotter. If Najma was driving on Highway 90, she would not be far from their current position.

He depressed his talk switch. 'Fly alongside Highway 90. Stay on the southwest side. Maintain three thousand feet above ground level.'

'If she's down there,' said Brush, 'she might spot the chopper.'

'On the off chance we do find her, we'll keep flying and get a drone overhead to track her. Lots of military choppers headed in and out of Fairchild.'

Brush nodded, 'Yeah, the risk is acceptable.'

They both moved over to the left side of the Huey.

The pilot said, 'I always liked that boxy Bronco model. Which year was it? It shouldn't be hard to spot. Not many of them around anymore.'

'Early '70s. It's better off-road than on the freeway, so she won't be going fast,' said Brush. 'Popular where I grew up. That and the Chevy Blazer.'

'To avoid cops, she'll be just below the speed limit,' said Jim.

'Fingers crossed you see her,' said Sheilla, who was

monitoring from the command center at the BWC but tied directly to both Jim and Glenda.

Glenda was constantly in contact with dozens of agents. After the Wilbur convenience store video, there were no sightings in any direction. She studied a map. There was a small airport to the west of Wilbur. Her breathing increased as she searched the map. The only roads to it were west of Wilbur from Highway 2. And there was a small road south of the convenience store that trailed off to the west, over a creek. From there, one could eventually return to the entrance road to the airport. What got Glenda excited was that it was so indirect, such a convoluted way to the airport, that none of her agents had investigated it. It would be just the thing Najma would do.

Glenda leaned over to Brees. 'Get people to the Wilbur Airport.' She pointed at the map.

Brees jumped up and walked the ten feet to Sept. 'Glenda wants agents to this airport ASAP.' Then she moved back to her chair and typed in the airport on her number two monitor. Glenda was talking again, then disconnected.

'It's perfect,' said Brees. 'Nearly 4000 feet. Good condition. Good for lots of airplanes. No tower, so no records. I have Sept getting our people to the airport. He'll monitor their progress. I gave it to him as I'm struggling with the feeds from the cams. I want them live to us.'

'You have time still before she could get to Spokane.'

'I like the airport idea. Perfect ruse. No one would think about going back to the airport by that out-of-the-way route. No one, including us. Until now, that is. If she flew, we could track her better in the air. It would be nice to catch her, nice to rescue the boy, and nice to be able to have a

Christmas. I didn't manage it last year. I like the lights and color and snow back home.'

'Only one more day… We better get used to having our holiday in he Bus.'

'Voyage to another universe. Christmas in our very own Battlestar,' said Brees with resignation.

Sept toggled the intercom connecting him with Glenda. 'First agents are pulling into the airport. They report no sign of the Bronco. There's four hangars.'

Glenda switched to the frequency the agents at the airport were using.

'One hangar is a crop duster,' reported an agent. 'No blue Bronco.'

Another voice reported nada behind the hangars.

'There are two locked hangars. There're enough cracks in the metal siding that we can see that the suspect's car is not inside.'

'A crop duster pilot said he had been here all day waiting for a part, and he saw no one matching the suspect's description and no sign of an old Bronco.'

'Damn! Where in hell is she?' said Glenda, sounding irritated.

'You want a cup of coffee?' asked Brees. 'It was a plausible idea. We'll spot her with the cams.'

Glenda looked at the GPS tracking map. 'Coffee sounds good. Another fifty minutes before she could make it to the cams.'

'We've got the problem solved and should have live coverage in a few minutes,' said Chen.

'Kitty, you want some coffee? Let's talk,' said Glenda.

'Green tea for me. I'll meet you at the table,' answered Kitty.

Glenda sat down, her mind instantly lost in thought, hardly realizing that Brees had handed her a cup of black coffee. Her thoughts cleared as Caitlin, the slender, five-foot-six dark-haired special agent who despised her name, walked to the small round table. Caitlin wore jeans and her usual oversized sweatshirt. For the last two days, she'd sported her favorite burgundy UCLA sweatshirt with large white letters on the front.

'What do you want to chat about, boss?'

'What are we missing here, Kitty?'

'Nothing. I can't think of anything we haven't discussed.'

'There's always something.'

'There are dozens of ways she could try to elude us. But with all the agents on the ground, she'll only elude us temporarily, I think. We're looking for tire tracks on every dirt road. This is probably the most extensive search in the history of the FBI.'

'Name the ways. Be creative. Don't worry about repeating. You might come up with something we haven't thought of.'

'Well, flying out is one. Bus, maybe. Hitching a ride. She could have had someone meet her, so she's in a separate vehicle or maybe in the back of a van or truck. Without roadblocks, we'd never catch her.'

'She's a loner. I don't think so. Keep going.'

'She could switch cars.'

'My guess is she will. The old blue Bronco's distinctive. She wants us looking for it.'

'She could be holed up someplace.'

'We've got dozens of agents checking every house and building along the routes,' said Glenda.

'Unless she's doubled back, and we've missed her. Okay. How about this? She disguises herself, maybe as a rancher. Like in what movie? Oh, yeah. *Victor Victoria.*'

'Psychologically, I don't think it's her style,' said Glenda.

'Here's one we've not discussed. She's got a truck and trailer stashed. It could be a big rig or big enough, like an eight-foot-wide by sixteen. Drives the Bronco in and hauls ass to wherever.

'You're right. We haven't discussed that one, and it's been done before. Could be a horse or cattle trailer. Get the word out to ask if any rigs or trailers have been parked and then picked up. Check cattle feedlots, auction sites, fairgrounds, trailer or truck sales,' said Glenda, as she drained the last of the coffee in one swig and walked back to her station. She tapped Brees on the shoulder before sitting down. 'Thanks for the coffee. Nice of you.'

'We'll have the live feed piped in shortly. What happened to the stud you overheard talking about the "senior agent with the big boobs?"'

'I try not to pay any attention. There are way too many of them out there. Misogynists who think we're drooling over them. Macho idiots who don't give us credit for what we can do. I don't miss them and don't have them with my new group.'

'Got a job for a black woman at BWC?'

'You mean a black woman with a brain. Brees, I'd take you on in a second. My group is a pretty small field operations unit, but I think the general and Colonel Johnson are always looking for competent people.'

Brees pointed at a video monitor. Static, a quick image of a freeway, more flashing and static, and then the image settled down to show close-ups of cars headed toward them.

Chen moved behind them. 'I'll help you get this organized for close-ups and getting the other two cameras up. I think the problem is going to be how fast they are moving when we get a close-up. I think we have an idea how to solve that.'

'Work on it. I've got some calls to make.'

'Jim, what's your ETA?'

'Fairchild's out the front window. We're landing at hangar eleven. The MPs will escort you when you arrive. No sign of a blue Bronco along Highway 90.'

'She could have taken Highway 2. We have cams set up just past where they merge.'

'Even though I think we are right about direction, she could have doubled back.'

'We're checking every property, road, house, barn, security cam, and garage in all directions from where we last spotted her. I think she picked the Bronco so we would look for it. But she isn't in it anymore. We're also checking for any trailers that could hold a car. If she's in a big rig, we'll never know. Hundreds of them.'

CHAPTER 42

Although she felt somewhat secure in the old beige station wagon, Najma didn't like driving on the main east-west highway while it was still light. Her hair tucked into her tattered rancher hat, she looked more like a youngish man than a woman. She was camouflaged. It was still a risk even with Pedro hidden in the back.

Better to keep going forward. Stalling was a losing proposition. Sooner or later, they would find the dead couple and Colbert's Bronco. Keep moving. It would be dark soon enough. She didn't need to stop for food or gas. Getting to the compound as soon as possible was the right choice. She looked at the speedometer as she merged onto Highway 90. Trucks crowded the road on both sides for as far as she could see. The lumbering Buick felt tiny next to the long-haul trucks. So as not to attract attention, she maintained a speed of seventy although she wondered if it was wise with so many vehicles passing her. Cars, tractor-trailers, and even an oversized bus emblazed with the name of a rock group, passed her.

If Najma had doubled back or had decided to take Highway 2 east, north of her current position, another bus traveling toward Airway Heights and Fairchild Airbase would have put Najma and Glenda Rose Stuart only feet from each other. Neither Glenda, Brees, Kitty, or Sept, ensconced inside *The Bus*, would have known Najma was within their reach, any more than Najma would have recognized them. Ironically, prey and predators, brushing so close to one another, would have remained as oblivious to each other as they currently were, separated by fifty miles of sagebrush and black lava fields.

As the roads merged toward Spokane, in approximately an hour, the separation would be less than seven miles from where the Huey waited for either news from Glenda or for her arrival. While Jim paced a hundred feet away from the helicopter, the pilots stood smoking, talking with Brush. The colonel sensed Najma would be located soon. As long as his and Glenda's guess was correct concerning Najma's direction, Fairchild was in the perfect launch position for all manner of air support. If they were wrong in their surmise, and she was headed west or in another direction, the Air Force could move them fast.

Jim could feel the first hit of adrenaline in his blood. With so many people chasing a lone fugitive, the probabilities of not finding her were slim. He would soon be facing her. Nevertheless, Najma's skills would likely postpone the eventual showdown. Jim didn't speculate who would win the confrontation. His real concern was keeping Pedro from harm. Najma was determined to inflict damage on Jim. If she failed to kill him, she would take revenge on Jim by taking his boy's life.

Jim visualized scenarios. In each one, Najma was

holding the child close. He pictured her executing Pedro before he could get near. The more he thought about it, the more convinced he was Pedro's execution would be part of her plan. He shifted his satellite phone to his left hand and punched in Sheilla's number.

'I need two of Neilly's watchers, Garcia and Roberta, as soon as you can get them.'

'On it.'

Jim disconnected. Up until now, he had concluded it would be a one-on-one face-off, and that Najma was setting the stage for such. He chastised himself for not thinking clearly. Jim had an emotional side, something he concealed from outsiders. He had always been able to separate that side from his prudent, more rational mind-set. It was what had kept him alive all these years. That and luck. *The unknown factor*, he thought.

What people saw of him was the rational part: cool, collected, and efficient. Some even viewed him as cold and lacking empathy. He found small talk a waste of time. What mattered to him were serious, significant issues. Not the scratches in life, not the broken bones, but problems that had a major impact. He solved those and dismissed the others. It had been his mission in life.

'Whatcha thinking, buddy?' asked Brush.

'Until a few minutes ago, I haven't been.'

Brush tilted an eyebrow and waited. Jim valued critical thinking. He was always hard on himself in the rare times when he fell short. 'Explain.'

'Najma will inflict as much suffering as possible.'

'It's her modus operandi.'

'I'm her target. She's unfulfilled until she kills me. First, she needs to see me suffer, and I failed to see that as anything other than her besting me and watching me die one-on-one. She's planning an encounter, but only after she's punished me by killing Pedro.'

Brush thought for a minute and then said, 'Makes sense. She will kill him when she knows you're watching. So, what's your plan?'

'Fluid. We don't know where we will catch up with her. I've requested Garcia and Roberta. Then, when we locate her, our advantage is that Pedro will be safe until I'm present. Roberta and Garcia find their spot before I make an appearance. We control the events rather than her.'

'They take her out if they have a clear shot?'

They looked at each other. Brush knew what he was thinking: the effect of Najma's head gushing blood and brains. Jim wanted Najma killed with as little impact on Pedro as possible.

Jim said, 'If it's the only way. No matter what I want.'

Brush understood Jim would not be able to rest easy until he had personally dealt with Najma. He also knew that his buddy would act so as not to endanger others.

They'd spent much of their adult life together. Long years when they'd been friends and partners in the army, in Vietnam, and on dozens of missions with the BWC. Surprisingly, Brush remained more complicated than Jim. He left much of the planning to others, especially to Jim. But he was the guy who was always there when the action started. To look at him, you would think he was the simple, straight-line shooter. And, in some ways, he was. But with one difference: he had never compartmentalized his thinking as Jim had. That made him both simple and complex.

The two parts of Jim's brain allowed him to approach

their battles with an unimpeded clarity. He naturally refrained from mixing the linear pragmatic side with its opposite, the circular emotional side. Brush had never specifically analyzed what he knew about Jim's processes. It was not his way. That was Jim's way. He only knew they both trusted each other with their lives. They both had unique skills. They both inherently understood their luck would someday come to an end.

CHAPTER 43

Sheilla had never before questioned her boss, Colonel Johnson. But with his request, she wondered why he'd requested only two of the snipers. Would it not make more sense to have all three of Neilly's watchers ready to be deployed?

She could have contacted Neilly directly, but she could just as well go through General Crystal. 'General, Jim asked for two of Neilly's watchers, Roberta and Garcia.'

The general hesitated briefly. He might have expected Sheilla to ask him to arrange a deployment under certain circumstances. This felt out of sync somehow. 'What's on your mind?'

Now Sheilla hesitated. Will Crystal had seen through her. She took a deep breath. 'Would it hurt to have the third sniper standing by, maybe even Neilly's full team?'

The general understood Sheilla was slightly off course, but he'd enlisted her to apply her brain. Since their first encounter in Seattle, she had far exceeded his expectations.

She had proved her worth and dedication. When she was still with the FBI during their first dust-up with Najma, he had witnessed her competence. After recruiting her, she had become a key member of their mission team.

'Neilly was deployed on a sensitive mission to the Middle East. Diverting even the two snipers puts Neilly and his team in danger, and Jim would not request it lightly. That's why he asked for two, not all three. Glenda has snipers from the FBI available as well as the FBI's best special weapons teams.'

'Oh, dear! I didn't mean to…' The general cut her off.

'Listen carefully. To my knowledge, you have never questioned the colonel or myself. You've discussed options with him and with me. You didn't this time because your mind is casting him as a victim. You don't want to inflict more pain. You might imagine that he is not thinking rationally. You are showing compassion and it makes you moral. That makes you good.'

'Ouch. I'm underestimating him. Falling into a learned behavior and letting it influence me.'

'That's about it. Jim is not typical. He will handle the pain. The loss of Heather only gives him more resolve about the worth of things remaining. It's a bad paraphrase of something from a philosopher I remember from my school days.'

Sheilla sat spinning in her chair. Her vision slightly blurred. A physically induced mantra. Her long auburn hair drifted out at each push as she turned around and around. She did not notice her door open.

'Are you dreaming or planning?' asked Katarina.

Sheilla blinked. Her twirling slowed when her foot stopped accelerating. 'They're the same thing for me. I'm not sure what the difference is when I'm focused on a problem.'

'Don't you get dizzy?'

'I used to wonder that too. When I learned to accept it and embrace the light-headedness, it feels like I enter a different space. What's up?

'Just thought I would stop by before our FBI briefing to see if you had any special thoughts on what I should say. There will be experienced profilers and a psychiatrist present. I don't want to mess up. I didn't mean to disturb you.'

'No worries.' Sheilla was thinking about what the general had just told her. In essence, he trusted her judgment. She was not to be dissuaded by old conventions from expressing what she thought. She shook her head. Katarina wondered what she was thinking.

'I just assumed that, because of Heather, Colonel Johnson might not be thinking clearly. I just found out I was wrong. We've both been given an opportunity here to be ourselves and do our jobs. I don't have any pearls of wisdom for you, Katarina. You are skilled and, as far as I'm concerned, as good as any of the FBI profilers we'll be talking to. You'll be fine. In fact, you'll be so good that I will have to worry they might try to steal you away to D.C.'

Katarina laughed, brushed her curly blonde hair back, and said, 'That'll never happen.'

'Fred's got everything set up. Let's pad our way down the hall.'

The door to the room that doubled as their conference

room and, less frequently, as their war room was ajar. If the ground effort caught up with Najma, the room would quickly convert to a command center. All the key members of the staff would be there: Captain Kramer, their lead analyst Fred, their IT manager, Katarina, their profiler Mark, Sheilla's administrator, and his assistant Bridgette. Only their two elite computer geeks—Misa and Vidya— might not be present. Their unique abilities meant they were given wide latitude to do as they pleased, and since they disliked meetings, they rarely attended them.

Sitting in the corner was a foot-tall artificial Christmas tree with miniature lights. A bittersweet touch, reminding them of the holiday. The members of the BWC mission team had accepted there would be no festivities this year. Celebrating would have to come after the mission had been completed. In many ways, this omission didn't bother those without family. Seasonal celebrations were just another reminder of their isolation from society.

It was not widely known that, along with Heather, Misa and Vidya had both been held captive by Najma and members of the Mexican cartel. They'd been forced to watch the rape and killing of two of their friends. Just as Martin was after his encounter with Najma, they were personally involved. They fervently wished for Najma to be eternally silenced.

Fred had set up live conferencing with the FBI and the CIA. Many of the participants knew Najma's basic background. Katarina was going to provide everyone with the details of her history. The participants were then charged with analyzing the pooled information and building a report about what she might do to stay hidden, what her intentions might be, and when cornered, what she might do. Profilers were not eager to work this fast. But when the head of CIA wanted their reports in the hands of the ground forces by midnight, they complied.

Sheilla had just talked to Martin Pearson. He had become her official counterpart at CIA. He had wondered whether, with so many people involved, the analysis would become diluted or compromised.

The two now talked quite frequently. Only Barbara, the lab manager at BWC, had noticed their mutual attraction. Sheilla normally didn't have time for romance and, before coming to the BWC, she had rarely met anyone who seemed worth knowing. She hoped the two of them would someday have another occasion to meet personally.

Sheilla had concluded that, before meeting Martin, she had been either too fussy or too independent. Gloria Steinem, an author she adored, had written a few short words that frequently ricocheted through her thoughts: 'A woman without a man is like a fish without a bicycle.' The emotions evinced while talking with Martin had shocked her. She was a woman, after all. And her mantra for years, she now replaced with another favorite Steinem quote: 'The truth will set you free, but first it will piss you off.' Later she would find out that Colonel Johnson had read Steinem's book too.

Katarina's presentation broke through her thoughts. It wasn't like her to be distracted like this. *Is this what a man will do to me?* she thought annoyed with herself. 'Born 15 November 1959, as near as we can determine, in Tashish, Iraq. We know nothing about her mother except reports that Najma's father beat her. Najma's physical description has been sent to all of you, along with any photos in our files. Note, she has a red, raised birthmark behind her right ear, five centimeters across and shaped like a starfish or a gecko's hand.'

A male voice cut in, 'We have this in the written document in front of us. Do you have anything new to add? Otherwise, I would like to get to it.'

Without missing a beat, Katarina said, 'I've learned several bits of information since the written report was sent, which I would suggest you have transcribed. So as not to waste time, I'll continue.'

On the monitors, Sheilla watched the man who had spoken. Seated with several other men, his cheeks turned red. Sheilla tried, with difficulty, to keep her expression neutral and not laugh.

'Father is Iraqi. Illiterate but wily. A leatherworker, but mostly involved in petty crime, drugs, and arms smuggling. Mother Turkish. Died when Najma was thirteen, beaten to death by the father. Najma was molested and beaten by her father. Father forced her to provide sex to his male friends for money. Father taught her to hunt. She learned to kill domestic stock with a knife at an early age. The father gave or sold her to a gun smuggler who taught her more about shooting and weapons. The smuggler raped and abused her. She killed the man with a knife after torturing him. Considers Pedro her son. Why she has this delusion is open to discussion. Could possibly be possession or transference or sexual.

'I'll summarize two other observations, first about her personality and second about her modus operandi. She displays typical psychopathic personality traits. Feels no emotions for anyone else. Preoccupied with herself. An egotist who never pretends to be other than what she is. Trusts and depends on no one. A loner. Has a complete disregard for human life and sees others as pawns or puppets to be used for her ends. Proud, ruthless, callous, remorseless, sadistic, motivated by power over other people and over life and death. She enjoys and seeks out sexual power. She is aroused by the primal connection between sex and violence. She has no ambition other than to assuage these desires. Bisexual. Unknown. Can control and ignore her physical pain.

'Najma is, first and foremost, concerned with self-preservation. Like a lioness, she stalks her prey, observes it, senses its weakness, then chooses her moment. She enjoys killing, as we know. Kills slowly, causing as much pain as she can, teasing her victims with hope, humiliation, and torture. Gets erotic pleasure from murder. A killer of exceptional brutality for whom the mental anguish of her victims is as important to her as their physical torment. Kills for the feeling of dominance it provides her. Wants to see into the minds of her victims, their struggle between hope and despair. Enjoys watching others' brutality and often encourages or orders others to rape and murder. Does not like to be bested and savors pitting herself against a capable opponent. Focused, professional, resourceful, skillful. A survivor and a contrarian. 'Any questions?'

An older male from the FBI's Terrorist Screening Center asked, 'We have a hostage situation. How will she react with the boy if she is cornered? It's the paramount question we need to answer.'

'Deputy Director of Intelligence, Martin Pearson. From my encounter with her, she is, as Ms. Jenson indicated in her report, a stone-cold assassin. She calls the boy her son but, if it were to her benefit, she would kill him without hesitation.'

'How is it you are alive, DDI Pearson?' asked one of the FBI agents who had not heard of Martin's capture by the cartel and subsequent torture by Najma.

'Luck.'

CHAPTER 44

Jim looked west as the sunset deepened. There was a thin crescent moon pasted on the dusky-orange sky. Between the horizon and the moon, a star-sized sphere of white: Venus. Then he noticed a smaller point of white not far from the crescent. It could only be Mars. He and Heather had often watched the planets on the ranch and in the mountains. The thought of never sharing with her again made him angry. He clenched his jaw and stepped into the helicopter, while Brush went back to talking with the pilots. In the growing darkness, the red ember of a cigarette danced like a firefly as one of the pilots waved his hand, recounting some past adventure.

Jim put his headset on just as Glenda said, 'Hi, "six."'

'What's up?'

'ETA eleven minutes. Pretty funny, Colonel. You knew what I meant by six. How d'you know?'

'Remember it from studying World War II tactics. Sometimes used in call signs currently, with the second in command called five. Also, an abbreviation for the pay grade of six or colonel.'

'Hmm. It had a nice ring to it when I read it. I thought it was only used a long time ago. Hold on, Jim.'

A few seconds passed. 'We found the Bronco in a garage south of Wilbur. An old couple dead in the kitchen. She has their car, a 1971 cream-colored Buick station wagon.'

The big old Buick cruised quietly down the middle lane of Interstate 90. As she passed through downtown Spokane, she held the speed at the reduced sixty miles per hour. She heard Pedro stir under the plastic tarp. Even if he woke up, he would be groggy. Since it was dark, she was not as worried about someone seeing him inside. *Better if he is unconscious.* He might do something stupid if he came to. *Like unlock the back door and try to jump out.*

She was now past the downtown and on a stretch of highway bordered by car dealers, truck stops, and fast-food joints. She shook her head at the American fascination for fat, and at those who would frequent a restaurant displaying a yellow and red clown. In a few minutes, she would pass the state border and be in Idaho. Pedro stirred again in the back. 'Khara, the little shit is waking up,' she said annoyed. A large sign announced "Welcome to Idaho, the Gem State."

She saw a truck weigh station but couldn't pull in, or even off to the side, as the station would have cameras. Passing a camera near the entrance, she tipped her head down and pulled the brim of her cap lower. Not far past the weigh station, there was a sign that said "Rest Stop." They would likely have cameras too, but she wouldn't go to the parking area. She would just pull in and off to the side.

She reached behind her and unlocked the rear door. More noises below the blue tarp. She pulled it up. His eyes were still closed. 'Thirsty, boy?'

There was no response, so she lightly slapped his cheek. Still nothing. She changed her mind and decided against giving him any more of the sleeping draft. Instead, she decided to tie his wrists and legs. She reached in front and pulled her rucksack back, opened it, and found what she was looking for: a plastic Ziploc bag. She took out four snap ties and a roll of duct tape.

If she were stopped by a cop or had a breakdown, she did not want Pedro crying out. It was still a risk, as he could kick and squirm, causing a noisy ruckus in the back. As a further precaution, she took out another two snap ties and secured the one binding his wrists and ankles to a metal protrusion under the front seat. She smiled. This would be his second lesson in pain management.

'Review the Spokane cams for the Buick. It should have passed, according to the GPS projection, between 1645 and 1745. We've adjusted the projections for a thirty-minute delay at the ranch house.'

'Chen, supervise reviewing cameras on all the highways. She could have turned back north, or gone west, or south. My guess still is she's going east.'

'What's your reasoning?' asked Brees.

'Idaho. Lots of survivalists with a disdain for government. A good place for her to have disappeared to over the last few months.'

'Same goes for eastern Oregon.'

'Could be. We cover all bases, but I will be surprised if we don't pick her up on the Spokane cams.'

'Assuming we do, or she has already passed Spokane, let's get a head start reviewing cameras available on the east side. Just like before, I want the ground teams to be behind her. I don't want to do anything to alert her of our presence.'

'Fax report on the Bronco,' said Chen.

Glenda started reading. No vehicle identification number visible. Stolen Washington license plates. A search through states with registered blue Broncos uncovered 1,621 of them. Three hundred were in Idaho.

'Brees, I want to increase the research on all likely places in Idaho and Oregon. Add in the search registrations of Broncos in survivalist areas.'

The command bus pulled to a stop about fifty feet from Jim's helicopter. Glenda put on a radio headphone and grabbed her sat phone, cell phone, and another hand-held radio. Jim and Brush were walking toward the bus as she climbed down the steps.

Brush walked directly to her with arms out and gave her a very tight hug.

'Disconnect, big guy. I don't want to make a scene.'

'What scene? It's dark and no big secret.'

'Nothing new,' said Glenda.

'You look wired enough to be the first to know,' said Brush.

'I need to be. We don't know where she is, but something tells me we're close. Let's talk through options in the bus. And for you, Major McGuire, Brees has kindly volunteered to put on a fresh pot of coffee.'

'How you fixed for food in that thing?' asked Brush.

'I knew you would ask, my hungry man. Plenty.'

'Good deal. We've got lots of fine gourmet edibles: box rations, peanuts, granola bars, chips, etc.'

'Same for us,' said Glenda, smiling as she lightly punched his shoulder.

'For just a second, beautiful, I believed you.'

As they arrived at the steps, a fuel truck pulled alongside. The bus driver said, 'Welcome to the Titanic' and then uncapped the fuel tank.

'We're fine on fuel. The Air Force already topped us off after we landed,' said Brush.

'Alternate transport here?' asked Glenda.

'Everything our hearts might desire,' said Jim. 'Helicopters, fast movers, scout planes.'

'I'm hoping for something on the freeway cams, and the drones should be picking up something soon too,' said Glenda.

They sat down at the round table. Brush sighed as he sat and took hold of the blue coffee mug emblazoned with gold letters—FBI.

'Help yourself to whatever you want in that cupboard or the fridge,' offered Glenda.

'Agent Stuart,' said Sept as he rolled his chair toward the back table. 'They've identified the car east on 90, entering Spokane at 1705 and thirty-nine seconds. The image is not clear. One driver, no passengers.'

Glenda looked at Chen who nodded and started giving orders to the tech teams. Kitty was doing the same with the ground teams.

'She's headed to Idaho,' said Brush.

'She's in Idaho,' added Glenda. 'We're only minutes behind her. Idaho is less than thirty minutes from the cams.'

'Question is, where in Idaho?' said Jim.

'We've lots of analysts working on the possibilities.'

Sept rolled his chair over and passed Glenda a fax.

She quickly scanned it and passed it to Jim.

'Most likely an area north of Coeur d'Alene. Adjusting the GPS plotter for the time she was sighted, Najma would already be to Coeur d'Alene on the interstate.'

Jim studied the map, 'It makes sense. She turns north on Highway 95.'

'The second drone should be there in a few minutes. Let's assume you are right, and she turns north, heading toward the preferred survivalist area south of Hayden Lake. We'll position the drone just north of where she could be.'

'Won't do much good at night,' said Brush.

'Technology is leapfrogging ahead. Our drone guys said that, with its dimensions and shape programmed in, the drone can find a specific type of car.'

'Car recognition software, like facial recognition, eh?' said Brush.

'You got it. We've only a few minutes. When we're fueled up, let's hit the road,' said Glenda. 'While we're waiting and face to face,' her eyes crinkled as she looked directly at Brush, 'Let's discuss scenarios again. We catch up to her while she's on the road. What action do we take?'

'Mostly what I have been thinking about,' said Jim. 'Boils down to two possibilities. Before she arrives at her destination or after. We need two very different solutions for each.'

'If she's headed to where you're suggesting, she is going

to get there very soon,' said Brush. 'If we get lucky and find her in the next few minutes, we can effect an ambush. It won't be easy in the dark.'

'I'd opt for that,' said Jim. 'It will be hard to get people positioned, but we will have the advantage in the dark. We spot them and get intercept teams in front of her. Pick our spot. Trap her. The main problem, we don't know Pedro's status. We don't know how she is holding him. My guess is if I'm there, she will kill him.'

'It fits her profile,' confirmed Glenda.

'If she gets to her destination, we lose a lot of control. She's had time to prepare. Less time if we take her out on the road.'

'What if we catch her,' said Brush, 'while she is slowed down like at a stop or construction zone and we snipe her.'

'What if she has rigged Pedro up with a self-detonating device?' asked Glenda.

'Whatever we do, it's a gamble,' said Jim. 'We have to be ready for all options and take them as they come.'

Najma reached the freeway exit for Highway 95 north. She turned and pulled over to the side. The more time passed, the closer she got to what had been her home for the last several months. She understood that, as the clock moved forward, her pursuers would be catching up with her. She reached into the rucksack and down near the bottom, she found three grenades, which she set next to her. Then she pulled out the micro-Uzi and set it on the seat. Although close to her destination, she didn't relax. Instead, she became more alert.

She planned to strap two cell phone detonated explosive devices on the boy as soon as she arrived at the compound. The vest's tiny charge would have just enough power to kill Pedro. Even if Najma were within a few feet radius of him, she would be spared.

Najma would use the boy as a decoy to lure the colonel inside. Then she would have her way with her nemesis, holding the detonation trigger while the boy watched. Would Jim be as aroused as she? Leave his seed inside her? She had never had an orgasm with a man except for sitting atop the Viking vet. She remembered it fondly. Seeing the fear in the vet's blue eyes, while at the same time imagining the colonel's eyes fade into darkness.

She held her hand over her breast. She pinched a nipple and could feel it grow hard. She shouldn't waste precious time, but she couldn't stop massaging, stroking, kneading . . . losing herself in thoughts of the colonel. Faster now. She could feel herself on the verge. Pressing. Pausing. Teasing herself until she could no longer stay the pulsations. Her hips thrust up into the steering wheel. She closed her eyes and sat still for a few seconds before putting the car in drive and accelerating onto the road.

Jim could not know that there would be two devices. After having seduced the colonel, Najma planned to retreat a short distance away and detonate the smaller bomb as the colonel watched. Naturally, the colonel would rush to what was left of Pedro. Then, from yards away, Najma would set off the larger device, thereby assassinating the colonel. She didn't want to kill him that way. The second bomb was simply insurance. A precaution in case she had failed to kill him with her knife. What she really wanted was to use Pedro to seduce the colonel and then to kill them both.

Jim would see his boy die. And one way or another, Najma would see Jim, her archenemy, die. She had been assured by an explosives expert that the small detonation would not set off the larger one in a chain reaction. After having murdered the boy, she wanted to see the effect on Colonel Johnson. She wanted to see his eyes. Either way, she would do what the situation called for. She would triumph. In killing this man, she would have conquered her nemesis.

CHAPTER 45

Najma proceeded north on Highway 95. Having checked the odometer when she left the freeway, she found she had driven six miles, leaving approximately thirteen to go. A mile a minute. Her pursuers had thirteen minutes to catch her.

~

'The drone is moving along Highway 90 going east. It will be at the junction of 95 in about four minutes. What do you want to do, Colonel?'

Jim and Glenda were maintaining constant contact on a dedicated frequency.

'According to the plotter, where would Najma be if she continued east?'

'About five miles ahead.'

'Move the drone ahead ten miles and come back to Junction 95. Let's eliminate her heading straight. If we don't spot the Buick, then north up 95.'

'We're on the same wavelength. It will take about four minutes. I've started it already. Thanks to another nifty little program from Misa and Vidya, I can call for a drone, mere moments in advance, by simply selecting a destination, clicking my requested start point, and dragging the cursor along the route I want. Brad then executes it. I can't control the drone directly. You sure it's worthwhile to do this and not just head up Highway 95?'

'No. Could be a mistake. But it seems prudent to eliminate her going that way first. How far north would she be on your plotter?'

'Eight miles north of the junction. Near a place called Hayden. According to the briefs I'm receiving, it's a hotbed for preppers.'

'New term for the survivalists, eh?'

'Turn the drone up 95. If we can't find her there, we can check the other roads.'

Najma passed the abandoned fun park before turning left to the Coeur d'Alene Airport, better known by the locals as Pappy Boyington Field. Two minutes later, she pulled up behind a long aluminum gooseneck stock trailer hooked to an '80s blue and silver Chevy pickup. She jumped out and lowered the ramp. Moments later, she set the parking brake and squeezed out the Buick's door. Outside, she raised the ramp and flipped the hinges that secured it. Almost there. She looked up at the stars. The Milky Way was brilliant. There was little moonlight, but with all the stars, a ghostly silver lit the frosted grasses and patches of snow. High mounds of dirty slush lined the parking area. It hadn't snowed for days, but she knew there was a storm front moving in from the west.

'The drone is flying north to south on 95, starting from farther north than she could be at eighty miles per hour. Our best guess is she is staying right on the speed limit,' said Glenda. 'That only puts us four minutes ahead of her.'

'There are not many secluded spots to land our bird. I think we'll go to the Coeur d'Alene Airport and set down,' said Jim. 'We'll stay up for another fifteen minutes.'

'Risky if we are right about where she is heading. A local will spot us and word will get around.'

'See any alternatives?'

'No.'

'If we don't have her, she has likely gone another direction. If she's headed to survivalist land, she is close and won't likely switch cars again. We need to stay close.'

'Could have pulled under cover to wait for a while,' said Brush.

'Doubt she will,' said Jim. 'She's smart enough to know she is being tracked. She would lose her advantage if she sits while we catch up to her. She lives nearby. This is where she has been hiding.'

'How far are the ground teams from the junction of Interstate 95 and 90?'

'Approximately an hour. They are working their way in this direction. Not leaving anything to chance.'

Brush looked over at Jim in the dim red night-light and raised his eyebrows as if to say, what's next?

'Drone has passed all logical points on Highway 95.'

'Fly over the airport,' said Jim.

'Will do. Damn it, Jim. I was sure I was right.'

'Just because she's not on the road doesn't mean she's not there. She's there. It makes sense. We just don't know where,' said Jim.

The key to the Chevy truck was under the floor mat, as Colbert had said. Najma pulled back onto Highway 95, turned north for a short distance, and then went east on a road heading toward English Point. Three miles down the road, she made a left on a gravel road and drove for seven miles before turning into a gravel drive with an orange steel ranch gate. A heavy chain and lock secured it. The hinged side of the gate also had a heavy chain and lock.

An attached sign warned "NO HUNT" in rough hand-painted bold characters on splintered wood. It was the same sign she remembered from when she had arrived in the Mexican's black popping machine. Another plastic store-bought sign demanded "No Trespassing."

With the hand-lettered sign, the preppers intended a clear message: we have guns, we're uncouth, and we will shoot you. The message also conveyed that its authors were not educated. Backwoods Neanderthals that were not to be messed with. Otherwise, the notice might have read "No Hunting" rather than "NO HUNT" in dripping black letters. The chain and the lock on the hinged side also had a meaning. The experienced survivalists and ranchers knew that, with a simple wrench, one could loosen the hinge bracket and slip the gate off the hinge in a few seconds.

Najma opened the gate, and a bell rang nearly two miles

away in the main house as well as in the underground bunkers of the compound. Several pairs of eyes looked at monitors with multiple images on each and noted who it was and that the gate was closed and secured behind her. Some were not too happy about her return. Most wished she had never moved in and had hoped she wouldn't come back.

Glenda Rose Stuart sat staring at her computer monitors. They'd lost her. They had checked all truck weigh station cameras on the freeway, gas station cameras, even some security cams at rest stops. Hundreds of ground staff were checking houses, garages, and anywhere that a car could be parked or abandoned. The drones had flown along all routes and found nothing. Satellite images, when available, showed nothing. The last sighting was in Spokane and then at a truck weigh station, which showed her driving east on Highway 90. *Damn, damn, damn. I can feel her. She's close,* thought Glenda.

Glenda needed a new idea. She said to Jim, 'If she has stopped, the ground agents will overrun her. We'll lose the element of surprise.'

'She knows we're coming after her. She doesn't have any idea what the task force size is or how close we are.'

'Or aren't.'

'Perhaps it doesn't matter as long as we don't catch her before she gets where she is going.'

'Where do you think that is?'

'She's a survivor. I think she's drawn a line. Best guess is she wants me and is willing to sacrifice whatever it takes to accomplish that. She won't care who gets hurt. There's no surprise possible anymore. Get the agents into the open and focus on interviewing every person in this area. The airport is our command center. It's only a slightly different game now.'

'Okay, Colonel.'

'Sheilla, get Misa and Vidya on the line.'

'No need, Colonel. We wrote a little program that sends an alert to our monitor if our names are mentioned when you're using the BWC comms,' said Misa.

'The situation is this. Najma has disappeared. Both Glenda Rose and I, without any real evidence, are guessing she's staying in Idaho. Personally, we both think she's close to our current location near Hayden. If that is true, best guess is she's gotten in with a survivalist group.'

'Makes sense. They're secretive. Good place for her to hide.'

'I'll buy that,' said Vidya.

'What can you do to find her?' asked Jim.

'I want to talk to Jason and Jake at Huachuca. Call you back in a few minutes.'

'If it were only Najma, we could storm in and flush her out.'

'It's not the first time we've dealt with a hostage situation.'

'Jim, we're going to work on some other ideas,' said Misa, 'but to start, Jason and Jake are going to tap into the phones and Internet at a store that seems to be the hub for local gossip and merchandise. Vidya and I are going to explore some other options.'

'Well, we don't know for sure, but we're thinking some survivalist types might have satellite Internet and TV. If they're as paranoid as we believe, they may have security cameras connected through Wi-Fi.'

'Even if you can tie into them, how many people will you need to monitor multiple sites?'

'We think just the two of us. I'll keep you advised, of course, if we can do what we want. And, to answer your question, if there are multiple sites, we'll try to monitor them with facial recognition. The same one that we worked on for the cams on the highway. It's pretty primitive, but it will alert us if someone with her general facial characteristics shows up on a cam. It will save the screen image, and then we will be able to review the saved stills to verify it's her.'

'Thanks, Misa,' said Sheilla. 'This sounds like maybe the best option we have of finding her without putting Pedro in danger.'

CHAPTER 46

When Jim and Brush landed, the Coeur d'Alene Airport was full of the night's quiet. A billion stars lit the crisp air. As the evening advanced, cars, agents, fuel trucks, and planes filled the stillness with activity.

The bus had arrived. Jim, Brush, and Glenda sat at the round table in the back. Brush was content to have Glenda close. What more could he ask for on Christmas Eve? He was as relaxed as Jim and Glenda were tense. The two could feel they were close to finding their quarry.

Misa, Vidya, Jason, and Jake worked tirelessly, refining computer programs to track Najma. The drones had been fueled and were searching the area with no results.

~

Jason Colbert walked toward the Quonset hut with mixed emotions. His feelings toward Najma had always been conflicted. He liked her. He wanted her. Logic, however, told him he was being foolish. Deep down, he knew she was trouble.

She had not told him why she needed his blue Bronco, only letting him know she would be gone a few days. Colbert could see Najma squeezing into a car inside the trailer. Then she backed the car—not his car—out of the trailer and stopped. Instinctively, he knew he would never see the Bronco again.

Colbert was a hardened combat veteran and had enjoyed few romantic relationships. He hated the tingles she caused in him. Along with most at Bright Light, he had hoped she would never return.

He opened the door, pulling her out and into an embrace. She playfully pushed him away, and walked to the rear door of the car, opened it, and pulled back a tarp.

'You have a surprise for me back there?'

Najma didn't answer and, a few moments later, pulled out Pedro, squinting at the bright lights in the Quonset hut. 'Straighten up, boy. You are looking at a real man, not some play colonel.'

'Colonel? Who the heck is the boy?' asked Colbert.

Najma looked him in the eye and said, 'He is my son.'

'No, I'm not,' said Pedro, who received another backhand.

'You've got some explaining to do, woman.' Colbert took hold of Pedro's wrists. Pedro tried to pull back, but Colbert was too quick and strong. Pedro winced.

The deep grooves from where the boy's hands had been restrained were an angry red. Colbert turned toward the house and motioned for someone to come out.

'I'm going to get him attended to.' He wiped a smudge from Pedro's cheek, and Pedro didn't pull away. The man looked odd with his full brown beard, but Pedro was inexplicably drawn to him. Perhaps he sensed a similarity in this man's bearing to his adopted father. Perhaps anyone seemed better than Najma.

'Phil, find a warm body and get the truck and trailer back to the airport. They could fly in with the shipment at any moment.'

'We're getting nothing,' said Glenda. 'Agents are canvassing all stops. We're monitoring all cams. Agents are out in the open now, interrogating cashiers at markets, truck stops, and airports as well as traffic controllers. We're monitoring all radio frequencies. The BWC should be back to us with communications in and around Hayward. The state and local police have been alerted with a "do not apprehend" if they spot her.'

'We sit and wait,' said Jim. 'I'm going to review the FBI's reports on survivalists.'

'Chen and Kitty have been sifting through them. Oh, one other thing. We're looking for any murders committed in the last several months. We're talking to the sheriff, but even law enforcement here seems to want to keep their distance from anything federal.'

'My guess,' said Brush, 'if she's here, she will know soon enough.'

Colbert looked down at Pedro as they walked toward the main house. Bambi met him about halfway. She smiled at

Pedro. 'We have a visitor, and I'll bet you're hungry? Thirsty too?'

Pedro still wasn't sure if these people were friends. He turned and looked back at Najma who was staring at them. *If Najma belonged here, how could these people be good?* he asked himself. He nodded. He was very thirsty and hungry.

Bambi reached down and took his hand. 'Well, let's go cook something up for you. What do you like to drink?'

'Fanta,' answered Pedro.

'We have that and also some Christmas cake for dessert.'

'No sign of her.' Glenda shook her head.

'That means she's probably close. She might have switched vehicles again. Your agents could have missed her. Probability is, they haven't found out anything because she's right here under our noses with preppers.'

'Misa, Vidya, and our Huachuca boys said they have tapped into most communications. Some security systems were tied into Wi-Fi. Some have records of movement archived and they will be able to get to them. They're getting voice prints for Najma and adapting some programs to scan calls.'

'Shut-eye time,' said Brush.

Glenda shook her head but smiled at him.

'Can't do anything, honey. Best get some sleep.'

'Go on, you big lug, I know you need your beauty sleep.'

Jim sat at the table and went through reports on the preppers in the area. The FBI had been keeping records for years. There'd been one standoff not far from here three years ago. The Bus's generator hummed softly. Keys tapped. After several hours, he couldn't keep his eyes open. He woke up when Brees accidentally dropped her coffee mug.

She looked apologetic and said, 'Sorry, sir.'

Jim looked at his watch. Roy would be up. With cow calving, he may have been up all night. If there were premature calves, they would suffer from the cold weather. It did not make for restful winter nights. Roy checked in on all the cows every two hours through the night. His only respite was if Jim or Ben helped. And in the past, Heather and Duane. Shuskin and Ben helped during the day, but Roy didn't yet know how much he could trust the old man.

'Didn't wake you, did I?'

'Nah, Jim. I wish that were possible this time of year,' said Roy with a little chuckle. 'Did you find our would-be cowboy yet?'

'Not yet. How are things with the ranch?'

'All good. Lola and Shuskin are spending a fair bit of time keeping each other company. Lola still grumbles about him. Don't think those feelings run very deep. She pretends, but I think she is fond of the old coot.'

'She needs someone to cook for, or she's not happy.'

'Yep, and the old guy brings in firewood and is helping with the cows. I'd sort of like it if Ben stayed up there at the house.'

'Do what you think is best. Ben can have my bed. It will give you more on-site help. If we're lucky, I hope to be back with Pedro soon and be able to give you some relief.'

'Sounds like it's as good as it can get then.'

'If this is like other years, there's more cows going to plunk out their young ones tonight and tomorrow. Sometimes I think they know a thing or two and are trying to give me Christmas presents.'

'Holidays for us are never what we expect them to be.'

'Iffen I can, Loretta and Betty Lou are going to have Ben drive them up tomorrow. It looks like Christmas dinner with them two, Ben, the old man, and Lola. Six altogether. Guess I'll get to eat well. You okay with that?'

'Just fine, Roy.'

'Of course, that's just when a calf 'll wanna pop out. Still, lots of leftovers. Don't you worry none about a thing. You just take care of finding that little guy, and then you need to take care of him. We can handle the ranch.'

'I'll call as soon as we have him. Lola, Ben, and Shuskin are going to want to know he's safe.'

'You close to finding her?'

'I think so. Talk later, Roy. Say hi to Ben and Lola for me. Thank them, if you would.' Then he paused and added, 'Same for Shuskin. Heather saw something in him and I'm starting to see that she was right.'

Jim stood, stretched, and walked outside. The first hint of dawn hovered on the horizon. A drone was silhouetted on the runway. Warm light slipped through the cracks and small curtains of portable trailers that had been airlifted in throughout the night.

Jim looked at the mass of buildings and at the few people walking between them. Beyond, there was a large marsh on the northeast side of the runway. It was partially covered with gray-white swirls of ice formed by the water's movement as it froze. The surface textures, illuminated by the increasing light, reflected the never-ending freeze-thaw cycles. Tufts of tawny stalks were trapped in the ice. On the far side, birches emerged like white slashes against dark green-needled trees. About a mile away, he could make out a house near an opening. A small flicker from a window, a lantern, or maybe a flashlight appeared and quickly disappeared.

At one a.m., the town's chief of police had arrived for a briefing with Glenda. He arrived with one deputy, having left his other deputy in town. There was no complaint from the sheriff about jurisdiction. The overwhelming number of people, the size of whatever this was, told him it would be futile to argue.

The drone left the runway. Its objective: to fly grids covering a square twenty miles by twenty miles. The entry roads to the airport were now blocked and guarded. Since the operation had gone public, the press would be arriving en masse.

Jim slowly inhaled a deep breath of the cold morning air. He looked at his satellite phone and decided to call Maria Dakine. He knew that she was in touch with the BWC and that the inoculations were proceeding with the FARC. Without having to ask, he also knew that Maria was leaving him to concentrate on finding Pedro.

'Nice to hear from you, Colonel. Merry Christmas, by the way. Any news?'

'Nothing yet, but Merry Christmas to you too. How are you doing? The FARC cooperating?'

'They're great. I even had a chance to go to Bogotá. I really like this country and its people. Don't concern yourself about anything here. It took a little time for everyone to start trusting each other. WHO, the FARC, and the government have found a common cause. It's gratifying.'

'See much of Jago, Lobo, or Cherry?'

'All the time. Cherry has decided to be my protector. She can be a bit, a bit…'

'I understand what you mean,' said Jim.

'The thing is, it's as if we're becoming close. She wants to know all about America and other places. She asks about Brush too.'

'You can tell her that Brush is fine and so is Glenda.'

'Yeah, well, she knows that Brush was never in reach. She just likes him. I think she sees him as a kindred spirit. She asks about you too. And I think she and Jago are going to stay an item.'

She paused. 'We're all so sorry about what happened. I still can't believe it.'

'Thank you, Maria.'

'I gotta go. Tell Ben hello if you have a chance. I enjoyed entertaining him on the boat.'

'When we find Pedro, I'll bring him down to visit.'

'I'd like that. Oh, and by the way. I think another lady would too.'

'Who?'

'Angel has been here. I guess she is first lady of the Ecuadoran government now. For her, it's been quite a few months, rising from errant daughter to head of state. I think she wants to, um, keep in contact with what is going on with you.'

Jim sighed.

'I know what Heather meant to you, to me too. And I know that Angel doesn't understand.'

'She's done well. Pulled off quite a trick in Ecuador. Talk later.'

'Bye, Jim.'

CHAPTER 47

Just before the sun broke onto the horizon, Colbert started the well-used yellow 580 B backhoe. He had an affinity for the machine. It was over twenty-five years old and was in meticulous running order. The scars were evidence that it had performed many duties over the years. He drove it out of the Quonset hut and onto a narrow track. Bruce followed along in the Buick. They moved slowly along the track and through the trees to the edge of a small meadow.

Colbert left the track and proceeded a short distance along the edge of the trees on the west. That side received sun most of the day, so the ground was less frozen. The long grasses were brown and bent. Skillfully, Colbert lowered the outriggers and extended the arm, curved the bucket back toward him and, pushing as carefully as he could, scraped a layer off the frozen top. He scraped squares of the grass and weed into the bucket and set them out in the meadow. He raised the outriggers and moved back several feet, continuing until he had exposed a sod-free rectangle—twelve feet wide by twenty-five feet long.

The meadow contained few rocks. Still, there was always the possibility of a large boulder below. He extended the arm out straight and dug the bucket into the dry soil. His leather-gloved hand pulled two levers simultaneously, one with his fingertips and the other with his palm, while his foot pushed on the left pedal. At the same time, the arms rose and started to close. The arm swung to his left, while the bucket continued to rise. Colbert looked completely relaxed while the arms extended, closed, the bucket scooped, and the contents released under the trees.

The size of the hole increased to nearly eight feet deep. He had moved to the other end as the arms could not reach the full length of the grave. He stopped and nodded at Bruce, who backed up the car, stopping inches from its future grave. Colbert couldn't help himself. He jumped down and walked to the Buick.

'My dad had one of these. A pretty fancy wheel back in the day. Kind of hate to bury it.'

'It's in good shape too. Almost a classic.'

'I'm tempted, but we can't take a chance. Don't know what my lady did to get it, and I still don't have a clue about who the boy is.'

'That woman is going to cause you trouble. We all know it.'

Bruce disliked her more than most. He tolerated her begrudgingly because she had become Colbert's woman.

Bruce hooked up a chain to the shiny chrome bumper of the old Buick Electra. He then walked the chain around the hole and hooked it to the front bucket. Neither of the men noticed the speck 20,000 feet above.

Colbert sighed and walked back to his machine. He tightened his jaw and it backed up. He lifted the chain as high as he could into the air, just enough to lift some of the weight off the station wagon. The car's back wheels went over the edge. As he continued back, small amounts of dust rose as the dirt was pushed into the car's grave. A few seconds later, the front wheels went over the edge. The front followed, dropping into its final resting place.

Colbert wondered whether he might dig it up sometime in the future. *I should have brought tarps*, he thought. He began scooping buckets of dirt and dumping them on top of the Electra. When he had the right amount, he skillfully moved the bottom of the bucket across the surface, smoothing out the soil. With Bruce helping on the ground, they moved the half-frozen sod back on top.

'Pretty fair job,' said Bruce.

'We need some snow cover and by spring, it will be hard to detect. Take the truck and trailer back. Sweep the inside. I'll finish up here, scattering the left-over dirt under the trees.'

'You could scatter some branches and maybe slide over some leaves.'

'I'll do that, and then we can get breakfast. Maybe some eggnog.'

Marcy Williams was beside himself. He lived on the other side of the airport. While driving into his supply store, he couldn't help noticing the barricade on the airport road. He pulled up to see what was going on. The two men stationed there told him a private plane carrying a dignitary needed to make an emergency landing.

Marcy looked around and counted dozens of parked vehicles. Emergency landing. How did all these vehicles get here so fast? The story did not add up. He dialed the police station to talk to the chief. The only person present, though, was the radio operator who doubled as a secretary-receptionist.

'Jennifer, Marcy here. Hi.'

'After all these years, I recognize your voice, Marcy. I expect you calling this early is not a social call?'

'You're right. What I want…'

'I know you want to know why the FBI is out in such big numbers.'

'Yeah. I stopped at the airport. It's blocked off, and they gave me some cock and bull story about an emergency landing.'

'Well, I got nothing I can tell you.'

'You mean you don't know or won't say?'

'Both. Now I got work to do.'

While she didn't tell him anything, she had mentioned Feds were all over. He called Fred, who lived several hundred yards from the other side of the airport.

'Good morning to you.'

'You too. Bet you're calling about the hubbub at the airport.'

'Yeah. What's going on?'

'Don't know and ain't none of my business. Chief didn't say. Big sortie, though. Feds, I think.'

'Did you see an emergency landing?'

'Nope. Lots of planes landing, though.'

Marcy was getting worried. He had lots of friends and customers who could be on the wrong side of the government. He decided to start calling to warn them and, at the same time, to wish them happy holidays. His fourth call was to Bright Light. To Colbert.

'You heard about the Feds?'

'What Feds?'

'There's a bunch of them at the airport. Looks like they've set up a command post there.'

'Don't know why they're there, huh?' asked Colbert.

'Nope. Just letting you know.'

The hair on the back of Colbert's neck started to prickle. Najma. It must be Najma. What had she done during the last couple of days? Did she kidnap the boy? Even if she had, there would not be a big operation like the one Marcy described. He called Fred.

'Why's everybody calling me fer? I ain't got nothing to do with nothing.'

'Calm down, old man. Tell me what you see at the airport.'

'A bunch of em.'

'Planes. Yessiree! Heli birds about a dozen. Lots of funny-looking trailers with antenni's. Maybe aliens. A giant RV.'

'You see any uniformed men? Army?'

'Nope.'

'How many of them?'

'Don't know. Lots. I got things to do.' And he hung up.

Colbert ran his fingers through his thinning brown hair. Not looking into Najma's background had been a big mistake. He wondered once if she was law enforcement but then dismissed the thought. His group had strong anti-government views. They might have some illegal armament, but nothing that would warrant an undercover agent infiltrating the compound.

He stood and walked back toward their room. *I need to know. I need to find out her story.*

CHAPTER 48

G lenda opened the door of the Bus and yelled at Jim. 'We got the car.'

Suddenly, everyone was in high gear. Researchers were digging into ownership records of the property where the drone had spotted the car. Sheilla had passed the word to Misa. Both Misa, Vidya, Jake, and Jason dropped what they had been doing and focused on finding out the sort of communication links they could hack into at Bright Light. The FBI had found archived reports on Colbert's group and was compiling dossiers of members and their affiliations.

'Used parts have been delivered for a Ford Bronco. Same location,' said Chen.

It would only be a matter of minutes before the fax machine spewed paper nonstop. Within two hours, the full force of the FBI, the CIA, the National Security Agency, and the BWC produced a massive amount of information.

Jim and Brush sat at the table, looking at a detailed map of Colbert's compound. The drone had provided video of the cream-colored Buick Electra pulled into its resting place.

The distance was too great and the angle not good enough to discern the license plate, but no one doubted it was the right car. The video images showed the backhoe cleaning up the burial site and driving back up the small road to the Quonset hut. Two men then left the Quonset hut and walked to a house about a hundred yards away.

A thought crossed several minds. *Had they buried anyone with the car?* The agents hadn't uttered their thoughts aloud.

'Pedro's not in the car,' said Brush.

'It would make no sense to take him and then bury him.'

'What do you think, partner?'

'Sort of in favor of you and I and the two snipers working our way in.'

'Glenda told me the FBI's special TAC forces are good. As good as anyone,' she said.

'I'll meet up with them while you get our gear checked.'

Jim opened the door. Ten feet away, Roberta and Garcia walked toward him, stopped, and saluted.

Jim smiled and returned the salute. 'Nice to see you two again.'

'Wish it were under different circumstances, sir,' said Roberta.

'I'm on my way to talk with an FBI SWAT team. Tag along and tell me what you think of them.'

'It shouldn't take long,' said Garcia. 'Those guys are always dressed up like Darth Vader. Maybe they're better than the local cops, but I bet not by much.'

'Keep an open mind,' said Roberta. 'We're a little short-handed.'

'Better off that way.'

'There's twenty-plus in Colbert's compound. Some are

former Army Special Forces,' said Jim. 'You two up to speed?'

'Got the briefings on our flight here,' confirmed Roberta.

'We'll make this a short meet. Brush is loading a chopper. Sheilla set up your comms?'

'Yep, we're live.'

'Let's walk. We see what's up with this FBI group and then get your gear. Our chopper's close to the command bus. We've got an insertion point picked out. A small meadow close to eight klicks from the buildings. We're going to make a wide circle and come in from the north, so you'll have time to get the gear organized in flight.'

'Roger that,' said Garcia. 'I'd be better off checking the gear now. Roberta has the open mind.'

Roberta shook her head. 'He's right. One of us is enough to assess the FBI's black outfit, boys and girls. Now that we know what we're planning, Garcia might want to switch some things around.'

'Meet you at the chopper,' said Jim. Garcia walked away with his Barrett snuggled in his arm. On one hand Jim understood and on the other, he had to laugh. In the field, Garcia always kept his sniper rifle close

Several minutes later, 'Not what I expected,' said Roberta.

'Sometimes our expectations get in the way of clear thinking,' said Jim.

'They were more like us. No macho types. It also made me happy to see they have four women. Making a guess. High skill levels.'

'FBI thinks of HRT as special SWAT. They started out as a hostage rescue team. Their primary mission now is tangling with terrorists on U.S. soil. I've heard they're good,' said Jim.

'I give them a green light. I trust them for backup,' said Roberta.

The Huey flew southwest from the airport, steadily gaining altitude. After ten miles at over 8,000 feet, it turned north. After another fifteen miles, it flew south toward a small wilderness area to the east of English Point where Bright Light was located. The maps had shown no buildings north of the compound. Nevertheless, the pilot had been instructed to make a steep descent, starting just ten klicks north of their insertion point.

LZ's in sight. They would spend as little time as possible unloading. They were wearing tan camouflage fatigues. Brush jumped out alongside Roberta. Jim passed their gear out to Brush while Garcia did the same to Roberta. They cached some of it near the drop zone. On the flight, the team had divided up extra ammunition and supplies they would leave as backup on the off chance they retreated. It was an extra precaution that had proved useful in the past. To monitor the compound, Roberta and Garcia had positioned themselves about a football field apart.

Having slung on their seventy-pound packs, they moved below the top of the ridgeline above the meadow. Jim pulled out wide-angle ten-power binoculars and began to scan south toward the compound. Without the aid of binoculars, Brush did the same. Roberta and Garcia used their sniper scopes to scan as far as they could see.

None of them expected surveillance cameras this far away from Colbert's compound. Still, they would exercise caution in their approach. At this point, they were more concerned about humans in the woods whose heat signatures would be blocked from the drone. As they neared the compound, they would be increasingly concerned about defenses, cams, and people.

In the Huey, they had decided on the approach they would use. Jim and Brush would stay together. So would Garcia and Roberta. As they neared the compound, both snipers had selected positions they would move to from satellite images. They would adjust as needed. Nothing ever looked exactly the same on the ground. The dense forest surrounding the compound required them to get close.

The team assumed that, with the training Colbert and his three SF members had undergone, they would be worthy opponents. They might also have wireless cams or listening devices. If camouflaged, they would be difficult to spot on the ground. Jim hoped that Misa and Vidya would be able to obtain access to Wi-Fi connected devices. If so, the locations of such devices could be determined. Jim would prefer to avoid them, not disable them.

'Sheilla, radio check?'

'Loud and clear. We have your location and will track you. The second drone is above. You will have continuous coverage. Infrared shows no one between you and the compound. There are currently two heat signatures outside their buildings. We've tagged each and hope that we can get a full count on all present. Vidya has worked out a method for determining the strength of the heat signal and correlating it to mass. As the system is dependent on clothing and several other variables; it's not foolproof. But at least with it, we may be able to distinguish between adults and Pedro.'

CHAPTER 49

Colbert would not say anything about the feds. He was not one to divulge information. He was a seeker, not a giver. He made an exception, however, for the other three veterans. They had complete faith in one another. The four vets shared the kind of trust that could only come after years of reacting to extreme stress.

With Najma, he had let his heart overcome his brain. Or was it his libido? He'd fooled himself into thinking she cared for him. But now he realized she cared neither for him nor anyone. He'd deceived himself.

Colbert was a fan of science fiction. Some authors related the psychology of psychopathic behavior to humanoids, artificially enhanced robots. Were they the psychopaths of the future, like Najma, reading human emotions and coldly responding accordingly? Or would AI robots become capable of empathy?

Empathy was beyond Najma. To her, it was a foreign concept, inimical to her interests. Her present goal? To pit herself in a life-and-death battle against her fictional lover, Colonel James L. Johnson.

'Who is the boy and what is his relationship to you?' demanded Colbert.

'He is my son.'

'Your what?' exclaimed Colbert. 'You never said anything about having a child.'

Najma said nothing. She didn't care what he thought, and in any event, he would soon be dead.

Colbert was perplexed. It made no sense. A kidnapping would fall under the mandate of the FBI. But unless Pedro were the son of a high official, the size of the operation at the airport was overkill. And Najma would tell him nothing.

'I want to see my son.'

'Sit and don't even think about leaving.' He walked out of their room slamming the door. He didn't know how close he had come to dying. If he had been less abrupt, exited more slowly, he might have drawn his last breath. As it was, Najma was ready to take his life. If Colbert hadn't moved out the door so quickly, this would have been as good a time as any.

Colbert sat down on the edge of Pedro's bed. 'Are you feeling better? Is there anything else I could get you? You were very hungry.'

Pedro didn't know what to say. He was still traumatized, having witnessed the killing of his mother. Heather's death had been a severe blow, and he was still reeling. But the people here seemed to care about him. He was confused.

'No, sir. I am full.'

Colbert had asked Bambi to come in. She seemed to get

along with Pedro. Having her here might soothe him. Colbert wanted information. He had to know whether the presence of Feds at the airport had anything to do with Najma and, by extension, the boy. The future of Bright Light could be at risk.

'Hi, Pedro. How are you feeling?'

'I'm okay. Can you call my father?'

'We will try. Who is your father?'

'Jim.'

'Can you tell us how to contact him? Do you have a phone number or the name of the place where he works? Do you know where that is or what it's called?'

'He is a colonel.'

'In the Army?'

'Sí. He is a pilot.'

Colbert started to relax. An Army pilot would not be important enough to bring so many people to his area.

'Do you have a mother?'

Pedro's eyes teared up, and he looked down.

'Could we try to contact her or your father? Can you tell us how?'

Pedro didn't look up.

Bambi put her arm around Pedro. He leaned against her and started to cry. He tried hard not to. Bambi sensed the conflict he was feeling.

She said, 'Crying is okay. I cry.'

'You're a woman. You can cry.'

'Whoever told you that?'

'A boy at school.'

'Where is your school?'

'It's Twisp grade school.'

'Jason, get a map. I don't know where Twisp is.'

'Washington,' said Pedro.

'The state of Washington, or Washington D.C.?'

'The state with mountains.'

Colbert brought in a gazetteer with state maps. He opened it up to Washington State and asked Pedro to show him his home. Pedro pointed to Twisp.

'Is it very pretty there?' asked Bambi.

'Very,' and then his head dropped, and he started to bite his lip.

'It's okay. What makes you sad?'

'My mother. She is dead.'

Bambi hugged him and said, 'There, there. Mine is too. I understand. I feel awful for you. I know how much you must miss her. I miss my mom too.'

'Can you tell us about your mother?' asked Colbert.

'She likes animals and plants. Her name is … was Heather.'

'It will always be Heather,' said Bambi. 'Her memory will always be in your mind. You can talk to her there.'

Pedro looked up at her. He liked her. 'Why are you friends with the devil lady?'

'Who?' asked Bambi.

'Najma?' asked Colbert. What the boy had said so astounded him, he wasn't sure if he had heard right. He shook his head, not wanting to accept that the woman he had loved for a while was the person the boy described. But he did believe it.

Pedro clenched his jaw. 'She killed my mothers. She killed my family, my brothers and sisters, my dog, and my papá.'

Bambi's mouth dropped open. She could hardly speak but managed to force out, 'Oh. Oh, that's awful.'

Pedro turned toward Colbert and then Bambi. 'She is a bad woman. Una diabla.'

Bambi looked up at Colbert. Her face said everything. Colbert knew the others had never liked Najma. Bambi had been more vocal than most in her dislike.

'How is Najma involved?' asked Colbert.

Bambi shook her head. 'We're going to rest a little. Are there any games you like to play, Pedro? It's Christmas, you know. We're going to have a big meal later.'

'My dad, he come to rescue me. He rescued me before in Mexico. He will kill her.'

'Bambi thought it a little extreme to have Pedro saying his dad would kill the woman. 'Where was it your parents passed?' she asked.

'Passed?'

'Died.'

'In Mexico. Najma killed them.'

'But you said your dad?' Bambi didn't understand but didn't want to push it further.

'My new dad saved me. We live on our ranch.'

Colbert turned and walked out. He went to his computer, signed onto the Internet, and searched the town of Twisp. He found the phone number for the Twisp police. He dialed the number.

'Twisp police. How can I help you?'

'Can you tell me how to contact a Colonel Johnson?'

'One moment.' She put the call on hold. 'Chief, someone asking about Colonel Johnson.'

'I'll take it. This is Chief Thomas. How can I help you?'

'I'm an old army buddy of Colonel Johnson's. I know you probably have more important things to do, but if you could tell me, Chief, how to contact him, I would be grateful.'

'Let me pass you to someone that can look in our town's registry.' Chief Thomas had been directed to put all calls through to a number he had been given. 'Hold for a minute and I'll connect you to someone that can help.'

Colbert sensed trouble. Maybe it was the chief's voice. It sounded tense. The police would likely know everyone in a small town.

'Sheilla, call from the compound,' said Misa. 'It was Colbert calling the Twisp police and asking about Colonel Johnson.'

'Thanks, Misa.'

'Colbert just called the Twisp police. He hung up before they connected him to the CIA.'

CHAPTER 50

Colbert went outside. Phil and Rob were sitting on the porch. A string of multi-colored Christmas lights adorned the edge of the roof.

'Where's Gab?

'Down below.'

'Phil, stay here. Go upstairs to the box and keep a lookout.'

The box was an observation platform they'd built like an old-fashioned widow's walk. It was partially concealed, constructed alongside the fireplace. The box was low with small slits in all directions. Inside, it housed a screen that monitored their security devices, including images from the cams and alerts from motion detectors and listening equipment.

'Rob, get Gab. Have him find a position off the entrance road and out by the main highway. You go to the deer blind.'

'What's up?'

''There's a large contingent of Feds at the airport. Otherwise, I don't know.'

'The boy and the woman have something to do with it?' asked Rob.

'Don't know. Maybe. Check-in every thirty.'

'Shit! I knew she was trouble.'

'Save it,' said Colbert. 'Hustle up.'

Rob walked to a small shed, went inside, and opened a trap door. He climbed down a ladder and walked through an underground chamber where he found Gab. Several rifles and pistols were lying on a table. Fanatical about maintaining their gear, Gab was scrupulously cleaning and oiling an M16.

'Jason wants you down by the main road. Bunch of Feds in town and it might be about Najma.'

'What'd she do?'

'No idea. But maybe it has something to do with the kid.'

'If you see anything out on the main road, call it in.'

'Should I put on full camo?'

'Up to you.' Rob knew he would. Gab liked nothing better than his

ghillie suit and its matching shaggy tendrils hanging over his rifle.

'Not enough snow for the white ghillie. Tan it is,' Gab said contently, as he yanked up the puffy pants and put on the top. He looked like a cross between a shaggy bear on hind feet and a sunburned Sasquatch. He grabbed a scoped AK-47 and stuffed it inside a mass of the same tan-colored tendrils.

Rob started up the ladder. 'You gonna go naked?'

'Camo won't do me much good in the blind. Chief

wants me there pronto. No time for costumes. Later, buddy. Watch yourself. Colbert seemed a little tight to me. Could be serious.'

In the command center, Sheilla watched as the four blips on their GPS tracker showed the progress of Jim, Brush, Roberta, and Garcia heading toward the compound. They were still six klicks out.

'Colonel, two heat sigs just left the main house. One went into the woods toward the main highway. No longer visible. The other is walking in your direction along the same road that the backhoe took.'

The radio clicked twice in the command center at BWC. Glenda said, 'Roger that. We have it on our monitors. Confirm SWAT team is standing by.'

The fuzzy blips on the monitors diverged. Jim and Brush stayed together while Roberta and Garcia split up. It would take at least an hour before the two snipers settled into position.

'The blip heading toward you has moved into the clearing where the car was buried and is heading toward a small tower,' reported Sheilla.

'It's a deer blind,' said Brees. 'My dad hunted.'

Thirty minutes later, Brush approached the meadow from the far side in view of the blind.

'I'll signal when I'm behind it,' said Jim

'I'm the decoy, eh?'

CHAPTER 51

'Tell me about your mom. This is your stepmom?'

'She nice. Lola nice. Grandkin nice. Everyone nice but the devil lady.'

'Who's Lola?'

'She help me in Mexico and then come to our ranch. She cooks good. She is my aunt now.'

'Who was the other one you mentioned?'

'He's an old man. My friend. We take care of the animals together.'

'So, you have animals. You like them.'

'I love them, especially my new baby llama.'

'Wow! Llamas! That sounds really cool.'

'We have many llamas and other animals too: horses, cows, and two camels.'

'Really? Wow!' said Bambi. 'Two camels. What are their names?'

'Sharifa and Benji.'

'Nice names. Does your dad help with the animals?'

'Sometimes. But he's gone a lot with missions.'

'What sort of missions?'

'Secret ones.'

'Jason, you out there? Come in. Pedro is telling me about his animals and dad. His dad goes on missions for the government.'

Colbert walked in. 'That sounds cool. A secret agent.'

Pedro didn't know that much about what his dad did and said, 'No sé. He go all over the world. He save me from Najma, and he will come here too.' In his nervous excitement, Pedro had slipped back into his clipped English. He bit his lip as Heather did and said, 'He will be here soon. I hope he kills her.'

'You really want him to?'

At that moment, Najma walked through the door.

'He won't,' she said as she raised the small PPK 380 she had hidden in the bedroom.

Pedro closed his eyes a fraction of a second before the gun fired. He could feel Bambi collapse next to him. He could hear rapid footsteps and then another gunshot. Colbert didn't hesitate. He had charged straight at Najma as soon as he saw the pistol. He knew if he stayed put, he was dead. One 380 round might not kill him unless she shot him in the heart or head. He had to chance it. He lurched right and charged her. She was left-handed and moving the gun away from her body to her left would be more awkward than moving it across her body.

The bullet hit him in the chest between his shoulder and heart. It didn't slow his charge, and his large body slammed into Najma, knocking her into the wall. He could hear the air expel from her as she hit the wall. The gun thudded on the floor and skidded a few feet away. Colbert's two meaty hands were around her throat. His fury overcame any emotions he'd had about her. He didn't turn. He couldn't risk looking at Bambi. She had not been a menace to Najma. She was an old hippie with a kind heart.

He pressed hard and dug in his thumbs to crush Najma's larynx. Then he gasped as she grabbed his testicles and squeezed. Through his nausea, Colbert tried to press his thumbs into her throat. He forced himself to continue. He closed his eyes against the pain for a fraction of a second and, when he opened them, an index finger and thumb were all he saw before Najma pushed her thumb into one eye socket before sticking her index finger into the other eye. This time he relaxed his grip but didn't move away. Najma pulled the left thumb out and hooked her index finger behind the bridge of his nose. She placed her left hand on his chest and violently jerked her finger, breaking the bone and forcing his nose to pull away and down, exposing his brain. The eyeball came out with it, dangling obscenely. Standing on her toes, she slammed the palm of her hand up toward the dangling nose. The blow forced the broken bone into his brain.

Pedro had opened his eyes and couldn't believe what he was seeing. Bambi lurched next to him adding to his fear. He fled in terror out the door. Najma gasped and slid down the wall next to Colbert's grotesque head. She hadn't wanted it to end this way. She hated him. She hated every moment his large hairy body had used her as she'd pretended to enjoy their coupling. She had wanted to kill him every time he entered her. She'd planned and dreamed of slowly watching the life fade from his eyes, as she had done to so many men and women before him. She tried to stand. She couldn't get air into her lungs. She breathed in hard. Her throat made a groaning noise, followed by wheezing as a small amount of air entered her collapsed lungs. She thought he might have crushed her larynx.

Seconds passed, and she started to get more air through her throat. The collision with the wall had knocked all the air out of her lungs, and her throat had swelled from Colbert's chokehold. With short, raspy breaths, she forced air through her esophagus and into her lungs. Oxygen entered her bloodstream, allowing her to stand, bend over, and pick up the black Walther pistol. She stood on wobbly legs and stumbled through the door into the living room just as Phil came running down the steps. He saw her with the pistol. He knew if he stopped on the steps and tried to turn back, he would be an easy target. Instead, he didn't try to stop his downward momentum. He increased it and leaped the few remaining steps onto his outstretched hands, took the shock as his elbows flexed, and somersaulted forward to the edge of the front door. He scrambled, alligator crawling toward the front door. He didn't make it. A bullet hit him in the back. It grazed his spine, instantly paralyzing him from the waist down.

Najma ignored him. She would have preferred to watch his eyes as she smiled at him and fired a final shot. However, she needed to save the limited bullets in the PPK in case someone tried to interfere with her capture of the fleeing boy. It was crucial to her plan that she have control of Pedro and get him into the vest hidden in a box in the bedroom.

Her strength started to return. She jumped off the front porch and saw a woman run into the shed that was the main entrance to the underground bunkers. She was pulling Pedro behind her. Najma bolted toward the shed. Too late. The hatch had been locked from below. She turned and sprinted back to the main house where the third entrance was located. Too late. It, too, had been secured from below.

She slammed the closet door and turned toward Phil who was pulling his limp lower body through the door, using hands and arms. She stepped over him and onto the porch, where she sat down with her back against a heavy post that supported a section of the roof. Phil stopped. Crawling toward her was the last thing he wanted.

Najma could tell that, even with his paralyzed body, he was a fighter. 'How do I get into the underground bunkers when the hatches are sealed?'

Phil shook his head.

'Where are there more than the two entrances?'

'You know there are only two. The design is to keep people out. You won't get in.'

She lifted the Walther in her left hand and fired a bullet into his knee. Phil felt no pain as he positioned himself to see where she had shot him. Blood was oozing out of his knee. He looked at her. She smiled, raised the pistol, and squeezed a round at his thigh. He looked. Blood pulsed onto the floor. She smirked. 'How do I get in?'

'You won't.'

She moved closer to his head and stared into his eyes. She raised the pistol and fired into his groin.

'Thermals show a signature that would be consistent with a child and an adult entering a shed before the signal disappeared. It was accompanied by an adult signature. Another ran part way and turned back to the house.'

'Najma?'

'Unknown.'

'Garcia, position?'

'Approaching south side of the compound.'

'Eyes on the house,' said Roberta. Adult male down, alive on the porch. Unknown figure sitting … It's her.'

'Najma fired a shot at the male on the porch.'

'I have a line of sight. Should I take her out?'

'She's raising her pistol.'

'Your call,' said Jim.

'Roberta looked through her scope. The image was stable and crystal clear. She adjusted her new scope. There was no wind at this short distance. It wasn't a consideration. *A holiday present for you, Jim. And for Najma too. I'm not used to shooting to wound.* She squeezed the trigger. The force of the heavy .50-caliber bullet struck Najma, causing the World War II Walther pistol to fly up and strike the side of the house before clattering down onto the porch, only inches from Phil.

Roberta had made her call as Jim had told her to. She knew that Colonel Johnson wanted Najma alive. She also knew that having been hit anywhere with the .50 would most likely send Najma into shock. There were no guarantees that she would survive. Najma's left arm dangled by her side. Her shoulder was shattered and nearly severed from her body. With the loss of blood and shock, she might not survive the next few seconds. Phil forced himself to stay focused. His hand was slowly moving toward the pistol.

It was a determination bred in the army through countless battles. Phil was weak from loss of blood. At the same time, he was grateful not to feel pain. He had expected to die long before this. Dying did not scare him. Pain did. Not the pain one feels from a sprained ankle or even a broken rib, but rather the excruciating pain he had often witnessed among the wounded and dying.

Thoughts moved in slow motion through Phil's mind, equaling the slow, steady pace of his hand pulling him over the rough wood porch toward the black metal gun.

In the same few seconds that Phil's thoughts and hand moved ever more slowly, Najma slipped back into consciousness. Barely comprehending, she saw the Walther. Clarity eked its way into her thoughts. Najma moved her left hand toward the gun, but nothing happened. She looked to her left and saw why. Her brain was trying to make her move, but the impulse was not getting to her hand or arm. As the shock wore off, searing pain broke through. She struggled to overcome it. To accept it. To continue. Like the man who lay before her, she had trained to never quit, never give in.

Roberta caught sight of a movement to her left. Almost simultaneously, Glenda said, 'Heat signature moved across the access road, one fifty meters from Watcher One, end of straight away. Only ten meters from Watcher Two.' Roberta clicked once and Garcia clicked twice in response.

The colonel came into view by the Quonset hut. Roberta watched as he began to jog toward the porch. Then she looked back to the porch where Najma fell half sideways to her right, moving closer to the pistol. Then another motion to Roberta's left. She shifted her eyes and looked in the direction the movement had come from. There was nothing there. A motion meant danger. The heat signature that command had reported was camouflaged. She kept her head still and shifted her eyes between the porch and the unknown heat signature. She was well camouflaged in a shaggy ghillie suit similar to Gab's. But as soon as she'd fired, she revealed her position.

Gab had heard the first pistol shot that came from inside the house. He immediately abandoned his position near the main road. Staying in the shadows, he moved up along the south side of the road, hunched over in a fast walk. He looked like Mr. Snuffleupagus. As he approached the compound, he heard two more shots. A pistol, he thought. A long straight stretch gave him a view of the compound. He dropped into the dead winter grass alongside the road. He bunched up the ghillie wrap surrounding his rifle and rested the AK-47 barrel on it. He looked through the scope at the porch and saw Phil lying in the doorway. He was still moving. Alive. A figure, a female, leaned against a post, her arm lifted. She was holding a pistol. *Fucking Najma,* he thought. He released his safety and before he could take a shot, the woman's shoulder exploded. He heard the shot and, turning to his right, scanned for the shooter. Gab had never been a sniper, yet he often fantasized about being one. He loved the camouflage outfits, the long tendrils of the ghillie suit. He often went into the woods and practiced blending in. He was like a child playing solo in the forest. Using his imagination, he spent hours happily hidden from the world.

The long hours of play had provided him with a discerning eye for his surroundings. He scoured the area where he thought the shot had originated. He squinted. There was a small movement near a tree. Roberta had moved her head slightly when she saw Jim. Gab was not in a good position. He moved forward to get a better view of the shooter. He made a new mound on which to rest his rifle and looked through his scope. Roberta shifted her rifle toward the movement and found Gab. Since he had pulled the rifle wrap off to make a barrel rest, his rifle was exposed.

Now that Roberta was motionless, Gab was unable to find her. He was uncertain what to do, so he shifted, looking back to the porch. Roberta saw the movement and released the pressure on the trigger. Gab had been moments from taking his last breath when Roberta saw a ghillie-suited figure appear behind him. Gab saved himself by first looking at the porch. Only a fraction of a second before Roberta's squeeze on the trigger would have passed the point of no return.

'Watcher Two, four meters behind the unknown heat source,' reported Chen.

Garcia settled to the ground. He could clearly distinguish the camouflaged figure from the grass alongside the road. He looked through his scope and positioned the crosshair where the figure's head would be. 'Move, and you are history, pal,' said Garcia. 'You, in the ghillie suit. Lay down your weapon and very slowly lift off your headgear.'

Gab was so shocked by the voice that he let go of his AK and reached up, carefully lifting off his head covering. Both the voice and his missing headgear made him feel exposed.

'Arms out. I need to see your hands, raised and open.'

Gab did as he was told. He could tell the male voice was close. 'Slowly lift off the jacket.' Gab did so. 'Now pull the pants down, step out, and face down on the road.'

Garcia snap tied his hands and told him to be quiet and not to move.

Inside the bunkers below the compound, the preppers watched on their monitors, mesmerized. The security cameras were not clear, but of good enough quality for them to see some of what was happening. Mostly women and children, they had practiced shooting and survival techniques, but none had any real experience in firefights. A camera mounted on a post and aimed toward the front door had permitted them to see Najma's shoulder explode. Even on their low-resolution black and white screens, they could see her flesh, bone, and blood erupt.

They couldn't see the shooter. They had figured it was Gab before the camouflaged figure appeared behind him. Two of the men and one of the women climbed the ladder and opened the hatch. They walked out of the shed as Jim approached the porch. Roberta scanned the area. No weapons visible.

Roberta caught another movement back down the dirt road past the Quonset hut. Brush was escorting another man toward the compound. Roberta couldn't see that Najma had won the race to the Walther as Phil slipped toward unconsciousness.

Roberta glanced back to Gab, the would-be sniper, lying on the road. Behind Gab, she could just make out Garcia's ghillie suit. Then she covered the men and the woman as they walked out of the bunker.

Suddenly, several voices came over the comms. Two helicopters circled above the compound with door gunners strapped to the sides. Both Roberta and Garcia would stay hidden, searching for anyone who might prove a danger to the colonel or the major. They were doing what they had done dozens of times: safeguarding their brothers.

Several figures rappelled down thick ropes near the Quonset hut. Three took up defensive positions, facing away from the compound's house. Others secured the house, the main house, while others covered the people exiting the bunkers.

Jim reached the porch. Najma moved her head up and, although barely conscious, saw him and weakly smiled. Her look was almost tender. A look that did not match Jim's. His teeth clamped. His MP5 pointed at her.

'Pedro. Where is he?'

Brush came up to the porch with his MP5 trained on Phil. Jim did not turn away from Najma. Najma swung the Walther toward him. As the pistol arched toward Jim, she whispered, 'I love you.' A second later Jim depressed the trigger and a red hole appeared in the center of her forehead.

'What did she say?' asked Phil. 'Did she say she loved him?' before he passed out.

'How many more are still below?' The preppers were lined up outside the shed. A man looked at the group.

'I don't know for certain. Two, I think, the boy, and the other six children.'

'What's your total headcount?'

'Twenty-eight,' said a woman. 'Not counting Najma and the boy.'

'Three dead in the house, one on the porch. One below, counting Pedro and the other kids. Leaves twenty-two.'

'Twenty-two standing here.'

The lead FBI SWAT team leader said, 'How many entrances to your bunker?'

'The man said, 'Just this one.'

Gloria, who had given him the count said, 'Shut up,

Bruce. Don't be stupid. There's three total and three connected bunkers below, and an exit into the woods.'

'Show me.' The woman took him to both houses.

The SWAT leader posted guards at both entrances and motioned for another to follow them. 'Show me the one in the woods. And tell me who is still below.'

Brenda held Pedro. Having watched Najma die on the porch, she felt distraught. There was no sign of Colbert. *My coven, my coven,* she repeated over and over.

Pedro struggled free from Brenda's grasp and scrambled up the ladder. Hearing a person ascending, an HRT SWAT member tensed, her finger on the trigger. Pedro's small hands, and then his head, came out of the opening. The HRT SWAT member relaxed. She said over her comm, 'The boy is safe.'

Pedro went outside the shed, turned toward the house, and yelled, "Dad, Dad,' as he scampered as fast as his legs could propel him.

Jim's long strides moved him toward Pedro, who grabbed Jim around his thighs. Jim bent over and scooped him up, holding him out for a second before pulling his son into a hug.

With a torrent of tears, Pedro managed to say, 'I knew you would come. From over Jim's shoulder, he stared at Najma. 'She kill Mom.' Tears poured once more from his eyes.

Gently, Jim set Pedro down. He dropped to a knee and looked into the boy's moist red eyes. He didn't know what to say. A tear coursed down his cheek. Then Jim said, 'We have each other.'

The End

ABOUT THE AUTHOR

RS Perry has written six psychological thrillers combining adventure, mystery, and romance. Dr. Perry trained as a NASA Astrobiologist and founded an educational charity that explores issues of the environment and space. He is also the chairman of an educational company in the UK. He is a script writer and a member of the Writers Guild of America West in Los Angeles. And a director of Athene Films, a Vancouver based film company. In the pursuit of science and adventure, he has crossed the Atlantic in a small sailboat, plunged to the bottom of the Pacific in Alvin, the Woods Hole deep submersible, climbed in the Andes and the Himalayas, enjoyed the solitude of deserts from the Mojave to the Atacama, the Yukon, and explored the Amazon. He is a Vietnam veteran who is a trained fixed wing plane and helicopter pilot. He has a continuing fascination with the Earth's wild areas and their preservation. Educated at the University of Washington, he has held fellowships at University of Oxford and Imperial College London. He splits his time between New York City and London.